TROLLS

TROLLS

STEFAN SPJUT

Translated from the Swedish
by Agnes Broomé

FABER & FABER

First published in the UK in 2019
by Faber & Faber Limited
Bloomsbury House
74–77 Great Russell Street
London WC1B 3DA
Originally published in Sweden by Albert Bonniers Forlag in 2012

First published in the USA in 2019

Typeset by Ian Bahrami
Printed in the UK by CPI Group (UK) Ltd, Croydon, CR0 4YY

A CIP record for this book
is available from the British Library

ISBN 978-0-571-34105-4

2 4 6 8 10 9 7 5 3 1

The snowmobile track was a sharp line across the white sheet of the fens; the wolf was running below them. Appearing and vanishing like a pale ghost dog in the shrouds of snow stirred up by the rotor blades. Anders put one leg out through the cabin door and found purchase for his boot on the landing gear foot step. The wind rushed through his hair and the collar of his jacket whipped against his face when he strained his eyes not to lose sight of the blurred creature.

'Would you look at that!' he shouted. 'That's no bloody hybrid, that's for sure!'

The helicopter had moved in so low he could see the waves rippling through its fur. Its tongue, flapping out of its long snout like a wet rag. Ears pressed flat against its head. He leaned as far out as his harness allowed, pushed the butt of the stock against his shoulder, turned the ring on the scope one notch and tossed his head to push his ear protector out of the way. His index finger slid down and curled around the trigger; then he fired.

With snowshoes strapped to their boots, they followed the tracks that led in among the spruce trees. Geir went first, striding through the snow as though in a race to reach the wolf first. Anders got winded and called out to him, but

Geir strode on, arms pumping, seeming not to hear.

The wolf had gone into hiding under the skirt of a large spruce. It was lying on its side; when they creaked their way in under the branches, it raised its head. Its nose was spackled with snow. The spark behind its eyelids slowly dimmed. The dart with its red fletch was buried like a pimpernel in the animal's hip. Geir pulled it out and slipped it into his breast pocket. Then he pushed his hand into the fur and turned up the undercoat, which was pure white. He examined the claws on the enormous paws and noted that they were black. With his knuckle, he pushed his foggy glasses further up the bridge of his nose and then he sat quietly, deep in thought while Anders praised the wolf's remarkable size. He had come across wolves that weighed more than he did himself in northern Canada, and this looked to be of the same stock. Without a doubt, it was the biggest wolf he had ever seen on Scandinavian soil.

'This is incredible! What a giant!'

The vet said nothing, but when he pulled out the syringe with the anaesthetic, Anders noticed his hands were trembling.

The snowmobiles had tracked them across the fens and there was much excitement when Anders and Geir arrived, hauling the animal. A crowd formed around them but dispersed at a few barked commands from Geir.

A woman from the Environmental Protection Agency was with them; she handed Anders coffee in a plastic cup. Her name was Åsa. She had gathered her hair up in a ponytail that danced against the hood of her puffy snowmobile over-alls as she walked around like an astronaut, serving coffee from an aluminium thermos. From Geir's muttering earlier in the day, Anders had gleaned that she had been lobbying hard for this, more or less unilaterally ramming through the decision to move this wolf immediately, without the legally required quarantine. Which also explained why the Norwegian silently shook his head when she tried to offer him coffee from her thermos.

The wolf had been placed on a blanket with a scarf wrapped around its head. Geir snapped on a pair of light-blue nitrile gloves and tied the animal's fore and hind legs together. He fastened the rope to a big-game scale, which he hooked onto the shaft of a snow shovel. Then Anders and one of the snowmobile drivers raised the shovel above their heads like a couple of weightlifters. Geir read the dial, studying it carefully. The result, 170 pounds, quickly spread through the stunned assembly.

Geir was on his knees, working intently. He pushed back the scarf and shone a flashlight in the animal's eye; he moved the polished silver bell of his stethoscope across the furry ribcage that was slowly rising and falling. He measured the teeth with callipers. From time to time, he made pencil notes in a protocol fastened to a writing board with a metal clip. People thronged around him, asking him questions he wouldn't answer.

A man from the county board was present, pacing in circles while talking on his mobile phone. Satin military jacket. Dark leather patches on the shoulders, corduroy-lined collar and a napoleon pocket. Squinting at the sun that glowed red behind the jagged treeline on the other side of the fens, Anders pushed a portion of snus up under his lip, figuring the man had probably worn that jacket during the hunt as well. Topped off with a feathered hat. Was he even one of the regular field agents? Doubtful. And yet, here he was. In that get-up. Probably so he would have something to brag about.

'Cheers then!' Åsa exclaimed; a whisk of steam rose from the cup she raised.

'Cheers,' Geir said quietly, tightening the bolts on the tracking collar with a pair of pliers. 'Cheers to echinococcus.'

He was talking to himself, but Anders heard.

Echinococcus was also known as the hydatid worm. A horrendous parasite. He had seen pictures. Scary pictures. An x-ray of a human head with equal parts worm and brain inside the cranium. It had turned his stomach. And it was turning now too. Because he realised he had put his snus in without washing his hands first. He had worn gloves, of course, but taking them off, he had touched them. And he had been the one to carry the hind part. Who knew what might have been caked in those long tufts of fur? He thought about white fettucine, about eggs and cysts. Cuticles lined with invisible ribbons of roe. Horrified by these images, he sank into a squat, dipped his hands in the snow and dug his fingers around. Then he spat out his snus, cleared his throat and spat again.

They wrapped the wolf in the blanket and loaded it into the helicopter. Anders leaned back in his seat and felt the vibrations reverberate through him. His eyelids drooped. It had been a long day and he was terribly tired. How long before he could sleep? Best-case scenario, they would reach the release site by 6 a.m. In bed by nine. Best case.

[4]

The moment the skids sunk into the snow, Anders grabbed his rifle bag in one hand and backpack in the other and dashed, at a crouch, through the miniature blizzard stirred up by the helicopter in the dark. He pushed the remote Åsa had given him. The headlights of a large Mitsubishi turned on. He threw his equipment on the back seat and opened the bed cap. The transport crate was inside. A metal box with a steel grate in the front and a sliding hatch with air holes in the back. He placed it on the ground and ran back to the helicopter.

People made way for them as they carried the wolf between them. They put it down in front of the cage. Then all that was left to do was wait.

The temperature had dropped, quickly. Anders had pulled on a hat and was stamping his heels hard in the snow to keep warm. They were on a road in a frozen fox forest, somewhere north of the Kaitum River. They had followed the directions from the snowmobilers, but the venerable male had confounded them for a good long while. While he stood there, trying to come to grips with the geography, a cricket started chirping under his jacket. He pulled out his phone and poked at it with cold fingers.

'Is the wolf all packed up and ready to go?'

It didn't exactly sound like a question. More like an accusation. He said he couldn't answer that; he even said he had no comment. It made him sound like a politician, so he added: I know you'll be able to see why, Micke.

When he had finished the call, he hurried over to Geir and Åsa. They stopped talking when they saw the look on his face.

'They know we're coming!'

'Who?' Åsa said.

'Micke Moilanen from Hunt & Hunter. The entire hunting community, in other words.'

'Okay, but wasn't that inevitable?'

'Was it?' Anders said and looked over at the snowmobiles and the anonymous bunch huddled by them in yellow hi-vis vests. 'I reckon you should be a bit more careful what kind of people you employ. To do the tracking. Are those guys from the Sami village or are they just regular wolf-haters?'

The look Åsa shot him signalled that she thought he was getting worked up over nothing. He took a deep breath, and when the air came back out it was as white gas through his nose.

'The more people,' he said, 'the worse for the animal. All the eyes and scents. We have to put the animal first.'

'We do,' she said. 'That's why we're here.'

The wolf was awake now. It was sitting up, head gently swaying from side to side. Geir hooked his fingers under the collar and led it to the crate.

'Get in, old chap,' he said.

The headlights ploughed the darkness aside, clearing a strip of road. Here and there, the light from a window or a lantern flickered, wandering sparks in a night that seemed infinitely deep. Geir had kept both his jacket and his hat on. He had been fiddling with his phone for a while, but now he was leaning against the window, possibly asleep. Anders had tuned in to a station playing golden oldies. He tapped along on the steering wheel from time to time and whenever he knew the lyrics, he sang along, though without ever engaging his vocal cords.

A shudder ran down his spine; he shrugged his shoulders to shake it.

'What's the matter?' Geir mumbled and sat up straight.

'I was just thinking about what it would be like to live here. To be trapped in this darkness. In this bunker!'

'You mean Sweden?'

Anders chuckled. Geir had been strangely quiet all day, but now he recognised him, his dry, minimalist sense of humour, and so he unleashed the barrage of questions that had accumulated during the day.

The county board had acted unusually quickly when reports about the immigrated wolf had reached it. The Sami village wanted it removed from their year-round grazing land immediately and had probably delivered some kind of unspoken ultimatum, because just one day after the animal's genetic value had been established, Anders had carried his rifle bag onto a plane headed to Gällivare like some kind of hitman. He had instantly sensed the tension surrounding the decision. Relocating a wolf without putting it through quarantine was a severe breach of regulations. Potentially fatal, according to Geir, who initially had refused even to help.

Geir, however, didn't seem to want to talk about it.

He sat staring out the window, silent.

'I can tell you're angry,' Anders coaxed.

'What makes me *angry*,' Geir replied, 'is that the authorities in this country ignore their own rules and endanger the public. Not for the wolf's sake, but for political reasons. Because they can't stand not being number one in the EU.'

His voice had a disdainful tone to it when he spelled out E-U.

'At the end of the day,' he continued, 'it's about status. About prestige. And that pisses me off. If the hydatid worm is brought into Sweden, we'll get it in Norway too.'

'Not my doing.'

'It's worth asking whose wolves are more inbred in this colossal mess.'

'Sure, okay. But this guy, he doesn't look particularly inbred. And he's definitely not a dog. That much we know.'

'I'm actually not sure what he is.'

'It's not a dog, it's a wolf. As the Phantom would put it.'

'He weighs a hundred and seventy pounds. A hundred and seventy! Wolves like that don't exist. Not west of the Urals. This wolf doesn't exist. It *can't* exist.'

'You mean someone released it here?'

'I don't know. All I know is something's wrong.'

'Speaking of which, it's probably time to check on him.'

Geir looked at his watch.

'No, keep driving.'

'I kind of need to drain the lizard.'

The reflective rectangles of Geir's glasses turned toward him.

'Piss. I need to take a piss.'

Anders fumbled the fly of his insulated trousers open and drilled a glittering rod into the snow bank, where it quickly rotted out a steaming hole. The cold seized him by the scruff of his neck and refused to let go. He raised his eyes above the tree tops. The stars had come out.

The car door slammed shut behind him. Then there was a scraping sound from the flatbed; when he turned his head, he saw that Geir had opened the cap and the crate as well. It surprised him. Wolves needed their privacy during transport, so they usually only peeked in through the grate to make sure they were all right.

The vet was studying a thermometer in the light of a miniature flashlight. The wolf was lying down, and Anders could both see and hear that it was breathing rapidly.

'It's warm,' Geir said and turned the light off. 'Very warm.'

He stuck his hand into the cage and ran his fingers through the fur. Turned the torch back on and aimed the beam at the wolf.

'And it's shedding. See?'

They each grabbed a handle and backed up a few paces to avoid the worst of the exhaust fumes; as soon as they had put the cage down, Anders dashed over to kill the engine and hit the button with the emergency triangle.

In the fruit-punch red light pulsating across the deserted road, Geir was kicking the snow bank; for a brief moment, Anders thought he had flown into a blind rage. That he had lost his mind. Then he realised it was the snow he was after. The animal obviously needed to be cooled down.

Geir picked up a few lumps of snow and crawled into the cage with them. That set things off in there. Something banged against the metal and Geir cursed. Then he came crawling back out, bum first. He fitted the hatch into its grooves and only just managed to slide it into place before the wolf hurled itself against it.

Geir was on his knees with a frozen smile on his lips.

'I tried to feed it a bit of snow,' he said. 'It didn't much care for that.'

He crawled around to the other side of the crate and pointed his flashlight in through the grate. The wolf was sitting up, glaring at them. Its eyes had cleared. There was no fear in them. No hostility. But something else. Something hard.

'Are you going to give him something?'

Geir turned the light off and stood up.

'Let's leave it here for a bit. Let it cool down a little.'

'But you said he was shedding. That's not good, is it?'

'That was . . . a mistake. I got it wrong.'

Anders phoned Johanna and paced up and down next to the snow bank while they were talking. He told her he thought they would reach the release site around six and be home by nine. When she asked him how it was going, he heard himself say it was going well. He didn't have the energy to tell her the animal was likely in hypothermic shock. Not now. Not when the poor reception broke their words into fragments and the cold was gnawing his fingers to the bone.

Before long, they were back in the car, encapsulated in darkness, silent and dazed. Judging by how Geir stared fixedly at the road and the snow grains crashing into the windscreen like asteroids, he was deep in thought; Anders assumed he was casting about for a medical explanation for what had happened. For his part, Anders was struggling with an anxiety that was suddenly raging inside him.

He had experienced mishaps before. Drugged animals that staggered into rapids and were swept away. Vomit and swallowed tongues. These things happened. But this was different. All eyes were on them this time. If this wolf didn't make it, they would be in for it. From every direction. Even the hunters who wanted zero wolves in the country, preferably not even in zoos, would lay into them. Most of their ire would be directed at the Environmental Protection Agency, naturally, at Åsa, to be precise, if it was true that she had lobbied for the relocation, but internally, the spotlight would be turned on him and Geir. On Geir in particular. He, of course, had the option of retreating into the haven known as his native Norway. Anders had nowhere to hide. He would be told he was nothing but a lowly field technician with a dart gun he was not fit to operate. There were many within the veterinary field who felt a veterinary degree should be a requirement for tranquillising animals and this would provide one more argument for them to point to. It would be insinuated that he had messed up. This would reach him in the form of jokes and barbed comments, which was actually worse, because you couldn't defend yourself against that.

'The car behind us,' Geir said. 'Hasn't it been there for an awfully long time?'

Anders' eyes shifted to the headlights in the rear-view mirror.

'You're being paranoid, Geir.'

He said it quietly, to underline that he did not want any tension in the car. His own anxiety was simmering just below the surface. Against his will, he was now picturing an armed mob. Merciless men, maybe masked. Like a bloody western. It was not entirely unlikely. He knew that. Wolf-hatred was fierce and ran deep. At times, he wondered if it was genetic, if there were men who hated wolves. Besides, he couldn't deny that there *were* rational reasons for stopping them. An intervention of this kind would draw no end of attention, and would once again highlight the absurdity of transporting wolves halfway across the country at enormous expense to the taxpayer.

'Listen to me, Anders. They want us dead.'

It was such a weird thing to say Anders pretended not to have heard at first. But the words hung in the air and after a while he had to ask what Geir had meant by them.

Geir didn't reply and seemed so paranoid Anders realised he had to calm him down. They were not being followed. The roads were practically empty, so it made good sense to keep a constant distance to the car in front, wouldn't he agree? But the Norwegian was not persuaded; he didn't even seem to be listening; he just stared into the wing mirror and the head-lights that were burnt into it.

Anders eased off the gas pedal. The dial on the glowing plate of the speedometer dipped from sixty to fifty-five and then down toward fifty and the car, a big Volvo with a thick crust of frozen snow on the roof, overtook them.

But that did nothing to help matters. Because now its tail lights morphed into a pair of red eyes that hypnotised Geir.

'They want us to die,' he said quietly.

'No one wants us dead!'

'This is dangerous,' he whimpered. 'It's dangerous.'

Anders was getting seriously worried now. Geir was acting very strange. Should he call someone? Åsa maybe? He pulled out his phone but ended up just holding it in his hand.

What had he meant to do again?

Had he meant to call Micke Moilanen? Or Johanna? Fragments of what he had just thought whirled around, but there was nothing to tie them down. His eyes darted between the road and the screen of his phone. The clock showed 6.68 p.m. He knew that was wrong and waited for the digits to correct themselves.

But they didn't.

He swallowed hard. Tried to focus his eyes.

Six sixty-eight.

'Anders. You're bleeding.'

It took him a moment to understand what Geir was saying. Bleeding? He pressed his thumb against his nostril and when he felt it getting wet, he reached up to the ceiling and groped around for the light switch.

His thumb was red. Why did he have a damn nosebleed? He never had nosebleeds. He sniffed and wiped his nose on his hand. A red streak along his index finger. He placed both hands on the steering wheel, raised his chin higher and swallowed.

'Who hit me?' he said.

When there was no reply, he glanced at Geir, who was sitting with his head at an odd angle. Blood had trickled out of his nose. A thin rivulet across his lips and down his chin.

'You're bleeding too.'

Geir nodded.

'I know.'

The car pulls over and comes to a stop, tyres skidding. Anders gets his door open and staggers out, one hand pressed against his nose. His throat emits short, rumbling noises when he sucks the cold air into his lungs and he realises he has had a headache for quite a while without being aware of it. The pain is a sound, a torturous squeaking that is drilling further and further into him. He squeezes his head with his hands and pleads for mercy.

'Go away,' he says. 'Please, go away.'

He falls to his knees and spits and spits. Coins of blood that are absorbed by the snow while his thoughts flap around. A lorry with a shining halo thunders past; he shuts his eyes tight. Why won't it stop? Why won't it stop?

Someone is speaking to him. It is Geir, who is staggering about in the dark, saying they have to release the wolf.

Anders' mouth is open. Everything has started dissolving inside him; the only permanent thing left is the sharp sound inside his temples.

A shout is heard from the car but it is so far away it doesn't concern him. I should call Johanna, he thinks to himself and pats his jacket; I need to tell her there's something wrong with me. That my nose is bleeding and I can't stand up. So she can call an ambulance. Because I think I've bloody pissed myself too. He looks for his phone by patting his jacket and trousers. When he has felt all his pockets, he starts over again, mindlessly.

After a while, he notices that there is someone standing behind the car, watching him. A hunched-over and emaciated little old man. Who is stark naked. He gets it into his head that he is an elderly person lost in the night and remembers his father, the way he looked toward the end of his life. How small he became. A shrivelled child with anxious eyes. His legs won't carry him, so he crawls; his only thought is that he needs to help this poor sod immediately.

Geir is lying in the snow, curled up like a foetus. He has pulled his hat down over his face and is holding it with both hands as though trying to stop someone from pulling it back up.

Anders is on all fours now, watching him blankly. Then he looks up at the monstrous creature standing on misshapen wolf's legs in the red light of the tail lights. Wrinkled and cross-eyed like a witch of old, with the transmitter like some kind of extravagant, futuristic piece of jewellery around its neck.

He turns and crawls away, whimpering in horror. Eventually, he gets to his feet and runs as fast as he can down the snow-streaked road that leads into the distant darkness.

SATURDAY TWENTY-FIRST OF JUNE
TWO THOUSAND AND FOURTEEN

Seated in a plastic chair in the exercise yard, Lennart studied his severed arm. Blood filled the grotesque creases of the scar tissue and was dripping down into the grass, where a small puddle had collected.

He wiped his mouth with his fingers and glanced over at Dennis, who was standing by the door, head bowed, mesmerised by his mobile phone. Then he sank his teeth into the mangled stump. The bits that came loose he gathered up with his tongue and spat out.

He was not entirely steady on his feet; he stood swaying for a short while before setting off toward the door. He shuffled across the lawn in his plastic slippers; a thin rope of blood dangled from the arm he was holding out in front of him. He was breathing heavily, wheezing with deep, rattling undertones. Dennis tore his eyes away from the screen and stiffened. Took a step back. Slipped his phone into his pocket and cursed.

They put him on a gurney. Wrapped his arm in towels; Dennis stood next to him, keeping the bundle elevated. A rose of blood bloomed on the white terrycloth, growing bigger and bigger. He stared at the fluorescent ceiling lights while Dennis jabbered in his ear, pouring sour coffee breath over him.

'Bloody hell. This was pretty unnecessary, don't you think? Seriously.'

Johan came out with his phone in his hand, informing them that the prison transport service was currently in Härnösand and that it would be at least a couple of hours before they would deign to show up. Dennis suggested they drive him to the hospital themselves and after a while, Johan acquiesced.

The injured giant showed no signs of being aware of what was going on around him. He lay completely still, studying the ceiling through his dark glasses. But he was listening the whole time, listening closely.

The A&E was a hangar. Ventilation pipes wriggled across the ceiling like metal entrails. The light streaming in through the windows of the roll-up door drew a pattern of rectangles on the concrete floor. An ambulance was parked under a basket-ball hoop; Lennart looked at it as though he had discovered some kind of mystery. A woman in a white smock placed a disinfected little hand on his arm and asked, needlessly loudly, if he wanted to lie down.

They helped him onto a gurney; once he was on his back, he started rocking his head from side to side as though he was in the grip of despair; the woman asked him if he was in pain and then said he would be given pain relief in a little while.

'So the hand is gone, obviously,' Johan explained, 'but that didn't happen now. What he did today was bite himself. The stump, so to speak. And it's not the first time. It's something he does, more or less regularly. It's bleeding, but I don't think it's particularly deep.'

That Lennart had bitten himself didn't seem to faze the woman; she asked about his medications and then wheeled him off. He was pushed through a din of voices. Man, born 1914, he heard someone say, then the din subsided. The lamps in the ceiling slid by like train cars made of bright light. The gurney made a sharp turn, a sliding door was opened and now he was in a small room with bare, green walls. The nurse told him the doctor would be with him shortly; then she left, pulling the door shut behind her.

He lay there, still, like a corpse. The only sound was the gentle rush of wind from a vent. A surgical light loomed over him and he could see himself in its dome, his dark glasses and the bloody smear around his mouth.

The pillow sighed when he lifted his head up. A mirror and a sink. An empty polished steel table on casters.

He climbed off the gurney and went over to the sink. Turned the water on and put his hand under the tap. Hit the pumping lever of the soap dispenser and scraped the suds from the edge of the sink, cleaning himself up as best he could. The water eddying down the drain was pink. He grabbed a paper towel, wet it and rubbed at his mouth. Grabbed another one and rubbed hard. The blood had dried into his stubble, so he smeared soap between his fingers and lathered up his lips and chin. Scooped up hot water and splashed his face.

There was a folded sheet on the gurney, a white square against the red mattress cover. He took it and draped it over his injured arm, which he held against his chest to hide the bloodstains on his shirt. He opened the sliding door a crack, then stepped out.

With the sheet folded over his bent arm, he hurried down the corridor like some kind of shabby waiter. He exited through the front doors, walked around the hospital building and angled across a lawn. A footpath skirted the hospital grounds; he followed it until he glimpsed the car park. At that point, he turned off into the woods.

Old planters had been scattered across a gravel patch. Decorative shrubberies of various kinds were growing into one another; their clustered blooms shone with remarkably vivid colours and behind them a pallet stood on end like a mysterious portal to a different forest space. He sat down on the edge of one of the planters to catch his breath.

'Lennart?'

His name pronounced in Norwegian. The rise of the final syllable. He looked up to see a man striding up the hill.

Abraham stopped and studied him. One of his eyelids drooped like a crooked blind.

'We should get going.'

It was stuffy and dark inside the motorhome. Drawn curtains covered its small windows, another blocked out all but the faintest trace of light from the driver's cab. He raised his chin slightly and sniffed the air without making a sound. Then he removed his glasses and waited for his eyes to adjust to the gloom.

The old lady was lying under a blanket, watching him.

'Come sit down, Lennart.'

He squeezed in behind the table and sat down on the bunk, by her feet. A small, gloved hand rose slowly, not toward him, toward the curtain. In the light that streamed in, blazing a trail across a face crinkled by deep wrinkles, he could see how thin her hair was. How thin it had become. He could almost count the individual hairs above her forehead.

He lowered his gaze, let it rest on the table. There was a phone on it. A blister pack lying foil-side up. The heavy, black plastic sunglasses with the gold details on the temples.

'How are things with you?'

Before he could respond, the door to the cab opened. He could hear Abraham climbing in behind the wheel through the curtain. Shortly thereafter, the diesel engine rumbled to life. Grete had to raise her voice to be heard now; it made it shrill.

'You look so sad, Lennart. Why are you sad?'

He shook his head.

'Don't be sad.'

Smiling made her cough. She closed her eyes; her chest heaved. At the end, it sounded like a dry laugh. She pushed herself upright with her hands and then sat propped up against the wall, watching him. Her yellow eyes with their piercing pupils were deeply embedded in the swollen folds of her skin.

There was movement under the blanket. Ripples running this way and that. He let his hand slip in under the edge. All activity ceased instantly. He wiggled his fingers and soon felt the cold touch of a tiny nose. He pulled his hand out, shaped like a bowl; a mouse was sitting in it. A wood mouse, with black seed-pearl eyes. He slowly tilted his hand. The little one stiffened and then poured down his thumb to sit on the back of his hand, poised to keep running. When he turned his hand again, the mouse had had enough and jumped off.

It scuttled up the blanket and paused for a second on Grete's stomach. Then it was gone.

'How many do you have?'

She made a resigned hand gesture.

'Why are they not with Skabram?'

'It's no help.'

'You have to give it time.'

She started coughing again and while she coughed, he sat with his head bowed, studying his arm. The blood had seeped through the terrycloth wrapping, spotting the sheet.

'I think I need to lie down for a minute.'

'We have a lot to talk about, Lennart.'

'Not now. My head. I'm not feeling well.'

'You've been asleep for ten years.'

'I feel like I need another ten.'

'Help him. I don't want him looking like this.'

Only now did he realise there was a person further in, watching him. It was Ingvill. But she was not a child any more; she was a woman. She was holding an animal in her arms; when she set it down on the floor, he realised it was a very old hare.

The terrycloth towels were stiff with dried blood and the innermost one didn't want to come off. After announcing that it was stuck to his wound, she ripped it off with a firm tug.

'Did it hurt?' she said without looking at him.

Under the towel was a fleshy crater glazed with coagulated blood. She took out a roll of gauze, wrapped it around the arm and tied it off with a neat bow that she folded in under the bandage.

The shirt she lay out for him was black and the logo on the chest read 'MEKONOMEN' in yellow letters. She cut a four-inch slit in the sleeve. When he had put the shirt on, she grabbed his upper arm and helped him stand up; he then supported himself with one hand on the wall, moving slowly toward the innermost darkness of the camper. A curtain was pulled closed behind him. He couldn't see much. But the smell was unambiguous. He rummaged around among the blankets until he felt coarse fur against his fingertips. He gently pushed the old animal aside before lowering himself onto the cot.

He soon noticed that it was not just the hare that had found a bedding spot among the blankets. His presence caused astonishment. The little ones pitter-pattered around him and darted back and forth; it was not long before they were scurrying all over him. Just like children, they soon overcame their shyness and grew affectionate and then intrusive. The scratching of their claws had a relaxing effect on him; he was soon lost in deep sleep.

It was a Monday. I had just opened the shop and nothing much was happening. Out in the square, on the other hand, things were lively. They were putting together the frame for that gigantic beer tent they have every year during the festival. Any day now a tent was going to appear smack dab in front of my shop window too; one always does. They block me out, plunging my shop into darkness; the tourists can't see that I exist but what is there to be done about it?

For the time being, though, I had a view and as I sat there on my stool, craning my neck to see if Ella was among the gaggle of teenagers hanging about the square, Roland appeared from behind a building site fence. He zigzagged between transport racks and steel crates and the bikes the teenagers had left strewn about with quick strides, and since he usually moves at a leisurely pace, I figured something must have happened.

'Have you seen this?' he said.

'What?' I said, not bothering to get up.

'He's escaped. The cult leader.'

He handed me his newspaper, one of the tabloids. When I saw the headline, which read 'LENNART BRÖSTH ON THE LAM', an icy wave surged through my gut and it was probably a good thing I was already seated.

Lennart Brösth, the leader of the so-called Jillesnåle Cult, has escaped from Sundsvall Psychiatric Hospital. Brösth absconded last Saturday from the local A&E, where he had been taken after sustaining an arm injury.

The police have added helicopters and canine units to the search for the escaped prisoner. They also welcome information from the public.

'A nationwide alert has been issued; members of the public are advised not to approach the prisoner,' says Robert Öhman, from the county police.

At the time of absconding, Lennart Brösth was dressed in a grey top and black trousers, both bearing the logo of Västernorrland County Council.

'A lot of people will have seen his picture in the paper, but he also has a very distinctive gait; he walks a bit like a movie villain. And he's big: over six foot three, and powerfully built,' Öhman says.

That Lennart Brösth was supposedly born in 1914, as his barrister claimed during his trial, and therefore a hundred years old, is something the police take with a pinch of salt. So too, Börje Bratt, interim medical consultant.

'We have always suspected that the information we have about the patient's age does not correspond with his real age; this incident would seem to confirm that suspicion,' he says.

The Jillesnåle Cult kidnapped children and raised them in isolation on a farm outside Sorsele in inland Västerbotten. The children were given new names and in time forgot their true identities. Lennart Brösth was identified as the cult's leader and, in 2006, sentenced to prison for kidnapping and arson. A few years later, he was moved to the Sundsvall Regional Psychiatric Hospital.

When I had finished reading, I pushed the paper away and looked at Roland, who had his hands in his pockets and was eyeing me searchingly. He put his hand on the paper and turned it ninety degrees.

'Doesn't he look a bit like that terrorist,' he said, 'what was his name, the Jackal? In those dark glasses.'

I stood up and paced up and down between the shelves, trying to collect my thoughts.

'It just doesn't seem real. Here I've been walking around, waiting for him to die in prison. And then he escapes. Did you know they'd moved him to the psych ward? Let those alone; they're decorative!'

Roland was standing by the shop window, gazing out at the square; when he straightened up after putting the fruit back in its place next to the orchid, he accidentally bumped into a ptarmigan suspended from the ceiling on fishing line. It swung back and forth like it had come to life; I wrapped my arms around myself.

'Isn't it odd,' I said, 'that no one from the police has been in touch?'

'They probably don't see any reason to,' he said and stilled the white grouse with his hand.

'They're clueless!'

I had snapped at him; he made a lengthy pause before responding.

'In that case, it's no wonder they haven't been in touch.'

'I have to warn her.'

'Gudrun. The last time you went out there, you were depressed for a month afterwards.'

'So what am I supposed to do then? I have to do something!'

'I find it hard to believe he would go after Susso.'

'You finding it hard to believe is not a great comfort.'

'She's taken the website down, though, right?'

'But he was caught because of her! Do you think he's forgotten? Well, you might think so, but I don't.'

Customers had entered the shop, so I had to stop talking and slap on a welcoming smile instead.

I spent the rest of the day in a numb haze. When I got home, I went straight to my bedroom and changed. Then I sat on the edge of the bed and looked at the picture of Susso on the wall. It's a school picture. She is thirteen or fourteen in that picture; it was before she moved away from Riksgränsen. Away from me. Down here. That girl no longer existed and I was trying to remind myself of that fact. I tried to squeeze out a definitive grief that I could fold across my face like a veil. I really tried. It wasn't easy. The pictures clashed, and the one on the wall was incredibly powerful.

Roland was standing in the doorway with his glasses in his hair like an Alice band.

'Keep sighing like that and there won't be any oxygen left in this flat,' he said and sat down next to me on the edge of the bed.

'How are you doing?' he said.

I shrugged.

'My hands are cold.'

He grabbed my hand but said nothing about its temperature. His hand was warm and rough, as ever.

'And I'm feeling dazed. I had a customer today; he wanted to buy one of those little wooden table flags, a Sápmi flag; he put it down on the counter and I just stared at it and didn't understand what he wanted until he pushed it forward with his index finger like this. And then when we were waiting for the payment to go through, he said, "So, it's finally starting." And it scared me that he seemed to be able to tell what I was thinking. So I asked him, "What do you mean?" and then he gestured at the square and it turned out he thought all the closed-off streets and the chaos in the square had something to do with the relocation of the town. Which was pretty funny, but I didn't even have it in me to correct him, I just said, "Yes, yes, it's finally starting."'

'They'll catch him in no time. It's a nationwide alert. And he's on the front page. Everyone knows what he looks like.'

'Maybe it's already too late.'

'Do you want to head over there? If it's what you want, it's what we'll do.'

I shook my head.

'Then what do you want to do?'

'I don't know.'

Roland said nothing for a while.

'Have you talked to Mona?'

'No. God, no.'

'If he's looking for revenge, which I doubt, and I want to be clear about that, shouldn't he be going after Magnus? He was the one who testified against him. He was the one who got him convicted. Not Susso.'

'It's not really Lennart Brösth I'm afraid of. You know, to be honest, I'm not actually afraid. I'm just tired. Tired of walking around with this secret like a millstone around my neck. Tired of having to joke around with people who come into the shop to see the picture.'

'People come in to see the picture? You've never told me that.'

'It happens. From time to time. And sell-out that I am, I play along. I turn mysterious like a fortune-teller and tell them not to ask questions they don't want to know the answers to. Whatever that's supposed to mean in this context. They think it's all a gimmick to lure in more customers. And I play along so hard I don't know what to believe any more. Can you understand how hard that is?'

'Don't dwell on it. It's not good for you.'

'They come into the shop and ask me if I believe in trolls, but I can tell what they're really asking is if I'm an imbecile. And whatever I tell them, it comes out wrong. One time, I said: "Look, I wish I did." And that's the truth. I wish I believed in trolls. Because a person who believes in trolls is just an oddball. But if you know they exist, you're cursed.'

'Cursed?'

'It's a curse.'

'There's no such thing as a curse.'

'My father brought a curse on himself when he took that picture. When he soared away in his plane until it was nothing more than a tiny letter in the sky that dwindled into nothingness. He abandoned his family to snap pictures of the wilderness, and abandoning one's family comes at a cost. It always comes at a cost. As far as I can tell, that's a universal law. That's why things are the way they are. There was a price for taking those postcards, and we're paying it, even now.'

'If there's a curse, it's in here, in your head.'

'I know what I know, Roland. I can't unknow it. The only thing I can do, to stay functional, is to not think about it. Look the other way. And I'm so bloody tired of it. My neck hurts from the strain.'

He threw a pillow down on the floor and when my bottom had slid down onto it he moved in behind me and pressed his thumbs into my shoulders, pushing hard like I have taught him. It crackled like electricity in my head and a warmth that seemed magically curative branched out through my body.

'Then maybe this might help?' he mumbled.

'I hardly think so, but it can't hurt.'

A patient. That was Diana's immediate thought when she spotted the little old lady who closed the gate to the animal enclosure behind her and came waddling toward her. One in the endless procession of embittered faces she encountered at the hospital. No name came to her, so she simply shot the woman a polite smile before turning back to the laminated note on the cage.

'Their eggs are white,' she said, 'and weigh approximately thirty grams. Hens often take good care of their chicks.'

Kiruna was a bit scared of the rooster strutting about on the other side of the fence, brandishing his silky-smooth feather swords over the hens that huddled in a corner, round balls of an unremarkable shade of brown. She disliked him because she knew he could crow terribly loudly and that there was no telling what would set him off. After he sauntered off to the other side of the cage, she dared to move in closer. She hooked her fingers into the wire fence and asked where the chicks were. Diana said she didn't know. The girl felt they should go look in the henhouse.

'We're not allowed,' Diana said and prodded the padlock, making it rattle. 'It's locked. And if the chicks are in there, we shouldn't disturb them. They're resting after their meal, like you do at nursery.'

The little old lady had stopped right next to them, unpleasantly close; Diana was just about to take Kiruna by the hand and lead her off to the shed the goats were filling with their braying when she realised this wasn't a patient at all, this was Susso's mother.

'Oh my God, hi,' she exclaimed. She was surprised, but above all mortified, which she tried to hide behind a stunned expression. Which Gudrun saw straight through. At least that was what it felt like when she met her eyes. Gudrun had called several times and left messages; Diana had planned to call her back, but had never got around to it, and now here they were, face to face.

Many of her old schoolmates' parents came into the clinic from time to time and it often depressed her to see how frail they had become. But Gudrun looked more or less the same. Glamorous designer glasses and spiky hair with dyed tips. She wore a hooded jacket and trainers and was holding a Lindex bag.

Diana pulled Kiruna closer, placing her between them like a shield. For some reason, she tore off her hat as well. Which the girl immediately wanted back; when Diana held it up, out of her reach, she started climbing on her.

'This is Kiruna,' she said.

The girl was given her hat back and pulled it down over her ears. Tilted her head back to look out from under the edge.

'And how old are you?' Gudrun said.

The little girl pressed herself against Diana, butting at her, rubbing the top of her head against her hip. Felt the phone in her pocket and immediately wanted it.

'She'll be five this summer,' Diana said and fended off the little hand trying to get into her pocket. 'In July.'

Gudrun nodded and Diana knew there was no way around it.

'Hey,' she said. 'How is Susso doing?'

She had used her professional voice. The solid doctor's timbre that was about an octave lower.

'Well,' she replied. 'If only I knew.'

'What do you mean?'

'She's moved away. Maybe you heard?'

'No, but I haven't seen her about in a long time, so I suppose I might have suspected. That she wasn't here any more.'

'You suspected.'

The old lady was cornering her. There was no question about it.

'How about a cup of coffee?' she said and nodded toward the brown hut that housed the park's café. She put a hand on Gudrun's shoulder to guide her, gently but firmly. She sent Kiruna off to the playground, which was under siege by a swarm of toddlers in hi-vis vests.

A couple of big bird dogs were stretched out on a rag rug by the hut. Their tails started wagging automatically when Diana went up to the counter, but only one of the dogs had the energy to lift its head up to look at her. Its jaw was chewing air.

She ordered coffee. And a juice box for the little girl. To avoid Gudrun's level stare, she gazed off toward the black ridge of the mining mountain. She studied her wallet and her nails. The dogs' water bowl was a clear plastic tub, wholesale packaging that had once held foam bananas; a leaf was floating in it; she could see its shadow moving across the bottom of the tub like a flatfish.

She carried the steaming plastic cups over to the wooden benches on the edge of the circle where they made a skating rink in the winter. The goats brayed dejectedly from inside their shed; the shrubberies around them were full of twittering bramblings. A child suddenly hollered shrilly over by the playground. Ship ahoy! Ship ahoy!

'Now tell me,' she said and sipped her coffee.

Gudrun was cradling her cup in her hands, looking down at the gravel.

'I don't know how much you know about what happened to us.'

'Only what I read in the papers, actually.'

'Quite a bit then.'

'I know Susso helped find that boy who was kidnapped. That she took some kind of photograph that helped the police.'

'I know what you think, Diana. About us. About our family.'

'What do you mean?'

Gudrun sighed.

'I suppose you could say Susso was damaged by what happened.'

'What do you mean, damaged?'

'She's not herself. To put it succinctly.'

'But what is she doing, is she on sick leave or is she working . . .'

Gudrun shook her head.

'She does nothing.'

[36]

'Nothing?'

'Yeah.'

'But how does she get by?'

'Would that I knew. She lives in Vittangi.'

'In Vittangi! Why?'

'She wants to be left alone. The last time I went out there, I couldn't believe my eyes when she opened the door. She had lost so much weight I barely recognised her. Her clothes were hanging off her. And her eyes were so black; she looked like when she was little and woke up from the anaesthesia after they took her tonsils out. She looked at me with those big eyes, but it was as though she didn't see me, or know what dimension she was in.'

'Could it be drugs?'

'Drugs. If only.'

Diana raised her eyebrows.

'She let me into the kitchen and we sat there staring at one another like two strangers. I felt about as welcome as a vacuum salesman. It was obvious she wanted to know why I'd come, but I also had the distinct feeling she wasn't entirely clear on who I was, and that was deeply unsettling.'

'My God.'

'She's a different person, Diana. It's not Susso.'

'Is she living with someone?'

Gudrun didn't answer straight away. She sipped her coffee and stared off into the distance. The wind soughed through the birch trees and a flock of cumulus clouds drifted into view, spreading a black blanket over the mining mountain.

'It depends on how you see it.'

'Does she have a boyfriend?'

'I have a hard time picturing that.'

'Is she not in touch with Tobe at all any more?'

'She's not in touch with anyone. She doesn't even have a phone.'

A toddler was trying to climb up the slide, her shoes squeaking against the metal. Kiruna was sitting at the top, patiently waiting to go. And then she went. Straight into the toddler. Diana put her cup down on the bench. But she stopped when she realised there was no crying, and none of the other adults sitting on the benches by the playground reacted.

Gudrun watched the children.

'Don't blink, Diana,' she said. 'Because when you open your eyes again, she'll be gone. That's how fast it happens.'

'Do you want me to go out there?'

It was pretty clear that was what she was angling for. That was the reason she had been calling and calling. Diana was Susso's best friend. Had been at least. And a doctor to boot.

But Gudrun was lost in thought.

'I have thought a lot about that, you know. About love, I guess. The limitless love people have for their children. That you can't imagine not being together forever. The bedrock of love is that darkness at that distant horizon. It grows out of it. Do you understand what I mean? It's what makes it strong. The inevitable end. The seconds tick by while we hold each other. All the time, we can hear the seconds ticking by. But we ignore that sound and we don't talk about the end because it can't be talked about. We ignore the end. Instead we hold each other, as tightly as we can. While time just slips away.'

Diana wanted to interrupt but couldn't bring herself to.

'Your little girl doesn't know anything yet,' Gudrun pressed on. 'She's too young. Later on, the end will enter her life and reshape her, from the bottom up. Which is terrible when you think about it. You're a child and life is wonderful, and one day Mummy and Daddy lean over you and tell you you're going to die, but before you die, we're going to die and leave you all alone. It's like one of those permanent residence permits that is suddenly swapped for a temporary one. What a cruel system. Though I can't think of a better alternative. It comes out wrong no matter what you do.'

'It sounds like maybe you should go talk to someone,' Diana said. 'Would you like me to set something up?'

'Talking. According to Roland, that's all I ever do.'

'I meant to a psychologist. A therapist. Being cut off from your child, like you are from Susso, from both of your children in a way, because Cilla's not quite herself either from what I hear, must be incredibly hard.'

'There's nothing I can do. That's the worst part.'

'Do you have her address?'

'I don't know that I do, but I can give you directions.'

'Give me directions,' Diana said and pulled out her phone.

'When you reach Vittangi, you turn left, no, right, why am I saying left? You go toward Pajala. Past the lake with that fountain or whatever it is. Then you carry on for a mile or two until you see a big, red barn with three green doors on your left; that's why I said left. Before you pass that barn, you turn off on a smaller road that takes you down to the river. That's where she lives. In a red house. By the river.'

'Right, then left before a barn with three green doors.'

Gudrun nodded.

'I'm not sure how soon I'll be able to go.'

'And there's one other thing.'

She sat there for a while with her hands pressed between her knees, looking down at the gravel before continuing.

'Lennart Brösth has escaped.'

'Yes, I heard.'

'And don't think the police bothered to inform us.'

'Are you afraid he might do something?'

Kiruna came bounding across the lawn. Diana picked her up and pulled out the juice box and with her arms around the little girl's body, she pried off the straw and pushed it into the hole.

'You don't need to worry about him,' she said. 'He's a hundred years old. A hundred.'

'Is there really such a big difference between ninety and a hundred? And besides, a hundred years is not the same for Lennart Brösth as it is for the rest of us.'

Diana didn't understand that last part, but she didn't have time to ask Gudrun what she meant. Kiruna had grabbed hold of the juice box before she could stop her. The little girl stiffened and looked at the juice that had squirted out of the straw, forming droplets on her jacket. Gudrun quickly pulled a stack of napkins from her pocket and wiped.

'These characters,' she said quietly. 'They're dangerous.'

'What characters?'

Her sceptical tone made Gudrun press her lips shut. The little girl sat quietly, drinking; Diana seized the opportunity to sort out her insulated trousers. The foot straps had come off; she slipped them back under Kiruna's boots. One of the straps was about to break so she tore it in two and tied the pieces back together. Gudrun studied the napkin as she carefully folded it.

'I just wanted you to know he's on the run,' she said quietly and stood up. 'In case you do go out there. It's not a hundred per cent risk-free.'

'Of course I'll go out there. No question.'

'Be careful. Promise me.'

'Pinky swear,' she said and held her little finger out in the hope of eliciting a smile, but Gudrun didn't smile, just turned around and walked away.

After exiting the mess, Anders stopped in the middle of the lawn, suddenly unsure of where he was going. Then his memory returned, smacking him in the back of the head. He couldn't remember what he had said, but he remembered how they had looked away when he had spoken to them. He had thrown down his food tray with a crash that sent the cutlery clattering away across the floor; the whole canteen had fallen dead silent and he had wanted to scream at them, but he hadn't. Or had he?

Now he could hear footsteps on the gravel. Micke and that French scientist were walking his way. Close together and silent like two fucking monks in a monastery, they passed him. He followed them. The Frenchman whispered something to Micke but Micke didn't turn around. They didn't hold the front door open for him and were probably hoping he wouldn't follow them into the laboratory building. But he did. When he entered, they had made it into the post room. He watched them through the open door and at length, the Frenchman looked up.

'Hello,' he said timidly.

The post was sorted into pigeonholes with names above each one, and this was the honeycomb wall Micke was staring at. As though he had forgotten which pigeonhole was his. The charade was so ridiculous Anders had to chuckle.

In the middle of the day, like now, the hallway was quiet and where doors had been left open, broad swaths of sunlight swept across the floor. The door to his room was open too; he didn't like that. He had a clear memory of locking it.

The map, the big picture of Bergslagen with all its wolf territories drawn in, with which he had covered the wall by fitting together four topographical maps to the scale of 1:50,000, was gone and the sight of the bare wall, dotted by drawing pins, under which torn paper fragments were still stuck, made his eyes well up.

He leaned against the desk and tried to collect himself. He was aware he had rubbed people at the institute the wrong way since he came back from sick leave, but that things would escalate to the point where someone broke into his room to destroy his things, that was unexpected. This was proper harassment. Bullying.

He collapsed into his chair and looked out the window. Smooth, freshly mowed lawns. A sliver of Lake Bysjön glittering between the birch trees in the cow pasture. The view had a calming effect on him.

How many times had Johanna told him that he had gone back to work much too soon after the accident? This was proof she was right. He was crying in his office, and it wasn't the first time either. But he remained firm in his conviction that work was the best cure. Work and routines.

He nudged the mouse and his computer screen sprang to life. Without turning away from the window, he reached out and typed in his password with his index finger. But he wasn't logged on. Instead a notice popped up. He rolled closer to the computer and pushed each key with myopic meticulousness. The same notice. A red cross of rejection. And it was only then he noticed what had happened to his screen. The Post-it notes usually stuck to it like a wreath were gone.

He pushed his chair back and left the room. Curses came bubbling out of his mouth, but he had no one to heap them on. At the other end of the hallway, he spotted a figure. A PhD student whose name he didn't know. She quickly retreated; when he passed her room, the door was closed.

He went outside and got in his car. He sat there for a long time.

The rage wouldn't subside. He was so upset the key shook when he inserted it into the ignition. He shifted into reverse and pulled out. When he spotted Micke's Peugeot, he had a sudden urge to ram it, and in the next moment, he had. He heard the crunch. It just happened; these things can be honest mistakes. He had a hard time imagining that Micke had been the one to break into his office. But it made no difference. He thought about the way he had stood in front of the pigeonholes. Micke, who he had thought of as a friend. Or something along those lines anyway. A pleasant colleague. Who had now become an unpleasant colleague. Joining the rest of them.

He went home. William was sitting in his blacked-out bedroom with his earphones on, staring at his computer screen, where a little man was running down a corridor with a rifle in his hands. He was completely focused. Next to the mouse mat was a plate and tall glass. The dark-brown ring at the bottom indicated that he had been drinking chocolate milk. Like a little kid. Anders stared at his scrawny neck and wondered what it would feel like to snap it.

The kitchen looked much as he had expected. The milk and butter were sitting out, the bread was on the cutting board, halfway out of its plastic bag. Every single cupboard was open and several drawers were pulled out. Like a fucking poltergeist had torn through the room. Even the microwave was open. When he picked up the butter knife, yellow globs dripped from it.

He threw the door open and turned the overhead light on. William whipped around and stared at him, eyes wide. Then he took his earphones off and put them on the keyboard.

'You're going to clean up the mess in the kitchen.'

The boy got up immediately and almost ran to the kitchen. He smacked the lid onto the butter, yanked the fridge door open and put the milk and butter in. Shook the bread into its bag and closed it. Pulled out the cutting board and raked the crumbs into the sink. All with a haste that surprised Anders. He stared at his son. His fine, ash-blonde hair was stiff after a day of being flattened under a hat. A widespread growth of angry red spots fanned across one of his cheeks while the other was largely untouched. As though his face were divided into different growing zones. Or was maturing unevenly. He took a deep breath and tried to calm down. The boy avoided his eyes and seemed frightened.

'What's with you?'

'Nothing.'

'I know you worry about me, William. But you shouldn't. I'll be better soon. It's just been a difficult few months. But since I started working, I feel much better already.'

'You're working?'

'Of course.'

'Where?'

'What do you mean, where? In the same place I've worked the last thirty years, of course.'

The boy scowled at the floor.

'Hey. What's with you?'

'Nothing.'

The front door slammed shut and moments later Johanna entered the kitchen. She was carrying two paper bags bursting with groceries. She had on a puff-sleeve blouse; her upper arms were red. She put the bags down on the floor and looked from the boy to Anders and back to the boy.

She brought William back out with her to fetch the rest of the bags; when they came back, Anders was standing by the sink, eating pepper salami straight out of the packet.

'Sit down,' she said.

She sat down at the kitchen table and studied him while rubbing her forehead, which was shiny with perspiration.

'Anders. You don't work at Grimsö any more.'

'What do you mean?'

'The research station. You don't work there any more.'

The salami slices were stuck together; he pulled them apart and crumpled them into his mouth one after the other with trembling fingers.

'You don't work there and you can't go there. Are you listening to me? They're going to report you to the police if you go there again.'

Anders stared ravenously at the packet while he chewed.

'I haven't had anything to eat all day.'

Lennart opened the door and thudded down the steps of the motorhome. They were parked on a mountain plateau covered in rocks and gravel. Grete was gazing out across the water from her wheelchair, toward the sun hiding behind a thin frieze of clouds by the horizon. A scarf covered her head and she had a blanket wrapped around her shoulders. Abraham and Ingvill were sitting on camping chairs on either side of her and the hare was on the ground, its front legs stretched out and its head raised like some kind of sphinx. The eyes that turned to Lennart were completely blind. Like two white pupae. Its nose moved up and down without cease.

He walked to the other side of the motorhome, untied his trousers, took out his rock-hard member and peed while studying the treeless landscape. There was a village by the edge of the bay at the foot of the mountain. A hodge-podge of houses of various hues. Fishing boats along the breakwater. No people. The road that had led them there disappeared like a ribbon into the distance.

'You went to sleep Saturday evening,' Abraham said, 'and now it's Monday night. Or Tuesday morning, to be exact.'

He had his hands in his pockets and slurred his words a

little. He was squinting with one eye, but not on account of the sun.

'What time is it?'

He pulled his hands out of his pockets, pushed back the sleeve of his jacket and checked his wristwatch.

'Quarter past four. Are you hungry?'

'Bloody thirsty.'

Abraham stepped into the motorhome; when he came back out, he was carrying a plastic bottle. He twisted off the cap and handed the bottle to Lennart.

'Where are we?'

'Varangerhalvøya.'

Abraham nodded toward the sea.

'See that line way, way out there? That's Fiskerhalvøya. Or Poluostrov Rybachy as it's also called. That's Russia.'

Some way off, a concrete flight of stairs led down into the ground. Lennart pointed to it, but Abraham shook his head.

'It's a bit further.'

'How far?'

'A few hundred yards that way.'

'What are we waiting for?'

'We've been waiting for you. For you to wake up.'

'Sleep well?' Grete said when he walked over to her.

He made no reply.

'Aren't you happy? Now that you're going to see him?'

He gingerly squeezed his bandage. Then he looked around. Contours of bunkers and demolished sangars. A radio mast.

'How did you find him anyway?'

'The paper!' she said. 'It said a bear had broken into a cabin. In Jarfjord. Inside, it had trashed the furniture and eaten all the food and guzzled down all the beer. Like Goldilocks! Except in reverse. So Abraham went up there, tracked him down and drove him here.'

'You drove him here?'

'We felt it might be good for him,' he said. 'An environment he could feel at home in, right? This entire mountain is like a fucking rabbit warren with holes and tunnels everywhere.'

'Erasmus claims he'll never turn again,' Grete said. 'That he misses the other bears too much and that it would be better for everyone if he, well, if someone put him out of his misery, to speak plainly.'

'Erasmus said that? That he'll never turn?'

'Erasmus,' she said and fixed him levelly, 'has lost his mind.' She tapped her index finger against her temple. 'Insane.'

'It's the wolves' doing, you know that, don't you? They've realised the bears are gone. This is what happens. They come out to play. Who knows what feelings Erasmus has been pushing down all these years, roaming about with the wolves like a tinker in that wagon. Now it's bubbling up to the surface.'

'He's taken over a whole place. A village.'

'A village?'

'Yes.'

'What village?'

'It's called Rumajärvi.'

'In Finland?'

'No, Sweden. Mikko's there and that tall bloke, what's his name. Tony. And several others.'

'Näckstam? Tony Näckstam?'

'Yes. And there he sits. Like a ridiculous little king. With all the wolves. Stewing on old injustices. That we know nothing about.'

'What happened at Stava and Mauri's then?'

'They came to take Ransu, a week or two after they took Sakka from me. Two weeks. And when Mauri tried to stop them, they killed him. Stava stayed with me for a while, but then she moved on to look for Ransu. I've called a few times, but she's turned her phone off.'

'So he got away? Ransu got away?'

Grete nodded and pushed back a strand of her hair that was dancing wildly across her forehead, egged on by the wind from the sea.

'There was an accident a few months ago; a veterinarian who was killed by a wolf they were relocating, maybe you heard? Stava thinks the wolf was Ransu, and that the other person involved in the move knows a lot more than the newspapers reported. So she wanted to find him. That man. But I don't know. She's desperate. Just like me.' She sighed, attempted a smile. 'These are desperate times, old friend.'

'There's no guarantee Skabram can do anything about it. Now that they've learnt not to fear the bears. Besides, I can't force him to turn.'

'He will turn, I'm sure of it.'

'We can't imagine what this is like for him. There were always four thurses, we're talking hundreds of years. And now he's suddenly alone. All alone.'

'So imagine then,' she said, leaning forward, 'how he'll feel seeing you, Lennart. He probably thinks you're gone as well.'

'He may not even remember me.'

'Of course he'll remember you! You're his offspring.'

'You reckon?'

'You belong together. You're miserable, Lennart, and it's because the two of you belong together. Who are you without him? An aberration. A freak! Just like me, without Uksakka.'

'It's going to take time. It could take months.'

'Then there's no time to lose.'

Every time Anders tried to explain to her how he remembered things, or rather, how he didn't remember them, how they were like white spots in his head, she just nodded at him. Almost imperceptibly, but like she knew what he meant, even though she couldn't possibly; it really irked him. She just wanted to get rid of him. That much he had gathered. She wanted him to admit himself to the psych ward in Örebro.

A word she kept circling back to in these conversations was shock. She talked about shock as though it had taken over his body, consequently absolving him of any moral responsibility. It was the shock that had scared him into the car and made him drive all the way home after the wolf killed Geir. The police had calculated that it would have taken him approximately ten hours and that he had stopped for petrol in Örnsköldsvik; listening to their description of his journey was like listening to an account of what he had got up to during a monumental bender.

According to Johanna, there was nothing to be ashamed about. He had been through a horrific ordeal. The reason she underscored this was that a lot of people felt he should have intervened. A kick in the arse would probably have scared the wolf off. And the wound the beast had torn in Geir's throat was probably shallow enough his life could have been saved.

If he had tried. Instead of jumping in his car and hightailing it out of there. What thoughts had run through his mind during those ten hours?

None at all. It had been completely blank.

Pointing to the shock had made sense. Everyone knew shock made people act irrationally. Johanna had told him about a father who had dashed about on the motorway outside Fagersta, gathering up his dead child's scattered body parts, shouting at people to help him so they could start putting the child back together. A completely ordinary father, stunned by shock.

Yes, he blamed the shock. He could also blame the shame. When it was time for Geir's funeral, he had let it be known that he couldn't face Geir's loved ones and colleagues, who thought he had acted cowardly, and indirectly blamed him for Geir's death. I think I was already feeling ashamed in the car, he had said. It was something he had arrived at through speculation and Johanna had understood. Everyone had understood. Or at least they had made out as though they understood. During the weeks following the incident, he had been wrapped in a cocoon of understanding. The department had sent flowers. The police officers who came to his house to ask questions had put on their kid gloves.

And then he had been fired. That was what they were supposed to talk about. It was half past ten at night and a fine rain was pattering against the plastic roof of the veranda. She was concerned about his memory lapses and wanted him to seek help. That was what she was getting at. He tried to dismiss her concern and when that didn't work he changed tack and claimed William had misunderstood. Of course he knew he had lost his job. He had just gone out to Grimsö to pick up some things. Some personal belongings. A map, among other things.

'So you don't have memory lapses?'

'No, I do, but mostly from that night and the days that followed. That's blurry, but otherwise it's not too bad.'

'Do you remember acting violently?'

'What do you mean violently?'

'You've shoved me several times, and William too. He's terrified of you and to be honest, so am I.'

'There's no need to be.'

'One night when I tried to stop you from leaving the house, you grabbed me by the throat.'

'What on earth is that supposed to mean?'

She showed him her neck.

'Like this.'

'I grabbed you by the throat?'

'Yes.'

'I must have been sleepwalking then.'

She raised her eyebrows.

'I must have been. If what you're saying is true.'

'Are you implying that I'm lying to you?'

'It just seems so strange.'

She crossed her arms and smiled.

He leaned forward.

'I mean, how do you think it feels when someone tells you you've done all these awful things that you can't remember doing? Huh! Am I supposed to just accept it? You could say whatever the fuck you want and I'm supposed to be all like, oh really sorry, I was bad, I shouldn't have done that, sorry, sorry.'

She pulled out her phone. Opened something on it and handed it to him across the table. He pushed his glasses up to his hairline.

It was a picture of her throat. Her head was back and her chin tilted up. A small root system of red streaks fanned out across her skin.

'Did I do that?'

'How do you think it feels when someone who's hurt you denies it even happened?'

'I'm not denying it, I'm just asking.'

'It was the first night you left the house. Since then, I haven't stopped you. I'm sure you can understand why.'

He didn't respond. Her tone had hardened and he noticed it was getting his dander up, but he didn't want that to show.

'You don't remember this?'

He heaved a sigh.

'That's frightening. That you don't remember. And it can't go on like this.'

He pulled his glasses back down.

'You think it's frightening. How do you think it makes me feel?'

'It doesn't really matter how you feel. Because by tomorrow, you'll have forgotten. And then we'll be here again. I should start bloody recording it.'

'But I do have memories, Johanna. Faint memories. I can't sleep. I have nightmares and then I can't go back to sleep. So I go outside for some fresh air. What's so weird about that?'

She snorted derisively.

'It's nice in the woods. Relaxing.'

'Relaxing? Yeah, I know what relaxes you.'

She shook her head at his perplexed look.

'Don't play dumb.'

He was silent for a moment, pondering what to say.

'Let me explain what it's like. When I'm out there, it's kind of like a dream. Like being half naked. Half waking. It's hard to explain. I suppose it's the shock that hasn't worn off. These things take time, Johanna. But we can't let it get to us. It will pass.'

'You're sure of that?'

'Anyway, isn't it dangerous to stop a sleepwalker? Aren't you supposed to get out of their way? Because things like that can happen.'

She studied him through narrowed eyes.

'I think I've heard that,' he said. 'That you should get out of their way.'

'So you're sleepwalking, that's your explanation?'

He shrugged.

'Just now you said you couldn't sleep.'

'I obviously meant I must have been sleepwalking that time you tried to stop me. Since I reacted like I did and grabbed you. But normally I go for walks. Long walks. I'm aware of that.'

She looked at him with eyes sizzling with suppressed rage.

'I know who she is.'

'Who?'

'I've followed you, Anders. I've seen her.'

'Seen whom?'

'You go to that construction trailer.'

'Oh, come off it, will you?'

'It's that woman, that Finnish woman who came here. The wolf woman.'

'Wolf woman?'

'She was from some organisation. Some predator organisation or whatever. And she asked lots of questions about the wolf you were going to move. Maybe a month ago. You don't remember that?'

He shook his head, even though she had clearly meant it as a scornful swipe at him rather than a question. He looked at her, pleadingly. He was at the end of his tether, couldn't she tell? But there was nothing in her face, no trace, to suggest she intended to retreat so much as an inch.

He stood up and went back inside. He didn't know where to go, so he ended up in the bedroom and when he heard her footsteps, he quickly closed the door behind him. She opened it. By then, he had sat down on the edge of the bed. He was hunched over, with his head down and his elbows on his knees, as though inviting her to sit down next to him and maybe stroke his back.

She didn't.

She leaned against the doorpost, arms crossed.

'I can see why you'd be worried.'

The words came out in a slurred mass.

She laughed at him.

'Worried? That's how I felt the first few weeks, Anders. There's nothing left of that now, just so you know. Nothing but a lot of fucking anger.'

She was screaming now, venting the fury that had been simmering under the surface.

'You watch TV all day, feeling sorry for yourself, and at night you sneak out and fuck some bloody slag in the woods! And then you pretend nothing's going on.'

'But I don't, I don't know what you're talking about!'

'I don't know what you're talking about. That's all you ever say.'

'You don't know what it's like. What it's like in here.'

He slapped his forehead hard. His voice was breaking. She turned around. She couldn't even look at him any more.

'And this might be the worst thing,' she said. 'That you feel so damn sorry for yourself. First you deny everything, and then you sit here feeling sorry for yourself. It's a pattern. You come in here every time. Do you know that? You sit there, in that exact spot!'

'What am I supposed to do then? I don't know what to do . . .'

'You need to get help, Anders. Because this has got out of hand.'

He nodded and she left, and he stayed on the bed and looked at the floor and when he eventually got up, it was because he was wondering why Johanna hadn't come to bed even though it was past eleven.

Diana sat in front of her computer with a referral open, but she wasn't looking at the screen; she was gazing out the window, at the forest of downy birches and willow thickets covering the slope outside the house. A lettuce-green jungle that reached all the way to the dark band of spruce trees and mountains that bulged up under a grey blanket of clouds to the north. Grey, grey, grey. The rain hurled itself in rattling showers against the glass and she felt sorry for Kiruna. When she finally got to ride the dragon, it rained.

She had been happy but not particularly surprised to suddenly one morning find a merry-go-round and a rollercoaster in the park. The day before Midsummer, the lawns in the park had been white and they had built a small snowman and crowned him with a wreath of frostbitten birch twigs, and in the girl's wondrous world the sudden appearance of the carnival seemed like a similar phenomenon. Something that just happened. A natural kind of magic.

Merry-go-rounds were not the only thing to appear out of thin air. While the festival was on, the city teemed with returnees; it was like Christmas Day. That's why she had opted to stay home. She hated when people came back to town. And she was tired. That was what she had told Håkan and it wasn't an outright lie. She didn't want to meet a horde of drunken ghosts and she was tired. As usual. Håkan claimed it was chronic, maybe one of those illnesses the evening papers were always writing about? A hidden epidemic. That only afflicted working women.

Her real reason for staying at home was something else: she had got it in her head that she would bump into Susso in the crowd. She knew it wouldn't happen, but the premonition was so vivid and insistent that she had let it influence her decision to stay home. You go, she had said. I have to get some work done before I go on leave.

After her run-in with Gudrun in the park, she had started thinking about Susso and with these thoughts, an older image of the city had surfaced. This image seemed like an overexposure and given the nostalgic atmosphere the returnees generated, she wasn't sure which Kiruna was waiting outside their front door. Was it present-day Kiruna, or Kiruna in 1998?

She tried to visualise Susso, but her face kept slipping away. Did she even have a picture of her?

She watched the screen. Moderate ethyl consumption. No family history of dementia. Somatically healthy. The marker blinked in the diagnosis field. Retrograde amnesia and nascent dementia, she had written. Now she typed: Something else?

Then she opened her web browser and typed:

Susso Myrén.

TROLL HUNTER'S PICTURE POLICE'S ONLY CLUE. The article was from January 2005. There was no picture of her. She clicked on a link. There she was. She was standing in front of a snow bank. Rosy cheeks and squinting eyes. Inca hat and Lovikka mittens. And that coat. It was the same one she had worn in secondary school. Or was it an identical one? Neither possibility seemed less distressing than the other.

She closed her laptop and pushed her chair back. Opened the door to the walk-in closet and pulled out the moving box lurking in the dark under the clothes that hung in there. It contained stack upon stack upon stack of papers and was so heavy the handle on one side had ripped. This is where Håkan and she had mingled their lives together. Implicating them. The way Kiruna was an implication of their genes.

Håkan's yearbooks looked virtually untouched. Had he even opened them? She flipped to ninth grade, scanned the grey faces until she found him. She found his name too. Håkan Hellström. He had a side parting and his shirt was buttoned all the way. He was, in fact, the only person in his class wearing a button-down shirt, aside from the teacher, who wore both a shirt and a waistcoat. They had probably had a great relationship. Håkan had always had perfect grades. Not good, like hers, perfect. From the first term to the last. It had probably made him a strange bird. At least that's how he looked, squeezed in between lads in Adidas jackets and young men with intense stares and black crosses on their hands. In medical school, on the other hand, he had found his peers and blossomed. He had been a shining star. Who had he been before he started studying medicine? She didn't know. His yearbook picture offered no answers.

She didn't have any yearbooks. She and Susso had vandalised theirs. Writing nicknames, established and made up. Drawing devil's horns. Goatees and Hitler moustaches. Boils and warts with hairs growing out of them. Big, flappy ears.

Speech bubbles full of obscenities. Anna Hedlund and Carina Aaro's faces had been overlaid with so much ink the paper had ripped. They had drawn a sombrero on Jerry Brynerfors, who was so inbred he looked Mexican and who they therefore called Diego, and next to Odd Enoksson, who was a head taller than everyone else in his class, including the teacher, she had written 'PATHETICALLY TALL', and level with the top of his head she had drawn a stickman with round specs and an arrow and written 'Robert Pershing Wadlow'. He was the world's tallest man. Eight feet eleven inches he'd been. He hadn't stopped growing until he died. If he hadn't died, he might have hit nine feet. Maybe ten. At least that's what Susso had claimed. She had read about him in *The Guinness Book of World Records*. There hadn't been a lot of books in the freezing little flat where she lived alone like Pippi Longstocking, but she did have *The Guinness Book of World Records*, several editions even; they had been lined up on the shelf where she kept her CDs and video cassettes as well. Every year, her dad had given her that book for Christmas up at Riksgränsen and now, thinking about it, it struck her how depressing that was. How paltry. He bought his abandoned daughter one book and one book only, and that was the one he picked. *The Guinness Book of World Records*. Diana had read the books too, but hadn't found anything to support Susso's claims that Robert Pershing Wadlow could have reached ten feet. She had not been convinced a person could grow that tall. Probably not even nine feet. For the same reasons trees had to stop growing eventually. There were limits. Gravitation imposed limits. But she had never disputed Susso's claims. She always kept her doubts to herself. She never called Susso on anything, and that had been a prerequisite for their friendship. It had been built on the fact that she never called Susso on anything.

Now she was sorry she didn't have the yearbooks any more. She would have liked neatly stored memories too. Like Håkan's. Memories you could show others. Representative memories. For Kiruna's sake, if for no other reason. What was she going to think about her mother? True, destroying the yearbooks had been hilarious. That was some consolation. To be honest, she couldn't remember a time when she had laughed more. Tears had streamed down their cheeks; Susso had lain prone on the table with the pen in her hand, paralysed by silent laughter. No, she had never laughed like that again, laughed so hard she didn't know what to do with herself. That was something she had only ever experienced with Susso.

She dug deeper into the box and pulled out a handful of stapled A4s that said ART IN KIRUNA. By Susso Myrén and Diana Sillfors, class 8B. She couldn't believe her eyes. An extant school assignment!

Someone had added an *F* in pencil before the word ART. Probably Susso, but she couldn't be sure; their handwriting was difficult to tell apart. Which was actually odd considering that they hadn't learnt to write in the same school. They had been influenced by each other later on. When Susso started writing the letter *E* like an *L* with two bars instead of an *I* with three bars, she had followed suit. Or maybe it had been the other way around. Everything between them was intermingled.

It was a school assignment about various works of art in the city. The assignment had been to select a number of pieces they were familiar with and write what they knew about them and then find each piece of art and describe it and see if they could learn something new, either by going to the library or by asking someone, anyone. Susso had been new in town and hadn't known any of the public artworks, not even the Northern Lights Obelisk; she had asked if that fat guy in *Asterix* had a cousin in northern Sweden. Diana smiled at the memory while she flipped through the papers.

This is what they had written about *The Thinking Sami*:

Location: By Park School
Year it came to Kiruna: 1927
What we knew before: It's next to Park School. It's of a Sami, thinking. It's nice. It looks at the church.

What we saw when we got there: It was made by Ingrid Geijen or Geijer. It's made of black stone. It has a knife with genuine Sami patterns in its belt. It has shoes with tassels. And it has mittens with Sami patterns. It's looking out at the town or at Restaurant Lapplandia or something in that direction. Not at the church, which is what we thought.

Interview with Kiruna resident number 1:
Do you know anything about it?
No
Do you know who made it?
No. I don't know anything.
But maybe you know the name of it?
No!

Interview with Kiruna resident number 2:
What do you know about it?
Well, nothing.
Do you know what year it's from?
Well, no.

We couldn't find a lot of facts about *The Thinking Sami.*

His name might be Olle. He looks pretty pathetic.

There it was again!

That word. They had used it in virtually every other sentence back then. Everything, absolutely everything, was potentially pathetic, in one way or another.

Wasn't she being pretty pathetic now, digging through an old box full of memories from her childhood while a cold rain pelted a city that was about to be torn down? That was going to be packed and then unpacked. Be resurrected, but not really. Not ever.

Granted, a sculpture could look pathetic – especially a sculpture of a Sami from the twenties, when people were still wrapping measuring tapes around Sami people's skulls. And the name. She obviously knew it alluded to *The Thinker* by Rodin, but given how the Sami were viewed back then, it acquired different connotations. Like how the unique thing about this particular Sami was that he was actually thinking.

But that's not what they had meant when they had written that he looked pathetic. They hadn't been capable of that kind of insight back then. They had slapped that word on to create distance to the assignment. To the requirement.

A distance signalling rebellion. Against the school. Against everyone and everything. At the end of the day, everything was meaningless, but what were you supposed to do about it? Suck on a shotgun like Alice Älvros' dad, who had made such an ungraceful exit it gave Alice bulimia. They had laughed about it behind her back, and the thought of that stung now when she wondered whether their jeers had ever reached Alice's ears. So callous! So incredibly callous.

Joking like that and mistrusting anything that was less morose than a heroin-infused grunge ballad had obviously been a survival strategy. A pact that offered a certain amount of protection from the mechanical, masculine force at work in the mining town, which ground people into identically sized gravel with identical technical skills. Come to think of it, their attempt at resistance had been pretty heroic.

She remembered the day Susso had sauntered into the classroom clearly; she remembered the exact moment, like a film. The unconcerned look in Susso's eyes when she shuffled down between the desks to her seat. That was eighth grade. Halfway through the school year, after the Christmas break, in 1994. An odd girl from the village school in Abisko who looked like she had walked all the way down to Kiruna on foot, because her cheeks were bright red and so was the tip of her nose.

She had worn a big Fjällräven coat, puffy and exclusive. Diana had had the same one; she had nagged her parents all autumn and been given it for Christmas in an enormous package.

They had found each other immediately. It was like fate.

And they looked so alike as well. Everyone had always

pointed it out. That they looked like sisters. Here come the sisters! Myran and Sillen.* Their coats gave them identical outlines, but it wasn't just the coats. They had the same kind of hair – mousy, if she was being honest. The same heart-shaped faces, the same upturned noses. The same height, the same physiognomy. They had even had their first periods the same month – unless Susso had lied about that. The same way of speaking. And the same laugh. Above everything, the same laugh. Whose laugh it had been originally she didn't know. It was something they had created together. The same was true of their way of speaking. They had their own language. An idiom. It was dead now, but she was certain it would be revived immediately and without effort when they met. Just like Sumerian would if two Sumerians rose from their graves and were brought together.

When they met.

Not if.

The phase they were in now, when they had, for various reasons – what you would have to call external reasons – grown apart, was just temporary.

But what if it wasn't?

Squatting there by the moving box, clutching the twenty-year-old school assignment, she suddenly realised she had taken that for granted all these years. Subconsciously, she had assumed they would be reunited, and there had been no reason to dwell on it. She had assumed Susso felt exactly the same way. That they mirrored each other in that too. In their feelings for each other. In their memories of each other.

* The girls' nicknames mean 'ant' and 'herring' respectively, and are a play on their surnames.

But what did she really know about Susso's memories? The way Susso viewed her? What she felt when she thought about her? Maybe she felt nothing at all.

The tensions had begun to appear after upper secondary school, that autumn when there was no school to go back to, which had come as a shock to most people. Some moved south. Mostly girls. She herself had applied and been accepted to medical school in Umeå, but Susso didn't seem to have any plans whatsoever. She worked in a shop and seemed content. Did sporadic shifts as a carer. Natta Simonsson worked in care too, so she and Susso started hanging out, drinking pretty heavily. Simonsson was friends with Sporty, and that was where Diana drew the line. Sporty had not earned her name by being into sports but rather by sleeping with a visiting floorball team from Sälen. The entire team. Not all at once, but over the course of the week she had worked her way through them all and played with several sticks at least once. At least that's how rumour had it. That Susso would go out and get trashed with Sporty, this infamous harlot, was incomprehensible. They had used to make fun of her! Joke she didn't just suck, she sucked a whole floorball team. This development had made Diana distance herself and as a consequence her move to Umeå had been less of an abrupt goodbye. They emailed a little bit back and forth, but then that petered out too. And when she moved back home to do her residency at the local hospital, Susso was still working in the same shop, virtually unchanged.

Except that she had become a cryptozoologist. In earnest.

The aerial photograph Susso's grandfather had snapped in Sarek National Park had exercised a powerful pull on them during the part of their teenage years when they were drawn to anything that was somehow eccentric. Anything that was odd. Susso had shown her the blurry picture, furtively, without her mother's permission, and it had filled her with a titillating and trepidatious horror that she could, in fact, still recall today.

The small photograph, which was kept in an unmarked manila envelope, had been a door to a different world. A portal to a supernatural realm no one else knew about or could be *allowed* to know about. This was something Susso's family had decided. The Picture wasn't even spoken of, and that's what made it so remarkable and exciting. Diana had been let in on the secret and she had felt like she had become a Myrén and she had even wished she were one.

However, over the years, she had come to the conclusion that the secrecy surrounding the photograph probably sprang from shame. An unwieldy shame that no one in the family knew how to handle. There was no other explanation than that the patriarch, the great nature photographer Gunnar Myrén, world-famous in the north of Sweden, had produced a fake picture and his descendants found that embarrassing.

Why it was such a big deal, she had never been able to figure out. She had never met Susso's grandfather, but had assumed he was a bit of a prankster. Wasn't it actually kind of funny? Why had it been such a sore point? Because it definitely was a sore point. Susso had always found it surprisingly difficult to talk about it. You didn't know Grandpa. That was her only argument. Diana thought she should pull herself together; in fact, she more or less kept waiting for that to happen. For Susso to come to her senses and abandon her childish fancies. Grow out of them. Was she really serious when she claimed she believed in trolls? Susso said she was, but it was hard to tell whether she meant it or was just being contrary. Torbjörn had always taken Diana's side, though he had been careful not to admit it. Susso had a temper on her, as he was very well aware. But he had giggled at Diana's comments and given her cautious backup, and thus they had formed a pact against Susso; maybe it was this pact that had driven her into the arms of Simonsson.

She had no idea how Susso had lived after she left for Umeå, but there seemed to have been a vacuum of some kind, and Susso had filled this vacuum with cryptozoology. For lack of better options. It had been a hobby at first. But it had grown. Assumed new forms.

And that was because of the internet.

She had made contact with people who shared her delusions on cryptozoological forums and bolstered by this community, she had constructed a website that revolved around the secret photograph. Which thereby became anything but secret, since now the whole world could see it. Diana had visited the website but hadn't even wanted to show it to Håkan. She didn't want him to slap some cynical diagnosis on her best friend.

Because that's what she was. Or at least there was no one else who could aspire to that title. But what kind of friend had she been to Susso? Since she moved back, they had barely seen each other and after what happened in 2005, when that boy disappeared and Susso was in the papers, she had outright avoided her. And not just her. All of Vänort Square and the surrounding area had been a no-go zone for her, and when she had to walk past the shop she had always quickened her step and stared at her phone to give her eyes an alibi. If Gudrun had managed to catch her eye from inside, she would have been forced to go in. And talk. And ask. And find out about the thing she didn't want to know anything about.

Not knowing was so much easier. Hiding behind that. Strangely enough, she hadn't given her own behaviour any thought. Not discussed it with herself, which she normally made sure to do as soon as she had an internal conflict that posed a threat to her conscience. After all, Susso and she had been practically joined at the hip all throughout their teens.

What Gudrun had told her in the park didn't make any sense. So it was after Susso had killed her website that she had started acting oddly. She figured it should have been the other way around. That she should have snapped back in. Besides, she had a hard time imagining Susso isolating herself like that.

But what did she really know?

They hadn't talked to each other in over ten years.

My God, could that really be right?

Why hadn't she been there for her? Talked to her? She knew why. Susso didn't fit into her life. That was the bitter truth. She had rejected her and when she put that into words, she was instantly filled with self-reproach that stung so badly it must have been gathering force at the back of her mind for years.

She tossed the school assignment back in the box and closed it. The front door had squeaked open and the hallway was full of Kiruna's chirping and Håkan's rumbling. He told the girl to take off her boots and then told her to put them away neatly. Both of them!

Diana went downstairs, still dazed by the feelings that had emanated from the box like swamp gas. The little girl wrapped her arms around her leg and clung on. Her hair was dark and she smelled like a wet little animal. Diana asked if the dragon had flown away and the little girl shook her head. The dragon was still there and she had gone on it twice. And she had found birds lying on the ground.

'Fieldfares,' Håkan said. 'Chicks. They're everywhere.'

'Dead?'

'I didn't perform a clinical examination. But they were on their backs in the grass, and none of them responded when spoken to.'

Diana looked at the little girl.

'They jump out of their nests too soon. Before they can fly.'

'Why?'

'I don't know. They just do.'

Lennart hung the headlamp around his neck and in the same movement removed his glasses and handed them to Abraham, who was staring at his eyes with unveiled curiosity.

The bunker had been blasted into the mountainside; the imposing entrance was neatly cut. Made of poured concrete now streaked with white lines of limestone tears. At the top of the pile of excavated rubble blocking the entrance was a crevice that had been stoppered with a tangle of rusty-brown barbed wire.

The first rock he put his foot on shifted, almost sending him sprawling. He grunted and continued, half crawling, with his injured arm pressed to his chest. When he had made it to the summit of the rockpile, he reached out and grabbed the barbed wire. It was jammed in tight; he had to tug hard several times to get it out.

The daylight barely made it past the opening. He could see the tunnel floor, a channel of brown, stagnant water. The tiny white limestone stalactites hanging from the ceiling. Further in, darkness. Solid, like matter.

As he crawled across the rubble on his belly, his body blocked the light; for a few moments, he could see nothing. But as soon as he started sliding down the slope, the tunnel became visible once more. He crawled down and got to his feet.

He stood stock-still, listening. The mouse sitting in front of him was listening as well. It gingerly poked the stuffy air with its nose and whiskers. Then it pattered off. It ran in a straight line, like a tightrope-walker. Suddenly it stopped and sat back on its hind legs. Apparently, that was as far as it would go, at least by itself, because it turned back and looked at him.

His nostrils flared, but the only thing he could smell was wet concrete and stagnant, subterranean air. Rusting iron.

He strapped on his headlamp and switched it on.

Further on, the tunnel turned sharply and in the wavering beam of the headlamp he could see the water ripple away from his feet and lap against the walls.

There was a door to the right. A small room. Some kind of rack on the walls. Bent iron pipes that looked deep-fried in rust.

He splashed on down the tunnel, led by the mouse, and after rounding the corner, he stopped. There was something there. He turned his head to catch it. A whiff of rot. He moved his head this way and that, sniffing, testing the air from different angles. Rotten meat.

A few paces further in, he stepped over a high threshold, entering a cave. Glassy bumps protruded from the rough cave walls. When the light hit the drops of water hanging from the ceiling, they twinkled like constellations.

Something lay on the floor in the middle of the room. He went up to it. A backpack. There was a water bottle in the mesh side pocket. A small stuffed moose with a rounded muzzle dangled from a string. He studied the backpack and the ridiculous moose for a long while.

He let the beam of light from his headlamp sweep across the uneven walls, but there was nothing to see. Except a staircase.

He stayed where he was, pondering. Then he filled his lungs with air, rounded his lips and whistled. A high note that he held for as long as he could; when the echo had subsided and remained only as a memory in his ears, he whistled again, but lower. He waited and repeated the signal. The same two notes, one high, one low. A desolate melody for the gutted insides of the mountain.

Then he listened.

As though expecting a reply.

And he got one.

A thud. From above.

The beam of light swept across to the staircase, its smooth steps littered with mounds of gravel.

A low rumbling. The crunch of gravel.

Now he could smell the old one. He was near. He might be standing at the top of the stairs.

'Adja?'

He waited. The bear was moving above. Pacing to and fro with a heavy, dragging tread. Snorting. Growling deeply.

'It's me. Lennart-bardni.'

The big one panted.

'Can I come up and join you?'

He slowly moved toward the stairs.

'Do you want me to turn off the light? I'm turning off the light.'

Darkness enveloped him and he continued on with his hand sweeping through the air in front of him. The old bear's scent was so powerful he could follow it to the stairs.

After reaching the top, he stopped. There were shades to the darkness. The scents multiplied and grew stronger and the strongest of all emanated from the bear, rising like steam from its fur.

'*Skabram. Lea go jur dådas dån.*'

The big one breathed heat and blew it out. Grumbled and rammed its head against his chest, rammed it hard. Almost knocked him over. He reached out and tried to put his arm around the massive neck in some kind of sentimental embrace, but the bear wouldn't have it; it rolled its head away and snorted Lennart's face wet and foetid.

Slowly, it moved away from him. He heard the pads of its feet rasp against the concrete further away. He was leaving now.

Lennart fumbled his way to the wall and put his palm against it.

He pulled off his headlamp, shoved it under his shirt and found the button with his thumb. A light flared to life in his chest; he cupped his hand over it, as if to protect a precious flame. Eventually, he was able make out contours in the dark, contours that slowly filled with content. The length of the corridor. A long passage of smooth rock. The bear that stood watching him with its enormous head. The hump on its back.

He took a few more steps toward it.

'*Boade deike,*' he said. '*Rahkis guoibmi.*'

The erect ears. The black toad skin of its nose and the cavernous tunnels leading into it. The drooping lower lip.

'Karats is gone. Urtas is gone. And Luttak. *Leat javkan.* But I'm here. Lennart-bardni.'

The old one backed up a few steps.

'*Tjåvo mu.*'

He chanced another step closer as he surreptitiously pulled the headlamp out from under his shirt. He let it hang down so its beam hit the floor. Two concentric circles dancing across the concrete.

'You have to come out of this mountain. To the children. *Jurddes unnoras asiide.*'

Now the old one rattled out a noise.

'You can't stay here. *Gal dån ipmirdat, adja.*'

A displeased sound.

'You just disappeared. When I came back, you were gone. So I never had a chance to talk to you about what happened. What happened to Karats. Do you want to know what happened to Karats? *Sorbmejädji. Nu dat lei. Sorbmejädji.*'

The bear turned around and lumbered off.

Lennart hung back a moment. Then he followed.

The old one had moved into a chamber and lain down. Lennart stopped in the doorway and cast the light around the revolting room. A human was on the floor, facing the wall. Fully dressed. Boots with deep-tread soles. Blue windbreaker down to his thighs. Strands of hair that had rotted inside the hood.

Skeleton parts from God knows what creatures were scattered across the floor. Bone sticks, bone hooks. A curved bone column. A small ribcage. And over there was an entire cat. Except without its abdomen. Like some kind of miniature cheetah. The stench was a noxious gas; he coughed discreetly as he walked over to the bear and sat down on the floor next to it. After a while, he reached out and placed a hand on its wide brow.

'*Badjan, Stuora Skabram.*'

The bear's eyes were closed, the slits invisible.

'I'm here. I'm here with you.'

Ingvill started in fear when she heard someone coming out of the mountain. She quickly stood up and stared at the crevice. Once his upper body was through, he turned around and slid down on his bottom. The sunlight was strong; he was squinting.

'Was he there?'

He put his sunglasses on and nodded.

'The little one didn't come out.'

She scooped the mouse out of her jacket pocket.

'It came out a long time ago.'

Lennart prodded it with his index finger.

'You can't just run off like that.'

Grete was eating. Tuna with pasta spirals in an old plastic container. She put her cutlery down and swallowed.

'That was quick.'

'There's a human in there, did you know that?'

'A human?'

He held her gaze until she understood what he meant.

She waved her hand dismissively.

Lennart sat down and stared at her.

'What are you saying we should have done? We had to find a way to cheer him up.'

'There are better ways.'

'We felt it was worth a shot.'

'He has retreated very far into himself. It's as if he can't find his way out. He might not even be aware that he can turn.'

'You can help him, I know you can.'

Lennart sat in silence for a moment.

'If we could get that human,' he said. 'The one with the website. What was her name, Myrén? If we give him her and we can get him to understand who she is and what she's done, I think that might do him good.'

'That's easier said than done,' Grete retorted.

'Just go get her.'

'She's protected,' Ingvill said.

'Is it that bastard fox?'

'A squirrel,' Grete replied.

'A squirrel?'

She nodded.

'What fucking squirrel?'

'We don't know.'

He stared at the plastic container she was eating out of. A winged child with golden curls holding an ice cream cone in each hand was depicted on it.

'Have you seen it?'

'Abraham has,' Grete said softly. 'When he went down there, when was it, a year ago? And he took it hard. That's why he looks the way he does.' She ran her fingers along her cheek. 'Food sticks in the corner of his mouth. And he's almost blind in one eye.'

'What's the situation at Torsten's?'

'Well now,' Grete said and dabbed her lips with a sheet of kitchen roll. 'Last time we were there, he threatened us with a gun. Elna has moved out, the children too, I think. There's nothing for us there.'

'What about Carola? Carola Fjellborg?'

'All the lemmings are gone. Since the fire at Öbrells'.'

'Isn't that just something she's saying?'

'She's shaken, there's no doubt about it; she just sits at home, smoking cigarettes. Besides, I don't think the lemmings are equal to the task anyway.'

'They're not to be trifled with.'

'We need something bigger.'

'What about the hare?'

'That one?' She snorted out a laugh. 'He's blind. And not always to be trusted either.'

Lennart quietly turned the problem over in his mind for a while.

'Remember Frans?' he said. 'Frans Fagervall. We were there after the war, after Urho died? His, what would that be, nephew, Rune – we could ask him. He's a bit tricky, but it might be worth asking. Because he has a wolf.'

'A wolf?' Ingvill said.

Lennart nodded.

'I thought all the wolves were with Erasmus and Stava,' she said with an inquiring glance at Grete, who had started rubbing and scratching the fingers of her gloved hand.

'Sure, because that's what Rune wants you to think. He wants nothing to do with Erasmus and Stava.'

'Does it turn?'

'What do you mean?'

'If it doesn't turn—'

'It does. Last time I was there it was wearing clothes.'

'Clothes? That's promising.'

The old lady took off her headscarf and patted down her hair.

[80]

'And do you think he would help us?'

'Rune? Well, what choice does he have? If Erasmus finds out about his wolf, he's going to claim it. So I guess we're going to have to threaten him, between the lines. It's in his interest, too, to have Skabram turn.'

'Where does he live?'

'In Dorotea.'

'Then let's make for Dorotea.'

When I walked out onto the square, I spotted Roland at one of the long tables lined up outside the beer tent. He was all alone.

'Fancy finding you here,' I said and sat down across from him.

'They've raised a flag,' he said and nodded to the flagpoles outside the Cultural Centre. 'The rainbow flag.'

'This won't do,' I said.

'What?'

'We can't have you sitting here. Outside.'

'I'm crashing the festival,' he said and tilted his plastic cup of beer as if to examine the viscosity of the liquid.

'Honestly, it feels more like the festival's crashing us.'

He laughed and I seized the opportunity to go on the offensive.

'I ran into Susso's childhood friend the other day. Diana. She's a doctor at the hospital. And I asked her to go visit Susso. Because I'm afraid to. That's the truth.'

Roland took a small sip from his cup and then sat staring at the stage as though someone were performing on it.

'And now I feel guilty.'

'Why?'

'What if something happens to her?'

'You're thinking about the cult leader?'

I shook my head. Then I changed my mind.

'Well, yes, of course I am. But not just him. You know it's not actually Susso I'm afraid of. There's a reason why she turned out the way she did.'

I glared at him until he caught my meaning. Then he grinned at me, as much as he dared to. He had shoved his hands into his trouser pockets and was moving his sandals about restlessly under the table.

We had never made it past this point. The reluctance to take this conversation further was so intense I was breaking out in a cold sweat. My fingertips went numb and I was over-come with a powerful urge to change the subject. Just then, they turned on music: clattering rock started streaming out of the speakers and when I raised my voice to make myself heard, I somehow seemed to break through the barriers that stymied me whenever we tried to talk about the trolls.

'You've seen it for yourself,' I shouted. 'She's had it for ten years. And Barbro had it for twenty-five before that. Would you say that's normal?'

'But we don't know if that's true.'

He looked away with a cocksure, indifferent expression; I leaned across the table.

'Why can't you just believe me? You know as well as I do what it's done to her. She's completely changed. And Cecilia too. That's proof, isn't it?'

'Proof of what?'

'That they're real. That they're actually real.'

He picked up his plastic cup and downed its contents, ran his index finger over his lips and then sat there rubbing his thumb against the part of the finger that had got wet.

'She was damaged by the things that happened, that's obvious and hardly all that surprising, given what you went through and what the papers wrote. But to say it's because of the . . .'

He broke off abruptly.

'I don't want to talk about this,' he said.

'You know what? I don't either.'

'Then why are we?'

'Because we have to, Roland. Don't ask me how it works, but we're somehow prevented from talking about these things. Can't you sense it, the resistance, the almost physical aversion? I've been thinking it must be part of their cover. It's like some kind of mental block.'

Roland had crossed his arms and was studying me; he was clearly waiting for a chance to speak.

'Would you like a pint, I'm going to go buy a pint.'

The door to his office was locked; it was so unexpected Anders pushed the handle down over and over again and even yanked it hard. Then he took a step back. Why was the bloody door locked?

While he stood there just staring at the closed door, something happened inside him. It was like a shifting, inside his head. He waited for things to clear. They didn't. The feeling lingered, but when he tried to grasp it, it retreated inward like a cat under a sofa.

Nothing remained of the good humour that had had him whistling on his way to the laboratory building. Now he felt almost sick. He grabbed the clutch of keys hanging by his stomach. The key slid into the lock but he couldn't turn it.

Why couldn't he get in? He looked at the sign to the right of the door. The tag with his name was gone. Puzzled, he looked around. The sign on the next door over said 'Per Ahlqvist'. So he hadn't gone to the wrong room.

He ran his hand over his head and felt himself losing his footing. Lost and scared, he walked down the hall to the rotunda that housed the department's library. It contained a display case with a collection of craniums that were reflected in the glass. The skulls were of different sizes, but they all looked alike. As though they had been created by someone who wanted to practise doing different scale models. Hollow-eyed capsules in various shades of yellowy white. The smaller animal craniums were so tiny they looked like something you'd collect at a beach.

The sensation that had just eluded him slithered by once more in the ever-shrinking nook of awareness he had access to, and this time it left something in its wake. A feeling that he had committed some sort of crime. But what had he done?

Powerlessness swelled within him. He sank into a squat and grunted and pressed his hands to his head. Then he jumped up and gave the display case a shove. The craniums responded by executing a hastily coordinated relocation. He grabbed the edge, rocked the case up against his chest and hurled it away. It tipped over, so slowly he had time to see the skulls gather in a grinning heap that tumbled around and around before the display case smashed against the floor. The glass shattered with a loud, symphonic crash and before he knew it, he was running down the hallway like a hunted madman.

Johanna was in the kitchen when he came home. He waited in the hallway for a while, watching her, before he could work up the courage to enter. He tried to touch her, but she pulled her arm away and looked at him like he had groped her.

'I know,' he said. 'I don't work there any more.'

'Do you know what time it is?'

'No, what could it be? Seven? Half seven?'

'It's four, Anders. Quarter past four. That's when you get back.'

His eyes veered to the digital numbers on the microwave.

'Yes, well, I did think work seemed a bit deserted.'

He met her eyes and leaned forward with his head in his hands, supporting his elbows on the table.

'I think there's something in my head,' he mumbled.

'There's no tapeworm in your head,' she said. 'We already checked.'

'I mean something else. Something worse. It's like there's someone in here.' He screwed his index finger against his temple. 'Another person. I don't know how to explain. It's kind of cramped. It's really scary.'

'I'm going to bed,' she said and stood up.

'Okay,' he said. 'I think I'm going to sit here for a while.'

Just before she shut the bedroom door, he called out:

'Are you hungry? I could make something to eat.'

He walked through the woods aimlessly. But then there it was. A red construction trailer wedged among the spruce trees. Its chimney like a periscope. Black, empty windows.

He got out the key that hung on a nail under the wooden deck, climbed the steel mesh stairs, entered and shut the door behind him.

Everything seemed familiar yet strange. The ear protectors that had been hooked onto a pair of rugged, brown ram's horns that cast long, pointed shadows on the wall. The glasses and plates in the washing-up bucket. The white bell shade and motionless glass prisms of the kerosene lamp. A silly miniature gold hat neatly folded from a flattened beer can.

There was an open sleeping bag on the mattress on the lower bunk and a toiletry bag next to the bed. He looked under the bed. There was a suitcase there. When he noticed the clothes in it, he was suddenly terrified. He even walked over to the door, ready to leave. But he stayed.

The whisky bottle was mounted upside down on a stripped wooden log and had a tap. He poured a slug into a coffee cup and sat down at the table. A few maps were scattered on it. A cube of writing notes. He looked at the top one and was relieved to see it wasn't his handwriting. A shopping list, scribbled in ink. Kerosene. Coffee filter holder. Paper plates. Terminal clamps.

He tore off the note. Picked up the pen but put it back down. Sat there with a smile on his lips. Without drinking, almost without moving. Hours passed. Flies were crawling on the window, but he saw nothing.

Then he suddenly stood up, opened the door and said:

'Come in.'

It was early morning when they arrived in Dorotea. They parked a few hundred yards from Rune's house, which they could glimpse at the edge of the forest on the other side of a meadow where a listing maypole stood. A percent sign in the pale light of dawn. Lennart walked down toward the house alone. A brick bungalow with a black concrete tile roof. Two cars were parked in front of the attached garage. A van and an old Saab. A rose inside a cone of transparent plastic wrapping could be seen through the Saab's rear window. It had been there so long it had withered into a black horror flower. There was a car seat in the back; Lennart stood staring at that for a good while before climbing the front step and knocking on the door. Music was coming from inside. *Through the years, we all will be together*. He peered in through the textured glass sidelight. The only thing moving in the disorienting sea of refractions was his own face. *Hang a shining star upon the highest bough, and have yourself a merry little Christmas now.*

The door opened a crack, revealing a topless human. A youth. The beard around his mouth split into two ginger feelers.

'Where's Rune?'

'He's not here.'

Lennart grabbed the handle and tore the door open. The

young man backed away. His arms were covered in tattoos that looked homemade. He was holding a boxcutter.

'You're not allowed here,' he said.

Lennart glanced into the kitchen. A brown refrigerator door reflected the fluorescent ceiling lights. There was post on the table, a fan of white envelopes. He pushed past the young man and followed the music into the living room.

He was sitting on the sofa. The wrinkled face that had been Rune's was streaked with brown discolouration and a yellow eye was staring out through one of the roughly cut holes where Rune's eyes had once been; looking into that eye was like meeting the gaze of a lunatic through a keyhole.

A skinny girl was sitting pressed up against this horrifying figure. Her head was shaved and her arms verdant with meandering tattoo tendrils. She was clasping the old man's hand, which was hidden inside a work glove, between her own.

For a second or two, Lennart stood motionless, staring at them. Then he turned without a word and walked briskly back to the hallway and out through the front door.

Grete was sitting outside the motorhome and saw him lumbering back up the road. When he drew near, she grabbed her crutch, an aluminium pipe with a cuff of solid plastic, and stood up.

'Wasn't he home?'

Lennart sat down, panting.

'Both yes and no,' he said.

The narrow strip of forehead that was visible between her sunglasses and headscarf furrowed.

[90]

'I've never seen anything like it. Rune's dead. And the wolf has used his face to make a mask. He's pulled the skin from his skull and made a mask, with hair and all the rest.'

The motorhome door opened and Ingvill came out and sat down on the steps. She was wearing a men's shirt and knitted hat.

'You can't do things like that with claws,' the old lady said. 'He must have had help.'

Lennart nodded.

'A boy and a girl in their twenties. They have a little one too.'

'A child,' Grete said thoughtfully and dug the crutch's rubber tip into the gravel while she studied the house on the other side of the meadow with newfound interest.

Then she turned to him with a smile.

'Are you telling me you've never seen it before? A mask.'

He shook his head.

'Not that kind. Made from a human.'

'No,' she said, nodding agreement, 'it's likely a wolf thing. Were you scared?'

'I don't know about scared. But it wasn't exactly what I had expected, put it that way. The question is what we do now.'

'But what did he say?'

'There didn't seem much point in talking to him. Given what he's done to Rune.'

'But we don't know that he killed him. He could have died of natural causes. The mask could be an expression of grief and loss. No?'

'So you think I should go back?'

'I'll go with you.'

*

The girl opened the door. She was holding a toddler in her arms. A boy who was breathing through his mouth. Sweaty curls were plastered to his big head. There was a plaster on his cheek and a sock had been put over his right hand and taped in place around the oedemic arm.

She looked at them for a second before stepping aside and letting them into the hallway. The wolf man was still sitting where Lennart had left him on the sofa and the same Christmas song was playing. When Lennart and Grete stepped into the living room, he turned his head to them. Then he tilted it back a little, so he could see out with both eyes. Sliced by the blinds, the light from outside drew a ladder across his face, on which Rune's features appeared in a twisted, helpless expression.

The girl sat down on the sofa next to the old man. She had set the child down on the floor.

'He knows you,' she said. 'You're the bear man. Why is there a thread around your hand?'

'It's a bandage.'

'He doesn't like it. That you're wearing that bandage.'

'It bleeds. If I remove it.'

'Rune,' Grete said. 'We've come to ask a favour.'

When she spoke Rune's name, the old man tilted his head to the side like a heeding dog.

'If you come into the kitchen,' the girl said, 'we get out those little cups from the cabinet and you could have sweets from the box that's a rattle. I mean sweeteners. Would you like some sweeteners?'

'Yes, please,' Grete said, inclining her head, 'we would love that.'

They went into the kitchen and sat down. The girl got cups from the cabinet and set them out on the table, opened a small jar and poured tablets into their cups. Then she picked the boy up and rocked him in her arms.

'How are things up at Torsten's?' she said.

Lennart glanced at Grete.

'At Torsten's?' he said. 'I don't know. I haven't been there in a long time.'

'It's bad,' Grete said and shook her head sadly. 'It's all bad. Very, very bad.' She wet her index finger, fished a tablet from her cup and put it in her mouth. 'As I was saying before. We've come to ask a favour of you.'

'Why do you talk so funny?'

'Funny? I'm Norwegian.'

She took off her sunglasses and put them on the table, then she leaned forward so Rune could see the unhuman sheen in her eyes.

'There is a human in Vittangi who scares me so much I can barely talk about her. She wants to do very bad things to me. Which means she wants to do very bad things to you. Because you and I are siblings. You and Lennart are also siblings. He is your brother. And I am your sister. And surely you want to help your sister?'

The figure on the other side of the table sat stock-still.

'But there's a problem. A small problem. Because she has a little one helping her.' She showed with her hand how small the little one was. 'A squirrel. He is old and knows much, and we can't quite handle him, and we're afraid of him. I'll admit as much. But I'm certain you aren't. Which is why we're here. We have travelled far to see you, Rune.'

Lennart studied the girl, who was leaning back against the kitchen counter, rocking the little boy in her arms. The arm with the sock on moved up toward her mouth; she turned her head away as if to escape a fly.

'He doesn't understand,' she said. 'And he doesn't like that you talk funny.'

'Maybe we should do this in Swedish?'

'He thinks you're trying to trick him,' she said.

'We're not,' Grete said. 'We just want you to come with us to Vittangi. And help us with this squirrel. Before it's too late. For your own sake. Rune. For your own sake.'

'Who's Vittangi?'

'It's the place where she lives,' Lennart said. 'The girl with the squirrel.'

'He doesn't want to go there.'

'We really do need your help,' Grete said.

'He doesn't want to. He doesn't like Vittangi and he doesn't like you and he doesn't like the bandage on his hand. You're just trying to trick him. You're thieves.'

'Thieves? We're not thieves.'

Silence fell in the kitchen. The only sounds were the music from the living room and the little grunts coming from the child as it tried to twist out of its mother's grasp.

'I think you'd better leave,' the girl said.

Grete stayed in her seat. But when the young man appeared in the doorway, she nodded, stuck her sunglasses into her hair, grabbed her crutch and got to her feet.

Lennart held the front door for her but she was in no hurry. She had pulled out her phone and was tapping it with her thumb. Then she aimed the glowing screen at the young man.

They didn't have to wait long before the door slammed shut and he came outside. Grete asked his name and he said Elias. For fear of being overheard, he wanted them to move further away from the house, but Grete said that wasn't necessary. He looked terrified. His eyes darted this way and that and he was unable to stand still.

'What's her name?'

'Fanny.'

'Is she your girlfriend?'

'Yes. Or. I don't know. She used to be, anyway.'

'And the boy? What's the boy's name?'

'Malte.'

'If you want us to help you, Elias, you have to help us first. If you help us, we can look after Malte. I promise we'll look after him if you do.'

'She'll never hand him over. She won't even take him to see a doctor.'

'And I can see why.'

'But there should be something they can do . . .'

'There's nothing *a doctor* can do for him. She's right about that. He will be better off with me. And Fanny will understand that, in time. He will be better off with me.'

'What do I need to do?'

'You have to make Fanny see that you're not safe here. That you will never be safe here, and that Rune has to come with us.'

Elias nodded.

'Would you like me to talk to her?'

He nodded.

'When does he sleep?'

'Rune? During the day, mostly. It depends.'

'Take my phone number. And give me a ring when he's asleep.'

'Okay,' he said and pulled a phone out of his pocket.

'When he's asleep. Not until then.'

An hour later, Grete's phone rang and Lennart went over to fetch Fanny. She was waiting for him out by the road. She had put on a hoodie and pulled the hood up.

'We want to talk to you,' he said.

She walked about fifty feet behind him to the motorhome. He opened the door for her, but she stopped outside with her hands like lumps in her jacket pockets. Her mouth pressed shut, her lips pale.

'She's in there,' he said.

'Why can't she come out?'

'She's resting.'

Her eyes darted away. She was thinking. Then she walked up to the door and climbed the little steps. Grete's voice croaked from inside.

'Hi there, Fanny. But where's your little boy?'

Håkan took off his watch and put it on the shelf where they kept the spices. He always did when he was about to do something in the kitchen. Diana sat on a chair, watching him. The hairs on his wrist were curly with sweat under the metal links of his wristband. He wore his jeans, which were the perfect length, with a leather belt, and his shirt was tucked in. It was always tucked in. How he managed that was beyond her. He was filling the frying pan with pinches of mince from the packet. The pan hissed when he dropped the red dollops into the butter and the fan was humming so loudly she almost had to shout to make herself heard.

'His blood pressure won't budge even though I've given him the whole shebang; I even have him on spironolactone!'

'Have you done any tests?'

'Of course I have. The screen lit up like a Christmas tree when I opened the module. MCV was high and his triglycerides and transes. He had a CDT of nine!'

'Because he drinks. You know that, right?'

'I've asked, I ask every time. But he denies it. *Snaps* at Christmas and a glass of wine or two on the weekend with his wife.'

'Speaking of which, I bought wine,' he said and chopped at the mince with the spatula.

She opened the door to the laundry room. The bag was on the floor, next to the box of detergent. Håkan always put alcohol in the laundry room. Maybe because he was ashamed of the bags, maybe it was the closest they had to a wine cellar. She pulled out a bottle of red, set it down on the kitchen counter and rummaged through the drawer for the bottle opener.

'I ran into Susso's mum the other day, in the park. Last Tuesday.'

She turned the roar of the fan down a little, sniffed the bottle and then filled two glasses she had placed on the table.

'And I realised something I hadn't understood before. Which is that she's a few sandwiches short of a picnic. No wonder Susso turned out the way she did with a mother like her. All of it comes from her. From Gudrun.'

'Like a kind of heritage, you mean?'

'What's it called, a delusion shared with another person, something in French.'

'*Folie à deux.*'

'*Oui. Folie à deux.*'

'Though that's exceptionally unusual, just so you know.'

'More unusual than trolls?'

'Pretty much on a par, I reckon.'

'She's worried Lennart Brösth is out for revenge.'

'On her?'

'On Susso.'

'Why? Cheers.'

'Cheers. Because she helped catch him. Do you want me to cut the vegetables?'

'It's done.'

With her wine glass in her hand, she sat down on the floor with her back against the fridge.

'Wasn't it the other way around,' he said, 'that the picture she took had nothing to do with the kidnapping? Shouldn't he be thanking her for pointing the police in the wrong direction? If there's logic to the madness? Or am I wrong?'

'She says they're not like other people. They're dangerous. A hundred years is not to him what it is to us.'

'The old man certainly does seem spry.'

'See what I mean? She says things like that while at the same time claiming Susso's been acting weird.'

'Though you have to wonder what acting weird entails, given that we're talking about a person who actively and openly is searching for actual trolls. Minus plus minus. Maybe it means Susso has come to her senses?'

'She's moved to Vittangi.'

'That's actually how *folies à deux* work,' he said. 'It's always one person sucking another into their delusions. And if the other person creates distance, like by moving away, the spell is broken, so to speak. And that seems to be the case here.'

'I think she's doing drugs.'

'Drugs? How come?'

'Gudrun says she's a different person. That she's skinny and no one seems to recognise her. On the other hand, maybe that's to be expected if Susso's doing her best to reject her. If it's true that she's realised she's kind of been brainwashed.'

'Who are her friends?'

'She doesn't have any. According to Gudrun she doesn't see anyone.'

'Addicts are not usually loners. Or does she grow her own? Was she good at chemistry in school?'

A clay fridge magnet was digging into the back of her head; she took it down. A flattened ladybird with big, rigid eyes. She held it in her hand; it was amazingly smooth to the touch. She counted the dots on its back. Couldn't remember if she had made it or Håkan. Which one of them had laboured over placing the dots on it. She didn't answer his question and he seemed to assume he'd gone too far because he used a different voice when he then asked if they had been classmates in upper secondary or before that.

'Secondary school,' she said. 'But we were close after too. Until I moved to Umeå. Since then, we basically haven't talked at all. We ran into each other once or twice just after we moved here. Swapped numbers and all that. But then it just didn't happen.'

'And this thing with the trolls, how did she get into that?'

'Her grandfather was Gunnar Myrén. The photographer. Surely I've told you this before?'

'I know you had a friend called Susso, and that she took that picture that was in the newspaper. That's all I know. You never talk about her. You've never talked about her.'

'But you know who Gunnar Myrén is?'

He nodded.

'What's with the face?'

'What face?'

She grimaced.

He had cut the bag of seasoning open and was sprinkling it over the mince.

'Isn't he a bit kitschy?'

'Either way, he took a picture of a troll. An aerial photograph. In Sarek. It's a bear and there's someone sitting on it, riding it. But it's impossible to say what it is.'

'And this is a photograph we're talking about, a proper photograph?'

'Yes, to the extent that a photograph of a troll can be a proper photograph.'

'Which it can't be. And I'm fairly convinced I have all of science on my side when I say that.'

'I've seen it.'

'All right.'

'It looks very real.'

'Photoshop?'

'This was the eighties.'

'There were obviously ways to doctor images back then too.'

'Could you stop putting him down! He's kitsch and the picture's fake. I'm Håkan and I'm a doctor, I'm scientific and everyone else is stupid.'

'I'm sorry, I thought we were talking about Susso's grandfather.' He pointed the spatula at her. 'Not your grandfather.'

'Regardless, it was something she did. For a while.'

'Trolls.'

'She wanted to know if they were real. She had a website, a cryptozoological website, where she wrote about these things and posted pictures. That she had taken or people had sent to her. And through this website she got in touch with an old lady in Jokkis who had seen some dodgy creature in her garden. So Susso went down there and installed one of those cameras that take pictures by themselves. A trail camera. And it snapped a picture of a little man.'

'That was the one in the paper, when that kid had been kidnapped?'

'Yes, they suspected him of having taken the boy.'

'But he hadn't?'

With a mouth full of wine, she shook her head.

'He was innocent?'

'Yes,' she said and put her glass down on the floor.

'So who was he?'

'Who was who?'

'The person in the picture! The little man.'

'No one knows.'

'He hasn't come forward?'

'Not as far as I know.'

'Why didn't he come forward, if he didn't have anything to do with the kidnapping?'

'How should I know?'

'That's weird though, right? You're going to have to move your *belles fesses*.'

Without getting up, she scooched sideways so Håkan could open the fridge door.

'But you think he's real?'

'Real?'

'Yes, you don't think Susso conjured him digitally, so to speak. Carrying on the Myrén family tradition.'

She pondered that with her eyes on the floor.

'The thought has crossed your mind?'

'It might have.'

'But you know her. Would she, in your opinion, be capable of producing a counterfeit photograph for the purposes of misleading the police and general public?'

'As I said, I haven't talked to her in years.'

'Because of her delusions.'

'Partly, but there are other reasons.'

'I see.'

'I don't see you being super close with your childhood friends.'

He had cut open a packet of sour cream and threw the tab in the bin.

'In Kiruna County I have, let's see, zero childhood friends.'

'How convenient.'

'You've distanced yourself. On account of the trolls.'

'Because I knew you would make fun of her.'

'So it's my fault?'

'The two of you are not compatible.'

'You sound very sure of yourself. Almost like you've made your mind up we're not compatible.'

'It's like me and your sister. Cat and dog.'

'Millan tries. But you don't. You've made your mind up it's not working.'

'I know you would make fun of her.'

'Can't we invite her over then? So I can prove you wrong.'

'Because you want to meet her or because you want to prove you're right and I'm wrong?'

'Because I want to meet her, obviously.'

'You're such a liar!'

She laughed so hard she splashed wine on her shirt – a white cotton shirt she was fond of – which made her pull an angry face.

'Call her.'

'She doesn't have a phone.'

'Then go out there,' he said and held out the salt packet to her.

She pulled off her shirt, poured salt on the stains and threw the shirt in the hamper.

'I told Gudrun I would,' she said as she dug through the pile of clean laundry. 'But I really don't feel like it.'

'What are you afraid of?'

'What am I afraid of?' she said and pulled the shirt over her head. 'I obviously want to preserve her.'

Håkan opened his mouth but didn't have time to get a word out.

'The way she was! If it's true that she's completely broken. You get that, don't you?'

'Can I talk now?'

'No, you can't,' she said and topped up her glass.

'You're being really selfish. You know that, right?'

'You're selfish.'

'If she goes off the deep end properly, you'll never be able to forgive yourself. You are going to want to be able to tell yourself you tried. That you at least did everything you could.'

'You know what junkies are like, you can't save them, they have to save themselves.'

'You can do enough to be able to tell yourself you tried. Go out there. Invite her over for dinner. Let her meet Kiruna. And I'll meet her too.'

At this point, the little girl entered the kitchen. She looked at them wide-eyed.

'Kiruna Sillfors is wondering why you're shouting,' he said.

'I'm shouting because I'm starving.'

Håkan pulled the cling film off the bowls; the little girl

climbed onto her Tripp Trapp chair. But he ordered her back down: first she had to turn off the TV and wash her hands. In that order. He held out the breadbasket with the taco shells. Diana said thanks, but then he put one hand behind his ear and she corrected herself. It was an idea of his, that you weren't allowed to say thank you when you ate tacos, you had to say *gracias*. Kiruna thought it was hilarious and became unusually polite, so that was good at least. Though she didn't eat much. The mince and sweetcorn went down okay. And some cucumber she munched away on.

'Then I'm going out to Vittangi tomorrow.'

'You'll miss the festival.'

'Oh no.'

She turned to the little girl.

'I'm going to go see a friend.'

'Who?'

'Her name's Susso.'

'I didn't know you had a friend called that.'

'But I do. When we were little, people called her Myran.'

'Because she was small?'

'No, because her last name was Myrén. And do you know what they called me?'

The girl shook her head, full of anticipation.

'Sillen. Because my name is Sillfors.'

The little girl giggled.

'And do you know what I was called?' Håkan said and took a big, crunchy bite. 'I was called Håkan.'

'Håkan Hellström,' Diana whispered.

The little girl giggled. Then she said: 'If you hadn't named me Kiruna, my name wouldn't have been Kiruna.'

'True,' Håkan said, 'then your name would have been something else entirely.'

The little girl nodded.

'Is that weird to you?' Diana asked.

She nodded again.

'Yes, it's pretty weird. When you think about it.'

'Can I come with you?'

'To Vittangi? I don't know if that's such a good idea. I haven't seen her in so long. And she's not feeling too well.'

'Is she sick?'

'That's what I'm going there to find out.'

Anders was sitting on the sofa in the living room, trying to figure out why he was home alone. He was, quite clearly, at home. In his living room. He was sitting in it. In the middle of the day. But it wasn't a weekend, because then Johanna and William would have been home too. He knew he had a lot of leave saved up. Was he on leave, was that why he was sitting there? He swallowed hard and made a new attempt at driving his thoughts forward, but he didn't get anywhere.

When he turned his head, he felt he could make out shapeless figures coming at him from both sides. Quick, stealthy shadows with evil intent. It was highly unpleasant, so he sat dead still to avoid it. Then he turned his head, but he did it stiffly and slowly like an old-timey robot.

He remembered something now. Something had happened at the field station. After the wolf incident, he'd been put on sick leave. Sick leave, he had that phrase to hold on to. But then? Had he broken something? Yes. He had a memory of glass shattering. People shouting. Several people talking over each other and attacking him with vicious tirades he had no way of defending himself against, a bombardment of accusations. Or was that something he'd dreamt? It was impossible to say. It was like there had been a merging in his brain. Everything blended together in a blurred mass and he knew he had tried to explain this to Johanna, what it felt like and how insanely difficult it was to put it into words and how it affected him, but she didn't want to listen, the only thing she wanted was for him to seek help.

You need help, Anders.

You're going mad. This is what it feels like.

Still, he felt he could remember more and more when he really put his mind to it. When he sat like this and searched his recollections. He had talked to Johanna, was that yesterday? She had said he ran about outside in the night. He remembered that. Not that he did but that she had said he did and he remembered exactly what she'd looked like when she said it. That was a step in the right direction. Maybe things were clearing up. Blue skies ahead.

He closed his eyes for a few seconds and the moment he took the leap into sleep he jerked like he was being electrocuted.

There was a notebook on the kitchen table. It was open and he could see that someone had written something on it. Words meant for him. How many lines? The paper was blue all over. Johanna's handwriting. It was not a greeting, not a message. It was a letter. She had written him a letter and put it on the kitchen table. That was very ominous; he only reluctantly went up to the notebook and prodded it to make the writing turn the right way up. His fingertips strayed to his hairline but his glasses weren't there. The only thing he found was a small piece of bark. A flake from a pine tree that he crumpled to dust between his fingers. He picked up the notebook and calibrated a distance at which he could make out the letters.

When he had finished reading, he put the notebook down on the table. Practically threw it. Then he went into the bathroom and closed the door and tried to cry, but he couldn't. Nothing came out. His mouth was ugly and twisted in the mirror, but no tears came.

Their bed was made; she had even arranged the decorative cushions in a pile on the bedspread. He stood and looked at the bed and tried to connect this level of care with what she had written in her letter. Is that really something you do if you've given up? If you're so afraid of a person you are unable to sleep in the same house as them?

He pulled the blinds down and closed them. Shut the door and lay down on the bed. He didn't have the heart to either move the cushions or pull the bedspread aside and he lay on the side that was usually hers.

A low wailing woke him. It couldn't really be called a howling. He lay still, listening. The house was dark. Night. Had the sound come from inside his head, or outside? He often snored so loudly he woke himself.

He was unable to go back to sleep; he couldn't even keep his eyes closed. The tension was too powerful, it was coursing through every part of his body. Eventually, he got out of bed.

He twisted the blind wand and widened the gaps. He couldn't see much. The black contours of the garden furniture. The rotary washing line like a dead tree.

He went into the living room and over to the terrace door, turned the key and opened it. Stepped out into the night. Stood there in his stocking feet, waiting. Even though his mouth was open, he breathed solely through his nostrils; there was like a block of some kind in his throat.

A human figure materialised out of the darkness of the woods. A short woman with a wimple of dark hair. She moved gracefully and silently like a shadow. Stopped a few feet from him.

'Why do you look so scared?' she said.

He backed up toward the house and almost fell over.

'Anders.'

'I feel so weird.'

'I noticed the car's gone.'

'What car?'

'Her car.'

'Yes,' he said, 'she's gone.'

The sound of a lorry reversing woke me. A cruel honking sound that found its way into my dream, where it morphed into some kind of klaxon. Not at all a nice sound to wake up to and I was cross with Roland for opening the window. After the rock music had finally died down, people had roamed the streets shouting like lunatics half the night. And now this. It was unbearable. I tried to go back to sleep but I couldn't.

Roland was already up, of course. And vanished without a trace, as I discovered when I went into the kitchen. He hadn't even read the paper. I licked my thumb and flipped through the news. Nothing about Lennart Brösth. Not a word. I had a shower and then sat down on the balcony with my coffee cup, shivering with cold. Four boys walked down the street carrying a section of a fence; they were heading toward the main stage in Ferrum Park, where Status Quo were booked to play. Thrilled shrieks were drifting up from the spinning rides at the carnival.

It was going to be a busy day; Ella was coming in to lend a hand and I knew she was looking forward to it. Not only because she needed the money. She liked manning the till. Taking payments and using her English. And spending time with her grandmother.

She was waiting for me in the foyer. Dressed in a short-sleeved shirt with a printed outline of Kiruna's two famous high-rises, and the text 'The Erskine Skyline'. The shirt was from the shop; I'd given her it for Christmas and I welled up picturing her back in that grimy, chaotic flat, picking this out as something suitable to wear. I squeezed out a smile but immediately realised she saw right through me with those shy, worried eyes of hers.

I unlocked the door and went over to the counter and put my handbag down. Ella went and picked up a book. A picture book. She always looked through the children's books, she was still that young.

'Well then,' I said, 'how's your mother?'

She shrugged.

'She's at some spa. In Piteå.'

'Again?'

'She said she needed to pamper herself a little.'

'Well then. Right. Have you seen these? Pretty, don't you think?'

She looked at the cloudberry I was holding out and then she took it in her hand and weighed it.

'What's it made of?'

'I should probably know that. What do you reckon, glass? So you're home alone now then?'

She nodded and I sighed.

'It's okay. I like being alone.'

I put the cloudberry back in its little box, then pulled out the drawer, put the box in it, closed the drawer and locked it.

'He was in the paper. That old man.'

'He was. But they'll catch him before you know it.'

The girl was quiet for a moment.

'That picture your dad took, do you have it here?'

'What picture?' I said, even though I knew very well which picture she meant.

'The one with the troll.'

'No, it's not here.'

'Then where is it?'

'It's gone.'

'Gone?'

'Oh look, customers.'

Lennart peered into the reeking darkness of the back of the van. A patchwork of newspapers and flattened cardboard on the floor and at the far end, a small armchair with upholstered buttons.

'Have you ever driven him?'

Elias shook his head.

'What about the girl?'

'Huh?'

'Fanny. Has she driven him?'

'No, I don't think so.'

Lennart slammed the doors shut and walked around the vehicle. A yellowed newspaper lay on the front seat. An evening paper. He took it out and was eyeing it when Fanny approached with the toddler on her arm. The little boy wore a hat that shadowed one of his eyes, the skin around his mouth was jaundiced and his eyes were darting around as though he'd never been outside before.

Elias installed the car seat in the front cab. It was a struggle. His trousers sagged under his wide behind, revealing the crack between his white buttocks. A belt-clip keychain snaked from his wallet, which was shoved deep into his back pocket, in under his shirt.

Now Rune was walking toward them. He moved his feet

slowly. A bent little creature in a chequered shirt that hung down to his knees. Lennart backed away and when the old man with the dead, distorted face strode past, he noticed there were still tufts of fur in his ears.

He didn't want to ride in the back; he put his gloved paws on the front seat as if to show that he was going to sit there, in that exact spot. But Fanny managed to persuade him that it would be better if he sat in the back. She stroked his luscious silver mane and looked in through the mask's eyeholes. Let's do it that way, okay? she coaxed.

When she had helped the old man into the back of the van, she shut one of the doors and gave him a smile and some encouraging words before closing the other. Then she jumped up next to the little boy in the front seat.

Lennart watched the van as it slowly reversed out of the driveway. Then he lumbered back across the meadow.

Abraham was standing outside the motorhome with the milky-eyed hare on a lead. His hood was up and his face grim. Lennart stomped up the stairs, pulled the curtain aside and climbed into the seat next to Ingvill, who was behind the wheel, waiting with her foot on the gas pedal.

When they reached the E4 motorway, the skies suddenly opened; the rain continued to beat down on them with un-diminished force mile after mile. The three wipers sweeping across the windscreen only managed to keep the lower half clear of water, tirelessly drawing wavy triptychs that instantly filled with new droplets. Lennart looked out at the dark spruce tree palisade. Clearcuts with solitary, scraggly pine trees rising from the broken terrain. Gravel pits and desolate sandy heaths. Game fences rushing past. One trampoline after another in garden after garden. Ingvill was silent like an animal and he was too.

Diana ended up setting off later than planned. They had lingered in bed and even managed to pull off touching each other a bit while the little girl watched TV. It had been kept simple by necessity. Quiet, goal-oriented side sex that could quickly and easily stiffen into an embrace if caught. Håkan had entwined his fingers in hers and gasped and grunted his way to climax. Then he had breathed warm air on her neck and pressed his lips against her shoulder and pulled out. Her nether regions were still throbbing. And she was hungry. And warm. A combination she hated.

The roadworks meant the car shook and jolted its way to Restaurant Gruvköket. Which was closed, of course it was closed. She should have bloody known. She decided to turn in to Svappavaara. Thanks to the mine, the town was expected to flourish again, that's what they had told her on the local news, so maybe she'd be able to find something to eat.

Long rows of construction site cabins. A pointless fence that was rotting into a bank. Brownfield land lush with weeds. A lone petrol pump and a newsstand without newspaper placards, without any colour whatsoever. Car tyres, a mountain of them in the greenery. A hatchback parked in the middle of a lawn that a person in shorts was watering with a hose. The only person in sight. Egg-white caravans hidden behind birch trees. Sofie Lindmark Road. How common was the surname Lindmark in the village? Probably inappropriately common. More caravans. A shuttered shop with windowpanes blinded by sheets of Kraft paper. Damn local news. There was never any nuance. It was either depopulation and shrinking tax bases and doom and gloom, or it was new jobs and budding hopes for the future. People didn't mind working here, but living here? No, they stayed well clear of that. She drove out of town with the same feeling she had every time she visited one of the villages around Kiruna. That this was tissue death. Necrosis.

She got back on the main road, floored it and had soon caught up with a lorry. Which irked her, because her empty stomach was starting to affect her mood. Soon her brain would stop working. She was tempted to overtake, but the straights were short and the right moment refused to occur. When the enormous equipage swerved out and touched the centre line only to then glide over into the oncoming lane, she took her foot off the gas pedal and had a vision of her immediate future, how she'd have to drag some overweight trucker out of a crumpled driver's cabin. A flock of children were riding their bikes along the side of the road. He had swerved to avoid them. Each and every one of them had a helmet on. As if that would make any difference if a lorry driver were to receive a text message at the wrong moment. What were their parents thinking? Of other things or not at all?

After passing the signs with the town's Swedish and Sami names, she briefly considered the OKQ8 petrol station, picturing a slimy fried hotdog, but she decided to push on, into the village that was under siege by men in hi-vis clothing who had jackhammered the pavements and blocked the streets with signs and diggers.

She rolled past the pizzeria. There was a supermarket further down the street. She pulled up outside and ran in for a yoghurt and a pear. It was an unexpectedly hard pear; she ended up having to hold it between her teeth until she started drooling.

By the barn with the three green doors, she turned off and followed a gravel road leading down to the river. There was no car outside; she was relieved to see that. She had brought pen and paper and even a plastic folder and a thumbtack. Tools to alleviate her guilty conscience.

She slammed the car door shut and looked up at the house. A red wooden house with a tin roof and richly mullioned windows that looked transplanted from an older house. Down by the river, a shed encircled by chicken wire. Nothing moving inside it, just weeds and bric-a-brac. The shaggy grass sprinkled with yellow buttercups. A snow sled propped against the railing of the front porch.

She thought she saw something moving in an upstairs window. The curtain twitched. As though the fabric were experiencing a spasm. She stood there for a long time, looking up toward the window, but the curtain didn't move again.

She knocked and waited a few seconds before trying the door. It was open.

'Hello?'

She stood motionless, listening.

'Susso?'

Clothes were hung on steel hangers on a rail underneath the hat rack. A sailing life jacket. A raincoat, a proper raincoat of dark-green vinyl. A crocheted long cardigan with a belt that had ended up uneven and was touching the linoleum floor. She glanced at the shoes. Nothing with high heels. There was a baseball cap on the hat rack.

A loud, tinkling noise made her cross the threshold to the kitchen. The tap was on; a thin jet was thrumming onto a laminated placemat in the sink. Turning the tap off was like turning on the silence.

She had figured it would be messy, filthy even, but it wasn't. At least no messier than her own house. Even the windows, through which different sections of the river could be seen, were clean. Unlike the Sillfors' windows, which were more akin to pieces of modern art. No syringes, no empty bottles. Because that was what she had expected. She realised that now.

She touched the dishrag hanging over the tap. It was rigid. She went into the hallway, glanced at the stairs leading up to the first floor, where the sun formed a floating window on the wallpaper. For some reason, she didn't want to go up there.

She opened a door. A closet. Then the bathroom. There was nothing to suggest she was in the home of a drug addict in either room, and she was ashamed at having thought that. She had made an assessment of Susso's situation based on what Gudrun had told her. Gudrun who was, by all appearances, clinically insane.

A red, heart-shaped rug. An open box of tampons next to the toilet brush in its plastic holder. A handful of crime novels, a folded-up gossip rag. A foot file. A toothbrush sitting all alone in a glass. A small brown medicine bottle with a dropper. She picked it up and read the label. Nail and cuticle oil.

One drop per fingertip twice daily strengthens nails and promotes growth. She smiled as she put the bottle back down on the sink. Anyone bothering with nail and cuticle oil couldn't be too far gone.

She put the lid up, undid her trousers and sat down. Bent over and dug her phone out of her pocket. But her thumb stiffened before it could touch the glass of the screen. A thin, squeaking sound had reached her ears.

Old brake pads.

A car.

Anders studied the strange woman lying in his bed. The soft curve of her spine, a trail of clearly defined vertebrae. The dark cascades of her hair, tumbling across the pillow, greying from the inside. Under the little lamp that used to spread a mild glow over Johanna as she read at night.

This was it. Rock bottom. It was always overwhelming during the aftershocks of his orgasms, but it could come over him any time. In this moment, he wished she would go away; he wished her hair would turn blonde and curly and that it would be Johanna lying there. He closed his eyes and wished it so intensely his eyes welled up.

But she didn't go away.

Stava. With an open, Finnish *a*.

Did she exist? Was she really real?

Yes, she was real. As surely as there was a pine needle in her hair. A yellow hair grip being swept away in that black river.

He looked at the clock radio. He had been awake for almost an hour, torn between violent repulsion and burgeoning desire. The door was ajar and the parquet floor outside a radiant plane. Dots of light stacked on the blinds.

'You're looking sad again.'

Anders swallowed hard before replying.

'How do you know?'

'Am I wrong?'

'I don't know. I can't see myself.'

She rolled over and looked at him.

She was almost beautiful. But just almost. Something about her nose was off. Her darkly squinting eyes were placed oddly far apart. He figured she might be around sixty, but it was hard to tell. She moved so quickly and in the areas where women usually had fat deposits, her skin was taut. Touching her was like touching a starving animal. She weighed nothing.

She reached out and pushed her index finger against his cheek until it hurt so much he had to turn away.

'Don't be sad. I forbid it.'

'You forbid it?'

She sighed.

'My aunt used to tell me that. I forbid it. She couldn't cope with sadness. So she forbade it.'

'And that worked?'

'It probably did for her.'

She had rolled onto her back.

'Is your mother alive?' She pinched the lampshade and scrutinised it. 'Where did you buy this, IKEEE-A?'

'Yes, she's alive.'

'I've been to IKEA once. In Haparanda. Twice. But I didn't buy anything. A bag of tealights, but that's it. Do you go to IKEA a lot? The happy little family?'

He had grown used to her sarcasms, which seemed to spring from searing envy, and didn't bother to make a reply; he just shook his head. She spun around to lie on her front. Balled the pillow up under her chin and looked at him between the dark curtains of her hair.

'Have you changed your mind, are you pining for Johanna? Do you long for her sweet scent?'

'Stop.'

'Then why are we here, Anders? Why are we in this bed? In this bedroom that is so bright and harmonious it makes me gag. Dad is waiting for us.'

She put the nail of her pinkie against his nipple and scratched it.

'Why did you ask if my mother's alive?'

'I know she's alive all right.'

'Yes, because I told you.'

'No, I can tell.'

'How?'

'A man doesn't become a man until her mother dies.'

'Her mother?'

'Fine, his mother. *Vittu!* You know what I mean.'

'Then what am I? A boy?'

'Yes, a bald little boy who wants to crawl back inside the beachball. Where it's so warm and cosy and the food comes through a tube.'

'I'm not bald. My hair might be thinning a bit, but I'm not bald.'

'And what about this little boy? Oh my, so soft.'

His prick lay limp and wrinkled on his stomach, but soon swelled between her bony fingers. She pulled back his foreskin without mercy, tugged it down, again and again, and laughed as he writhed to get away from the pain. In the end, he had to heave her off him. He ended up on top. He looked down on her. Her hair across the pillow. Her lips parted in a mischievous grin. The sharp shadows of her ribs and her four

[124]

hard teats. A shaggy patch of fur below her bellybutton.

At first, he had found her four nipples unsettling. She barely had any breasts, only those four colourless buttons that were always stiff. Now, they made him insanely horny. Her strange appearance filled him with a feeling he'd never experienced before. It was as though he'd found something unknown and forbidden in the forest, which he could stick his cock in as often as he pleased. Some kind of folkloric hulder in heat, risen from the decomposing remnants of a porn mag, hidden for years under a spruce tree.

She waited for him to enter her. But he made her wait. His cheeks were hanging down and growing heavy with blood. His small, gold identity tag dangled between their mouths. His upper arms trembled with the effort. In the end, she couldn't take it any longer. Her head shot up, she sank her teeth into his shoulder and once she bit down, she kept biting until she drew blood; that much he had learnt. He thrust his hips; it was like driving a stake into the heart of a vampire. Her scrawny body stiffened into an arc and her face tensed. He gathered up her arms and pinned them down above her head and picked up a leg and pushed it down into the mattress by holding it under the knee. He thrust a few more times before picking up the other leg as well. She was unresistingly bendy; her legs went back as far as he wanted, and she let him bend them; she let him do whatever he wanted. The headboard banged against the wall. She lay there, rubbing her fingers on her genitals, trying to catch his eyes with a mesmerising, dangerous gaze. The smell emanating from her bushy slit was so concentrated he turned his face away. She growled, that was the only word for the sound she made.

He closed his eyes and let out a dark groan; in the next moment, he was overcome with a sense of acute revulsion. It happened every time. She tried to stop him when he wanted to pull out, but he tore free so violently he almost fell out of bed.

In his aroused state, his ears had caught a sound he'd been able to process. He snatched up a towel and wrapped it around his waist while he ran toward the front door.

William was crossing the yard at a brisk pace.

Anders called out after him and he turned around.

His backpack slung over one shoulder. An uncomprehending, grief-stricken face.

He knew he should go over to him and say something and hug him, but it was as though he couldn't leave the house. Like the gravel was a sound. They just stood there staring at each other from opposite beaches and eventually, the boy left. Trudged off with his head bowed.

Anders sank down onto the front steps. He couldn't go after him and he didn't want to go back inside, into the twilight of the bedroom with its powerful sex smell.

After a while, she came outside. She sat down next to him, wrapped in a cotton shirt. He looked at her furtively.

'Do you dislike me wearing her clothes?'

He made no reply. He sat watching the opening between the lilacs, where the spectre of William seemed to linger like the trembling remnants of a mirage.

'Her H&M clothes. That reek of fabric softener. Smell it. Can you smell the shiny green apples?'

'Stop.'

Her fingers were brown like an Indian's and she pulled them into the sleeves of the shirt.

[126]

'You're wondering if he saw us. He didn't.'

'How do you know?'

'I heard him coming. And he didn't venture beyond the hallway. But he did hear us.'

'Why didn't you say something?'

She giggled at him.

They sat in silence for a while.

'We can bring him if you want.'

He looked at her.

'We can bring him with us when we go.'

'No, we can't.'

She got to her feet.

'Then stop sulking.'

Grete sat gazing out the window, her scarf-covered little head propped against the wall. Filled with light, her eyes beamed like two yellow lamps. Her red lips had stiffened in a melancholic smile. Lennart took a seat and studied her, but she was in a world of her own.

'How's your hand?'

He looked at the bandage but said nothing.

'When I was young, I chopped off my foot. I did it two or three times. Two times. Then I gave up.'

She pulled off her glove and held her hand up to her face, turning it this way and that. Her ring finger and pinkie were grey and woolly and bent like an old monkey's.

'I never tried it with my fingers. Not like that. They only started looking like this when I was a teenager, and by then I'd realised it wasn't the best idea to cut things off. I've obviously groomed them; for a while I did it daily. And I've painted my nails. If I can call them that. I've put plasters on them too.'

She put the glove back on and immediately started massaging her fingers, methodically and vigorously.

'How did you get him to come?'

'I promised Fanny they can stay with us. That they can live with me. All of them.'

'Where? On Andøya?'

She nodded.

'It's the only place the little boy will feel at home and have a decent life.'

'Is Erasmus going to leave you alone?'

'You and the thurse could live there too. Nearby.'

'This business with Susso Myrén,' he said. 'It's just a shot in the dark. A straw to grasp at. And we both know it. We don't know if he'll turn and in the unlikely event that he does, we don't know what he'll be like. He's never been alone.'

'Do you hate her?'

'Who?'

'The girl. The troll hunter.'

'Why do you ask?'

'I've wondered where the idea came from. If it came from the thurse or from you. But maybe you don't know yourself.'

'It was the only thing I could think of. And he's angry. He's furious. But he can't get it out. It's like it's stuck inside him.'

'I'm tired,' she said. 'I think I might try to have a little nap.'

She made sure the pillows were where they should be before leaning back. He watched her disappear behind the table and then he sat staring at the table top like a wiped-out gambler.

The car was turning around when Diana stepped out of the house. It was slowly reversing into the shade under the trees. Then it just sat there, with glaring red brake lights. A green Mazda with a dark semicircle in the grimy film that covered the rear window. She went down the front steps and walked into the yard to show herself. Even so, nothing happened. What if she doesn't recognise me? Or it's not her?

The next moment, the door swung open.

The person climbing out of the car was sickly pale. And skinny. Her collarbones were sharply etched and her clothes baggy. She wore a frayed denim shirt with a thin top underneath. No bra. She stopped. Stood there with a plastic carrier bag hooked onto her fingers. The same angular face, just emaciated. The same glasses. Something had changed around her mouth.

'I'm sorry I went inside. I just really needed to pee.'

Susso didn't speak; she just stood there.

She doesn't recognise me, Diana thought to herself.

'Dana.'

There was no pleasure in her voice; there was nothing. Except maybe vague wonder at rediscovering a name long forgotten.

For Diana, the word was a signal. She stepped forward and

put her arms around Susso and when she smelled her warm hair, which was pulled back into a messy bun at the nape of her neck, she teared up and was overcome by a sudden vertigo. Because it was really her. An older version of Susso, anaemic and anorexic, but even so, it was her.

'I'm sorry,' she squeaked.

Susso stared at her. Her jaw muscles worked underneath her skin. As though she wanted to say something but instead chose to grind it up between her teeth. She wore no earrings, just the pinpricks in her earlobes.

Diana followed her into the kitchen and watched her put the groceries in the fridge. She didn't know what to say, so she just stood in the doorway in silence. The walls were a shade of apricot and the cupboard doors yellow with brown knobs. A bench and four stools encircled the kitchen table. She sat down on a stool. When she did, Susso looked at her. She tied the carrier bag into a knot and threw it into the cupboard under the sink.

'Did Mum ask you to come?'

She instinctively shook her head. Then she shrugged.

'She's worried. And I am too.'

She regretted it instantly. Saying you were worried about someone was a kind of reproach. A moral reprimand. Which Susso's feelers instantly picked up on.

'Why?' she said.

'I think about you. A lot.'

Susso was holding the percolator, seemingly pondering whether to accept that explanation. She rinsed out the coffee pot and while she filled it with water, she gazed out the window. At the slow-moving river. A viscous, grey mass.

Diana was dead certain she was going to mock her for opening up like that; when no comment seemed forthcoming, she apologised.

'You know what it's like. Old age makes you sentimental.'

After a while she continued.

'But it'll all be over soon!'

'Into the ground we go, finally.'

'Not one day too soon.'

They shared a quiet smile. Once upon a time, that had been the pillar of their worldview. That everything was really shit at heart and it was incomprehensible that people didn't see it. The percolator started hissing and spitting. Susso had her arms crossed and was looking down at the floor, the rag rug. She had pulled one foot out of its slipper and was lifting it with her toes, up and down. Diana looked at the slipper as well. A red Croc. It was the only thing moving in the kitchen.

'So how are you?'

She shrugged.

'I've seen ghosts with healthier tans.'

After saying that she immediately tried to think of something to say that wasn't about Susso's health. To show her she had come as a friend, not a doctor on a home visit.

'I have a daughter.'

'I know.'

'Her name's Kiruna.'

'I know.'

Susso fetched the percolator and poured the coffee into two drinking glasses that she put on the table. Then she sat down on the bench.

'So are you divorced yet?'

'Me and Håkan? No, it looks like it might be a while yet.'

'Everyone gets divorced.'

'Not us.'

'Give it some time.'

'Well, it's never too late to give up.'

'Besides, you weren't supposed to get married.'

'I know.'

'We weren't supposed to ever get married.'

'I know. But,' she said and raised her index finger, 'we're both called Sillfors.'

'Because he was sick of being called Håkan Hellström.'

'True, but still.'

'Traitor.'

Diana giggled.

'So that's why you're living like this?'

'Like what?'

'Here, all alone?'

'How do you know I'm all alone?'

'I assumed. I used your bathroom. It looked feminine.'

'Maybe I'm living with a woman.'

Susso's steady gaze suddenly made her feel awkward and she looked around the kitchen.

'Are you renting this place?'

'No.'

'It's yours?'

She nodded.

'Where did you find the money? Well, I guess you owned a flat. Though I thought that was actually your dad's.'

'It was. But he gave me the money.'

'That was nice of him.'

'He's nice now. In his old age.'

'How long have you lived here?'

'I don't know.'

'You don't know?'

'A few years.'

Silence fell in the kitchen and it was painfully clear Susso had an easier time enduring it than her, whether due to habit or because they were on her turf.

'It's lovely. Lovely location.'

'Are you still on Villagatan?'

'Villastigen? No, we're on Duvvägen. If you know where Stina Taube's mother used to live.'

Susso shook her head.

'Well, that's where we are. The house next door. To the house where she lived.'

They sat in silence.

'So why did you move out here?'

'It's lovely, you said so yourself.'

'But what do you do?'

'What I do?'

'Yes. Are you working as a carer or what?'

'You might say that.'

From time to time, there was a secretive glint in her eye that Diana didn't recognise at all. It made her feel unsure of herself. Uneasy.

'Well, as I said, your mum's really worried.'

'You said you were worried too.'

'Yes.'

'Why?'

'I thought you were doing drugs.'

The words just came out and she almost wanted to clap her hand to her mouth afterwards. But Susso didn't seem offended.

'Why would you think that?'

'Your mum told me you'd gone weird. I ran into her in the park, in Gruvstad Park. And she said you were living out here all by yourself and that she didn't recognise you. And my mind immediately went: drugs. But I've since realised your mum suffers from delusions and that it's probably her fault you started believing in trolls and did cryptozoology and all that stuff. It's called *folie à deux*. So I really get that you wanted to make a clean break with her.'

What she said was true. Every word. But she couldn't understand why she'd blurted it out like that. Unvarnished, no sugar-coating. It was something about the look on Susso's face. Her pale, drawn face, and all the memories that were surfacing. It had the effect of a mental enema. It all just came out.

Susso seemed to ponder what she had said.

'She let me move down to Kiruna after Grandpa died. I was fourteen,' she said and illustrated the journey from Riksgränsen to Kiruna by drawing a line across the tablecloth with her index finger. Not even fifteen, I was. Fourteen.'

'I thought you wanted to? I remember you being over the moon about not having to live up there.'

'So what? I was fourteen years old. I didn't even have a legal right to fuck. You can't let a child go off on its own like that. Then, after the divorce, she came after me, in a sled full of Grandpa's photos and all kinds of nonsense, and moved into my building.'

'I think that was kind of sweet. Her wanting to be close to you.'

'My mother. She just feels sorry for herself and demands that I do too. It's all about her, actually. And now, when I've moved out here, up she pops again, spinning those apron strings like a lasso.'

She made a whistling sound to mimic a lasso whipping through the air.

'She thinks that Lennart Brösth guy is going to hurt you. He's escaped. Did you know that?'

Susso said nothing.

'Are you afraid he might hurt you?'

'Do I seem afraid?'

'It took you long enough to get out of your car. I got the impression you were hanging back in there so you could speed off. If I'd been someone else.'

'I just didn't know whose car it was.'

'Won't you tell me what happened? You and Tobe were the ones who found those kids, weren't you? In Sorsele.'

She had dreaded this moment. Aware of the risk that Susso might buck and possibly kick her out. But she didn't. She just sat there in the bright kitchen, studying her.

'How come you were the ones? That old man you snapped a picture of, he had nothing to do with the kidnapping. How did you find the children?'

'They weren't children. Not any more.'

'Sure, but they were children when they were taken.'

She nodded.

'How did you find them?'

Susso kept her eyes fixed on her. Her pupils were so dilated it made her brown eyes look black. She looked at her for a long time without speaking; eventually, Diana started feeling uncomfortable and just then, it was as if Susso released her hold on her.

'We had help.'

'From whom?'

Susso sat with a hand over her mouth, as though she were pondering something. Then she moved her hand, slowly extending it and unfurling her index finger to point to somewhere diagonally behind Diana.

Diana turned around, but it took her a moment to spot what Susso was pointing at. It was a squirrel; when she saw it, she let out a surprised yelp. It was standing on all fours on top of the fridge, between a roll of kitchen towels and a packet of crispbread, staring at her. The bushy plume of its tail pointed straight up and was twitching rapidly.

'A squirrel.'

'He's secretly not a squirrel. Or at least not just a squirrel.'

Diana bunched her eyebrows together.

'You're being weird again.'

'It's a very old squirrel.'

'Yeah, he looks a bit mangy.'

'Watch what you say. He understands Swedish and he holds a grudge. He never forgets.'

She couldn't tell if Susso was pulling her leg or if she really believed the squirrel was as old as she claimed. And understood Swedish to boot. That kind of conviction would be very much in line with what she had used to believe, which was why Diana was neither worried nor even surprised. She had figured the charmingly eccentric Susso she'd grown up with was gone forever and that a disillusioned spinster had taken her place. But that evidently wasn't the case, and it made her want to laugh.

'What's up?'

'Nothing?'

The look on Diana's face drew a half-muffled chuckle from Susso and then they both burst out laughing. Susso got up and put the glasses on the counter.

'May I offer you a Chinese gooseberry?'

Diana made a resigned gesture; she had no idea what she meant.

'Would you like a kiwi? I bought kiwis.'

'Of course I want a kiwi. Can I have two?'

'Yes, you can.'

Elias was sitting outside Frasse's, alone under a parasol that was being inflated by the wind, making it look like an undulating jellyfish. From time to time, he put his burger down on the tray and drank from a paper cup and gobbled down clutches of French fries. Lennart looked around before crossing the car park. A newspaper placard on the wall. Nothing about the escaped cult leader. A sandwich board outside the shop. Special offer! Cantaloupes ten kronor per kilo. He sat down across from the young man, who instantly drew back in fear and lowered his eyes.

'Grete's going to take good care of the boy. No one's going to find him odd in any way. He's going to be fine there. And you and Fanny, you can start a new life.'

The young man stared at his burger.

'Let me see your ear.'

'What?'

'Let me see your ear.'

Elias lifted the ring dangling in his earlobe.

'Fuck,' Lennart exclaimed, 'there's a hole through your ear. Like an African chieftain. Have you seen it on TV? How big is it?'

'Eight millimetres.'

'Fuck.'

Elias took another bite and Lennart watched him eat. Then he put his hand on the table and tapped his knuckles against it until the young man realised he was trying to get his attention. He opened his hand like a lid; crouched underneath it was a wood mouse. It raised its nose and long whiskers in the air and ran over to the edge of the cardboard container where the golden-brown potatoes glistened with salt. The dejected look vanished instantly from the young man's face.

'Do you think he's hungry?'

Lennart shrugged. Then he turned to the window, through which two surprised faces were staring. The women on the other side of the glass ogled the little creature sitting on their table. Lennart glowered at them until they resumed their meal. Elias had torn off a flake of meat from his burger and was trying to feed it to the mouse; Lennart walked away.

The little boy was sitting with the black straps of the car seat harness over his shoulders, examining a bunch of keys. Jabbing it with his sock mitten. The window was half open and he could hear the kid's loud mouth-breathing and the jangling of the keys.

'She lives down by the river,' Abraham said, 'about a mile from the village, and there are no neighbours.'

'Are we going to put her in here?' Lennart said. 'Because she can't go in the van.'

'Don't you think it would be okay if Fanny's there?'

'I don't know,' Grete said. 'Who knows what might happen in that dark van on the way up to Finnmark? It's a long drive. A lot could happen. It might end in a drama triangle, the consequences of which we can't imagine. At least Fanny has a measure of control over him.'

'Then I guess she's going in the boot,' Abraham said. He was holding a drinking cup and amusing himself by pulling his straw up and down through the hole to make a squeaking sound.

'Yes,' Grete said with a nod, 'I think that's for the best.'

Abraham pulled the curtain aside and climbed into the driving seat and tried to push the cup into the cup holder, but it wouldn't fit. Then he slurped down what was left in the cup and discarded it on the floor. The engine rumbled to life. Lennart glanced at Grete and was met by a smile. Her teeth were long and her gums were turning black around the edges; the enamel was a shade of grey like old china.

'It's probably for the best,' she said.

Anders was standing in front of the bathroom mirror, inspecting the underside of his tongue. The frenulum was completely severed. His tongue moved about his mouth freely and he could extend it surprisingly far. Almost down to the tip of his chin. Like that rock singer. It was yellow with coffee stains and tremblingly striving toward its most extended state. Stava had chuckled when he crawled up to her in bed and demonstrated his new ability. She claimed a person could determine the level of a lover's dedication by looking in his mouth and that she felt heart-rendingly sad for his wife, who had shared a bed with a man with an unliberated tongue for twenty years. Then she had gone on to dismiss their entire marriage and he had lain next to her, humming agreement and licking her shoulder without paying attention.

His face had been covered in stubble for days. Now he had a full beard. It was actually longer than he'd ever had it before. The hairs hung down, covering his top lip, and his chin was pure white; it looked like he had dipped it in flour. And he had lost weight. His cheeks were hollow and his eyes too; they had retreated into his skull, as if to get away from something.

It felt like the change had happened overnight, but the reason for that was obviously that he hadn't looked in a mirror in a long time, at least not properly.

He leaned closer to the glass, with his hands on the edge of the sink. He saw his own reflection in his pupils. Two miniature versions of himself. They were standing behind the windows of his pupils like some kind of microscopic dark elves, watching him, disliking him being so close. So they leaned out, and they leaned further out than he was leaning toward them.

He jerked his head away and when he saw his terrified face, he felt it belonged to an insane person. A paranoid junkie who jumped at the slightest sound.

Shaken, he turned his back on the mirror and put up the toilet lid. She had said the nervous and unpredictable state he was in would soon come to an end. It was a process that couldn't be rushed. At least his memory lapses had stopped, in the sense that there were no new ones. But the things that were gone didn't come back. Though that might be just as well.

Now he heard Stava's voice.

He flushed and left the bathroom.

She was standing by the kitchen window.

'Your wife's here,' she said.

The silver Citroën had materialised in the driveway. It was undeniably sitting there. Johanna climbed out of it. She was wearing a blouse and a white summer jacket and leather loafers with white gold buckles, and he thought it was strange that she had dressed up.

'What day is it?'

'You're not going to let her in, are you?'

'What am I supposed to do, it's her house . . .'

Before he knew it, Stava had gone into the hallway and thrown open the front door. Johanna stopped in front of the house. She looked scared and Anders suddenly felt incredibly sorry for her. It washed over him. He didn't want her to see him, so he moved to the side. He stood pressed against the curtain, breathing loudly through his nose.

Johanna was the one who broke the silence.

'What do you want with us?'

'I don't want anything with you.'

'Where's Anders?'

'He's at home.'

The reply seemed to confuse Johanna and Stava paused before continuing.

'I've stolen him from you. You're going to have to accept it.'

'Can't you see he's ill? Yes, he is. He really is. You don't know him.'

'Johanna. Sweet little Johanna.'

'Let go of me!'

When he got outside, Stava had pushed Johanna up against her car. She was rolling her boyishly narrow hips in some kind of taunting dance that continued until Johanna pushed her away.

He stood in the doorway, staring at the two women. Johanna took a few steps to the side and when Stava reached out to grab her hand, she ran over to Anders, hiding behind him, and for a few absurd seconds they stood together, like the married couple they in fact were, studying the odd woman who had wormed her way into their lives. Stava sank into a squat and watched them.

'My God, you look disgusting together. Pale and afraid.'

He had nowhere to go and didn't know what to say or do. He had gone rigid and in the end, Johanna dashed to her car, like from one sanctuary to another. She opened the door and looked at him, but her eyes slid across his face as though it were the face of a stranger and when she climbed into her car and drove off, he knew he would never see her again and that she drove off with a piece of him that he would never get back.

He went into the kitchen and sat down at the table. They hadn't cleared their plates from the night before. Chopped-up potatoes lay in a pool of balsamic vinegar and had turned dark. There was red wine left in the glasses, which were covered in fingerprints. She sat down in his field of vision, but his eyes were unseeing. Part of him thought she had been unnecessarily cruel to Johanna, but it would never occur to him to say anything about it. She gathered up balsamic vinegar from the plate with the tip of her index finger and painted tears on her high cheekbones. He knew what she would say: that being sad was forbidden. Was he sad? A mild melancholia was aching inside him, but it was like a pain that had been dulled by a significant amount of drugs.

'I want to leave now,' he said.

Susso told her she was going out for beer. Then she put the squirrel on her shoulder, got into her car and drove off. Diana sat on the front steps, tapping at her phone. Twenty minutes later, Susso came back with two plastic carrier bags full of beer.

'I didn't realise there was somewhere selling alcohol in Vittangi?'

'There isn't, but I have nice neighbours.'

Diana studied her surreptitiously. The muscles of her lower arms looked like braided ropes under her skin when she pulled the kettle grill across the unkempt lawn and ripped open the bag of charcoal. When she stood behind the heat and the rising smoky haze with a bottle of beer in her hand. In counterpoise. Except it wasn't her hip that was popped, it was the iliac crest. A sharply protruding ridge. Diana was fairly certain Susso knew she was being studied from a medical perspective. Though it didn't seem to bother her. Granted, she had always been like that. She had never cared what other people thought of her. A lot of people made out as though they didn't care, well, most people really, to a greater or lesser degree, but with Susso it had always been completely genuine, and Diana had emulated her. In her case, though, it had remained just an attitude. In Umeå, she had come to realise she actually did care an awful lot about what people thought of her as a person.

They were sitting at a rickety little plastic table, eating with sweat beading on their foreheads in the sunshine that created prisms in their drinking glasses. Salmon and potatoes wrapped in tinfoil with butter and cloves of garlic. Susso had caught the salmon herself. A plastic boat with an outboard motor was moored down by the jetty; she used it for fishing. When Diana heard this, she laughed so hard she did a spit take into her hand. Susso wanted to know what was so funny.

'There's something about this life you've made for yourself,' she said, making a sweeping gesture with her bottle. 'You live here, all alone, outside bloody Vittangi of all places. Together with – a squirrel. Who understands Swedish. And from time to time you paddle out and catch a salmon or two.'

She had, yet again, made her spill something she would rather have kept to herself. And, yet again, Susso seemed unperturbed.

'You feel sorry for me.'

'Yes, I do. I find it pretty tragic. But it makes me mad too, at your mum, because I think it's her fault. She's the one who made you think trolls are real. And talking squirrels.'

'I never said he could talk.'

'You've been brainwashed. By your mother.'

Susso got to her feet.

'I'm sorry! I shouldn't have said that.'

'Don't worry about it,' she said. Then she picked up their plates and carried them inside.

Diana gazed out across the garden. She had sucked down two beers while the tinfoil packets sizzled on the grill, but she felt like she'd had ten. Her head was spinning and there were grease stains on her thighs from all the food she'd dropped on herself. And all the things she had blurted out! It must have been lurking somewhere inside her. But it was the fact that Susso didn't seem to care in the slightest too. The old Susso would have been furious. And given as good as she got. This one, she just sat there. It was almost like she enjoyed it.

She pulled out her phone. She'd received a picture of Kiruna. She was on the merry-go-round, sitting on the back of an animal of an unidentifiable species, looking solemn. She tapped in a long row of hearts in reply. When she stood up, she lost her balance. That made her start talking to herself, which she continued to do while she cleared the table and carried the overloaded tray inside. The kitchen door was closed and when she tried to open it by pushing the handle down with her elbow, Susso came out of the bathroom.

'Don't open it! I trapped him in there.'

'What do you mean?'

'I've trapped him. So I know where he is.'

They carried their chairs down to the jetty. Susso fetched a bag of beer that she tied to a rope and lowered into the water.

'I didn't mean what I said,' Diana slurred. 'That you living here is tragic and that you've been brainwashed. But you know how I feel about all that. The trolls and stuff. Cryptozoology. You know what I think.'

Susso used Diana's snus tin to open another bottle of beer. Took off her baseball cap and put it down on the jetty and tossed the beer cap into it. When she realised the wind was threatening to carry the hat off, she anchored it with the bottle of mosquito repellent. She leaned back. Her eyes were fixed on the opposite bank of the river. There were no houses in sight.

'Do you know how many kids the Simonssons have?' Diana held up six fingers. 'The latest, though probably not the last, is called Arwen.'

'Have they become Laestadians or something?'

'Söderberg has four.'

Susso took a sip of beer.

'It's like that game,' she said, 'with the pebbles. When you predict how many children you'll have. Hey, look, I had zero children when I grew up.'

She had time to think: no, but you got a squirrel. But this time she managed to keep her mouth shut and she was grateful for it.

'They all have diagnoses. They're a pain in the neck. I think Ida probably wishes she'd got zero children as well. At least she looks like she does whenever they come into the clinic and run riot.'

'Ida Söderberg,' Susso said slowly. 'I'd forgotten about her.'

'They fade,' Diana said and pulled a bottle out of the bag. 'But they're there. They never go away.' She flicked off the cap and when she managed to get it in the hat, she gave herself a silent round of applause and Susso smiled at her.

When she exited the bathroom, it was like she got stuck in something; she kind of froze mid-step. She stood staring at the door to the kitchen. The grain of the wood in the mirrors. The rusty holes left by an old rim lock. The polished trim plate of the handle. The keyhole that was a shape that always made her think of that classic Swedish picture book about the red yarn that in mysterious ways leads all the way through a house to a kitten hidden in a vase inside a cupboard in the attic. Susso had reminded her not to open the kitchen door and she hadn't had any intention to. But now, standing here, it was hard to resist the temptation. Maybe simply because she wasn't allowed. Like in Bluebeard's castle. But there was something else too. She found the squirrel disturbing. Not the squirrel so much, perhaps, as the act of keeping it indoors. In the kitchen. It shouldn't be in there; not letting it out would be unnatural. She felt that very strongly. That it needed to get out. She even put her fingers on the handle. But she didn't open it. Instead she went outside and fetched her charger from the car, singing as she walked. She found an outlet in the hallway and plugged the charger in.

When she passed the kitchen window, she couldn't help but look. And there it was. Staring at her.

She walked up to the glass and bent down to get level with the tiny face. Tapped with the nail of her index finger and watched the funny faces her mirrored self pulled.

'You can't keep a squirrel in the kitchen,' she said and sat down. 'Pooping everywhere and stuff. Super unhygienic. Bloody impractical too, because it probably hides things, and you have to keep a kitchen neat.'

She pulled the plastic carrier bag out of the water and took out the last couple of bottles. Their labels had peeled off. Then she threw the bag back in the river.

'Now you have to tell me. Why do you have a squirrel?'

Susso didn't respond; she stood up, so quickly she wobbled. Diana grabbed her to keep her from falling. Then she noticed Susso was staring at something.

A little man was standing between the house and the jetty, watching them. No taller than a child. But his back was bent and he was wearing some kind of mask. Diana figured it was a local urchin who had put on a costume to scare them and asked Susso who it was, but got no reply.

Now he was walking toward them with a slow, shuffling gait. As though some kind of geriatric zombie had caught their scent in the summer night.

Diana tumbled off her chair. Sat on the jetty, barely able to breathe. When she realised the horrifying figure was not going to be explained through any concepts at her disposal or stop coming toward them, she slipped into a state she had never been in before. It was as if an unknown room had opened up inside her consciousness. Everything was so weirdly quiet. She could even hear the mosquitoes swarming around her. Susso had sunk into a deep squat; it looked like she was peeing.

Now the little figure reached out with one hand.

The monster grabbed Susso's hair and pulled it and she crawled after him without resisting, as though they were engaging in some sort of perverted domination game.

Diana clapped both hands to her mouth.

'Let her go,' she said. She wanted to scream, but all she could manage was a whimper. 'Let her go.'

Rune was hobbling around the lawn with quick, hopping steps. He threw his arms out in every direction in jerky, incomprehensible gestures. It looked like some kind of deranged dance. Fanny sat on the front porch with her hood up and her arms around her pulled-up legs, watching him. Her jeans were rolled up on her calves and she was scratching at her ankles.

One of the women stood looking stupidly at the ground with eyes that didn't blink. She had a small goatee of blood. She was being held upright by her friend, who wore glasses and didn't seem too out of it; she was even swatting at the mosquitoes.

Abraham was clutching a wad of tissues that he pressed to one nostril from time to time. Rune was intrigued and followed him when he walked off.

'What's that in your pocket?' Fanny said.

'Nothing,' he mumbled.

'You're sad about your face.'

Abraham made no reply.

'You're ever so, ever so sad.'

'I'm fine.'

'Rune wants to give you a gift.'

'I don't want any gifts.'

Her eyebrows shot up.

'Are you refusing his gift?'

'No,' he said. 'Of course not.'

'Would you like to know what it is? He's going to let you have a taste. Of them.'

She nodded toward the women.

'We're going to gut them and then you will get to eat some of the things we pull out. The little friend you keep in your pocket will get its share too. It's enough for everyone.'

'What kind of nonsense is that?' Lennart said.

Rune was standing stock-still on his bow legs. His back was slightly arched. The bulge of his tail moved underneath his trousers.

Fanny pointed.

'They're for someone else. Aren't they?'

Instead of replying, Lennart walked off, up toward the road Ingvill was driving down with Grete, who had the little boy on her lap.

The women were sitting next to each other on the ground. They looked like they were waiting for help to arrive after being in a car crash. The woman with glasses was taking small, shallow breaths. It was as though the automation of her lungs had stopped working and she now had to focus all her attention on breathing. Abraham gave her a kick.

'It's this one.'

'Yes, I know.'

'The other one, should we leave her here?'

Grete shook her head.

'We're bringing her.'

'Is she coming in the motorhome?'

'No, you're going to have to take her in one of those.'

She pointed to the cars parked under the birch trees. That was when they noticed the door on the driver's side of the van was open. There was no sign of Elias.

'What's his name again?' Abraham said.

'Elias,' Lennart told him.

'Elias!'

Grete waved her hand dismissively.

'Let him go.'

She got out of the wheelchair, leaning on Ingvill's arm.

'Lennart. You'll drive the van. It's an automatic.'

'What about the boy?'

'The boy will go with you; he'll keep you company.'

Abraham took the boy and buckled him into the car seat; when he was done, he dug his fingers into the child's puffy stomach and made a sound that was supposed to amuse the boy, but he neither laughed nor smiled, just looked at him. When Abraham shut the door, the child turned its eyes to Lennart. His bottom lip was wet with saliva and white splinters were poking through his pink gums. The little boy raised his sock-clad hand and rubbed it against the plaster on his cheek.

'Don't do that. It's not a good idea,' Lennart said and turned on the engine.

When Diana opened her eyes in the dark, she had been dozing for what felt like hours, thinking she should open her eyes any moment now. For some reason, she had put it off, again and again. She had been busy with other things. Entangled in something that had seemed so important she hadn't been able to tear herself away from it.

But now she lay there, blinking. It wasn't completely pitch black and she knew she was in a car. The sound of the engine had penetrated her sleep. Though it hadn't been proper sleep. More like some kind of numbed stupor. Which she was still under the sway of. Because she didn't panic. Not even when she realised her hands were tied, and her feet too.

Susso, she thought to herself. Did I go to Susso's house?

She tried to rip the tape around her hands apart but was unable to, and the tape around her feet was every bit as tight. When she wiggled around, she spotted something she recognised. She blinked and tried to focus.

Kiruna's denim skirt.

She was in her own car.

The boot cover prevented her from getting up, so she rolled over on her back, bent her knees to her chest and pushed her feet upward. The cloth yielded and let in light that blinded her. She kept kicking with flaring nostrils; the effort was helping clear her head.

'Diana! Stop that.'

She lay still. A Norwegian man. Who knew her name. And was driving her car? She started kicking again, and this time she screamed too, filled with terror and rage: she roared so loud her ears popped.

The car slowed down. Stopped.

She lay still, waiting.

A door slammed shut. Footsteps against the asphalt. The boot opened. The man stared down at her. He had curly black hair and a furrowed face, with stubble like a shadow across his cheeks.

'I'm going to have to ask you to stop that,' he said pleasantly.

To get some idea of where she was and what was going on, she tried to catch a glimpse of what it looked like behind him. A dead straight road with sparse forest on either side. No houses, no signs.

'We don't really need you, so if you make trouble, I'm going to leave you here.'

It was only then she realised there was something wrong with him. Half his face contorted with spastic tension and he was staring at her with one eye like an old sea captain.

He motioned with his head toward the gravelly side of the road.

'Do you understand what I'm telling you, Diana? I'm going to dump you here like a bag of rubbish.'

He sounded so friendly she didn't know how to take his threat. A car was approaching; as it drove past, she started kicking again. That made the man grab the boot cover and pull it off. She immediately calmed down. He was going to free her now.

He looked at her with his lopsided face. In her panicked state, she had to admit he was good-looking, despite his defect. A tall man in jeans and a red shell jacket with a standing collar. It was a Tierra jacket, she could tell from the tiny ice axe on his chest, and her dazed mind told her that Håkan had a jacket of that same brand, so he couldn't very well harm her.

He leaned in over her and put a hand on her shoulder. The fear that he would hurt her slipped into her awareness but had no time to trigger a reaction. Because her field of vision was split by lightning and after the lightning, there was nothing.

Every now and then, Lennart's eyes slid from the road to the little boy. His head had flopped to one side and his curls billowed sweetly in all directions like on a classic cherub and his domed eyelids were fringed with dark, curved lashes. It made him look like a doll.

He poked his right foot and when there was no reaction, he pinched it. That made the child turn and bury his head into the car seat's headrest; maybe there was a bit of shade there. It didn't look comfortable but in any event, he seemed to be sleeping soundly. Despite the nocturnal light, which was slowly intensifying. Soon, the car would be filled with sunlight.

His head started moving and suddenly went rigidly still. Lennart glanced over and was met by a pair of eyes that had opened in wonder.

The boy didn't seem scared, just sat there looking at him. His dummy lay between his legs. Lennart picked it up and held it out in front of him until he reached for it. It was not long, however, before he started whining. Lennart picked up his phone and thumbed his way to the right number.

'He's hungry or something. I can grin and bear it, I guess, but the question is what happens in the back if the kid starts howling. If Rune's asleep, we don't want to wake him. We're going to try to ride it out.'

After ending the call, he handed the phone to the boy, who was entertained by it for a moment or two. Then he started squirming in his seat, emitting displeased puffing sounds. He wasn't crying yet, but it wasn't far off. Lennart tapped the phone against the buckle on the child's tummy.

'Look,' he said. 'Look at this.'

They stopped at a petrol station and Lennart carried the boy into the motorhome. Fanny had a bag full of clinking glass jars. While the microwave hummed, the boy sat with the old lady. She rocked him on her knee and sang softly in his ear: Hooray for me and you I say, hooray for me and you. Fanny watched them with a weary expression. She didn't seem able to keep her eyes open properly.

Lennart stepped outside. It wasn't even five yet. A reindeer with brown, plump horns was standing under the petrol station's roof, glaring at nothing, and beyond that there was another one and two more on the other side of the car park, grumpy-eyed and bored, speckled like feral cats.

Abraham and Ingvill were waiting next to the Audi. A weasel was skittering up and down and around Abraham's arm. Its back was brown and its belly white and it moved so quickly it looked like a living tail. With the same good sense as a tail, because there seemed to be no purpose to its windings. Then it suddenly stopped. Perched on his shoulder, looking at Lennart with its black nose like a third eye.

'Have you checked on them?' he said.

Abraham made a beckoning sound with his tongue against his teeth and tried to catch the animal, which shied away and slipped over to his other shoulder.

'Do you think it'll work?' he said in his slurred voice. 'If we give her to him?'

'I don't know.'

'Can't we send in our friend with the mask instead?'

Abraham smiled. Or did he? It was hard to tell. Either way, he was decidedly unconcerned. He was playing with the weasel, doing his best to persuade it to run over to Ingvill, but it didn't want to.

'The main thing, though,' he said, 'is that we get him to turn, right?'

Lennart had spotted something in the car. The sole of a shoe bracing against one of the windows. The woman had managed to heave herself out of the boot and was wriggling into the back seat. He drew Abraham's attention to what was happening with a nod. Then he looked around to make sure no one could see them.

Just as Ingvill managed to get the car door open, the woman hurled herself forward between the seats, trying to get to the start button with her taped-up hands. She managed to reach the button with an extended finger. The engine started. But now Abraham caught hold of her. He grabbed her by the hips and pulled her out of the car. After slamming her into the asphalt, he lifted her up by the hair.

'Did you not understand me?' he said and rammed a fist into her stomach.

She doubled over and collapsed and then sat leaning against the car with terrified, staring eyes, while the weasel dashed about on the ground, hissing at her menacingly.

'Did you figure I was playing around?'

Abraham was standing over her, trying to catch her eye,

but she jerked her head away and averted her eyes. That made him pinch her ear and stretch her earlobe out.

'You'd better listen to me.'

From out of nowhere, he suddenly conjured a knife. An all-purpose knife with a red plastic handle.

'If you don't do as I say, I'm going to cut off your ear and put it in your mouth and tape it shut. So you don't forget what happens when you don't listen.'

Ingvill had pulled off a piece of duct tape that she now put over the woman's eyes. Then she wrapped her whole head until nothing but the top of her nose was visible. Abraham pinched the nose and released it, pinched and released. The woman tossed her head from side to side to escape the torture.

When they wanted her to crawl back into the car, she resisted. Abraham shoved her to the ground and heaved her into the boot, sweating bullets all the while. He slammed the boot shut and then they stood there looking at the broken black boot cover. After no more than a few seconds, the head with the grey swaths around it popped up. Like some kind of futuristic mummy, rising from its grave.

'She doesn't seem to be getting it,' Abraham said.

He went over to the motorhome, opened the boot and pulled out the other woman, who was Susso Myrén. After throwing her to the ground, he opened the Audi, pulled out her unruly friend, led her over to the motorhome, shoved her into the luggage compartment and slammed the door shut. Then he gestured to Susso to get up, but she just stared at him.

That made him fly off the handle. He ran at her and kicked her as hard as he could in the ribs and then he straddled her prone body and shouted at her to stop staring at him. He ripped off her glasses and held the point of the knife to her eye.

'I'm going to gouge your eye out! Stop staring at me!'

When he plunged the knife in, she kicked her feet and growled furiously behind the tape covering her mouth. Then she lay curled up with her face against the asphalt, emitting a strange, humming sound. Abraham stood up and put the knife back in its sheath and picked up the weasel, which craned its long neck and squirmed around so as not to lose sight of the suffering woman.

'She shouldn't have stared at me,' he panted.

Ingvill squatted down, put a hand on Susso's arm and tried to make her turn around. After having a look at her blood-streaked face, she rummaged around the boot of the Audi. She found a small piece of clothing, a girl's denim skirt, which she folded up and put over the damaged eye.

'Hold this,' she said.

Abraham reluctantly sank into a squat and held the skirt in place while Ingvill pulled off a piece of tape that she wrapped around Susso's head. Then she continued wrapping her head in tape.

'She shouldn't have stared at me.'

Lennart walked away, climbed back into the van and sat there staring at the empty car park until Fanny came out with the little boy on her arm.

'All right,' he said, 'so he's fed and happy now?'

Anders had asked if he should bring anything and she had said valuables, but when he lugged the TV over, with its power cord dangling like a tail, she had giggled at him.

'Valuables, Anders. Cash and jewellery.'

As he moved to carry the TV back, she told him to just throw it on the floor. He hesitated at first. Then he did it. She laughed hoarsely at him and praised him. He was left wondering if he had dropped the TV.

There was a heart-shaped jewellery box on the dresser in the bedroom; he was gazing into it dreamily when she entered. She had a look in the box, pulled out an earring and looked at it like she'd found a dead bug. She muttered something in Finnish and he could sense it was a derogatory remark. Was this all?

He went into William's room, pulled out his desk drawers and rummaged through his papers and pens and tangled headphones until he found a black plastic box. It said 'Ceverin Jewellers' in embossed letters on the lid. Inside it, on a bed of cotton wool, rested a gold chain with a pendant in the shape of an ox. The boy had been given it for his confirmation, but he didn't know by whom, maybe his grandparents, and he had never seen him wear it. He held the necklace up for Stava to see. He figured it was gold at least, but she didn't even look at it.

'How much money do you have in your bank account?'

'I don't know,' he replied and tried to fit the lid back onto the tiny box. 'A few thousand.'

She asked if he had any weapons and he nodded.

They went down to the basement and he opened the gun safe and stepped aside. As if to make room for a potential buyer. She picked up a box of ammunition and shook it, then she took the .30-06 from the rack and picked up the shoulder bag with the ammunition.

When they stepped out the front door, the wolf was standing there, watching them with its head lowered. Anders stopped in the doorway, fearful. Stava opened the boot and the wolf jumped in like a German Shepherd.

They got in the car and drove off. Out on Bergslagsvägen and down road 68 toward Gävle. He opened his hand and looked at the tiny ox that had been pressed into his skin.

She held the wheel casually, with her elbow against her stomach. He could tell she was angry, but he didn't understand why. He could hardly be blamed for there not being more valuables in his home, now could he?

The air in the car was crackling with her displeasure. Anders sat shaking his head; he shook it incessantly. Like a mental patient facing the wall in a common room. As though his entire existence revolved around a single question to which he was doomed to answer no for the rest of eternity.

'We can't arrive empty-handed,' she said.

Anders said nothing. He was too busy shaking his head, convinced terrible pain would set in the moment he stopped moving it.

'Well,' she said. 'I'm glad we're in agreement.'

Her eyes roved across the landscape. Fields sprinkled with silage bales. Red wooden houses immersed in verdant greenery.

'Are there any rich people around here?'

'Rich people?'

She nodded.

'Not as far as I know.'

'No neighbour of yours?'

'Why am I feeling like this, what's happening to me?'

Lennart followed behind the motorhome. Sometimes he saw Ingvill's elbow moving in the rear-view mirror. They had crossed over into Norway. The fens and low-trunked birch woods disappeared, replaced by blue-tinted mountainsides and roads leading up and then down and then up again.

They stopped for petrol in Varangerbotn and then followed the road that ran along the stony shores of the sea fjord. Every now and then, a breeze smoothed dark fields on the water. Far out in the distance, there was a person in a boat, their life jacket like an orange dot.

The further out on the barren peninsula they got, the further apart the houses were, and the more derelict.

Once the boy woke up, he sat watching Lennart with enigmatic patience. Lennart told him to look at the sheep lining the road like grey rocks, but the boy never took his eyes off him.

The road up the mountain to the bunker was little more than a trail. A woman was walking along its edge and when Lennart climbed out of the car, he heard a dog barking not too far away.

He followed Abraham into the motorhome. Grete was sitting on the floor by the sofa. Her shiny scalp could be glimpsed between her wilting strands of hair. Her top lip arched, wrinkled and taut, across the teeth of her upper jaw as she tugged at the blanket in an attempt to hide her legs. When Abraham knelt down to lift her up, she let out a sound that made him shy away. He straightened up, bewildered. Ingvill said something inaudible from over by the bed and Grete smiled without looking at them.

'I'm tired, lads. You'll have to come back later.'

They went outside and stood in silence, united in confusion.

'There's too many people around,' Lennart said. 'We have to wait for nightfall.'

Abraham took out his weasel. It lay curled up in the palm of his hand; which end was which was anyone's guess.

After a while, Ingvill came out with a camping mat under her arm. She walked around the motorhome and unrolled the mat on the ground. She hid her head in her hood and lay down on her side with her arms crossed, her knees pulled up and her eyes closed as the sea wind filled her jacket with folds and blisters.

The little boy toddled over to her but when he put his hands on her leg, she pulled it away. Her shoe hit him in the stomach and he sat down hard on his bottom. He didn't cry, just looked wonderingly at the woman who had kicked him, then he struggled back onto his feet and tottered off in the opposite direction; a golden plover called from somewhere.

I recognised the girl, so I knew who he had to be and naturally assumed Diana was nearby too, but the shop was so crowded and the queue to the till kept growing, so I didn't have time to look for her. I didn't even have time to ponder what her reason for coming might be. Had she been out to see Susso or had she just stopped by to say hi? To my surprise, I couldn't actually see her anywhere. It was just the little girl and her dad. He had been standing there, holding her hand, the entire time, but now he let go and came up to the till and from the grave look on his face, I could tell something was amiss. He introduced himself as Håkan Sillfors and having made sure I was Susso's mother, he got straight to the point. Diana had gone to see Susso the day before, on Friday. She had let him know she was going to spend the night and be back in the morning. Now it was almost five and she had neither come home nor been in touch. And she wasn't answering her phone and hadn't read any texts since last night.

'And we're getting a bit worried,' he said.

He must have sensed what I was thinking, because his expression changed. He had probably counted on me at least trying to calm him down and when I didn't, but rather acted as though I were about to pass out, he demanded, through gritted teeth, that I give him Susso's address.

'It's not what you think,' I said.

'Would you please give me her address.'

'Just let me close up and balance the till.'

He borrowed his father-in-law's car, swapping it for the little girl. Kent Sillfors' car was a red Skoda and having it in the rear-view mirror on the E10 motorway felt like being tailed by the police. Because I knew he was sitting there, thinking all kinds of thoughts about me, like the police do when they're keeping an eye on a car in front of them. Like heat against the back of my neck. He was a doctor too, and he and Diana had likely discussed Susso, and probably our entire family, and it wasn't hard to imagine what that conversation had been like.

I always used to be proud of my name, boastful even. I would pronounce it with a level of smugness in any and all contexts. When a stranger found out what my name was, I would follow up with he was my dad before they were even through asking whether I was related to Gunnar Myrén. I was that eager to bask in his glory. However, that glory had gradually faded and eventually vanished and these days I felt a pall had been cast over our name. I certainly didn't take any joy in telling people my name any more; it made me feel ashamed, because I knew people no longer associated the name Myrén with pictures of beautiful mountains; they associated the name Myrén with pictures of trolls. Faked pictures. Counterfeiting. And as if that wasn't enough, kidnapping and obscure cults too. That's what Margareta Oja had told me when she came in the shop one day, that someone had asked her on Facebook what our connections had really been with that kidnapper cult outside Sorsele. And she obviously didn't want to reveal who it was who had asked. She felt it didn't matter. And that was the worst of it, that she said it didn't matter who had asked the question, because that made it seem general. Everyone is wondering. Everyone is talking. That was why she had popped by and told me about it, under the guise of wanting to share a confidence. She probably thought I shouldn't look quite so smug, standing by my little display case in the village hall, for everyone to see, because as we all know, you must never think too highly of yourself, and definitely not of your father. And she succeeded, I'm sad to say. I took it to heart. It went straight in. I probably wouldn't have cared if it had been some random snide remark, but this was obviously something that had already gnawed at me for a long time.

For some reason, I took the fact that Diana's car wasn't parked by the house as a good sign, and I told Håkan she might already be on her way home. We would have met her on the road, he countered. I don't know why I assumed the role of optimist, maybe that's just what happens in difficult situations: if one person pulls one way, the other takes the opposite tack. I felt anything but optimistic on the inside.

Håkan barged through the door, calling Diana's name; the sound of his voice broke my heart. The worry I had carried inside for years had been just that, a worry. Something internal. Now here he was, shouting. It was suddenly serious. I didn't call out; I was already bracing for the worst and didn't know if I could even bring myself to enter the house.

Diana's phone was charging on the floor. He yanked the cord out and stomped up the stairs with the phone in his hand.

When I reached the upper landing, he had already gone into Susso's bedroom. He stood there, stock-still in complete silence and when I came in, I realised why.

There was a man sitting on Susso's bed. The bed was unmade but the man was fully dressed. He had a red beard and his arms were covered in tattoos.

'Where is she?' Håkan demanded.

'We're going to live here,' he said without looking at us.

'What?'

'We're going to live here.'

'Where the fuck is she!'

Håkan was instantly furious; he revved up like an engine. He kicked at the feet sticking out from the bed and when the man pulled them back and curled up in the foetal position among the pillows, he lunged at him and grabbed his throat with both hands. He straddled him and bellowed into his blood-filled face, where is she, where is she, what did you do to her!

Did I try to intervene? I might have mumbled something, but that was it. I stood there, watching Håkan Sillfors strangle that poor sod. I was invaded by the dark energies that were also filling Håkan with a murderous rage. But I was neither murderous nor rageful. I was nothing. I felt absolutely nothing. The man was emitting gurgling sounds and I just stood there, looking at his feet, which twitched and then stopped twitching. Pilled white socks that said INTERSPORT, I remember that clearly, and I suppose I'll never forget it.

Afterwards, Håkan slid to the floor and sat with his back against the bed, staring vacantly into thin air. Not at me; I don't even think he was aware I was in the room. I was also fairly certain he hadn't seen what I'd seen and if he had, he had no way of knowing what it meant.

'Håkan!' I said.

That made him look up. Then it was as though he suddenly realised what he'd done, because he leapt up onto the bed and tried to resuscitate the man, who lay there with his mouth wide open, his baseball cap still on his head, oddly enough. He carried on for quite some time, doing rescue breathing, which looked obscene, and trying to get his heart to start beating, but what good did that do, the guy's face looked like a prune. In the end, he gave up and slid back down to the floor and this time, he buried his head in his hands.

'What have I done,' he said, 'what have I done.'

'Håkan, it wasn't your fault.'

'How can you say that? I strangled him! I've strangled a person. And I don't even know who he is. And I strangled him. Oh my God.'

He held his hands up in front of him and stared at them like they were two alien instruments.

I put a hand on his knee and maintained that it wasn't his fault and that everything was going to be okay. Håkan pulled out his phone and moments later, Diana's phone lit up on the bed; he reached for it and sat looking at it as it rang. It seemed to give him comfort. Then he said he was going to call the police.

'Hold on,' I said. 'Let's think about this.'

He didn't want to do that, he wanted to call straight away.

So I took his phone from him and put it in my handbag, and then I took Diana's phone as well. I helped him up and led him out of the room, walking as slowly as I could make myself, only to then slam the door shut, quick as lightning, before the mouse could get out.

It had been sitting on the bed. A tiny little thing, not much bigger than a pine cone, and it was lucky I spotted it, because otherwise who knows what might have happened. There were bald patches in its fur, and it walked on two legs or four by turns. Håkan was calling Diana's name again and wanted to search the garden, but I told him there was no point.

After nagging and pulling at him for a while, I managed to make him sit down at the kitchen table. Broken glass crunched under my feet when I fetched him a glass of water. He sat with his head in his hands.

'Drink this.'

I pulled out a chair and sat down across from him.

'I don't know what happened.'

'No, but you see, I do.'

'What have I fucking done.'

'It wasn't you.'

'Gudrun. What have I done.'

'There was someone else in that room.'

'We have to call the police, we have to look for her.'

'We will look for her. But we're not going to call the police.'

'Give me the phone.'

He held his hand out across the table. It was shaking.

'Listen to me, Håkan. If we call the police, you're going to end up in prison for I don't know how many years, and Diana will probably never come back. Do you understand what I'm telling you? If we call the police, Kiruna will be an orphan. You don't want that, do you?'

He stared at me and at length lowered his hand.

'Calling the police,' I said, 'is a bad idea.'

'Then what do we do?'

I pondered that for a minute. Leaned back in my chair. And then I saw it. It was sitting on the threshold, looking at us. What had I expected? After all, a mouse can squeeze through cracks light can barely get through.

'Come on,' I said and pulled Håkan out of the kitchen.

We climbed into the car and I was quick to shut the doors and lock them. Then I studied him from the side. He looked broken.

'Did you by any chance notice a mouse up there? That there was a mouse on the bed. This big.' I showed him with my thumb and forefinger. 'Tail included.'

Håkan made no reply. He just stared vacantly into thin air.

'That's what made you strangle that man.'

'Gudrun.'

'Yes?'

'What have I fucking done.'

'I know it's hard to understand, especially for a doctor, but you understanding this right here, right now, is critical if we want to find Diana.'

He looked completely helpless.

'I want to turn back time.'

'You can't.'

'No.'

'There's no chance of that.'

'What have I done.'

'This mouse,' I said, 'it has some kind of telepathic power. I don't know how it happens, but they can get in your head and mess you up in there. Why do you think I did nothing to stop you, Håkan! Have you thought about that? I was affected too, don't you see? Do you understand what I'm telling you?'

He shook his head.

'Can you at least hear what I'm telling you?'

He nodded.

'Good. That's all I ask. For now.'

We sat gazing out at the river and I wondered where the mouse might be. It was probably sitting in the grass just outside the car, pondering how to get inside; the thought made me queasy. The windows were fogging up.

'You're probably thinking I'm nuts right now.'

He shrugged.

I sat in silence for a while before pressing on.

'Do you know what a stallo is?'

'No,' he said and put his head in his hands. 'No, no, no.' He was once again overwhelmed by the realisation of what he'd done; it was hitting him in waves.

'Håkan. Do you know what a stallo is?'

'It's something Sami. A troll or something.'

'Maybe Diana told you about the photograph my dad took in Sarek? It's a picture of a troll. An aerial shot.'

He nodded.

'They're real, Håkan. Listen to me. Trolls are real. That mouse is a troll. A small one, but still a troll. And it's absolutely deadly. We have to beware of it. Because it can do things to us and they won't be good things.'

'We have to call the police.'

'If you want to call the police, you can always do that later.

You'll always have that option. But the option to get Diana back, that is about to expire. So you need to listen to me. I don't want to hear any more talk about the police for a bit. Are you listening?'

'I'm listening.'

'Trolls are real.'

He nodded.

'Say it, I want you to say it.'

'Trolls are real.'

'The reason you can't find them is that they hide in animal form. They can shapeshift, as it's called. It happens like this.'

I snapped my fingers and then pointed to the house.

'That mouse is no mouse, and you can actually tell, because it seems to have only partly transformed. They come in all sizes. Some are mice, others are bears. But inside, they're something else.'

He swallowed hard.

'I didn't see a mouse.'

'But you felt it. It made you do something you would never have done otherwise. Didn't it? And that's proof it was there. You're not a murderer, are you?'

'I am now.'

'No, you're not. You're innocent. It's like that powerful drug, what's it called, angel dust? You don't know what you're doing. You're innocent.'

He covered his face with his hand.

'Who was that up there?'

'No idea.'

'He might have killed them, they might be around here somewhere.'

'I doubt it. I'm pretty sure Lennart Brösth has been here and taken the girls. You know who he is, the cult leader.'

He nodded.

'The thing is that trolls like children. Just like in the stories; in that respect, it's just like the stories. That was what the Jillesnåle Cult were doing. They protected the trolls and kidnapped children for them. And Susso was onto them. Through sheer happenstance, actually. And when they tried to kill her, she ended up killing a troll. I saw it with my own eyes. It turned into a bear the moment it died. That's why they're after her.'

'But Diana hasn't done anything,' he blurted out. 'She has nothing to do with this.'

'Oh come on, Håkan, don't be an idiot! Do you think it matters? That's like saying a person who gets hit by a car had nothing to do with the car. She was unlucky enough to be in the wrong place at the wrong time.'

'Then where are they, what did he do to them?'

'I don't know.'

He rubbed his face with his hand.

'If we're not calling the police, what are we going to do?'

'We're going home.'

'But we can't just leave him there. Or can we?'

I was quiet for a moment before answering.

'No, I suppose we can't.'

'So what do we do?'

'I think we're going to have to try to get rid of him.'

'How?'

'Let's see if there's a shovel in the henhouse.'

'Are you serious?'

'I'm exactly as serious as the situation requires.'

'I'm not burying anyone.'

'I'm trying to help you, Håkan. I didn't kill a man, you did. You're the one who strangled him, I just watched. Remember that. If we're looking at it from a legal point of view. The easiest and best thing for me would be to call the police. But I don't want to do that. I want to help you. And I want to find the girls.'

'Me too.'

'So let's bury him.'

'I can't.'

'We'll bury him and then we'll never speak of this again. We bury him and then we shake on never speaking of it, with another living soul, for as long as we live, and not afterwards either. And that means not speaking about it to each other as well. Do you understand what I'm saying?'

He nodded.

'It never happened.'

'Okay.'

'Is that a deal?'

'Yes.'

'Then say it.'

'It never happened.'

'Then let's shake on it.'

Abraham had stopped at the top of the ridge and Lennart panted his way up the last stretch to see what he was looking at.

A tent. A small, blue dome tent, no more than fifty feet from the entrance to the bunker. They looked at it in silence.

'How hungry do you reckon he is?' Abraham said.

Lennart turned around and motioned to Susso to head back down again; on the way down the slope, Abraham informed him there was another entrance, one that wasn't visible from the tent. It was sealed, but the rocks were reasonably loose and should be movable.

'This way,' he said, pointing as he jogged along a bank of excavated rock. Below the bank was a long, narrow ditch they climbed into. Further on, this trench turned into a tunnel. A gaping hole straight into the netherworld. Abraham stopped and was evidently not about to go any closer.

Lennart clambered over the sharp rocks, with a hand on the rough stone wall. Susso followed him. A mute, one-eyed companion with a face streaked with dried blood.

On the ground some way into the tunnel, he glimpsed something white; at first, he thought there was someone lying there. Then he realised it was a pile of snow. He went closer and peered into the darkness.

'He's not in there.'

A young woman was standing above him, looking down into the ravine. She had on a camouflage baseball cap and a blue thermal underwear top and was holding a rolled-up leather dog lead in her hand.

'We're just looking around,' he muttered.

She tapped the lead lightly against her thigh.

'Erasmus wants you to come.'

He stared stubbornly at the ground, at the crystallised snow that seemed to be inching its way toward the shade inside the tunnel.

'What did you do to him?' he said at length.

'He's with Erasmus. There's nothing here.'

Now the wolf appeared behind the woman. Grey and bony, it stood by the edge, gaping at him, and in the darkness of its maw the white row of teeth in its lower jaw glinted like a sharp smile.

'Come on already. You're supposed to come with me.'

'Where?'

'To Erasmus.'

'I have to bring her. She's a gift.'

That caught the wolf's interest. It leaned out over the small ravine and watched them. The collar that was just visible among its tufts of fur was made of dark, studded leather.

'So bring her,' the woman said. 'But we have to go now.'

Lennart started walking. Then he turned around and motioned for Susso to follow. The wolf followed them up on the bank, like a guard dog with its eye on a couple of suspicious types. When they climbed out of the trench, the woman was already a silhouette at the top of the mountain; there was no sign of Abraham.

*

He watched the woman while she broke her camp. The wolf padded around them incessantly as if to remind them that it was watching them. One of its eyes had a white around it like a human eye. She packed up her tent and pulled on her backpack, which was so tall it towered above her head when she started walking.

'Do you have a phone?'

He pulled his phone out of the pocket of his miserable track-suit bottoms and stared at it as though he didn't quite know what it was. She held out her hand and he put the phone in it.

'I'm Ipa,' she said. 'Though that's not my real name, my real name is Ida, but everyone calls me Ipa.'

They walked almost a mile to get to her car. A small, white off-road vehicle, a Lada Niva, parked on a diagonal with the sun on its windscreen. Ipa opened the boot and helped the animal scramble in. It wasn't a big space, but that didn't seem to bother the wolf, who immediately lay down and placed its head between its front paws. She put the backpack on the back seat and had Susso climb in next to it.

Once she was behind the wheel, she took her cap off. She pulled the hair tie out of her blonde hair and put it between her teeth, tossed her hair about, gathered it up, took the hair tie out of her mouth and made a new ponytail.

The car bounced along on the uneven terrain; Lennart hit his head on the ceiling. Then he hit it again.

Before long, they had reached the road.

'Disengage the locking differential,' he said, nodding at the dashboard. 'The left lever. No, the left one.'

'Fucking Russian piece of crap,' she said.

Anders looked at the house on the other side of the horse pasture. A big brick house with a gable roof. The pool like a gash of mareel in the lawn. The L-shaped stable was as tall as the main house and a row of cars was parked along its side.

He climbed out, shut the door behind him, accepted the rifle she handed him and loaded it with trembling fingers. One cartridge fell into the gravel; he didn't bother picking it up.

The old man he'd been too scared to think about was standing in the middle of the road, wrapped in a sheet he was holding closed under his chin with his clumsy, werewolf-like hand. His face wrinkly and ugly like a bog mummy.

Anders stared at the cartridge on the ground and couldn't move; he could barely breathe.

'What's the matter?' Stava said.

Anders didn't reply.

'You don't have to be afraid of him.'

'Who is he?' he mumbled.

'It's Ransu,' she hissed and wrapped the rifle in a blanket. 'And you're going to have to pull yourself together. It makes him sad when you don't recognise him.'

'I do recognise him, I do, I do, I promise, I was just a bit . . .'

'Get it together!'

They walked toward the house. The tape fencing in the horse pasture drew white lines through the twilight, and white was the shroud around the figure eagerly dragging himself along behind Stava, like a deformed child on its way to a fancy-dress party in a useless costume his tired mum put together at the last minute.

A man and a woman were sitting at the end of a long table on the patio, engaged in quiet conversation, with the light of a small lantern between them. When they spotted the trio crossing the lawn, they fell silent.

Stava said good evening, but was given no greeting in return.

The man and the woman stared at the little ghost limping up to the edge of the illuminated pool.

'You look like you're having a nice time,' Stava said and climbed the stairs to the patio. 'Could we have some wine too?'

'What?'

'Could we have some wine too?'

The man got to his feet.

'We were actually in the middle of a conversation here . . .'

'Yes, it looks lovely. Anders, come sit down!'

'No, hold on here now.'

Stava had already pulled out a chair and sat down. Anders snuck up with the blanket-wrapped rifle in his arms. He didn't quite know where he was and what they were doing there, so he wanted to stay close to Stava. There was a pain behind one of his eyes and he had started shaking his head again. When he put his bundle down on the table, the barrel of the rifle peeked out, which elicited a strangled noise from the old lady. The man was still standing up. An older man in a tennis shirt.

'Are you home alone?' Stava said.

'What do you want?'

'Are you home alone?'

'Yes, we are.'

'Sit down.'

The man sat down just as Ransu stepped up onto the patio, hiding his hideous face like a leprous pilgrim. There were a lot of planters full of geraniums at the end of the patio; he squatted down next to them like a sentinel.

'What's your name?' Stava said.

'Torgny.'

'And you?'

'Yvonne.'

'Are you home alone?'

'Our daughter is upstairs,' the woman said. 'And her boyfriend.'

'So there's four of you in the house?'

She nodded.

'And there's no one else on the premises? Some Polish person shovelling shit and living in a shed?'

Torgny shook his head.

'How many horses do you have?'

'Do you mean in the stable or how many are ours?'

'How many are yours.'

'Fourteen.'

'Are they pacers?'

'Yes, we have pacers.'

'Flat racers?'

'Yes, some.'

'Do they win?'

'From time to time.'

He nodded.

'So you must be pretty well off then?'

'No, not particularly.'

'I suppose it's all relative.'

The man said nothing.

'Isn't it?'

He nodded.

'How much money do you have in your safe?'

'We don't have a safe.'

'Sure, but how much money is in it?'

The man was quiet for a while.

'I don't know.'

'Ballpark.'

'Maybe fifty.'

'Fifty thousand?'

He nodded.

'That's not a lot.'

'No.'

'Maybe you could spare it?'

'Yes.'

'What's the code?'

It was buried deep, but in the end he reeled off six numbers.

'That's your daughter's birthday, isn't it?'

'No. It's the day after. The month after. The year after.'

Stava nodded.

'Splendid.'

The girl's name was Moa and the boy's Lukas and they were lying on their backs in bed, their faces illuminated by a computer screen. Anders stood in the doorway with sweat trickling down his face. The laptop was closed. When they noticed the rifle in his hands, they crawled up against the wall.

'You're supposed to come downstairs,' he said. 'And bring a pillow.'

'What?'

'Bring a pillow.'

They walked ahead of him, half naked. Moa hugged the pillow. When they reached the patio, they sat down and Torgny said everything was going to be all right and reached out and squeezed his daughter's arm, and Stava studied them with an enigmatic smile.

They sat there, around the table, for a long time. No one said anything and no one moved. The person who finally broke the silence was Moa. She had discovered the crouching figure over by the geraniums.

'Oh my God, what is that!' she sobbed.

'Something horrible is going to happen here tonight,' Stava said. 'You see, your boyfriend is planning to rob your parents and if they don't do exactly as he says, he's going to kill them. And you too, if you're not careful.'

'No, I'm not,' Lukas objected.

'You're going to go into the study and empty the safe.'

The boy looked at Torgny, who nodded.

'Do as she says,' he said.

'Do you know your girlfriend's birthday?'

He was completely dazed, so she had to repeat the question, then he nodded and looked around with a stunned look on his face.

'The code,' Stava said, 'is the year after, the month after, the day after. Six digits.'

'Other way around,' Torgny said. 'It starts with the day.'

'Naturally. It starts with the day. Is that clear?'

'I think so,' he said and looked down at his underwear. He had wet himself, and he pulled on the fabric and wiped his hand on his thigh.

'What's her birthday?'

'The nineteenth. Isn't it? Moa?'

Moa nodded.

'So what are the first two digits?'

'Twenty.'

'Put anything valuable in the pillowcase. If there are binders or passports or papers in the safe, you will leave them there. The only thing you're after is valuables. Cash and jewellery are the only things you care about. I don't suppose you have a weapon in that safe, do you, Torgny?'

'The stunner's in there.'

'The stunner?'

'Well, I mean, it's one of those bolt guns. With cartridges. And they're in the safe. The gun and the cartridges.'

'That sounds exciting. You'll obviously take that. We'll be here when you're done. Can we trust you not to go looking for a phone or try to escape or some other foolishness?'

He nodded.

'Good. Then you can go.'

'Should I do it now?'

Stava nodded.

He got to his feet.

'The pillow,' she said.

The boy turned around, took the pillow from Moa and went inside. Torgny and Yvonne looked down at the table; Moa cried silently.

After a while, he came back.

'I can't find a gun, there's just this black thing . . .'

'That's it,' Torgny said.

'Should I lock the safe when I'm done?'

'Either way,' Stava told him.

When he returned, Stava took the pillowcase from him and looked in it.

'Lovely little goody bag,' she said.

She took out the bolt gun and turned it over in her hands. A heavy cylinder of lacquered black steel surrounded by nuts and counter-nuts that lent it a curved shape. After putting it back in the bag, she pulled out a wallet and flipped through the notes.

'Take this,' she said to Lukas and handed him a thousand-kronor note. 'Put it in your pocket.'

'I don't want it.'

'As a matter of fact, you do. Here you go. And you, take off your rings. Lukas thinks they look valuable. They're probably eighteen carats. In Finland, the standard's fourteen carats. Everything's a little bit shitter in Finland.'

When Torgny and Yvonne had twisted off their rings, Stava received them into the palm of her hand.

'Are these diamonds?' she said and Yvonne nodded. Stava shook the pillowcase gently, stuck her head in and pulled out a gold ring.

'Whose ring is this, then?'

'It's probably my mother's ring,' Yvonne said quietly. 'Or my father's. Both were in the safe.'

Stava put the diamond ring in the bag and handed the rest to Lukas.

'Put them in your pocket,' she said.

Then she turned to Torgny.

'You're going to go to bed now.'

They didn't move.

'But I don't want to,' Torgny mumbled.

'It's late,' said Stava, who was still digging around in the pillowcase, examining its contents.

Torgny got up slowly. A small amount of blood had trickled from his nose; it looked like the dark cavity of his nostril had widened.

'Come on,' he said, but Yvonne angrily snatched her arm away when he tried to make her stand up. He spoke softly to her and in the end, she followed him into the house.

He had seen animals stunned with a bolt gun several times, before being exsanguinated, but he had never operated one himself. That was why he was now sitting on the sofa in the living room, trying to figure out how it worked. Lukas was sitting next to him. The boy wanted to know why it was called a gun, since it looked more like a stick than a gun. Anders found the boy's companionability uncomfortable and didn't answer his incessantly repeated, pointless questions.

He picked up a cartridge from the cardboard box on the coffee table and once he had figured out which way the primer should go, he slid the cartridge in and screwed the buffer on tight. Then he pulled out the bolt until he heard a clicking sound from the trigger. He grabbed the gun with both hands, held it against the table top and fired. The nail shot through the wood with a bang that made Lukas jump.

'Did you see how I did that?'

Guided by Anders' instructions, the boy unscrewed the gun and loaded another cartridge. When he put it against the table top, Anders shook his head.

'You have to pull it out first. All the way. Now you can do it.'

He let him do a few trial runs, on the table top and on the armrest of the sofa; the boy pulled the trigger with a feeble-minded smile on his face.

Torgny and Yvonne lay in their bedroom, staring up at the ceiling. Stava was standing by the foot of the bed and Moa was sitting on the floor, her face hidden between her knees. Ransu was standing by the window, hunched and naked, with a deranged look in his swivelling dog's eyes.

Lukas was holding the bolt gun.

'They're asleep,' Stava said.

'But their eyes are open,' Lukas protested.

'Close your eyes,' Stava said and they did, instantly.

The boy went up to the edge of the bed and put the bolt gun against Torgny's forehead. He opened his eyes when he felt the steel against his skin.

'No peeking,' Stava said.

'Isn't it going to be messy?' Lukas said.

'I guess we'll find out,' Stava replied.

The gun cracked and Torgny's feet danced wildly under the covers. It looked like he was being electrocuted. But it was a short dance. Within moments, he was still.

'Torgny?' Yvonne said.

Stava hushed her and Lukas pushed the nail back into the gun by pressing it against the nightstand. A lamp was knocked to the floor, but Stava told him to leave it. He shuffled around the bed, leaned in over Yvonne and placed the gun against her forehead.

'Torgny?'

Stava wanted Moa to go up to her room and get in her bed, but she refused. She had curled up in a corner of the bedroom and spit was bubbling out between her tightly shut lips. Lukas pulled on her arm, but couldn't get a good hold on her.

'There's no point,' Stava said. 'You're going to have to do it here.'

Every time Lukas aimed the bolt gun at Moa, she jerked her head away or pushed it aside with her hand.

'Moa, cut it out!' he said.

Anders left the room. He paced a circle around the living room because he couldn't stand still. He was suddenly overcome with an impulse to sit down on the sofa and stick the barrel in his mouth. He heard Stava's hoarse voice from the bedroom. She was explaining something to the boy.

'This is going to haunt you for the rest of your life,' she said, 'you can't live with these images.'

After a while, she came out and closed the door behind her, carefully, as though she had just managed to put an infant to sleep.

She stood with her arms crossed, watching him. He was sitting on the sofa, poking at one of the holes in the coffee table.

'Anders,' she said and sat down next to him. 'Don't you

think I know what you're going through? You want me to push that pen against your head too. Don't you?'

He nodded.

'I would never do that. What you're going through, it will pass. I promise you. This is just a phase. A transition.'

'I can't, I can't do this.'

'What can't you do?'

He nodded toward the bedroom.

'They're just humans,' she said and stroked his neck.

'I'm a human too, aren't I?'

'You're my human. That's different.'

They sat on the sofa for a long while without speaking.

'I want to go home,' he mumbled.

'We're on our way.'

Suddenly, she whipped her head around to face the bedroom door. A sound had made her react. She listened and after a while she went over and opened the door. What she saw in the gloom on the other side disturbed her. She cursed and spoke heatedly in Finnish and moments later the wolf came shambling out into the living room like an old dog who's been banished.

'We have to get out of here,' she said.

'What happened?'

'Grab the bag!'

They jogged back to the car. Anders didn't know why they were suddenly in such a hurry, but he assumed it had something to do with Ransu no longer walking upright.

He put the rifle in the boot and after the wolf jumped in, he closed the lid. She had already started the car; he didn't even have time to close the door before she drove off.

Diana couldn't see anything and all sounds except her own pulse were muffled. She never heard the child, but she heard the woman talking to it in a childish voice. A young woman. Not a local. The voice penetrated her numbed awareness in waves and when she had established that the woman was real and just outside, she started kicking. Inside the hood of warm and sticky scrim-backed plastic that enveloped her head, her screams turned into a wordless lowing. She kicked and thrashed until she heard the woman again.

'Yes,' she said, 'what was that?'

Her voice had been lowered to express breathless wonder.

'What was that? Is there someone in there? Hm! Is there someone in there?'

Diana realised there was no point making a ruckus. Her nostrils flared to their greatest circumference when she sucked in air and tried to think clearly. She was in some kind of cupboard, but she wasn't sure how she'd got in it. Her memories were slowly coming back, but it was like picking through the debris of a serious bender. She had been at Susso's. She remembered Susso's drawn face clearly. Her kitchen. And the squirrel. How it had fixed on her through the uneven window pane. And that figure coming toward her, closing in with jerky steps like something out of a horror film. But then there was nothing. The guide in her brain refused to go any further.

She had no idea how long she had been locked in the cupboard. Her hands were wrapped in a clump of tape, so she could neither get to her watch nor remove the tape covering her face. They hadn't given her anything to eat or drink and from time to time she thought they must have forgotten all about her. That she would have to sit in the cupboard until she was desiccated like an old fruit. Those kinds of thoughts frightened her, so she tried to push them back down. She was severely dehydrated and could ill afford to pant out whatever moisture she had left in her body. In her miserable state, she clung to strangely rational lines of reasoning. That they taped up my mouth is a good thing, she thought, because that helps me preserve fluids. That's to my advantage. That's to my advantage. The words got stuck in a feverish loop and she sensed she was losing the ability to think clearly.

She had sunk into a stupor when she suddenly heard voices outside. Several voices, and not quiet, like before. A woman speaking Norwegian. Diana took the fact that they were upset as a sign that they would soon let her out. And that turned out to be correct. The door opened and a hand grabbed her upper arm and pulled her out. Her legs buckled and she collapsed like a puppet whose strings have been cut.

She stayed on the ground, with the smell of grass in her nostrils. She thought she could hear the sound of waves from far away. A quiet conversation in Norwegian. That woman. She couldn't hear what she was saying; they were too far away and speaking too softly.

A car started, a big car with a rumbling diesel engine, the one she had been locked in. It idled for a while before driving off. It passed by her very close. They're running me over, she had time to think, before the sound disappeared into the distance.

Now she could hear the young woman who had been talking to the child. She was angry and her voice slid up into falsetto.

'That's your fucking problem,' she screeched.

A door slammed shut and silence fell.

Footsteps on the gravel. Someone was nearby and that made her uneasy, because whoever it was didn't make themselves known.

'This is going to hurt.'

It was him. The one who had driven her car, the one who had beaten her unconscious. What was going to hurt? She curled up and tensed her neck muscles, bracing for a blow. When her head was tugged to the side, she yelped, terrified at not knowing what lay in wait.

It took a while before she realised he was peeling the tape off her head. He did it slowly and not without care. Her head moved from side to side as he tore at the strips. She tried her best to stay upright but still fell over; he helped her up while talking soothingly to her.

'You don't have to be afraid.'

When he got to her hair, he immediately turned gentler.

'We don't want you to be bald. I'm about to wax your eyebrows now. Are you ready?'

But he didn't tug; he pulled slowly and held the skin in place with his fingers. She cautiously opened her eyes, expecting to be blinded by the light.

He was squatting down, watching her. With his dark curls

and brown eyes, he looked more like a French alpinist in a travel catalogue than a Norwegian. An alpinist with frostbite on his face. Behind him, there was nothing. Just a vast, hazy emptiness.

The place was barren like a fell. A mountain plateau without contours, covered in gravelly moraine. Heather and willow crept across the rocks like sparsely woven rugs.

The Audi was parked some way off; next to it was a van. There were no other people in sight, and no sun either, and she couldn't say whether it was day or night. The wind came at them in violent gusts and in the lulls, there was the faint sound of waves; far below them the sea cut a bay into the grey Arctic landscape.

To separate the tape from her hair, he had to rip it. The pain was superficial but it was as though the nerves in her scalp were hardwired to her tear ducts. He pulled off the tape covering her mouth last. He did it slowly, stretching out her lips. Afterwards, she felt completely raw. Pieces of tape lay in tangles on the ground around her, silvery on one side and completely white on the other; the hair that had been ripped out of her scalp stuck to it in lanky skeins.

He tore off strip after strip from the parcel of tape around her hands. She didn't want to be near his face, so she sat with her head lowered as if bashful.

The back door of the van swung open and Diana immediately looked over. A young woman. The face under the hood of her sweater was ashen like a dead junkie's. She shut the door behind her and when she realised Diana was watching her, she glowered back, and in those eyes there was no mercy because there was nothing at all.

The man handed her a plastic bottle, which she accepted with trembling hands and drank from while he gathered up the tape, which he then rolled into a ball.

'Let's go.'

He helped her up.

'Where are we going?'

'We're just going for a little walk,' he said and shoved the ball of tape into his jacket pocket.

They passed the cars; she glanced in through the windows. The sunshade with its suction cups. The hair elastics around the chubby gearstick. Seeing their car there was deeply confusing. It was usually parked outside the garage next to their house on Duvvägen and now it was here, at what felt like the end of the world.

The young woman was leaning against the van with her arms crossed, watching her. Diana was suddenly furious.

'What the fuck did I ever do to you!' she screamed. 'Leave me alone! Leave me the fuck alone!'

The man softly told her to calm down and ushered her on. Across a stony plain. Further on, she could see the roof of a small lighthouse, an orange cone sharply outlined in the haze. The sound of the breaking waves grew louder and soon she could hear gulls screeching mindlessly.

She limped on. Her left leg ached and didn't want to move. It was as though it had knowledge of something the rest of her was denying. He had given her water; he had been gentle with her hair. We don't want you to go bald, he'd told her. So they couldn't very well be planning to hurt her. Maybe if he'd been alone, a murderer who combed his victims' hair with deranged care. But this wasn't like that.

This was about Susso, that cult she'd crossed. She wanted to ask where Susso was, but was afraid of what his answer might be.

Disorienting swaths of fog were drifting in and the mountain seemed to rise up like a ramp toward the overcast sky. Beyond the sharp edge of the cliffs there was nothing but a hazy void. What could be out there? There couldn't be anything out there.

'I need to pee,' she said and after saying it, she stopped. She turned around and studied the man. He put his hand in his pocket and scooped something out. A slender, hairless body. Some kind of furless weasel with a deformed face and cruel little eyes.

'You don't need to pee,' he said.

'I'm afraid you're going to hurt me.'

'We're just going for a walk.'

'Where are we going?'

'I want to show you something.'

She limped on and when she reached the lighthouse, which wasn't much taller than her, she stopped. The sea was just about visible as a dark streak at the lower edge of the fog enshrouding the mountain.

The man stared at her until she walked on. Below the lighthouse was a concrete platform that may have supported a cannon in a different time and she thought to herself that there might be other relics further out. Maybe it was something along those lines he wanted to show her?

They came out onto a terrace where limestone cliffs had eroded into discs like the ruins of some ancient megalithic monument. There was no path; that made her uncertain. She turned around and the man motioned for her to walk on, toward the edge.

Her urine-soaked jeans were stiff and cold and she moved with short, faltering steps. As though her shoelaces were tied together, or she was disabled by some neurological walking impediment. Lichen-flecked polygons, pink like salmon-flesh, spread out around her. A small flight of concrete steps unexpectedly appeared among the rocks and beyond it was a primitive fortification with a wall made of stone shards. She was hoping there would be something behind that wall, but there wasn't, just scrap metal, inscrutable, rusty formations.

From time to time, the mist parted to reveal a stretch of coastline in the distance. A promontory like the black back of a whale. Leaden, wave-streaked water disappearing under a curtain of clouds.

The mountain sloped into the sea with geological un-ambiguousness. After dropping down from a small ledge, she ran a few steps to regain her balance and then carried on running. Her legs moved of their own accord. The cliffs on her right jutted out over a steep drop; below lay a belt of fallen rocks. She stumbled among piles of rocks the size of human heads and ran into hollows deep as cauldrons and up again. She had no plan, she just ran.

The fog lifted and the sea spread out before her, but that was as far as she got because sitting in her path on a hunk of siltstone was that animal. It glared at her with its cold lizard eyes and the will to escape drained out of her in the blink of an eye. Suddenly, she wasn't afraid any more and she didn't know why she had run. Her mind couldn't move so much as an inch, forward or backward.

A hand grabbed her arm and she was led back and she smiled, embarrassed by her inability to remember what she had done wrong.

The man put one of his boots up on a crag like a jaunty explorer and gazed down at the precipice.

'What do you reckon,' he said, 'would falling off the edge kill you?'

'Am I supposed to fall off the edge?'

'Do you reckon it would kill you?'

'I don't know.'

'Have a look.'

She walked over to the edge and peered down.

'Yes,' she said, 'if you're unlucky.'

He nodded and took a step back.

'Then let's hope you're unlucky, Diana.'

'I think you'd have to get away from the cliff.'

'Yes,' he said. 'You'll need a good run-up.'

'Abraham!'

The young woman was walking toward them, and she wasn't alone. When Diana saw who it was wobbling along behind her like a dressed-up child, it was as if she had slipped into a forgotten nightmare.

The naked little animal slunk down from the man's shoulder to the ground and vanished. It unexpectedly reappeared a few feet away, as if it had travelled at lightning speed through an underground tunnel, and had found time to put on fur as well. Because now the animal was a weasel and nothing else. Diana was staring at the weasel when the red jacket disappeared from her field of vision. It was as quick as it was unexpected. The man just stepped up to the edge of the precipice, shouted something into the wind, some kind of deranged pronouncement, and then he was gone.

Only then could she bring herself to have a proper look at the creature who had come to her rescue. She realised its face had once belonged to an older person. A jagged line of broken skin, joined together by a seam of irregular sutures, ran up the wrinkled neck, in behind the long-lobed ears and some way into the grey mop of hair. The chequered shirt hung down like a smock and the tip of a tail moved underneath. A broom of grey bristles. Every once in a while, it bent in under the fluttering fabric and she wished it would disappear for good so she could write it off as a mirage; when it didn't, she placed her hand on her throat and swallowed. It tasted of blood. When she wiped her lip with the back of her hand, it came away red.

The saggy old man's face turned, but not toward her, toward a little critter sitting in the grass, flaunting his snowy white chest. They looked at each other for a while. Then the old man walked away, back the way he'd come, up among the sharp, mist-shrouded cliffs, and the weasel followed.

Diana was shaking with cold. Her trousers were like a cold compress around her thighs and she had nothing but an idiotic denim jacket over her shirt.

The young woman left without so much as a glance in her direction. She was grateful for that. It was as though they'd forgotten all about her. As though she'd watched it all through a peephole and they couldn't see her. And soon, they'd be gone.

'Wait!'

The girl turned around but didn't stop.

'Do you know where Susso is? The woman who was with me?'

She shook her head but Diana thought it seemed more like a reflex than an answer to her question. She limped after her, trying to catch her eye. She pleaded with her.

'Please,' she said.

'They were going to someone called Erasmus. In Rumajärvi or Runajärvi or whatever it was. That's all I know.'

The young woman wouldn't say anything else and Diana watched her disappear between the labyrinthine cliffs. She stood still and then sank into a squat. She didn't move for a long time. Then she trudged back. It wasn't easy to find her way because all the cliffs looked identical, but eventually she spotted the lighthouse.

Since the van was gone, she sidled up to the Audi. It was locked, but she tried the handle anyway. Her handbag was on the seat inside. There was a knit jumper in it and she would have loved to put that on. She pondered whether she should try to break the window somehow. But her wish to keep the car intact was stronger than her yearning for warmth.

The person who appeared in the window reflection surprised her; she turned out the side mirror to inspect her face. She looked terrible. Her nose was broken and there was a violet monocle around her left eye. She palpated for fractures but found none. Her eye seemed able to follow all movements. She pulled up her top lip; her teeth looked intact. But she found it difficult to open her mouth wide. Her skull clicked and crunched.

She sat down with her back against the car and looked out across the damp, barren landscape while she pushed and prodded her jaw, as though the pain could be massaged away. How did you end up here? How the fuck did you end up here? Fucking Susso.

The mouse followed us everywhere. Closing the front door or the door to the kitchen was pointless. There was a brief respite during which you prayed it wouldn't reappear, but it always did.

I think it upset the little demon when I turned on the vacuum, because Håkan suddenly burst into tears. He was sitting at the table, sobbing uncontrollably and when I turned the vacuum off, it was almost like I turned off the tears as well. So I found a brush and pan instead.

He had stared at the mouse when he first noticed it and I had reminded him not to, and to be safe I had done so in English. 'Don't look,' I told him. The best thing to do was ignore it. Which of course was easier said than done.

'Gudrun,' he said.

The mouse had climbed up on his shoe. It was turning this way and that, seemingly unsure which way to turn.

'What do I do?'

I pulled an old milk carton from a paper bag sitting in the cupboard under the sink. I pulled the sealed flaps apart and started filling the carton with shards of glass. Several drinking glasses had been smashed.

'Maybe you could take this out?'

Håkan took the bin bag and got up, slowly, and when he

moved, he hopped along as though his foot were in a cast. After a few steps, the mouse had had enough and slipped back down onto the floor.

When he came back in and sat down, the mouse ran up his leg and onto the kitchen table, where it submitted to inspection by Håkan, who took off his glasses and examined its fur.

'Did you know Diana cheated on me once?'

I shook my head. He was speaking unnaturally loudly and I didn't like it.

'With an old course mate, at a conference in Gothenburg. I think that's why I reacted like I did. Because she'd told me it was just going to be her and Susso here. And then that bloke was on the bed. I just snapped.'

'You certainly did.'

'You can never trust each other again after something like that.'

'No, it can be difficult.'

'It can't be fixed.'

We had decided not to start digging until late that night. There were no neighbours around but better safe than sorry. A person could come sailing down the river. But when I noticed that the mouse was already beginning to burrow into Håkan, I realised waiting that long might come with risks.

'Maybe it's time?' I said.

He looked up, with a vacant, indifferent look on his face.

'Time for what?'

I went outside and walked over to the henhouse. There were some gardening tools just inside the door, including two shovels. One for digging and one for scooping.

Digging a hole deep enough to fit a full-grown man is not the work of a moment. And if the soil is stony and criss-crossed with roots that seem to serve no other purpose than to make digging harder, then it's terrifically tiring work. Håkan had to do the digging, of course. He was unwilling at first, but I turned the conversation back onto the topic of adultery; that got him moving. He dug with gritted teeth and boundless, furious energy.

I ambled about in the yard, on the lookout. Not primarily for people. A feeling of being watched had crept up on me and it wasn't hard to figure out who it might be. My eyes searched the pine trees, but furtively, because I had no inten-tion of appearing inviting.

After an hour or so, he was done. He stabbed the shovel into the turf and sank down onto the ground. His shirt was dripping with sweat and his hair was lank. I walked over and looked down into the grave. Roots were flaring out from the walls of the dark pit. Some were thick and knobbly, others hung down like black, blindly searching tendrils.

'Are you sure he's going to fit?'

'That's his problem,' Håkan said and got to his feet.

He hadn't moved while we were gone. It would, naturally, have been extremely alarming if he had, but it still seemed strange to me, probably a symptom of my guilt. He was staring at the ceiling in a way that was anything but peaceful; I looked away because I knew that face was going to haunt me until my dying day. Håkan, on the other hand, seemed unperturbed and I worried it was because the mouse was wreaking havoc inside him. That being said, he'd probably seen a thing or two, in his line of work. Dead bodies were likely nothing to him. At least that's the impression he gave when he grabbed the dead man's feet, pulled him down onto the floor and then paused to ponder how to proceed. He wore a belt with a box-frame buckle, which he took off and wrapped under the arms of the dead man and buckled around his chest. Then he grabbed the belt and dragged the body across the floor, out onto the landing and over to the stairs. Once there, he paused for another think. It looked like he was contemplating how to move a piece of furniture and I thought to myself that it couldn't be professional detachment, it had to be something else.

The mouse never left our side. It ran in circles around us, watching everything intently. Håkan pushed the body until it rolled down the stairs. Then he ran after it. The mouse zipped down the trim along the edge of the steps.

Håkan had squatted down next to the body and was holding a wallet that had fallen out of the dead man's back pocket. It was connected to a belt loop by means of a clip-on keychain.

'Don't do it,' I said.

'Why not?'

'Because it's better not to know. Makes it easier to forget.'

The wallet had a Velcro closure; he was turning it over in his hands.

'It never happened. Remember?'

That made him push the wallet back into the man's pocket.

'Would you mind checking?' he said with a nod at the front door.

My descent of the stairs was not half as nimble as Håkan's and the mouse's; it was more akin to the dead man's. At least that's how it felt, mentally. The determination that had filled me was fading now. I stepped out on the front porch and looked around; after I confirmed that the coast was clear with a look, Håkan grabbed the belt again and dragged the body outside. Halfway to the grave, he had to stretch out his back and rest for a moment.

'His baseball cap,' I said.

I hurried into the house and up the stairs. My heart was pounding. Fetching the cap was almost worse than fetching the man who had worn it. It felt so calculated. Murder, Gudrun. This is murder. I pushed all such thoughts down, found a napkin in my handbag and grabbed the vizor with it, because you never know.

When I got back down, Håkan had already wrestled the man into the pit. He was not going to have a comfortable eternal rest; he looked like he had failed to do a backflip.

'Should we try to turn him over?' I asked.

'Let's just fill it up. Throw his cap in.'

We grabbed the shovels and started filling the hole. The first few spadefuls of dirt were the worst; as soon as the body was out of sight, it got easier. I think we both drew strength from that.

The mouse was very interested in our work. It dashed about around the grave and when I accidentally almost ran my shovel through it, I had a sudden impulse to kill it.

I had no time to think, I just whacked it.

It probably died instantly, but I followed up with a few more blows, both to make sure and to vent. Håkan tried to stop me, but it was too late. Once he was sitting there with the little beast in the palm of his hand, it had been thoroughly dispatched.

[208]

I gave him a moment. After a while, he stood up and threw the mouse in the pit. Neither one of us said a word about what I had done or what he thought about it.

We filled up the hole, then studied our handiwork. A black rectangle in the lawn. A noticeable one. Not to say conspicuous.

'What were we thinking?' I said.

'We weren't thinking.'

'Well, we can't leave it like this.'

'No.'

'We're going to have to cover it up.'

'If we cover it up, it'll never grow over.'

The only thing we could think to do was to expand the rectangle and make a fake vegetable plot, located, somewhat oddly perhaps, in a spot that had virtually no sun at any time. But we figured idiots must try to grow potatoes too. We dug up the lawn and turned it and then we tramped back and forth, hacking and digging like a couple of bizarre moonlight farmers in the bright summer night.

I put the shovels back and Håkan went inside to wash his hands. He spent a long time at the sink. Rubbing and rinsing.

'You won't get it all off,' I said.

He carried on washing his hands.

'You know all that sanitiser people are always slathering on themselves,' he said. 'Like healthcare professionals. Particularly healthcare professionals. You pump a dollop into your hand before doing anything else. As though it were some kind of absolution. In a small pump bottle from the pharmacy. A magical ointment.'

'But it works though, right? Kills bacteria and whatnot?'

'I guess the alcohol is fine, sure. But it makes people sloppy about washing their hands. Because they think they don't need to. So the net effect is negative. From a sanitary perspective. In terms of public health. That's my opinion.'

'I see.'

'Soap and water, Gudrun. Soap and water's the thing.'

I kept an eye on the pine trees as we walked to the car. There didn't seem to be any life in them. A fact I noted gratefully. I quickened my step as we got close and jumped into the car. Håkan probably assumed I just wanted to get out of there and I was happy to let him think that. I rolled down my window, but no more than half an inch; there were a lot of mosquitoes.

'Now what?' he said.

'I need time to think.'

'Aren't we in kind of a hurry? If this is a kidnapping?'

I saw his face dissolve. He had been composed. Weirdly composed, I had thought to myself. Now he fell apart.

I experienced something similar on the way back. The further away I got, the worse I felt. You would have thought it would have been the other way around. By the time we reached Suptallen, I wanted to burst out crying.

We turned into a Statoil petrol station. Climbed out of our cars and stood in silence in the artificial light. Two crumpled individuals with ashen faces. I took his number and he took mine. Talk tomorrow, I said and he nodded. Then we went our separate ways. I had to drive the last stretch at a crawl, because the road was full of drunk people and I was scared of each and every one of them, even the girls.

Diana walked toward the sea, which was Barents Sea. Gulls perched on a cliff that jutted out into the water, black as slate. Maybe a hundred of them. There was always one in the air, but rarely more than one. They sat spread out with their beaks pointing in exactly the same direction. Toward the horizon that merged with the overcast sky to form a blurred band. As though they were waiting for something. They certainly didn't take any notice of her as she staggered along in her worthless clothes like an apocalyptic survivor on the shores of a dead ocean.

The pebble beach was an orthopaedic minefield so she crossed it very cautiously. The reek of rotting seaweed hit her and she had turned up her collar and was hugging herself in the cold wind.

Plastic bottles. Wooden boards and whitened branches. The jagged leg of a crab. A monstrous frond of sea wrack with ribbons as thick as leather belts. As though the slimy head of a sea gorgon had been washed ashore in this desolate place. A lone feather and over there a clump that had once been a shoe. All unique and conspicuous in the myriad of pale, wave-polished stones that crunched loudly under her feet.

She glanced up at the outline of the steep cliffs, pushing their jaggedly crenellated edges up toward the sky, but there were no landmarks up there to guide her in one direction or another. The mountainside was formed of stacked stone discs, deposited one on top of the other like compacted lamellae; when she got closer to the precipitous drop where birds swarmed like insects around the ledges, it was like climbing up a flight of stairs. From time to time, she passed a pool of lifeless water.

She found him in a crevice. On his back with his feet pointing out toward the sea like some kind of insane subarctic sunbather. His face had turned pale and his eyes were pointing in the wrong direction, but otherwise he looked much as he had in life. The ball of tape with her hair stuck to it was still in his pocket. A chapstick. She pulled a mobile phone out of his right trouser pocket. She pushed her hair behind her ear and shaded the screen. It had survived the fall. It said Sunday. Three missed calls. She held the phone in her hand for a while before pushing it back into his pocket. Then she leaned over him and squeezed the left pocket. Felt the bulge of his member and next to it a small hard bump. She stepped over the body, dug out the car key and walked away quickly.

Climbing the slopes leading up to the plateau was taxing. Before she could reach the top, she had to lie down on the crunchy grass and rest. With her hand closed tightly around the car key, she closed her eyes. The sound of a gentle surf rose from the sea below. Birds screeching. A wondrous serenity filled her; when she suddenly let out a giggle, she started, because she didn't realise the sound had come from her.

She climbed into the car and locked the doors. Violent shudders kept running through her body. She looked at herself in the mirror and then looked again. It was like seeing someone else.

Her hands were weak and trembling; she put them in her armpits to warm them and calm the shaking. After a while, she felt a bit better. At that point, she turned the engine on. She reversed out and followed the road leading down from the mountain. The car struggled over sharp stone shards and through small, water-filled cauldrons. She drove carefully. If the car broke down, she would break down too.

At some point, she had glimpsed the sun like an elusive lantern behind the clouds, but she was too exhausted to even attempt celestial navigation. She felt she knew which direction was south, but no road led that way, it was just an endless prairie. On her left, she could see a sliver of sea. Far away on her right was a sign. A sign with white text against a blue background. She decided to drive toward the sign because she figured it would announce the name of a village waiting on the other side of the ridge. 'Domen 410 ft above sea level', it read. Not a village. A mountain. And there it was, the mountain called Domen, barren and dark.

Pressing on seemed as good as turning back.

After a few miles, she spotted a rest stop with a picnic bench and an information board. She slowed down and turned around. The board itself was long gone; in its place a hyper-realist landscape painting of a few utility poles wandering in a straight line in the distance had been installed. At the top of its frame was written 'VARDØ – ULTIMA THULE'. She opened the glove compartment and snatched out the manual and papers and found the road map, a spiral-bound book. But Norway was nothing but a grey appendix to Sweden. She sat there with the map on her lap, thinking, trying to remember what the Scandinavian peninsula looked like in detail. Then she rolled back out on the road and drove back and when she reached the coast, she felt like she was on the right path.

She just wanted to drive. Put mile after mile behind her. Accelerate away from the terror. The thoughts racing around in her head hurt her. Flocks of screeching birds. Harpies. She had turned the radio on to drown out the mayhem inside her, but it didn't help. She was only able to find two channels. Nothing about missing women in Kiruna. Of course not. Why would they care about something like that up here? And were they even officially missing? She had told Håkan she'd be back for lunch on Saturday. That was less than twenty-four hours ago. It felt like a week, but it hadn't even been a day. Didn't a full twenty-four hours have to pass before the police would actually start looking for missing people, at least missing adults? She thought about Missing People, an organisation Håkan loathed. People in windbreakers who tried to show off with their silly police jargon and who conducted searches, not primarily to find missing people but rather for the thrill that was missing in their own meaningless lives. Had he had time to change his mind about them in the past twenty-four hours? Had he called the police? He would talk to her mum and dad first, she was pretty sure of that. And they would probably go to Gudrun. What would she say?

Regardless, they probably hadn't told Kiruna anything yet. They would shield her. For as long as possible. That thought had a calming effect.

Driving in her state was foolish. Nothing short of utter

foolishness. She was reaching the end of her strength and ability. What she should do was call Håkan and then try to sleep for a few hours before pressing on. It would just be priceless if she ran off the road, after everything she'd been through. Though she would probably be fine. If I crash, I probably won't die. The airbag will catch me, embrace me gently; I've seen how gentle it looks in the movies. Her train of thought was alarming and when she spotted a motorhome parked some way from the road, she slowed down. She was going to have to ruin this morning for some poor soul. Bang on their door and stand there with her battered face, like an emissary from the valley of the shadow of death.

It was a Norwegian vehicle, parked by the water's edge. The loungers in which its occupants had enjoyed the midnight sun were sitting outside.

She rapped her knuckles against the door four times, waited a while and then knocked again. Then she spat on the back of her hand and rubbed off the blood dried into her skin. The vehicle rocked. Someone had got out of bed. She assumed they were having a look at her and her car, because it took a while before the lock clicked.

A pale man in nothing but his underwear appeared in the doorway.

She told him she had been in an accident and asked if she could borrow a phone. A round-eyed woman in a knee-length nightgown was moving about in the background. She thought they were going to hand her a phone, but they invited her in. Then they sat in silence, watching her, while she tried to remember Håkan's phone number. It took a while for it to come back to her.

He answered with his full name and when he heard her voice, he broke off. Then he said hi. No joy whatsoever. Just a quiet hi, followed by static. No questions, nothing. At first, she was confused, didn't he understand it was her calling? Was he in shock? The thought made her angry. He had no right to be shocked, that right was reserved for her. But she didn't want to yell and she wasn't sure what kind of insane accusations might slip out if she did. The only thing she could think of to say was: What's the matter? An absurd question given what she had just been through. As though their roles had been reversed.

'Nothing. Where are you?'

'I'm in Norway. I think.'

The man and the woman nodded confirmation.

'But I'm on my way home.'

'Why are you in Norway?'

There was a stabbing pain in her jaw when she chuckled.

'I don't know.'

Strangely enough, that reply seemed to satisfy him. Because he asked no further questions.

'When will you be home?' he said.

'As soon as I can.'

'Good.'

She gave the phone back to the man. Call ended, it said. She tried to collect her thoughts and after a while, she had to sit down. They wanted to know what had happened to her and if they should call the police. Had someone attacked her, did she want something to drink?

'Thank you,' she said. 'Thank you so much.'

Smiling was painful, but she did it anyway. She felt they

may not have let her go otherwise. She staggered out of the motorhome, climbed into her car and drove away.

She hadn't gone far before she pulled over. She was in the middle of nowhere. Moorland, infinite in its emptiness. As though the sky were projecting a green image of itself on Earth.

She stepped out of the car, opened the back door, crawled in and lay down on the seat. Then she sat back up and lay down the other way, with the battered side of her face up. She wiggled around until she found the least uncomfortable position.

When her body started to relax, it was as if all her energy was redirected to her face. She could feel it growing, rising like proving dough. The moment she drifted off, she slipped into a dream, which she woke from immediately. Then she fell asleep once more.

Ipa was more or less constantly on the phone. Usually in rural Finnish. On one occasion, she spoke Sami, Northern Sami; that was the one time she used the white phone. Shimmering like mother-of-pearl, with a fine crack branching out across the back.

Layer upon layer of scars criss-crossed the hand she used to operate the gear stick. Her skin had healed imaginatively, with plant-like patience after being bitten to shreds again and again. The tip of her pinkie was missing and there was no nail.

The woman in the back was completely silent. Her head was leaned against the window and she hadn't moved in a very long time. He reached back and pushed on her leg. He had to push a few times before she shifted and crossed her arms. Her eyes remained closed. A trickle of bloody ooze had found its way out from under the taped-on skirt and dried on her cheek.

'A gift,' Ipa said and when he showed no interest in discussing it, she asked: 'What kind of gift?'

'Susso Myrén, if you know who that is.'

She shot him a quick glance.

'That's her?'

He nodded.

Ipa said nothing more about it; she didn't say anything else at all, but later, when they had stopped at a rest spot, he overheard her talking about the gift and she was making an effort to keep her voice down. She was sitting on a picnic table with her legs spread wide and her boots on the bench. A phone in one hand and a phone in the other. *Karhuntappaja*, she said and then she repeated the word. *Karhuntappaja.* She was asked a number of questions she couldn't answer. *En tiedä*, she said. *Ei. Ei.*

He walked away. On the other side of the road was a night-blue lake and beyond that loomed the distant hills of a mountain range. Ipa had helped Susso out of and back into the car, probably so she could take a piss, and now she was heading toward him.

'What happened to her eye?' she said, squinting at him with one eye as if to illustrate her question.

In Varangerbotn, Diana turned into an Esso petrol station and filled the car up; then she went into the shop and locked herself in the bathroom. She needed to pee, but also to hide in a windowless room where no one could watch her. The bathroom was a poorly cleaned cell without any decorative elements whatsoever. The only thing to rest your eyes on was a broken tile; she stared at it. Then her eyes moved on to the square light switch, which had yellowed against the white wall. It felt like her consciousness was fracturing.

She washed her hands and studied herself in the mirror. Her skin was punctured where the blow had struck her nose and the blood that had seeped out had dried like a black tear. She wet a napkin and gently dabbed it against the wound.

She saw a lone mosquito hovering behind her in the mirror and for some reason, the thought of someone other than her having let it into the bathroom revolted her.

The woman at the till was from South East Asia. A small pink flower floated in the black river of her hair. She avoided making eye contact and seemed cross. When Diana asked what kinds of snus they had, she opened the cabinet and turned away and when they waited for the card reader to approve the payment, she stared at the card reader. Then she suddenly slammed her hand down on the counter. Diana was terrified. She didn't realise the woman had been aiming for a mosquito until she cursed and waved her hand at it.

After a while, a little man appeared behind the till. He gave her directions in sing-song Norwegian and took out a small map that he unfolded and pointed at. Basically, she just had to follow the river. She was supposed to take the E6 motorway all the way down to Karasjok and then head toward Kautokeino and down toward Finland and once she got to Finland, she should drive toward Kilpisjärvi. That would take her to Karesuando. He repeated it like a chant: Karasjok, Kautokeino, Kilpisjärvi. And Karesuando. Four Ks. Five with Kiruna.

She got back in her car and emptied her carrier bag of supplies on the passenger seat. Three chocolate bars by the name of Hobby, two bottles of Coke and a tin of mint-flavoured Skruf snus. She scarfed some chocolate and washed it down with Coke. Every bite hurt so bad she grinned like a malevolent old hag throughout.

The road never strayed far from the river, which came and went behind the birch trees. She regretted not asking how far it might be. Three hundred miles, six hundred miles, she had no earthly idea. This was unfamiliar territory. The heart of Sápmi. She had never been north of Abisko before. Yes, she had. No, she hadn't. Her head, her poor head. One moment, she was thinking about the station manager who had imported a wife – a catalogue hag, or CH, as Håkan liked to put it – a woman who seemed to hate her work and maybe her whole life up here among the mosquitoes and reindeer in the Far North, and she wondered if they had any children and if so what they looked like and what identities they would develop as they grew up.

The next moment, her mind turned to deformities of all kinds. Circus freaks. Victims of nature's cruel sense of humour. Siamese twins and wolf boys. She wondered what had become of the most severely afflicted throughout history. Severely mentally disabled and misshapen like fantastical beasts. Curious products of incestuous procreation that had continued unabated for generations. In isolated environments. The strange things that could happen to a coccyx.

This could not explain the strange collapse that had occurred in her head. A curious twilight had enveloped her and it still lingered, making it impossible for her to think back. She had not been conscious but had also not been unconscious. She had moved through a shadow world. Without a will of her own. When she thought about it, she noticed a resistance. It was like trying to recall something really embarrassing. There was a strike in the archives.

From time to time, she heard Håkan's voice. None of the things she had been through had hit her as hard as the words he had mumbled on the phone. She had considered calling again, but had decided not to. She was afraid. It wasn't just the fact that his detached voice had intensified the feeling of being outside the fact-based reality he represented. He had sounded different. And what was more likely: that his voice had changed over the past twenty-four hours or that her impression of it had? The mental tribulations she had endured must have interfered with her perception somehow. She zoomed past a sign that read 'SUOSSJÄRVI' and when she soon afterwards ended up behind a car with the number plate SU 5025, she thought to herself that she was losing her mind. You're tired, she said out loud. You're seeing things that don't exist. You have to sleep. In your own bed – not in the car you were abducted in. Home, Diana. You have to get home. Home to Kiruna.

Anders was woken up by the sound of birds singing, thousands of them, judging by the volume. The windows were laminated with dripping condensation, but the car door was open onto a wall of shimmering green leaves. Stava was gone, but the blanket she had slept under was still on the folded-down back seat. He opened the door and stepped out with aching joints.

They were on a forest track. Somewhere just north of Sundsvall, if he remembered correctly. Or had they come as far north as Skellefteå? The sun was a burning ball at the top of a pine tree and the day was already warm. He took a few steps before bending over and vomiting. He had had a vision of the holes the bolt gun had made in the smooth, white surface of the coffee table. In a dream sequence, he had filled those holes with putty and evened it out with sandpaper, and an unidentified person had run their hand over the table top and said it turned out really good, no trace of the holes, and he had agreed. But the dream had restarted, with new holes and the same procedure, and his repairs had turned out worse and worse. He had been stuck in that scene all night. Well, not exactly all night. He couldn't have slept more than a few hours.

He glanced in through the rear window and then walked up to it. The wolf wasn't in there. He opened the boot. But the rifle still was. He felt his face twist into a grimace. His abdomen tensed up and then he cried silently with a hand over his mouth.

They came toward him down the little road, shaded by the trees. First the wolf and about thirty feet behind it Stava, with her hands in her pockets like a dog owner out for a walk.

Anders squatted down and held his head in his hands.

'What have we done,' he said, 'what have we fucking done.'

She opened the boot and waited for the wolf to get in. But the wolf was busy. It had found Anders' vomit and was gently lapping it up.

'This is the first day of your new life as a muuurderer,' she said with a hoarse laugh. 'We're like Juha and whatshername. The one with the French lops. What was her name?'

He sobbed.

'Anders! Listen to me! We haven't murdered anybody. He did it. That kid. Lukas. We just happened to be there.'

He nodded.

'We just happened to be there.'

'We should get going. And as soon as we get to my dad, everything will be all right. Everything will be all right when we're with my dad.'

'How far is it?'

'Get in the car.'

Stava drove and he watched the monotonous landscape glide past outside the window. Tightly packed spruce trees in never-ending rows. He did actually feel a bit better. At least physically. His headache had subsided. It still hurt, but it no longer felt like his head was about to explode. It might be because the wolf was asleep. Or at least keeping quiet in the boot. He badly needed to pee, but was afraid to ask her to stop in case that would disturb the balance.

She wore a thin, purple cardigan he hadn't seen before. It looked high-end and expensive and smelled of sweet perfume. A curly blonde hair clung to the fuzzy sleeve. He leaned forward and opened the glove compartment, but found nothing to throw up in. It was going to have to be his paper coffee cup. He tore off the lid and regurgitated slimy water that stuck to his lips. Afterwards, he sat holding the cup because he didn't know what to do with it. Then his window suddenly opened and he threw the cup out.

'It will pass,' Stava said.

He wiped his mouth with his hand and nodded. A blue sign appeared. They were almost in Örnsköldsvik. The effort of throwing up had filled his eyes with tears that he now wiped away.

'Did you go through this too?'

'I've seen others go through it.'

'And they were normal afterwards?'

The word made her smile.

'Remember me telling you about Mauri?'

'Was he the one who shot himself?'

'That you remember.'

'Yes, because I feel a bit like I've taken his place.'

She picked something out of her mouth and inspected it before flicking it off her fingers.

'I see,' she said. 'So you think I'm cheap.'

'No, it's just how I feel.'

'You should know, Anders, that you're special.'

'No, I'm not.'

'Ransu could have bonded with your colleague, that Norwegian man. But he didn't. He chose you.'

'Wasn't that just random?'

'You belong together, and that bond is forever.'

'But what about you. You belong together too, don't you?'

'That's different.'

'Because you're a woman?'

'I'm not a woman, Anders.'

'Of course you're a woman.'

'Am I?'

'Of course you are. What else would you be?'

When I entered the kitchen that morning, Roland was sitting there with the newspaper open in front of him. But he wasn't looking at the paper, he was looking at me, and he was very clearly trying to get a read on me. My entire body ached, but I didn't let on because I had no desire to be interrogated. I poured myself coffee and sat down. Glanced at the headlines.

'Any news?' he said; I shook my head.

He closed the paper.

'They must have gone somewhere on a whim,' he said, 'over to Narvik or something. Like a fun getaway. After all these years.'

He stood up, refilled his coffee cup and sat back down.

'I don't understand what's with you,' he said. 'They're fine and on their way home. And here you are, moping around.'

'Yes, I know. I should be happy.'

'I don't know about happy, but you should breathe a sigh of relief at least. Not heaving dark sighs of anxiety. You were tossing and turning all night. And sighing. And sighing.'

'I couldn't sleep.'

'Not even after you had that text from Diana's bloke. And what time was that? Five?'

'I can't just turn off my worries. They have a life of their own.'

He studied me for a long moment.

[228]

'Gudrun,' he said, 'didn't we agree we were going to be open with one another, about our thoughts and opinions, even though we may not always agree? That we weren't going to keep secrets from each other?'

His words were like knives. He might as well have used the word murderer. I kept a straight face and sipped my coffee. But evidently, my acting skills were less impressive than I had thought.

'How am I supposed to help you,' he said, 'if you don't trust me?'

'I don't trust you? I've told you everything, what we went through, me and Susso. Do you think those are things you'd tell a person you don't trust?'

'Then tell me what's wrong.'

'Nothing.'

He leaned back in his chair.

'You're limping around here, grimacing, looking like you're walking on nails. And you're normally loath to miss any opportunity to update me on exactly how much pain you're in. Take your feet, for instance. I get up-to-date observations from the southern regions of Gudrun twice an hour. But now, not a word.'

'That's just because you're being like this.'

'Like what?'

'Poking fun at me. For being in pain.'

'What I mean to say is that I can tell you're keeping something from me. It's obvious. So spit it out.'

'It's nothing.'

'If it can make you bite your tongue when you're in that much pain, I don't believe it's nothing.'

'What if you've made a promise to someone? Then do you think it's right to tell you? I would like to know so I can decide whether I'm right to trust you with things in the future.'

'Who did you make a promise to?'

'Just answer my question. Isn't it right to keep your promise?'

'That depends on the situation. In my opinion.'

'If I make a promise, I keep it. You have to respect that, Roland.'

'No, I can't. Sorry.'

'You can't help me.'

It just slipped out. And then, once I had started, more followed. The floodgates had opened.

'No one can help me,' I said. 'What's done is done.'

'And what is done?'

'I told you about that man Susso forced out of the car in Sorsele. That it was tantamount to murder. Because the bears were outside.'

'I never agreed with you on that. That it was tantamount to murder. Murder is something you do to do it. Murder's not what I'd call it. Besides, he deserved being kicked out, given what he'd done.'

'We murdered him. In practice, that's what we did.'

'You can't dwell on that, Gudrun. The statute of limitation on that passed a long time ago. Conscience-wise. That's what we agreed. That you should let it go. You told the police what happened and no one thought you or Susso had done anything wrong. If you had, you would have been charged, and you weren't.'

'I didn't tell them about the squirrel. The police.'

He leaned back and crossed his arms.

'No, because then the nice men in white coats would have come for you.'

'I've come to the conclusion – lying awake, going over everything again and again, like I've been doing almost every night for ten years now – that it was all the squirrel's fault. He's who made Susso do what she did. It's the squirrel's fault Susso's become what she's become.'

'Here we go again.'

'I've come to the conclusion that it's a monster.'

'I know.'

'But it's actually not that simple.'

My coffee had gone cold, so I put it in the microwave and while the cup rotated in there, I contemplated whether I should tell him what happened or continue to keep my mouth shut. I added a splash of milk and sat down and realised I'd passed the point of no return.

'When we got to Susso's yesterday, there was someone there. A man, a young man. He was sitting in her bed, saying he was going to live there; it was very unsettling. And Håkan, he strangled that man.'

'Now hold on.'

'He strangled him. Like this. And I watched.'

Roland took off his glasses and put them down on the table. He watched me without speaking. Picked up one of the temples of his glasses and tapped it against the table, and he did it thoughtfully. Like a tentative signaller.

'Then we buried him the garden.'

Without a word, he stood up and walked over to the pantry; I heard him take down a bottle and put his cup on the counter and fill it up and knock it back. Then he came back and sat down with the bottle. It was whisky. He poured me a slug and then another for himself.

'Håkan thought he'd done something to Diana at first. Something terrible. Because he just sat there on the bed, not speaking. Like he was ashamed of something. And he had tattoos. A spiderweb tattoo on his elbow and snakes and whatever else. He didn't exactly look innocent.'

'But he was.'

'Apparently. And that's why I didn't jump for joy when I got that text from Håkan this morning, which said they were fine and on their way back. If they had been in trouble and he had been involved somehow, maybe I could have lived with it. That's going to be much harder now.'

'It's not like you killed him.'

'True, but I didn't do anything to stop it either. And I helped bury him. It was actually my idea. Because Håkan wanted to call the police. And it all happened in my daughter's house. I'm certainly implicated.'

'Yes.'

'What's it like, Roland, living with a murderer?'

'I don't.'

I knocked my drink back.

'You've already left me?'

'You're not a murderer.'

'Then how do you explain my being involved in two murders? My witnessing them first-hand and up close.'

'There's something about you, Gudrun,' he said and topped me up. 'I've always said that.'

'The least common denominator in these two murders is

not me. The least common denominator in these two murders is the trolls. And I'm talking about the smallest ones.'

'So it was there? The squirrel?'

'No, it was a mouse.'

'A mouse.'

'It was the mouse that harnessed Håkan's rage and amplified it. Like a little transformer. And I was completely numb. I felt nothing. Even though he was killed right in front of me. It was like watching TV. And you know I don't even like seeing violence on TV, I look away when there's blood. But it wasn't the mouse's idea. It just harnessed Håkan's feelings. Do you see what I mean? The hatred didn't come from the mouse, it came from Håkan. And it was the same with the squirrel that time in Sorsele. It wasn't the squirrel that wanted to throw that man to the bears, it was Susso. It's as if they're triggered by strong emotions. Particularly strong negative emotions.'

'You have to understand, Gudrun, that this is pretty hard to take in.'

'You just have to swallow it. Because this is serious.'

He stroked his moustache thoughtfully.

'What happened to the mouse? I'd like to take a look at it.'

'I smacked it dead.'

'You smacked it dead?'

'Yes.'

Roland pondered this while cradling his cup. Sipping his whisky.

'Well, the mouse had it coming,' he said. 'Technically speaking. And you can't let a mouse that more or less incites murder run loose.'

'It wasn't premeditated, I just struck it with my shovel.'
He nodded.
'So now there's a corpse buried in Susso's garden.'
'Yes.'
'She's not going to appreciate that.'
'What were we supposed to do?!'
'The question is whether we should consider moving him.'
'Have you gone completely off your head?!'
'No, I'm trying to use my head. In situations like this, you have to keep cool. Very cool. If he is – was – one of Susso's neighbours or a boyfriend, there may very well be people who know he was there. Or who could guess. And if the police go out there looking for him, there's no telling what they might find. What with their dogs and everything. And if we're going to move him, we should do it as soon as possible. It's not pleasant, but we can't let that stop us.'

'I'm going to let that stop me. I'm not digging up a corpse. That's where I draw the line. When we buried him, we weren't ourselves entirely, I've realised since. I don't even think I could bear going to Vittangi now. I'm not doing it, Roland, I'm not doing it! I'd rather go to prison.'
'You mean that?'
'Yes, I mean that.'
He sat there, looking at me.
'Why don't you sleep on it.'
'I can't sleep.'
'Take this.'
'I don't want it.'
'Drink it.'
I knocked back the whisky and pulled a face at the oily

liquid that made my eyes tear up. Then I went into the bed-room. After lying down, I reached for my phone on the nightstand. Nothing new. My head spun when I closed my eyes and I could hear the tinkling of the bottleneck against the edge of a cup from the kitchen.

Ipa had ripped the tape off Susso's mouth and cleaned her battered face with wet wipes, gently and not without affection. Crumpled up and red with blood, the wipes were now littering the floor around Lennart's feet. They reeked of perfume as well.

The car slowed down. There was a sign by the side of the road. At the top of it, someone had written 'MURHAAJA!' in pink paint that had run down across the village's name and the rest of the sign.

They turned off on a shady gravel road. After a few hundred yards, they came to a boom barrier. It was brand new, a bright red and yellow symbol. Ipa climbed out, opened the barrier, got back in the car, drove through, climbed out, closed the barrier, got back in the car and drove on.

The village lay next to a lake and consisted of about ten houses. Spruce-covered mountains rose up on the other side of the lake, which was being clawed by a stiff breeze. Some of the houses were surrounded by tarpaulins that blocked them from view; they drove in through an opening in one of the billowing enclosures.

Ipa turned off the engine, pulled the handbrake, grabbed both phones with one hand and climbed out. She took the front steps in one stride, threw open the front door and called out. Then she stood talking to someone in the hallway who seemed not to want to show themselves.

Lennart opened his door and heaved himself out. The car sagged under his weight. A face slipped out of sight in a window. He scanned the yard. A horse trailer. A green Ford Scorpio with tinted windows in the back.

'Well now, we have fancy visitors, do we? The celebrity has come.'

Mikko Jokela had appeared in the doorway. He stood there for a moment before stepping out into the light. Under his unbuttoned military jacket, he wore nothing except a lot of gold necklaces of varying thickness and a pair of black plastic sunglasses that dangled from the chain that hung lowest on his chest. He pulled his hand out of his pocket and stroked the beard that was growing in a neat circle around his mouth. An enormous signet ring sparkled on his pinkie.

'Where's Erasmus?' Lennart said.

'Rasmus? There's no one by that name here.'

The look of theatrical puzzlement he had put on morphed into a smile that revealed an incomplete set of teeth.

'Where is he?'

'What happened to your paw?'

Ipa stepped out through the door and down from the porch. She motioned to Lennart to get back in the car. Mikko had put on his sunglasses. Stood there staring at him, glittering with gold, grinning scornfully.

They drove along the edge of the lake and stopped in front of a cabin. A dark cabin with gingerbread window frames. The garden looked like a scrapyard. There was a hob sitting next to the front steps.

'Is he in here?'

'Here? No, this house is empty.'

'Then what are we doing here?'

'You're going to live here.'

He stepped out of the car and after it left, he looked around. Paper bags bursting with decomposing newspapers in the tall grass. A picture frame with gilded embellishment. A moose shed gnawed to pieces by tiny teeth. It looked like the remnants of a truly terrible car boot sale.

A pungent smell of corpse greeted him when he stepped through the door. Every room was crammed with stuff; what the floor might look like was anyone's guess.

He located the bathroom and sat down with a snowmobile magazine that kept falling to the floor when he tried to hold it open in his lap. The dimmer switch was buzzing like a bug in his ear; he turned it off with a hard slap.

The fridge was empty but in a cabinet above the sink he found a tin of meat soup. He cradled it in the crook of his arm, wiggled his finger into the little metal loop and pulled the lid enough to fold it back. He scarfed it all down in two gulps, grinding the stringy bits of meat up between his teeth.

The bed was wide and had a tall headboard with turned bedposts. He lay on the side of the mattress that was not dark with dried-in bodily fluids. His eyes roved sleepily across the room. A white table fan. Stacks of CDs. An empty aquarium with grimy sides. A terrarium, actually. The heat lamp was stashed inside. A wood stove that wasn't connected to a chimney. His chest moved slowly up and down and the air generated one strange noise after the other on its rattling way to and from his lungs.

A chirping woman's voice. From inside the house. Ipa popped her head through the door. She patted a bag that was slung across her shoulder.

'I figured we should tend to that wound.'

Lennart grunted.

'Let's do it here,' she said.

'Fine.'

'Sit up.'

'You want me to sit up?'

'Yes, sit up.'

She got down on her knees and unwound the bandage from his arm, humming a song as she did. What emerged looked like a wet pork shank, but it didn't seem to revolt or even surprise her. She studied the weeping wounds meticulously and even sniffed them with her little nose.

'Did someone bite you?'

He said nothing.

'Let's hope it doesn't get infected.'

'It won't.'

A hand reached up and felt his forehead.

'A bit hot.'

'I just need some sleep.'

'And what are we going to do about this?'

She pursed her lips thoughtfully.

'Just wrap it back up. The main thing is to keep it from making a mess and me from getting at it and opening it up again.'

'I don't suppose there's any point sewing it up.'

'No. There isn't.'

She took out a compress and a roll of gauze from her bag; he studied her face while she wrapped the gauze around his arm. It was like a starry night sky of moles and tiny birthmarks.

'All right then,' she said, 'what's it going to be tonight, are you staying in, watching the telly?'

He said nothing.

'You don't watch TV?'

'Sometimes.'

'What do you watch then, do you have a favourite show?'

He shook his head.

'I watch whatever's good.'

His answer made her smile.

'Would you like something for your fever?'

'No. I just need to sleep.'

She gathered up the last of the gauze, put it in a plastic bag, stood up and watched him as he lay back down. As though that was something that required supervision. Then she left, without closing any of the doors behind her.

It was close to eleven at night when Diana rolled into Kiruna. The festival was over and an unnatural stillness enveloped the city. It made her uneasy to think that people had been partying while she was gone. Partying wildly. Chugging beer out of plastic cups. Belting songs out at the bright night sky in a collective, pagan frenzy. Status Quo had played. Like some kind of subtle propaganda. Dear local residents! We're going to tear down your houses and move the city but everything's going to stay the same.

Her dad had always been peeved the carousel would keep turning after he got off, but she had never understood why. Wasn't that just the way of things? Now, as she drove down Malmvägen and met a lorry that said LINDSTRÖM'S CARNIVAL, she felt she knew what he meant. The infuriating thing wasn't that the carousel kept turning, the infuriating thing was that you fooled yourself into thinking you were an inseparable part of it. She thought to herself it must be the remnants of some grandiose developmental phase. A psychological foetal membrane protecting humanity from the awful truth: the world is just fine without you. While you're trapped in the car boot of death, other people are clapping to the beat of Status Quo.

She parked in front of the garage and climbed out. She

had driven without breaks; her back hurt and her neck. A mild evening. Almost summer. They'd had snow just a week before. The ground had been covered.

Håkan was lying on the bed with his tablet on his belly, its light falling across his face like a blue mask. He had earphones on and was breathing heavily like an old man. Kiruna could be seen as a small lump under the covers. One foot was sticking out.

She watched them without announcing her presence. Stood there in the door like a recently dead ghost watching her old family. What was left of it. Normality like a membrane. Which she didn't want to rupture, so instead of announcing her presence, she went straight to the bathroom.

She inspected herself in the mirror while the tub was filling. Polychrome like a crime victim in a Polaroid picture. And the man who had caused her injuries, he was dead. Probably still out there like some kind of bizarre beach find. Maybe the gulls had found him. Though maybe they didn't eat people. Then again, maybe they did. They were probably pragmatic creatures.

She sat down on the toilet seat and stared at the floor tiles, the grid pattern of the grout joints, and tried to silence her thoughts, which kept returning to that beach. Every time she closed her eyes, she was transported back there. She took a deep breath, puckered her lips and exhaled slowly. I'm here. I'm home. That's my towel, that's my insanely expensive shampoo, that's Kiruna's wind-up hippo. I'm here.

Dazed, she undressed and stepped into the tub. The water was scalding; she sat up for a while to get used to the heat before sliding her bum forward, leaning back and letting her head sink toward the bottom, where it landed with a gentle thud. Maybe she should stay down here, just stay. She resurfaced with closed eyes and slicked back her hair, reached for the shampoo bottle and squeezed a dollop into the palm of her hand.

When she got back out of the water after rinsing her hair out and slicking it back once more, he was sitting on the toilet, watching her solemnly. He looked tired and ugly. The way he'd looked the first year after Kiruna was born. A face paralysed by the anaesthetics of chronic sleep deprivation.

In one of the many scenarios that had played in her head during the almost ten-hour drive, she had lain with her head in his lap, telling him a terrible story laced with supernatural elements. She had told him everything, every detail, and he had listened, without mocking, without even interrupting her, and he had looked empathetic because her facial injuries confirmed she was telling the truth.

Now he was sitting there on the toilet seat with his stubbly cheeks and she knew it wouldn't be like that. He hadn't waited up for her; he'd been watching Netflix. Detached from reality. And now he was keeping his distance. He almost seemed afraid of her. Of touching her.

'You shouldn't have gone out there.'

No questions, no sympathy. Just reproach. She realised she had never seen this side of him. He had probably been terrified. Likely still was.

'But I did.'

'What happened to you?'

'I was knocked about. Among other things.'

He said nothing.

'I've been locked in the boot of a car. My nose is broken, look, and I think I have an orbital fracture. Because it feels like I do when I open my mouth.'

'Did you call the police?'

She shook her head. Now he was going to get up and get the phone and call. Introduce himself as a doctor and file a report. But he didn't. He just sat there. There were food stains on his shirt.

'Who did this?' he said.

'I don't know.'

'You don't know?'

She shook her head.

'Does Susso know who they are?'

'She might.'

'Is she back too?'

'No, they took her. She's with someone named Erasmus. And don't ask me who that is, because I don't know.'

They sat in silence. The only sound was the water dripping from her hands when she gingerly touched the skin stretched taut over her cheekbone.

'I suppose it's that cult,' he said. 'Lennart Brösth.'

'Can we talk about it tomorrow? Look at me. I'm beat up, both physically and mentally. I barely know my own name and I need to sleep. I can tell you more tomorrow.'

'Do you want me to take off work?'

'There's no need.'

'Are you sure?'

She nodded.

'What are you going to tell Kiruna?'

He motioned toward her face.

'Sometimes you get assaulted. For no good reason. Children get that.'

He looked like he was about to object. But nothing came out.

'Have you talked to Gudrun?' he said.

'To Gudrun? I've barely even talked to you.'

He stood up but didn't leave.

'You shouldn't have gone out there.'

'Doctor Sillfors concurs with Doctor Sillfors.'

She was able to make a joke. Where did she find the strength? She didn't understand it herself. But she assumed it was some kind of defence mechanism. An attempt at redirection. Or was she happy? Baffled at still being alive? Despite everything. She lay still and watched the water lap against her knees. She had figured she would call Gudrun and tell her what had happened to Susso. The urge had overwhelmed her several times during the drive. But she had suppressed it each time. If Gudrun decided to call the police, what had happened would be translated into paltry police prose and registered and archived. That would make it irrevocable. There would be a file and that file would redefine her life. And she didn't want that. She still held out hope she might manage to wiggle out of the whole thing somehow. Find a way out. Trap the event between the brackets of a parenthesis. Her whole being was straining to achieve that. Working toward it, tireless, automated. Like smooth muscle tissue. Her eyelashes stuck together when she blinked; she wiped the water away with the tip of her middle finger, which had gone pruney.

He was still on his back with the screen on his chest when she entered the bedroom. But he turned it off and took out his earphones and watched her put on her nightgown, a gown of light-blue, almost transparent cotton. She lifted the duvet, gently pushed the little girl aside and slipped in next to her, feeling the heat from the tiny body. Then she pressed her fingertips against his shoulder and said they would talk tomorrow and he nodded.

Stava climbed out of the car and walked up to the boom bar-rier. She moved almost furtively and after realising the barrier was locked, she froze. Her slender body watchful and tense. With her long black hair, she looked like some kind of Native American scout at the edge of an unknown territory. Her sud-den insecurity was probably due in large part to them having dropped Ransu off, but he had also noticed that she spoke of her father with deference that bordered on fear. He wondered what kind of person he might be. Was he even human, biologic-ally speaking? Probably not, considering her constitution.

He had a pen in his hand and now he started jabbing it hard into the side of his head. He pushed the button in and out, in and out, in and out, but he stopped the instant she got back in the car.

She reversed off the road and parked.

'I don't know the code,' she said and turned the engine off. 'So we're going to have to leave the car here.'

They got out and followed the gravel road that led down to a lake that came into view, cold and smooth like polished metal, between the spruce trees. Stava moved so quickly Anders had to jog a few steps now and then to keep up.

Suddenly, a wolf materialised in their path. It was smaller than Ransu and had lighter fur.

Stava sank into a squat.

The wolf came closer but stopped before it got too near. It stood with its head lowered, studying her. Its nose practically touching the gravel. Another wolf was padding about behind it.

'Maybe I should leave,' Anders said. 'I can wait in the car.'

'These are my friends,' she said. 'They know me.'

After a while, the wolves withdrew and continued watching them from a distance. Stava didn't get up straight away.

Two children were walking toward them between two houses surrounded by tarpaulins. A girl with plaits. She had an otter on a lead, scuttling along with its back arched. The other child had a peculiar, jerky gait and kept in the background. It was wearing a mosquito head net and Anders soon realised it was no child's face hiding behind the dark netting. He backed up a few steps and then broke into a run. Stava chased after him and grabbed his jacket.

'Don't do that,' she said. 'It's dangerous.'

She took him by the hand and led him back.

'I'm looking for Erasmus,' she said. 'Do you know where he is?'

The otter darted this way and that and the little girl stepped out of the lead, which was wrapped around her legs. She yelled at the animal, which turned its funny, snub-nosed face toward her.

'They're barbecuing,' the girl said.

'They're barbecuing?'

'I said cut it out!'

The girl yanked the lead so hard the otter was pulled backward. It wanted to go into the ditch and stared at it longingly.

[248]

It soon made another attempt but the girl was relentless. The lead went taut and the animal swayed on its hind legs.

'Could you show us the way?' Stava asked.

'It's that house,' the girl replied. 'The yellow one over there.'

'Thank you,' Stava said and pulled Anders along.

The house the girl had pointed to was older than the other houses in the village. The porch roof was crowned by an elegant spire and the brick well had both a roof and a shadoof.

An old man came around the corner. His grey hair fell in flowing tight curls down his shoulders and his beard was combed and glossy. He was dressed in a striped work smock and on his head was a stiff-crowned felt hat. A wolf trailed him.

Stava sprang an embrace on him and after letting him go, she tried to take his hands, but they slipped out of her grasp. He didn't even want to look in the pillowcase she held open for him.

They followed him around the house to the backyard, where a party tent had been erected. Stava's father walked up behind a woman and kissed her on the head. One of the woman's eyes was covered by a large compress and she seemed drugged. She was staring at the grass with her mouth open. Anders stared at the grass too. Next to the kettle grill was a bottle of lighter fluid with no cap. A plastic lid with a round béarnaise imprint. Cutlery.

A man in a military jacket started heckling Stava in Finnish. His insults grew increasingly offensive until in the end, he got to his feet and picked up a beer can from the table. Stava managed to turn away; the can, which flew through the air with a tail of liquid behind it, clipped her shoulder.

The man started pushing her around and when she fell to the ground, he chased her around with kicks and poured abuse on her. Then he snatched the pillowcase out of her hands and looked in it.

'Did you sold the car? Do you think that all now is okay?'

He fished a ring out of the bag and examined it. Then he dug out a rumpled wad of cash.

'There's more,' Stava said, 'we can get more! A lot of money. We can get a lot of money.'

'Do you have a phone?'

She shook her head and he kicked out at her.

'I have one. But it's in the car.'

'What car?'

'It's a Volvo. It's his Volvo. But you can have it!'

He dropped the bag on the ground and sat down.

'We have nowhere else to go.'

'Where's Ransu?' said the old man, who had sat down next to the woman and entwined his fingers in hers.

'I don't know,' she said.

'So that is what you bring us? Lies and a bag of money.'

She said nothing for a while.

'We dropped him off. Further up the road.'

'Where?'

'Up by the main road. But I can get him. I can bring him down here. So long as you promise not to hurt him.'

She got up on all fours and crawled toward her father like a dog. The lid for the béarnaise sauce clung to her back like a sticker.

'Please, Daddy. We have nowhere else to go.'

I didn't recognise her at first. She wore a baseball cap and sunglasses and her cheek was blue, the way it only ever gets when you've been beaten up, and I figured it was a junkie who wasn't going to buy anything but definitely cause trouble, maybe even shoplift. So I glared at her as she approached the counter and when I realised it was Diana standing in front of me, I clapped my hand to my mouth.

'You were right,' she said, gesturing to her face.

I couldn't get a word out; all I could do was stare.

'You said they were dangerous. You were right.'

'Where is she?'

'She's with someone called Erasmus. In Runajärvi.'

'Who's Erasmus?'

'I don't know.'

'Then how do you know she's there? Maybe she's home.'

She shook her head and then she told me what she'd been through over the past few days. I asked a lot of questions, and then repeated each one even though she'd already answered them.

'And you didn't see Lennart Brösth?'

'I didn't see anything. I had tape on my face.'

She grimaced at the pain her smile caused.

'It's my fault,' I said.

'Your fault?'

'I shouldn't have dragged you into this.'

'You know what? I'm glad you did.'

'How can you be, looking like that . . .'

'It was a good thing I went out there. Otherwise she'd be gone now and we wouldn't have known. We wouldn't have known anything.'

'Do you really mean that?'

'Yes, I do.'

'How's Håkan doing?'

'Håkan?'

'He came here. Last Saturday. When you hadn't come home when you said you would. And he couldn't reach you on your phone. So we went out there. To Susso's. But we weren't sure what had happened. Since you were just gone. Given that you hadn't seen each other in so long, we figured you had probably gone off somewhere. Your car wasn't there.'

'Without letting him know? And without bringing my phone?'

I bent down and pulled out a drawer. Took out her phone and put it on the counter. She picked it up and checked the screen.

'Eleven missed calls.'

'It was ringing in here, so I turned the sound off.'

She nodded.

'He didn't tell you that? Håkan.'

'No.'

'Nothing?'

'We've barely spoken. He's at work.'

I got to my feet. Customers had entered the shop.

'And the little girl, is she at nursery school?'

Diana shook her head.

'With my parents.'

'Then you should go home and get some rest.'

'I can't.'

A woman came up to the counter with a stack of kitchen towels. Black moose stamped on unbleached linen. She put the towels down and pulled out her wallet and while I served her, Diana sat with her head turned away, gazing out across the square.

When we were alone again, neither one of us knew how to proceed, so we just sat staring at each other. At length, she asked what we should do.

'About what?'

'About Susso, of course!'

'I don't know, Diana.'

'You don't seem to care all that much.'

'How can you say that?'

'Because that's how it seems.'

'It's just that I've known this day was coming. I've known they would take her, sooner or later. That it was inevitable.' The incredulous look spreading across Diana's face made me lower my voice. 'That person you saw. The one with the mask. You do realise that wasn't a human, don't you?'

'He had a tail. So I kind of figured.'

'And what are your thoughts on that?'

'My thoughts?'

'Yes. About him having a tail.'

Diana crossed her arms.

'I suppose it's some kind of birth defect.'

'There's another word for it, and that's troll. You saw a troll, Diana. A real troll. They come in all sizes. Some are as big as bears and some as small as mice. Because they *are* bears and they *are* mice. On the outside. They can transform. This is something I've seen with my own eyes. Susso shot a troll, she shoved a gun into its mouth and pulled the trigger and the moment it died, the troll turned into a bear. I saw it for myself, so I know it's true.'

I glanced over at the door before carrying on.

'The unsettling thing about them is that they can force their way into your consciousness and make you not be yourself. That's what's happened to Susso; you've seen her, you know what I'm talking about.'

'They're not trolls,' she said, 'they're people. A cult or something. They spoke Norwegian.'

'Those are the humans you're talking about, they're the trolls' humans. Some of them are the trolls' offspring. Because sometimes trolls breed with humans and the result is true freaks. Lennart Brösth is one of those freaks. That's why he's so old. Remember how he sawed off his own hand? During the trial, they said he was trying to kill himself, remember?'

She nodded.

'He wasn't. He sawed off his hand so no one would see what it looked like. See it was furry. And had claws!'

'How do you know?'

'Because I've met one of those freaks. She came here, to the shop, an elegant Norwegian lady in a wheelchair. She looked like an old film star. The wheelchair was exactly where you're standing now, and she had a hairy finger with a claw on it and she scraped that little claw against the palm of my hand, like this; I'll never forget it.'

Diana was studying Dad's books, which were stacked in neat piles on the counter; it wasn't easy to tell what she thought of what I'd just told her. By all appearances, it had been too much to take in at once, so I told her to go home and rest. That made her shake her head.

'We have to agree on what to tell the police.'

'There's no point sending the police after them, don't you see? It won't accomplish anything.'

'Of course we're calling the police.'

'No, Diana. There's no point.'

'Then what do we do?'

I sighed.

'Other than sigh,' Diana said.

'I can't take this any more. Can you understand that?'

'The reason it's ended up this way is that you can't take it.'

'What do you mean?'

'You let her go. When she wanted to move.'

'What was I supposed to do, she's thirty-five years—'

'When she moved here! Here, Gudrun. In 1994.'

'But she wanted to.'

'And Kiruna wants to eat ice cream and sweets every day. Do you think we let her?'

'That's hardly the same thing.'

'Yes, it is, actually. As a parent, you have an obligation to stand firm. To resist! To not yield. You let her have her way because you couldn't take her nagging and that was weak, and a betrayal. Then she sat around down here, all alone, and started developing an interest in things that turned out to be very, very dangerous. And now, when you have a chance to do something about it, twenty years later, when you actually get that second chance, you're making the same mistake again. You're letting her down again.'

'I just don't know what to do.'

'Try to channel that guilty conscience and that *pathetic* self-pity into something useful instead, and be the parent you should have been back then.'

'I think you're being unfair.'

'You know I'm right; that's why you're making that face.'

Those words found their mark; I didn't respond, just fiddled with my watch strap. At that point, Roland entered the shop.

'This is Roland,' I said. 'My partner. And this is Diana, who was with Susso, up in Norway. Susso's still there. They've taken her, Roland.'

'Who? The cult leader?'

'I don't know,' Diana said. 'But I assume so.'

'They threw Diana in the boot of a car and drove her up to Norway. Then they tried to kill her. But she escaped.'

'As I can see.'

Diana pulled down the vizor of her baseball cap as though to limit what he could see.

'He knows everything,' I said. 'Can I tell him?'

While I told him what Diana had told me, Roland distractedly played with the items on the counter. Then he pulled out his phone, pushed his glasses down onto his nose and tapped at the screen.

'Runajärvi, Pangajärvi. Did I mean Rumajärvi? Could that be it? The Armasjärvi accident? No, what did I bloody type? Let's see now. Rumajärvi. Rumajärvi is a village in Karesuando parish, Kiruna County. It's five miles south of Karesuando.'

After a while, he continued:

'Suicide wave in Rumajärvi. That's from last year.'

He continued to read quietly; eventually, I was so impatient I took the phone from him. The article was from the local morning paper. It said three people in Rumajärvi had committed suicide during 2013 and that after that, the village had been abandoned.

'You have to ask yourself,' he said, 'why they took you so far north. There's that camping site up there. In, what's it called, Skippagurra. Maybe it could be one of those trafficking things?'

'Trafficking?' Diana said. 'You mean they were going to sell me?'

'I'm just speculating.'

'They were going to get rid of me. I'm pretty sure of that.'

'No one would drive a hundred and fifty miles just to get rid of someone.'

'But they would drive a hundred and fifty miles to sell me? A thirty-five-year-old woman with a child? There's no way I'd be worth it.'

'Hey. Listen to this. Suicide waves are extraordinarily rare, but when they do sweep the Cap of the North, it's virtually always the Sami, primarily Sami men, who follow each other in death after despairing in stoic silence for years. But in Rumajärvi, it was completely ordinary locals who took their own lives. Says a local politician they interviewed for the article. The population plummeted from eighteen to one over the course of just a few months.'

'Seventeen suicides?' Roland said.

'Three. The rest moved. Except one.'

He had picked up a blonde little girl doll in Sami trad-itional clothing and was lifting her skirt up to see what she was wearing underneath.

'Makes you wonder what they must be like,' he said. 'The one who stayed.'

'I suppose it's him,' I said. 'Erasmus.'

'Erasmus of Rotterdam,' Roland said. 'Well, since we have a name, and an address, let's just send the sheriff in after them.'

'No,' I said, 'let's *not*!'

'Why not?'

'There's nothing they can do. Don't you get it? Don't you remember what it was like last time? We had zero help from the police. You might as well ask them to do something about the weather!'

'I don't understand you,' Diana said. 'Of course we have to go to the police.'

'There's no point,' I said with a sigh.

I had locked myself in a bubble of feigned resignation and I stayed in it until Diana left. Then, I lashed out at Roland.

'How can you even think of getting the police involved! They're going to go out to Susso's and sniff around. With dogs and everything, like you said.'

'Isn't the most important thing that we get her back?'

'I don't want them going out there. Is that so hard to understand?'

'Then we'll have to move him first.'

'Fine, be my guest. You with your back.'

'Can we talk to the police if I make sure he's moved first?'

'Are you serious?'

He nodded.

'We can talk to them, but it won't accomplish anything. Firstly, because they think our entire family is full of lunatics; you can be sure that's down in some record somewhere. They think everything we say is lies. And secondly, there's nothing they can do. The creatures who have taken her, they're not human. Are you hearing me? They're not human. And whatever human traits they may have, they're external.'

He bent down and picked up the doll, which he had dropped on the floor.

'I keep dropping things,' he mumbled. 'Yes, I'm hearing you.'

'But you don't believe me. It was the same thing when I told you about the squirrel and the mouse. You sit there and you nod, but you don't believe me. In your heart of hearts, you don't believe me.'

He watched me silently with sad eyes.

'She's gone. I have to accept it.'

'For the life of me, I can't understand your way of thinking.'

'That much is clear by now, painfully so in fact.'

'You can't just give up and let them keep her.'

'My girls are gone. And it's my fault. And Dad's fault.'

I pushed over a stack of photo books that crashed onto the floor but instantly regretted it and squatted down to pick them up.

'Susso's in Rumajärvi,' he said, pointing to the handbags hanging on the wall. 'And chances are that bloke Brösth is there too. We have nothing to lose by talking to the police. So long as we clean up Susso's vegetable patch first.'

'We can't move him. It's sick.'

'It's five o'clock. Balance the till and close up. Then we'll head over to Manuella for something to eat. One step at a time.'

It was the intensifying, suffocating heat that eventually made Anders pull the jacket off his face. He was lying on the floor with a sofa cushion as a pillow in a room flooded with sunlight. It was cascading in through the curtainless windows.

Stava had rolled up on the loveseat that was the room's only piece of furniture. She was still asleep, with her head hidden under a windbreaker.

The walls were covered in thin wood panelling, but there were no mouldings and no trim on either doors or windows and where light switches and electrical outlets were meant to go, there was nothing but holes.

An insect was walking across the window pane. A large stink bug with long, sweeping antennae. He followed its path across the grimy glass. He couldn't determine whether it was on the inside or the outside. But he would soon find out. There was a sticker on the window. An oval with the text YAMAHA. The bug got closer and closer to the white patch, but just before it reached it, he turned the other way.

His back ached as he hobbled across the floor and his head pounded like the hangover from hell. She had said it would pass, but it wasn't passing. It was getting worse. The painkillers he had gobbled up made no difference. Luckily, there was no mirror above the sink, so at least he didn't have to look at himself. He sank down onto the toilet seat and studied his hands. They looked swollen and had a lot of tiny cuts of unknown origin on them. As though they'd been subjected to some kind of witches' ritual during the night and scribbled full of evil inscriptions. His fingertips were trembling and his cuticles were sore and it struck him that he hadn't had snus in days. He felt no hankering for it. What he did feel was a longing for something else, something he didn't know what it was. He figured maybe he was hungry, but stepping into the kitchen it was clear to him that food was not what he wanted. In fact, the idea of putting something in his mouth was revolting.

He stood in the doorway, looking around the kitchen.

Where the fuck was he?

He walked down toward the lake. The white hull of a plastic boat rose like a limestone cliff from the grass. The shore was lined with birch trees; he hid behind them and gazed out across the water, which was dark and rippling with white-crested waves. The forest stretched out across the mountains beyond the lake. There was a jet-black line where the spruce trees were reflected in the water. And over there, in the darkest spot, he glimpsed something.

A human figure.

He squinted and took a few steps to the side to see better.

It looked like a child. A naked child.

He didn't realise he'd waded into the water until his legs went cold and heavy. He continued until it was up to his waist. It was freezing; he held his elbows above water. The figure on the other side was no longer anywhere to be seen. He waded back up and ran along the shoreline and into the forest. His shoes squelched and he had trouble controlling his feet and he was running so fast his chest quickly started hurting. There was no path to follow. Whispering, he forced his way through whipping branches, pursued by mosquitoes drawn to his wet, steaming body. He didn't want to call out or even say anything. It couldn't be far now.

Ransu was squatting with his back toward him, partly hidden underneath a spruce. His entire body was smeared with clay, which had dried in uneven layers; spruce needles and other debris from the forest floor were stuck in the greyish-brown muck. His tail was thin and sparse like on a mangy fox and within moments, that too had disappeared in under the tree. The only sign that he was in there was the swaying of the branches, and that swaying was minimal.

He had seen a climbing frame outside one of the houses in the village; this is where he was now walking and sometimes running to. He sidled up to the corner of an outhouse and peered out. There was no one there and the house seemed vacant. The front porch was littered with so much stuff the front door was unreachable.

There was a tunnel to crawl through in the climbing frame, a net to climb. Two slides that had patches of rust on the edges where the paint had cracked. It looked like an abandoned world.

When he crossed the road, he spotted an old caravan. It had no tyres and lay like a filthy egg at the back of an ancient storage building. A plank with rungs led up to the little window. What caught his interest about the caravan was the chirping voice coming from inside it.

He wiped the sweat from his brow. He was sweating profusely, and not only because he had run all the way from the forest. Now the door swung open. A girl stepped out. It was her, the one who had greeted them the night before. The one with the otter. The girl shut the door carefully behind her and ran off, her plaits bouncing.

Anders stepped out and waved to her.

She stopped and looked at him.

'Hi,' he said in a shrill voice he didn't recognise, 'remember me?'

Lennart was lying on his back in bed, staring up at a ceiling made of thin, stippled pine panelling. It was morning, new light in the room.

He walked into the kitchen, opened the freezer and dug out a brick of mince, which he put on a plate and popped into the microwave. When it beeped, he took the plate out, slammed the door shut with his elbow and went out to sit on the front porch. There was still a frozen core inside the block of mince; he hacked at it with a spoon. Then he picked the whole thing up and ate it like a fruit.

After a while, he raised his head as though he'd heard something. He stopped chewing. Sniffed the air with flared nostrils. A smell of rancid decay in the air. He stepped down from the porch. Stood there sniffing with his injured arm pressed to his chest.

The trail led him to a house on the outskirts of the village. It was old and in a poor state. One of the upstairs windows was broken. There was a pile of mineral wool in the grass, swelling like a gigantic slime mould. Broken glass. Tangles of metal-coated electrical cables, their staples like thorns. He tramped through the debris to the back of the house.

The stench broke over him like a foetid wave; when he

pushed into the birch and willow undergrowth, he heard the flies.

It looked like someone had dumped a big dead pig in the woods.

Its head was gone and its body flayed. The pink musculature stained with membranes that had dried and turned yellow. Its claws had been pulled out but the fur on the paws was still there, like big, shaggy mittens, decorated with the smooth black stones of the paw pads.

A bare-chested young man with a motocross helmet sputtered by on a motorcycle and standing outside another house was a child with a doll's pram, who watched him as he staggered around, talking to himself like a drunk. He returned to the cabin, sat down on the bed and stared at the messy room, and that was how Ipa found him. She shut the door behind her. When it slid back open, she made another attempt and didn't give up until the door was completely closed. She went over to stand with her back against the wall and her arms crossed. The ceiling light came on and she turned around to switch it back off.

'I hear you went out for a walk,' she said. 'So I assume you found it.' She waited for him to say something; when he didn't, she pressed on. 'It was an accident, just so you know. It dying. Being transported was too much for it and Erasmus is very sorry about that. He wanted me to tell you that.'

She squatted down in front of him and put a hand on his knee. Lennart fumblingly reached for her pale blonde hair, which hung in greasy strands in front of her ear, but she pushed him away, kindly but firmly, and when his hand came at her again, she stood up and backed away.

'It was malnourished. And very, very old. I don't think it could have turned again. Do you?'

'You're just a stupid child.'

'Letting it die, it was the merciful thing to do. We all think so.'

She went over to the dresser and when she spotted the shed snake skin placed there like a brown paper table runner, she pulled a disgusted face.

'Someone's going to have to come over and clean this place for you!'

She looked around the room.

'You haven't seen a spider in here, have you? There are supposedly spiders here, those creepy tarantulas with hairy legs.' She held up her hand and waved her fingers up and down to illustrate how the hairy legs moved. 'Anyway, we're going to make this place nice. So you feel at home. We really want you to feel at home. How's your hand, by the way?'

He just glowered at her.

She walked over to the window and looked out.

'The whole village will be full of people soon,' she said. 'It's going to be amazing. You're going to like it here. I promise.'

A wolf followed him all the way up to the main road, but not beyond. It stood among the trees, watching him while he kicked off his boots. He picked the boots up and walked northward, barefoot in the gravel by the side of the road.

After walking a few hundred yards, he turned around. The wolf had stepped into the middle of the road. A while later, he turned around again. By then, it was gone.

Anders stood by the edge of the lake, trying to remember why he was in the woods. His trousers were wet and he was so cold he was shaking. He thought he'd seen Ransu, but he wasn't sure. Searching his memory inevitably stirred up an overwhelming nausea. It was like muddying a pool of water. The only state that wasn't decidedly unpleasant was when he avoided casting his mind either forward or backward. He rubbed his throat. It felt like he'd just vomited.

Stava was squatting outside the house. She was examining something on the ground and when Anders moved closer, he could see what it was. Two shrews were scampering through the grass, letting her hand chase them.

'Where have you been?' she said.

'What are you doing?'

'Your clothes. You're soaked.'

'What are those?'

'These? They're my mice. They lived with me and Mauri and they're homesick. But they're happy today. Yes, you're happy today.'

'I want to leave.'

'My lovely little friends.'

'Can't we leave?'

'No, we can't leave.'

'I don't want to be here.'

'There's nowhere else for us to go.'

'Of course there is. We could find somewhere, just you and me. A cabin or something. Where we could live.'

'You and me?'

He nodded.

'And what are we going to live off, are you going to rob people?'

He shrugged.

'It doesn't work in the long run,' she said.

'What did you live off before, then, you and that guy Mauri?'

'Grete gave us money.'

'Who's Grete?'

'It's my father's sister.'

'Is she dead?'

'She can't help us. Because she has nothing left. Dad has taken everything from her. He's taken Sakka, and he's taken her treasures.'

'What treasures?'

'Jewellery. Gold.'

'But then all that must be around here somewhere.'

'Mind what you're saying.'

She glanced at the mice running around aimlessly in the grass. When her hand swooped in to catch them again, they chirped like tiny birds warning each other about a predator.

'We can't hide anything from my dad. Do you understand me?'

Anders rubbed his forehead. His head was throbbing.

'I think I saw him before. Ransu.'

Now she was staring at him.

'Where?'

'On the other side of the lake.'

'You saw him on the other side of the lake?'

'Yes.'

'How do you know it was him? There are others here.'

'I thought it was him.'

'Why didn't you say something?'

'I don't know. You were asleep.'

She was walking away from him; he grabbed her.

'Where are you going?'

'I'm going to look for him.'

'No. Don't.'

'What's wrong with you? Let go of me!'

'I don't want you to go.'

'If he's there, I have to see him. I promised Dad we'd get him here.'

'But I was probably mistaken. It probably wasn't him.'

He held her hard and nestled his head in under her hair and kissed her neck and when she tried to wrest free, he turned rough, the way he'd learnt she liked. He ushered her toward the front door and into the hallway and shoved a knee in between her legs and pushed it against her genitals hard; she opened her mouth and hissed like a malevolent spirit.

'You can take those off now, Diana. We know what you look like. Underneath.'

'It's not that,' she said and put her hand on her baseball cap as she leaned her elbow on the table. 'I'm paranoid. I have it in my head that he's going to walk by on the street and spot me.'

'Here? On our street?'

'That's not a rational fear,' her father said.

'No, it can't be, since he's dead.'

'And now you're laughing, how can you laugh? My poor darling.'

Her mother reached out and put her hand on her hand and squeezed it; she squeezed it hard.

'We'll have to be grateful,' she said, 'that you came back.'

'I know you think I was mistaken, that I was exhausted and delirious. But I know what I saw and I'm asking you, begging you, actually, not to try to wear me down.'

'Wear you down?'

'Try to persuade me that what I saw wasn't real. He was this tall and had a tail and these people who have taken Susso, they're not *normal*. You have to believe me. Dad. You have to believe me.'

Kent Sillfors put his hand over his mouth, leaned back in his chair and studied his daughter.

'Maybe we should shelve this discussion,' he said at length. 'And focus on what needs doing instead.'

'What's to discuss,' her mother said, 'we have to call the police!' She leaned in and whispered. 'You were *kidnapped*.'

'Eva,' he said. 'Go easy on the girl. You never know how something like this can affect the rest of your life. Granted, I don't think there is any risk of legal consequences. But you never know. You never know. If Diana states that she was present when this Norwegian man killed himself and it turns out to be impossible to prove that anyone else was, things could get sticky. You're not likely to be convicted of anything, but you know how people talk. That doctor who was involved in that weird suicide up in Finnmark. Things like that never go away. They can be held against you for the rest of your life.'

Her mother leaned forward and when she spoke, it was in a voice that was meant to not carry to the living room, where Kiruna was watching a children's show on TV.

'But what if it's found out after the fact? If they catch Lennart Brösth and that Erasmus guy and start investigating what happened and Susso tells them what happened to her and they see a connection with a body found in Finnmark, won't it count against Diana that she didn't say anything? Won't that look suspicious? To have kept something like that from the police?'

Kent turned his arm over, pinched the loose skin of his elbow and studied it.

'This is quite a pickle,' he said.

'If that happens,' Diana said, 'I'll have to tell them, I don't know, I'll think of something. It doesn't matter. The important thing is that we help Susso and that means telling the police she's missing and reminding them that Lennart Brösth recently escaped and then tip them off about someone seeing him in that village.'

'Or we go up there ourselves.'

'No, Kent, you're not going up there!'

'They're dangerous, Dad. You don't understand how dangerous they are. They're not like anything you can imagine.'

'Then here's what's going to happen. I'm going to talk to Denny. Keep it informal, see what he says.'

'You have to do it today.'

He held up his phone.

'I'll call him right now.'

They walked back through the church grounds. The little girl frolicked through the undergrowth lining the footpath. She was looking for dead baby birds and found it strange that she wasn't finding any; just a few days ago, they had been everywhere. Where had they gone? She crept through the grass, calling them, making kulning calls with her tiny voice.

'Little dead bird babies, where are you? Come out!'

Diana pulled out her phone. Still no reply from Håkan. Her messages had been delivered but not read. Could he have left his phone at home? Considering what she had been through, she knew it was well within her rights to be furious with him. He should make sure to be available on a day like this one. At her beck and call like a hotel receptionist. But her anger never made it out of the theoretical plane. It didn't do anything to her.

A person leading a bicycle was walking toward them through the park; she turned her head away. But it was too late. The ticking sound stopped and then the bell tinkled. It was one of Håkan's colleagues. He wore a chequered shirt with rolled-up sleeves. Backpack and sturdy helmet. She could almost hear the processor in his brain rattling to life when he saw her. She was tempted to lie. Say she'd had a bad fall. Or crashed her car. So that the story about her battered face circulating among their co-workers at the hospital would be a story of everyday bad luck, possibly laced with unspoken suspicions aimed at Håkan. But she had already told Kiruna the truth. That she had been beaten up by some men who were angry at Susso. If she fibbed now, there was a significant risk the little girl might get involved and correct her.

'What happened to you?'

'I got beaten up. By some idiots.'

'At work?'

She shook her head.

'I have a childhood friend who's fallen in with the wrong crowd. It happened when I tried to help her.'

'Dramatic.'

'Right?'

'How's Håkan?'

'What do you mean?'

'He wasn't at work today.'

'He wasn't?'

His unbuckled chinstrap swung back and forth when he shook his head.

'I don't know, maybe he's not feeling well; I haven't been home.'

'He didn't call in sick. And he's not answering his phone. So things were a bit hectic in the clinic, put it that way.'

'That's odd.'

'Mm.'

'He must have thought he had the day off. Wasn't he on call last weekend?'

He shook his head.

'Very odd.'

Worry unfurled its tentacles inside her; they were cold and refused to retract. She clutched her phone and the little girl had to run to keep up.

'Why are you walking so quickly?'

'Hurry up!'

She had been home all morning, so she knew he hadn't been there. And she clearly remembered him asking if she wanted him to take off work, because it was as close as he had come to showing concern for her. It followed, then, that he had definitely been aware that he didn't have the day off. Could something have happened to him on his way to work? It was a ten-minute walk. Hardly likely. On the other hand, she had to admit the laws of probability seemed to be suspended since a few days back. It was as though all of existence had been decalibrated by an earthquake. She had left one Kiruna and returned to another. To the strange Kiruna of the Myréns. Kinura. Krinua.

The car was in the driveway, its number plate spray-painted with splattered bugs, as a reminder of her trip to the latitude of death. The front door was locked, but she still called out. Kiruna called out too, but rather than shouting Daddy, she mimicked her mother and yelled Håkan.

'Håååkan!'

The house was empty. Diana glanced out the terrace doors, but he wasn't out there. A film of rain on the plastic garden furniture and further down the slope their neighbour's sled like a forgotten temple in a jungle of weeds.

She went to the bathroom. Both the lid and the seat were up, which was odd because Håkan was always extremely meticulous about that and who else in their household would have put the seat up? But she didn't give the seat any thought until much later.

She tore off some loo roll and held it in her hand while she peed. Afterwards, she stayed on the toilet, tapping out yet another message to Håkan. Then she changed her mind and called instead.

It took her a while to realise the buzzing sound was coming from the other side of the shower curtain. She stared at the New York subway map, hanging near enough for her to reach out and touch it. A shuffling sound made her jump to her feet. She flung the door open and dashed out with her trousers around her knees.

Outside, she stopped and tried to collect herself, heart pounding. After pulling her trousers up, she took one long step back into the bathroom and tore the shower curtain aside. And there he was. Curled up with his arms around his pulled-up knees. Shirt and chinos. But barefoot. He was staring at the wall and only tore his eyes away from the tiles for a vacant glance in her direction when she said his name.

Diana closed and locked the door. Then she sat down on the toilet and looked at him. He didn't like that; he twisted away as though her eyes had emitted an unpleasantly strong light.

'What's the matter with you?'

It was the only thing she could think of to say, and if there was empathy in her voice, it was artificial. She wanted to scream at him that he wasn't allowed to act this way, but she curbed herself, for Kiruna's sake.

'Leave.'

'I'm fine right here.'

'Please.'

'Get it together,' she said and then she chortled loudly through her nostrils. She couldn't help it. It was so absurd. Him sitting there. If anyone should be crying in the bathroom, it should be her, shouldn't it?

'Can't you just leave me alone,' he said in a thick voice.

'Only if you tell me what's wrong.'

When he didn't reply, she took off her baseball cap and sat holding it for a while before putting it down in the sink.

'I get if you were worried, but I'm back now. Look. I'm here, Håkan. A bit black and blue, but mostly in one piece.'

He didn't look at her, and it didn't seem like her words were getting through to him. She had a mind to ask him what diagnosis he would give a father behaving this way. It was as though he was enacting a mental collapse of exactly the kind he liked to talk about with arch contempt during discussions about the rocketing number of people on medical leave and the failing work ethic of the general population. But she bit her tongue. Sarcastic digs were unlikely to help improve his state.

'How long have you been sitting here? Håkan.'

'Go away.'

'Can you tell me what's wrong?'

'It's nothing. I just want to sit here.'

'You just want to sit there? In the shower?'

He nodded.

'And how long were you planning on sitting there?'

'I don't know.'

'Wouldn't it be better if you went to bed?'

No answer.

'What do you want me to tell your daughter?'

His body twitched; she assumed it was meant as a shrug.

When she exited the bathroom, Kiruna was sitting on the stairs, watching her. Her eyes were bigger than normal and her mouth was open solemnly; she wondered how much the little girl had overheard. She shut the door behind her.

'Daddy's sick,' she said. 'Let's leave him be.'

When Roland told me he had asked a couple of friends of his from Malmberget to decontaminate Susso's garden, I was cross with him for having the gall to joke about something like that. But he wasn't joking and when that sank in, I had to sit down. A stool met me halfway, but mentally I continued down through the stone floor and straight into the abyss of the Kiruna mine, where I tumbled around in a darkness without dimensions.

'We can trust these lads,' he said.

He had a younger brother and I might have understood if he'd gone to him for help, but he just shook his head at that. There was no one in the world he trusted more than these boys. Two good old village lads, he called them.

Since I'd never heard him mention any friends of his, I had more or less assumed he didn't have any. At least none you could turn to with something like this. I mean: who does? So they were supposedly going to materialise out of nowhere and dig up and transport and dispose of a corpse, a corpse that had nothing whatsoever to do with them. Just like that, no questions asked? Was he going to pay them for it?

'First of all,' he said, 'they're not materialising out of nowhere, they're from Malmberget. And second of all,

Gudrun, you have to understand that these boys are very special. They're not like other people.'

'What do you mean, not like other people; are they retarded?'

'You might say that. But only in a positive sense.'

'Have you told them? About the trolls?'

He had fished out a sweet from the glass bowl on the counter and was trying to unwrap it.

'You can hardly think I'd ask them to help us with something like this without informing them about the risks?'

Aska had delivered a package that morning; I started tear-
ing at it to give my anxious fingers something to do. It was a
stack of table runners. I picked one of them up and ran my
hand over the cloth, studying the pattern, which consisted
of long rows of yellow, blue, red and green squares. She had
attached a note saying the pattern was called Kiruna.

'And what did they say to that?'

He tore off the sweet wrapper with his teeth. Then he stood
there, picking flakes of plastic out of his mouth. I was apparently not going to get an answer.

'What kind of people are they?'

'Their names are Harr and Ensimmäinen. Harr is my second cousin.'

'Harry?'

'Harr.'

'I don't think that's a real name.'

'You're clearly wrong about that, since it's his name. Harr
is a bus driver, but I think he's retired now. He's a troubadour as well. He's recorded a real CD. I'm not sure what
Ensimmäinen gets up to these days, but he used to work at
Gällivare Tractors.'

'You think he's retired? If you're such good friends, shouldn't you know whether he's retired or not?'

'With really good friends, regular contact's not a requirement. You know the other person's there for you come rain or shine and that's enough. The bond is so strong it doesn't need maintenance. It's a maintenance-free friendship.'

'I still don't think we should involve them.'

'Oh well. Too late.'

'Just tell them they don't need to go out there.'

'I can't.'

'Why not?'

'Because they were already there.'

I glared at him.

'You don't have to worry, Gudrun.'

'That's easy for you to say!'

'We can trust them.'

'But what did they do with him?'

'Do you really want to know?'

'No, I suppose I don't.'

'The only thing Susso needs to do, when she gets back,' he said and popped the sweet in his mouth, 'the only thing she needs to do is to ponder who dug a potato patch in her garden.'

'A potato patch without potatoes.'

'They planted potatoes.'

'Why? That's a bit over the top, don't you think?'

'They bought a bag so they'd have a reason for being there in case someone asked what they were up to. And then I reckon they planted the potatoes mostly as a fun thing to do. Minerva. Extremely hardy, according to Harr.'

I was about to make a sign for the table runners but instead I just stood there with the marker in my hand and I was so confused I wrote 'Minerva' on the sign.

'And I tipped the police off. About Lennart Brösth. About him being seen in that village. I asked a mate up in Karesuando to put the call in. Figured it was better than doing it anonymously. More credible that way.'

'But we don't even know if he's there!'

'Surely the main thing is to get them to head out there and look around. What you have to do, and you have to do it right now, is to report Susso missing, and to mention that you think Lennart Brösth might have taken her. Then we have to hope the police put two and two together.'

'You might have asked me first. Before you called the police. And before you asked your friends for help. I really don't like that.'

'What were you going to say? You would have said no. And Susso doesn't have time for that. I imagine.'

'Do I have to call the police? I don't want to.'

'All you have to do is tell them Susso's missing. And maybe remind them about Lennart Brösth's jailbreak.'

'I don't want to!'

'Why not?'

'Because I don't want to.'

'You don't think they'll believe you.'

I shook my head. Then I nodded.

'Then I'll do it,' he said and shoved his hands in his pockets. 'Or should we ask her friend, the doctor?'

'No, you do it.'

'They're going to ask what my relationship is with her.'

'So you'll tell them the truth.'

'And they will obviously send someone around her house. But you know that.'

'I don't like it. Even though he's not there any more.'

'You don't have to worry.'

'So they've moved him?'

Roland gave me a mischievous look.

'Maybe we should do something to thank them then,' I sighed.

'You'll have a chance tonight. Because they're coming here.'

'They're coming here? Why?'

'Well, Harr said they had some questions. We're meeting them at eight. At Momma's.'

'What kind of questions?'

'I don't know.'

'They want money, how hard is that to figure out? They're going to blackmail us! Or me, rather. They're going to black-mail me! Oh God, Roland, what have you got me into?'

My outburst baffled him; he even raised his eyebrows, making them pop up above the rims of his glasses.

'Then you'd better hike up the price on those tablecloths,' he said and shuffled off toward the door. 'See you in a bit.'

When I tried to put the cap back on the marker, my hands were shaking so hard I got myself on the knuckle and while I was rubbing the spot, I pictured the dark secret Håkan and I shared spreading from person to person; I envisioned the spread like a diagram. It seemed inevitable. Like all the misery afflicting me and my family.

A paralysing sense of inescapable fate had seized me. It was absolutely clear to me that we were dealing with forces against which resistance was futile. Doomed to fail. My eyes darted around the shelves before settling on the glass display case at the far end of the shop, right next to the front door. It showcased Dad's art treasures, gifts from the many Sami artists he had got to know in his day. That the artefacts were not for sale lent the shop a certain craft museum-like air, which I felt dignified the commerce, and encouraged it. There were boxes and *guksis*. Knives with elaborate sheaths. Ptarmigans coaxed out of the wood of the curly birch. A white, ghost-white, reindeer antler. And surrounded by all these objects, like some kind of chieftain, a strange wooden figure. The Hoarfrost Man was tall and emaciated like an old tree and his face was made of horn and from this hard face, grim like the face of a skeleton, stared a big, almond-shaped eye. It looked at me and I knew it would never blink.

Anders was in the kitchen, dressed in a fleece jacket and undies. He had discovered a pack of tortillas in the freezer. The paper-thin breads couldn't be separated, so he broke them into shards that he slipped in between his lips.

Then he heard a bang. A shot from a small gun.

He went out onto the front steps. Stava had heard it too. They exchanged a look. Stava walked up toward the road and Anders crept along behind her.

Someone was running toward them. A police officer. A woman with blonde, flowing hair. It looked like she had run at full pelt until her strength had given out, because she was stumbling along with her mouth wide open. Anders' first reaction was to want to hide. But there was no need. Even though she passed by just a few feet away from them, she didn't seem to notice them. Where the road curved, she tramped up into the forest.

Soon after, a wolf appeared and after it a woman at a trot. It was the one who had shown them to the cabin they were staying in. Ipa. She didn't seem to notice them either; it was as though they didn't exist. The wolf slipped in among the trees and she followed.

The police car with its jigsaw of yellow and blue squares was parked in the middle of the village. Like some kind of brightly coloured artwork touring the rural north. The man who had kicked Stava was standing a few feet away from it. He was holding a small pistol. He tried to spin it around his index finger like a gunslinger, but failed and almost dropped it.

'What happened?' Stava asked.

Instead of answering, he aimed the gun at Stava, pretended to shoot her and blew smoke from the barrel.

It was only at that point Anders realised there were people in the car. It was Erasmus and a police officer; they were in the back seat. The officer had his hands pressed against his ears. But it didn't look like he was covering his ears because he didn't want to listen to Erasmus; it looked more like he was trying to crush his own skull.

After a while, Ipa returned with the female officer, dragging her by the hand to make her walk faster. The wolf brought up the rear.

Mikko opened the driver-side door and shoved the woman inside. She just sat there with her hands on the wheel.

'I don't know if I know how to drive a car,' she said.

'You're a copper,' Mikko said. 'All coppers know how to drive.'

'I'm a copper,' she said and studied her uniform. Then she looked at her colleague, who was now in the passenger seat, gazing out the window. 'We're coppers.'

Ipa had her hands in her jacket pockets.

'I don't think she can drive. Not for a bit. We don't want them driving into a ditch up here, do we?'

This prospect didn't seem to worry Erasmus, who was scratching the wolf's neck.

[286]

'I'm a copper,' the woman said and squeezed the steering wheel so tightly her knuckles turned white. 'All coppers know how to drive.'

'Goodbye then,' Erasmus said and tipped his hat. 'I'm sorry we can't be of more help.'

'To be honest,' the woman said, 'I don't remember what we needed help with.' She looked at her colleague, a man with a brown beard.

'My God, I really feel like I know you!'

The man smiled awkwardly, clearly embarrassed to be so confused he didn't know where he was, and maybe not even who he was.

Ipa leaned in.

'Then it probably wasn't important,' she said.

'No, it probably wasn't,' the woman agreed and started the engine.

The police car rolled away very slowly and turned with blinking indicators. It took them a long time to turn around. Ipa waved when they drove past, but the woman was much too focused on the driving to see her and the other officer was crying into his hand.

Anders pressed himself against Stava.

'Are they looking for us?' he whispered.

'There they are,' Roland said as he zigzagged between the tables, so eager to greet his friends he left me in his wake.

They were at the very back of the room.

Harr wore a leather cowboy hat on his head. His nose was a big, hooked thing that looked like it had been burnt to a crisp in the sun, but it probably went deeper than that. He tipped his hat to me and lurking behind his curly grey beard was a moist little grin I couldn't read.

If Harr was the man with the hat, Ensimmäinen was the man with the hair. It tumbled down his back like a hard-rocker's and was more white than grey. It didn't match his angular face and steel-rimmed glasses at all and definitely didn't belong on a man his age; I thought he looked like a banker who had put on a zany wig for an office party. His long pale arms, which were resting on the table, were hairless like a woman's. He wore no watch and, naturally, no ring.

We sat down at the table and since they didn't say anything and seemed to be waiting for something, I forced myself to ask if they wanted beer, but they didn't even reply, and when, in a state of growing unease, I passed the question on to Roland, he didn't answer either. It was as if he'd suddenly gone over to their side, and it made me furious.

'Do you want a pint or not!' I cackled and that made him

snap back in and nod with a flat look on his face.

The waitress was a tired little girl with piercings all over her face and dyed black hair; when she left, I noticed Harr was watching me and that he was doing it fairly unabashedly. As though he felt free to take the liberty of inspecting me. He and his friend had an advantage over me that no one had ever had before. That was how it was. It felt like they owned me and that made me insecure and it made me angry. My face glowed hot from time to time and I was certain the flushes were fully visible on my cheeks, which did nothing to help matters.

'May I ask how business is going?' Harr said. 'Or is that intrusive?'

'Business? You mean my shop? Well, I guess it's going fine.'

'Rolle tells us you have competition now.'

'That man sells nothing but tat. He'll go belly-up in no time.'

'If he doesn't,' he said and adjusted his hat, 'Nänne and I would always be happy to go have a chat with him.'

During its fall toward the table top, my gaze touched his watery, light-blue eyes. Had he really said what I thought he'd said? No matter how I looked at it, the meaning was unambiguously clear: he had implied that they had resorted to mobster methods on my behalf and with that little dig at me, he was letting me know he had the upper hand. My face flushed again and this time the heat moved like a wave down through my body, like a hot flash. And Roland, he just sat there like a fool, picking at the label of his beer bottle.

'Do you sell records in your shop?'

'Records?' I said, my mouth dry.

'Music.'

'I have Sofia Jannok's CD. Her latest.'

Harr reached back and dug around the pocket of his suede jacket, which was draped over the back of his chair. He took out a CD case and after putting it down on the table, he placed his hand over it and pushed it toward me with a secretive look on his face. He was sitting behind the wheel of a bus. His elbow hanging out the window rockabilly style. His hat was blindingly white and around the high crown ran a concho hat band. The album was called *To Murjek and Back Again* and his name was printed at the bottom, Harr Honkaniemi.

'See who it is?'

I turned the case over and read.

'You might have heard "Give Me Your Hand". They've played it on Radio Gällivare a few times. I thought you might want to stock it.'

If this was the price for their services, it was low. The question was whether this was the final price, or just the start of a lifetime of blackmail. But I nodded. Thanked him, even.

Harr stroked his beard, looking pleased.

'You know, Gudrun, the only people singing about life up here are the Sami. And they just wail on and on about their roots and their lost pretend-country until your ears bleed. Now they rap too. On TV. It's Sami this and Sami that. Sami, Sami, Sami. And I know a lot of Sami people feel that way too. Sjul Jonsson, do you know Sjul, Roland, he likes to say: What's going to become of us old Lapps, now that the Sami have taken over?'

He tapped his index finger on the CD case.

'This here,' he said, 'is a different voice. You can tell them that. If anyone asks about the record and wants to know what the old man's about. You could put it somewhere people will see it. You don't have to advertise it or anything, but it would be nice if it sat out where people could see it.'

He took a sip of his beer and after putting his glass down he caught his moustache with his lower lip and sucked down the droplets that were stuck in the bristles. Then he asked in a quieter voice how my daughter liked her new potato patch.

They didn't know Susso was still missing, so I told them about Diana's little trip to Norway. I left out the part about her saviour wearing the face of a dead man and having the tail of a German Shepherd, because I was in no mood to be scoffed at.

They hadn't heard about the suicide wave in Tornedalen last spring, but they knew about Lennart Brösth and Harr wanted to know more about him and his kidnapping cult. I didn't know how to answer his questions; Roland had to ride to the rescue.

'Well, I did tell you,' he said, turning his bottle in his hands, 'what kind of people Gudrun and her daughter have got on the wrong side of. That they are tough to label. So to speak.'

'Trolls,' Harr said. 'That was the word you used.'

He said it loudly and with a naturalness that made me embarrassed; it was as though he had shouted out a four-letter word.

'Yes,' Roland said. 'But as I said, that's just a word.'

Harr unbuttoned the breast pocket of his denim shirt and dug around in it with his index finger, either looking for something or seeking to reassure himself something was still in there.

'We made fun of that word, you know,' he said and closed the pocket by pushing the button with his thumb. 'On our way to Vittangi. We had a good laugh at your expense, Rolle. For finding a woman on the internet who not only believes in trolls but is pestered by them too.'

That this man, a bigoted bus driver with swirls of lichen around his mouth, a tragic bachelor from Malmberget who didn't take his hat off in restaurants, who thought he was a troubadour, that he described me like that didn't bother me in the slightest; if anything, his ignorant arrogance gave me a soothing feeling of superiority. If only you knew, I thought to myself.

At that moment, the mocking glint in his eye vanished.

'But afterwards, when we were leaving,' he said, 'we didn't much feel like laughing. Did we?' He glanced at Ensimmäinen, who with a graceful movement of the hand caught a stray lock of white hair and pushed it behind his ear.

'Something happened while we were there,' Harr said without taking his eyes from me. 'And Nänne and I haven't been able to talk about it. We have tried to talk about it, but it's as if it can't be done.' He leaned forward. 'Why is it so hard to talk about?'

'What's so hard to talk about?'

'What happened to us. At your daughter's house.'

I really didn't want to talk about those things and I showed them as much by averting my eyes. Through the unwashed window above Harr's hat, I could see the building where I lived; I could even see my own living room window, the little lamp.

'How should I know?' I mumbled, somewhat absently.

'I think you do know.'

Something about his tone made me think he wasn't referring to the dirty work they had performed.

'You saw something.'

He nodded, almost imperceptibly.

'About this size,' I said and pointed to my pint glass. 'Plus the bright, bushy tail?'

'To tell you the truth,' he said, 'we only glimpsed it. Once, when it was sitting up on the ridge of the roof, like a weather-vane. So I said to Nänne, I said, look, a squirrel. But then we started suspecting that it wasn't that simple. That what we'd seen was something else.'

He glanced at Nänne, who nodded agreement.

'As I said, we barely saw it, but the whole time we were there I could sense it was looking for something. Under my hat. It was sitting up on the roof, but it was down here, under my hat. And that,' he said and scratched his beard, 'I didn't much care for.'

'It's incredibly fond of Susso,' I said. 'So it probably wanted to know if you knew where she is.'

'I felt like a pine cone. Do you understand what I mean?'

'Maybe not entirely.'

'Completely powerless.'

'Yes. You were lucky to get away.'

'I'm not sure we did.'

He bowed his head and took off his hat and after pushing his empty glass aside, he placed the hat on the table, and he did it all with slow, precise movements. His hair lay slicked across his head in sparse strands that came together in a silvery hook at the nape of his neck.

'It doesn't feel like we did,' he sighed. 'I still feel like a pine cone, just a used-up one. Pried open. And plundered.'

'He's a monster,' I said and quickly washed the slur down

with a sip of beer. 'That's what I've always thought.'

'A monster?'

I nodded.

Roland tilted his head, humming agreement.

'I don't suppose I ever really understood what you meant by that . . .'

'What do you actually know,' Harr said, 'about this creature?'

Sitting at Momma's bar, or steakhouse, as they called it, discussing with two perfect strangers from Malmberget the thing I had never before had the energy or courage to even mention to anyone, was exceedingly healing.

'I know he's old. Over a hundred years.'

'A hundred years?'

Harr leaned back and crossed his arms. They were alarmingly skinny; he didn't look like he'd done manual labour a single day of his life.

'The only thing you need to know is that he's dangerous. Because he won't let go until he feels like it.'

'Like a parasite.'

'There is nothing to be done about it.'

'We were lucky, Nänne. Do you hear me? He had no interest in us. Not even you, with your angel's hair.'

'He finds a secret way into your head and when he's inside, he goes looking for things. Things you've hidden. Every time I went over to Susso's, when she lived here, I left feeling lower than low. Everything turned black and I sat around dwelling on all kinds of misery that bubbled up, my divorce and other things, and you can back me up here, Roland, I got depressed. And it obviously took me a while to figure out the squirrel was causing it and I think he was doing it so I'd leave them alone. And he got his way, in the end.'

'Gudrun,' Roland said. 'Tell them about the mouse.'

'When we were there, at Susso's, that night, when it *happened*, there was a mouse there, and it was because of the mouse things turned out the way they did. It got into both our heads but especially Håkan's. And Håkan, he flew into a rage, because he thought that person had something to do with Diana going missing. And things went pear-shaped. It was the mouse's fault. One hundred per cent. I'm certain of it. That's why I killed it.'

'You killed it?' Harr said.

'Yes.'

'Wasn't that risky?'

I shrugged.

Now Roland leaned forward.

'The question is whether we shouldn't give the squirrel the same treatment.'

'If I thought it was possible,' I said, 'I would have done it a long time ago, obviously. This mouse, it was so *naïve*. I don't even think it was aware of what it was doing to us, it was just dashing about, completely high on all the hatred and confusion emanating from us. The squirrel, on the other hand, is anything but naïve. I don't even think it's *possible* to trick it. I wouldn't dare to try, anyway.'

'It has to go,' Roland said. 'If Susso's ever going to have a chance to be herself again, it has to go.'

'How many times have I told you just that? But you haven't believed me. But when your pals show up and tell you the squirrel is bad news, then you're suddenly on board.'

'If these two gentlemen tell me the squirrel is a troll, it's a troll. They would never lie to me.'

'I wouldn't go so far as to claim the squirrel is a troll,' Harr interjected, 'but I suppose we can call it that, for the sake of simplicity.'

'But I would?'

'Not lie, exactly. But you've grown up with this—'

'No I haven't! My dad took that picture in eighty-seven. I was forty-three years old! Surely that must qualify as being a grown-up!'

'It's emotional for you, this thing, with your family's reputation and all the terrible things that have happened to your girls, and I'm not above admitting that I've assumed you're exaggerating sometimes, seeing trolls where there are no . . . trolls.'

'You don't trust me. You trust them, but not me.'

He opened his mouth to protest but changed his mind. The conversation going off on a combative tangent. So he sat quietly for a while, looking at his bottle of beer, before continuing.

'If it is as you say,' he said, 'it has to die. The simplest way of removing it securely and permanently is to kill it.'

'And how would you go about doing that?' I said. 'It knows what you're thinking.'

'I guess we'll have to keep our distance,' Harr said and raised his hands like he was grasping an imaginary rifle. 'Nänne's an excellent shot. He can put a bullet through that rat's eye from half a mile away. So long as he can see it. Isn't that right, Nänne? No problem.'

'I think it might be a bad idea. Shooting it.'

'How is slaying a monster a bad idea?'

'It can be. If you need the monster's help.'

He looked at me uncomprehendingly.

'Is Susso back? No, she's not, and I have a very strong feeling the police won't be much help. They're going to go up to that village and then they're going to go home. And Susso is going to still be there. That squirrel gives me the creeps and I hate it for what it's done to my daughter, but I also know it's her protector. It's her protector. I've seen it protect her against a bear troll with my own eyes. Because you should know that trolls come in all sizes and if you don't believe me, you can head up to that village and see for yourselves. The internet says it's a ghost town, but I'm fairly convinced it should say troll town. And if I have to go there to get Susso back, which I fear it will come to, even if it will probably be the last thing I ever do, I want the squirrel with me.'

'I get that,' Harr said.

I shook my finger at them.

'So you can't shoot it!'

Harr put his hat back on and then he stood up and I realised he was considerably taller than I'd thought. He wore a denim shirt and jeans, an overall of washed-out denim it looked like, and I almost expected him to have shiny crocodile-skin cowboy boots on his feet, but he didn't, he wore trainers.

He left without a word; I assumed he was going to the bathroom. But after another minute or so, Ensimmäinen stood up too and left in silence as well, and when I turned around in my chair, I saw him head out the front door. A slender man with hair like a silver cape down his back.

'They left?' I said.

Roland nodded.

'Seems that way.'

'Are they staying in the hotel?'

'I don't think so.'

I made a puzzled face and he noticed.

'I told you they're not much good, in an everyday sense. They can be pretty difficult to be around. But when the going gets tough, there are no better friends on this planet, and nowhere else either for that matter. They're solid, to the core.'

'The one with the hair, is he mute or something?'

'Nänne. Nah.'

'But he didn't say a word.'

Roland took a sip of his beer and put the bottle down carefully.

'I guess he had nothing to say.'

'I think they're weird.'

'Sure. They are weird, no two ways about it. But this whole situation is bloody weird. So they should fit right in.'

We sat in silence for a while. One group of diners was unusually raucous and both Roland and I glanced their way from time to time; it was just impossible not to.

'So you believe me now?'

When Anders woke up, he was outside and it was night-time. The grass was damp with dew and made his feet chilly and the mosquitoes hung around his head like a veil. He had almost made it down to the lake. The dark water and the spruce-shaggy mountain beyond it scared him. He was cold. He only had jeans and a button-down shirt on. He peaked into his trousers. No underwear. The shirt was wildly misbuttoned.

He had a strong feeling of having been on his way somewhere. He no longer knew where to, but he could still sense the irresistible longing that had seized him in his sleep. This longing was now slowly dissipating and that made him desperately upset.

He continued down toward the lake at a trot. Could it be that Ransu had been calling him? Was he waiting on the other side of the lake like last time? It was impossible to tell; the spruce trees clumped together like a dark mass.

He knew he should go inside and wake Stava; he'd promised her he would if Ransu turned up again. But there was no time. What if he withdrew and disappeared again? She wouldn't want that. He ran along the water's edge until he reached the trees. At that point, he immediately began to proceed with more caution. The path winding around the lake was little more than an animal run, difficult enough to follow even in daylight; now it kept branching off, making him uncertain. It was as though the nocturnal light made trails appear where there were none during the day.

He thought the woods looked familiar. He scissor-jumped over a branchless log and skidded down a small slope and ducked under a spruce branch.

There was something on the ground.

A greyish-brown, moving mass.

Good God, what was it!

He crept a few steps closer to have a look.

A swarm of tiny rodents crawling over one another, faintly and elatedly squeaking. Mice, shrews, a lemming, two lemmings. He stared at it. Then he made a coughing noise and doubled over.

A shoe was sticking out of the heaving heap. A tiny trainer with flapping Velcro ties.

Anders' mouth started moving.

'No,' he moaned. 'No, no, no.'

His words triggered an irritated agitation among the little ones; when they shifted, the plastic bag that had been put over the child's face became visible and a lemming slipped from the swarm, got up on its hind legs and hissed at him with a clown mouth of coagulated blood.

Horrified, he leapt aside. He staggered backward and fell into a spruce tree. He didn't get back up.

When he finally crawled out from under the tree, he had cried himself empty and didn't quite know where he was. He had been somewhere else. Far, far away, in a place where only he existed and no one could reach him.

Now he walked slowly through the trees, carrying his hope like water in a cupped hand.

He stopped and stared at the abomination on the ground. Then he lunged forward, braying furiously, grabbed the plastic bag and started to pull it off; when the head appeared, he let go of the bag and ran away.

Diana sat with her phone in her hand, talking to her father. He was telling her the police had gone out to Rumajärvi but had found no sign of Lennart Brösth and when Diana put in that if that was true, they had done a poor job looking, he grumbled at her that the best thing would be for her to take some sick leave and leave the search for Susso to the authorities.

At first, she was furious. There was something about his tone that kicked her back in time twenty years, to the period when her grades were slipping and few weekends went by without her drinking her brain to bits. Back then, he had, on a handful of occasions, talked to her in a special voice, gravelly and low, vibrating with supressed rage, and that was the tone she thought she was hearing now. The fury that erupted inside her was, however, quelled when she realised he sounded like that because he was afraid.

'Don't get mixed up in this, Dana.'

'What's going on up there?'

'They're not going to tell me that. Denny just said she's not there. Which means there's not much we can do. At the moment. You're going to have to try to forget about it.'

'Forget?'

'Yes.'

'What did Denny say?'

'He said they'd been up there. That they went up there yesterday. And that they didn't find Lennart Brösth or Susso. That's what he said. Verbatim.'

'And what else did he say? I know there's more.'

'He said they'd got lost.'

'Who?'

'The officers. Who went up there.'

'The police officers got lost?'

'Yes, well, they didn't go home in any case. They drove south. Until they ran out of petrol. On the bridge in Lappeasuando, you know, that arch. Some kids from the campsite down there found them. Under the bridge.' He cleared his throat. 'At the foot of the bridge. They were just sitting there in the grass and were kind of, what's it called, catatonic. And with mosquito bites all over. And Denny said one of them was in a bizarre position, but I don't know what he meant by that. I don't know.'

Diana said nothing for a while.

'And you think that was a coincidence? That something like that happened right after they had been to that village, of all places.'

'No, I guess maybe I don't.'

'Then surely they have to go out there again. They must realise there's something wrong.'

'I don't know. I don't think so. At least that's not how Denny made it sound. He just doesn't see the connection. He doesn't think going to that place, to Rumajärvi, has anything to do with what they were like. He was talking about the police being understaffed and stress. Constant stress.'

'This isn't about stress.'
'No.'
'We have to do something, Dad.'
'What you have to do is get some rest.'

After the call ended, she stayed seated with her phone in her hand. Kiruna's untouched breakfast was on the kitchen table, a suspension of milk and dissolved cereal in a bowl decorated with fairy-tale creatures in light pastel colours. There was milk on the table, a small system of lakes. Through the window, she could see their neighbour's kid standing out on the street with a floorball stick in his hands, shovelling water out of a puddle; it felt like the blade was scraping the inside of her skull every time it scraped against the crust of the asphalt. Against that torment, painkillers were powerless to help.

She dragged herself upstairs. The little girl was sitting on the floor in her silent room, playing with something small she was cradling close to her body.

The curtains in the bedroom were closed and Håkan was in bed, facing the wall. A small rectangle of light faded on the nightstand, a sign that he was awake.

'I'm going out for a bit.'

He made no reply.

'Håkan?'

'Yes.'

'I'm going out for a bit.'

She pulled up the hood of her jacket and tramped up the steep incline of Adolf Hedinvägen. She passed the hospital without so much as a glance; it was like an anonymous rectangle at the edge of her vision.

Leaving Kiruna alone with him when he was in that state was perhaps not entirely appropriate, but she would be right back. Besides, she told herself the forced responsibility would do him good, make him pull himself together. She didn't know how to approach his collapse yet. That her disappearance had made him fall completely to pieces was in a way pretty touching and in time, she might learn to appreciate the vulnerable side of him he hadn't shown her before, but at the moment she was mostly angry. Angry he was lying there like a dissociative wreck but mostly angry because it was so unlike him. This was not the man she'd married, and she felt, to put it plainly, duped. At the same time, she was highly aware that it was unreasonable to walk around feeling duped. Especially now, given what they'd been through. She tried and for the most part succeeded in maintaining control by reminding herself that she had endured an extraordinary psychological ordeal. The medical terminology served as a warding spell against the panic that was constantly threatening to erupt inside her, but adopting a scientific perspective to understand what she had seen and what Gudrun had told her about also moved her toward a horizon from which the trolls could not be observed. That made them evaporate like swirls of mist. And so her brain had quarantined all thoughts on the topic until further notice.

Whenever she felt like screaming at the top of her lungs, she pictured Susso. Susso sitting on the jetty in her filthy fake-fur jacket with a bottle of beer in her hand, squinting at the ball of the sun lurking behind the screen of dark trees on the other side of the river. The picture was detailed and richly coloured, because she had filled it with all the longing that had accumulated over the years, which had never found expression outside of her dreams, in which she and Susso often ran into each other in both familiar and unknown places. Susso was always quiet and morose at first, but then they invariably found their way back to each other and when she woke up, she would feel sad because it hadn't happened in real life. Now, she drew strength from that sadness. It propelled her forward.

Gudrun was poking at her phone, which was on the counter. She was wearing a black, mesh-knit cardigan over a blue, shiny tank top that matched the agates in her necklace; when Diana told her what had happened to the police officers who had been dispatched to Rumajärvi, her hand kept tugging nervously at the cardigan. When Diana said they should drive up to the village themselves and get Susso, she walked over to a basket full of stuffed moose and started pointlessly reorganising them.

'The road to Rumajärvi,' she said, 'ends in Lappeasuando. If you get my meaning.'

'Then you know where to look for me.'

Gudrun turned to her and mulled that for a long time, all the while fiddling with her cardigan.

'I'll go with you, Diana. But we can't go alone.'

'Susso's dad might come. Don't you think he'd step up? Does he even know she's missing?'

The old woman wasn't listening. She had taken a step closer.

'When you were at Susso's, did you see the squirrel?'

'Yes, I did. It was in the kitchen.'

'What was your impression of it?'

'What was my impression of it?'

'Yes.'

'I don't know. I thought it was gross.'

'Did it seem to like you, or was it hostile?'

'I'd say it was fairly neutral.'

'It didn't make you feel anything in particular?'

'Not really, no.'

'Then you'd better go fetch it.'

'You want me to *fetch* the squirrel?'

Gudrun had taken off her glasses and was rubbing the lenses with a cleaning cloth. She was intently focused on what she was doing.

'We have no choice.'

'I thought it was creepy.'

'Yes,' Gudrun said and took another step closer. 'Look at my hand, see how it's shaking? See? Like an old drunk. It's because I'm thinking about the squirrel.'

'Susso claimed it understands Swedish.'

'Yes,' she said with a nod, 'he's very old.'

Diana turned away and shook her head, but Gudrun pressed on.

'You remember what I said about the trolls, don't you, that they hide in animal form? Underneath that fur, that lovely, brown fur, there's someone lurking. A creature? Yes, a creature I've never seen. But I can feel it looking at me. He stares at me and has thoughts about me and that's not all: he can affect how I feel and make me do things I would never do of my own accord.'

'It was strange, actually, now that you mention it. When I was at Susso's, I noticed I was saying things I didn't really want to say. It was like I was drunk and blurting things out. The kind of things I was thinking but didn't want to say.'

Gudrun nodded.

'Then you know what he's capable of. What he can do.'

'I don't think it likes me.'

'I thought you said he was neutral.'

'I don't know. I teased it a little. Susso trapped it in the kitchen and I looked at it through the window and I don't think it appreciated it.'

'Trapped him?'

'Yes. I think it was because it was ruining things for us when we were trying to talk. It butted in, in various ways.'

'Yes, exactly.'

'Wasn't he in the kitchen when you were there, you and Håkan?'

Gudrun shook her head.

'No, the house was empty.'

'Isn't that weird? Maybe they went into the kitchen then? And took him as well. He might not even be alive any more.'

'He's alive. And he's there.'

'How do you know?'

Gudrun made no reply; she just looked at her, pleadingly. Diana did a lap around the shop, inspecting the items on the shelves.

'What if he doesn't want to come with me?'

'Tell him you're going to go get Susso. That'll make him come, I guarantee it.'

'What's that smell?' Diana said, sniffing the air.

'There's a smell?'

'Something smells in here.'

'I don't know,' Gudrun said and wrapped the cardigan around her.

On her way home, Diana felt nausea rising. It was as though it was feeling its way, looking for a foothold. Her legs buckled but she didn't allow herself to sit down and rest, not even for a minute, because she didn't want anyone to see her. Even though her entire existence had been shaken to the core and everything around her seemed like a treacherous aspect of an enormous illusion, she clung to her reputation. Aside from Håkan's colleague, she hadn't run into anyone who knew her yet, which was a miracle in itself. She hurried home and when she passed along the back of the hospital, she hid her face in her hood like a conspirator.

Håkan was still in bed. She stood in the doorway for a while, studying the dark shape. Who was that lying there? And why didn't she care more about him? Something she didn't understand was at work inside her. She had figured it was self-preservation that had made her reject him emotionally. As an emergency measure. A red button. Now she was leaning toward it being something else. The feelings were there but couldn't get through. It was both eerie and pleasant.

Kiruna was on the floor in the middle of her room, propped on her elbows, looking at a picture book. Diana sat down in front of her and palpated her aching cheek. Then she lay down on her back.

'You're going to be with Grandma and Grandpa tomorrow.'

The little girl got up and when she stepped over her, Diana raised her hand to shield her tender face.

'I'm hungry.'

'I just need a quick lie-down. Give me one minute.'

Anders closed his eyes. Before, he had been sobbing uncontrollably, now he could only mime his crying. Erasmus looked at him. The light streaming in through the window set half his face alight. A glowing cascade of beard merging with a grey one. He was holding a dog lead, a plaited leather lead that he thumbed as though the interwoven straps were beads on a rosary. The tall, broad-shouldered man they called Näcken* was blocking the door. He was bald and had large, staring eyes with a cold, blue centre.

His ears were blocked; his own whimpering voice sounded like it was coming from another room. It was as though a frail, crying creature had been unleashed and was now speaking for him.

'How am I supposed to live, how am I supposed to bear having done something so horrible, something so incredibly horrible? I will never be able to forgive myself.'

'What you can't forget, you have to bury.'

'I can't. It's impossible.'

'I promise you it's possible.'

'I can't do it, I'm too tired.'

'You feel that way now. But in time, it will fade.'

---

* This nickname, which refers to a murderous water spirit from Nordic folklore, the Neck, is also derived from the character's surname.

'No,' he said, 'it'll never go away. I can't do it. I can't do it.'

'Anders. What is it you can't do?'

'Live with this.'

'So you want to die?'

Erasmus gave him a thoughtful look.

He said nothing. Strings of thick saliva hung from his mouth; he did nothing about it.

'That is the kind of thing,' Erasmus said and slapped the lead against the palm of his hand, 'you want to be one hundred per cent sure about. Because you can't change your mind afterwards.'

He nodded.

'So, how do you want it?'

Erasmus bent down slowly, very slowly. There was something shiny between the floorboards. It was a screw; after examining it, he placed it on the window bench like a very small ornament.

'You've developed a wonderful bond, you and Ransu. An unusually wonderful bond. Not all people are as open. So that is something valuable. Not to say enviable.'

'I don't understand why you're all cross with me.'

'Why would we be cross with you?'

'Because I did what I did.'

'Children,' the old man said, 'come and go. What will become of them? You never know what will become of them. But you, Anders, we know where you stand. We know what you're made of. You've proved it to us.'

The old man limped across the floor. A water tap was turned on. He returned with a glass and after giving it to Anders, he sat back down on the window bench.

'You can never go back to your old life.'

He nodded.

'In the world outside our village, what are you?'

'I don't know. A biologist, technically . . .'

'A murderer,' said Näcken.

Erasmus nodded agreement.

'A child murderer.'

Anders nodded.

'Out there.' The old man pointed. 'But not here. Not with us, no. We never have to talk about it again.'

'That guy Christer, her dad, he's never going to forgive me.'

'Never mind him,' said Näcken.

'Christer doesn't know what happened,' Erasmus said. 'He thinks the girl was dragged into the woods by the same creature that ate her. And there's no reason to tell him otherwise.'

'I thought everybody knew.'

'Everyone knows it was an accident. A tragic accident.'

Stava grabbed him the moment he stepped through the door. She wanted to know what her father had said and she had a nervous, intense look in her eyes he'd never seen before.

Anders sighed.

'We had a chat and I told them what I remember. But it's like a blank and I'm not lying about that. I didn't realise what I was doing until I saw her lying there in the woods and it wasn't clear even then. It was more like a feeling. The girl's father doesn't know who did it, and he won't find out either.'

'But what did he say about Ransu?'

'Nothing. It was an accident.'

Stava walked over to the window and looked out. First to

either side and then she put her forehead against the glass to try to see what was underneath the window.

'An accident.'

He nodded.

'Was she there?'

'Who?'

'The girl. The one with the eyepatch.'

He shook his head.

'Who is that?'

'Who is she? She's Dad's favourite. I'm probably going to have to call her Mother soon.'

'I actually feel better. After talking to him. He was very understanding. I was just doing what Ransu wanted, and he got that.'

'Of course he did.'

'I feel a lot better now.'

Seeing Susso's car parked outside her house was so unexpected that for a split second, Diana thought she'd returned. Having corrected her misperception, she felt a pang of sadness. She sat in the car looking at the house, the sun-drenched front with the mullioned old windows. The plastic table where they'd had their dinner. The little jetty and the dark band of the river. She had wondered if seeing the place would make her remember what had happened, but it didn't. And she was grateful for it. During her drive out to Vittangi, she had felt a mounting sense of unease, and now she was afraid in a way she hadn't been before. The engine was still running. She turned the car around, just like Susso had done when the sight of her own car had spooked her. But she didn't drive off. She let go of the wheel and chided herself through gritted teeth. Pulled out her phone and stared at the screen, trying to remember the music from that crestfallen, cold summer. 1998. When everything was over and there was nowhere to go. They had sat on the floor of the cabin in Kurravaara, singing at the top of their lungs. Drunk as skunks. Surrounded by melancholic music she hadn't listened to since.

When the forgotten, but oh so familiar notes of the acoustic guitar poured out of the speakers, transforming the car into a time machine, she put her thumb on the plus button on the wheel. She let it rest there. The music swelled and swelled.

The tin of snus she'd bought at the Esso petrol station in Varangerbotn was still in the cupholder. A white medallion that proved she really had been to Norway. Proof it had all really happened. This tobacco product may seriously harm you and is addictive. She twisted the lid off, fished out a bag, put it in her mouth, pushed it into place with her tongue, turned off the music and opened the door.

She wandered around the garden, keeping a close eye on the pine trees in particular. The wind set the branches swaying with slow, sweeping movements; she wondered if the squirrel was up there, watching. A little critter with black beads for eyes. It could be inside the house too. Gudrun had said it most likely had its own ways in and out so it could come and go as it pleased. It could be outside, it could be inside; you might as well predict where a swooping swallow would be at any given moment.

She really didn't want to have to enter the house. The thought of encountering the pint-sized creature in some unexpected place indoors scared her a lot more than the thought of spotting it in one of the pine trees.

The kitchen door was ajar. She stood stock-still, listening, while her eyes moved from the counter to the table and up toward the podium of the fridge where it had first revealed itself.

She carefully tapped her nails against the door jamb.

Did the squirrel have a name it answered to? It almost must have. Why hadn't Gudrun told her it? On the other hand, she didn't think she would have had it in her to call out to an ancient creature hiding inside a squirrel. The mere thought of shouting in the empty house filled her with unease.

She climbed the stairs and opened the door to a room with a sloped ceiling and walls covered in grey fibreglass cloth. There was a bed, which wasn't made, a small table and a wardrobe. A small black tapestry hung above the bed. 'Las Palmas de Gran Canaria'. The next room was just as bare. A bed, a couple of chairs. The same depressing fibreglass cloth. The ceiling light had an embroidered skirt; the canopy had slipped down the cord. The sheer curtains were closed.

She couldn't see any signs of the squirrel. What would a sign even look like, rat poop and half-eaten pine cones? What was weirder was that she couldn't find anything to suggest that Susso used either of the bedrooms as her own; the more she thought about that, the more the eerie feeling inside her intensified.

She peeked into a wardrobe. It contained a blouse and a shirt on hangers. A few jumpers on the shelf. In a wire bin lay a tangle of socks and three, four, five pairs of pants. She recognised the blouse. A peasant blouse of white crepe with three-quarter-length sleeves and gold embroidery on the yoke. In other words, it was over twenty years old.

So this was the room she slept in. But how was it possible to sleep in a room for so long without leaving your own stamp on it? She hadn't even bothered to remove the ugly tapestry hanging on the wall.

She continued down to the living room. It was posh. Upholstered hardwood armchairs turned toward a big black TV on a media bench with glass doors. Doilies. A few gold-framed oil painting reproductions, a cross-stitch sampler depicting a red cottage. Long curtains with enormous umbels.

She paused in the kitchen again. Looked down at the floor and started walking toward the door. Then she walked back and stared at the rug. It was a rag rug. She squatted down for a closer look. The knots on one side had been untied. Every last one. Was it supposed to look like that? She examined the knots on the other side of the rug. A complete row of tiny, white-haired Hottentots. She tried undoing one of the knots. It was tight. She dug her nails in and grimaced. She couldn't loosen it and felt immediately that her nails would yield before the knot did. Someone with strangely strong fingers and a lot of patience must have worked on the knots. Who would do such a thing? And why? And why on just one side, if you felt the need to do it in the first place?

She sat on the front porch, studying the trees while waving one hand about to keep the mosquitoes drawn to her at bay. She picked up her phone and stared at the jumble of icons overlaying Kiruna's face.

The urge to put her thumb on the local news app passed through her body like a shudder. Whether anyone had found a dead man on the Varanger Peninsula was something she both wanted and didn't want to know. She thought about what her dad had said, that she would be tainted by the incident, whether she had been involved or not. People would talk about what had really happened and draw their own conclusions and it would never be forgotten.

What had really happened. She didn't even know herself. Her fragmented recollections were floating out of reach, into a fog where everything seemed uncertain. Part of her wished the fog would persist, part of her didn't. She worried about what it would be like when it cleared.

She had no idea how long she'd been sitting there when she realised the trees were moving in a way they hadn't been before. A force that made their branches sway wildly was moving through the canopy along an unpredictable trajectory. She looked for the squirrel and soon spotted it. A reddish-brown streak. In mid-air, it turned into a hook that caught on a sprig of needles, setting it rocking.

It's here, she wrote to Gudrun. Then it struck her she might be mistaken. What if it was another squirrel, an ordinary one? It was certainly possible.

But that was wishful thinking. Of course it was that squirrel. The way it was going at it. When it sat still, she could only guess at its location, and it often turned out she had been off by quite a bit. It had a baffling ability of popping up where she least expected and after a while, she started wondering if it had tricked her into a weird game of hide-and-seek it might be risky to pull out of. It never seemed to tire of it; in the end, she walked over to the pine trees, which immediately stopped moving. She couldn't see the squirrel, but she knew it was watching her.

'You're coming with me!'

Talking to it felt unpleasant; maybe that's why she had sounded so brusque. She repeated her command, but in a gentler tone. Still fighting off the mosquitoes, she took a few steps to one side to try to catch a glimpse of the creature hiding up there.

'We're going to go get Susso.'

She figured Susso's name would serve as a watchword. But nothing happened. A gust of wind from the river hissed through the birch trees. The pine trees grew anxious; when shadows dappled their bark, a pattern of golden-red shards appeared on their trunks.

She walked down toward the water. The chairs they had carried out onto the jetty were still there. One of them had toppled over. She righted it and after a moment's hesitation, sat down on it. Having her back toward the house was unpleasant, but she forced herself to stay. A glass cylinder glinted in the gap between two of the jetty's wooden boards. A mosquito repellent stick. She picked it up, undid the cap and drew lines across her forehead and neck. Closed one eye tight against the sinking ball of the sun and gazed out across the river with the other.

She found boiled new potatoes in a plastic bag in the fridge, wrapped in blackish-green strings of dill that looked like wet hair. She sat down at the kitchen table and ate the potatoes straight out of the bag.

'I guess I have to stay then.'

'Can you?'

'Going home seems stupid.'

'Are you going home?'

She swallowed before replying.

'No, I said going home seems stupid.'

'Yes.'

After the conversation with Gudrun, she wrote to her mother that she wouldn't be back that night. The reply came in the form of a picture of Kiruna's face, closed in sleep. Her round cheek was sharply lit by the flash.

The reproach contained in the picture was not lost on her. When she dropped the little girl off earlier that day, her mother had looked at her like she was drunk. She was worried but knew she was unable to stop her. Now she was trying to call her home by reminding her who would suffer the most if something happened to her. She had told them nothing about the state Håkan was in; just said he was ill.

Diana looked at the picture for a long time and all of a sudden, she started to sob. Not because the picture triggered an avalanche of tender feelings, but because it didn't. She sat with her hand over her mouth, feeling nothing. Except the starch from the potatoes on her fingers.

It was almost midnight. She stepped out onto the front porch and looked at the pine trees standing motionless against a sky that was filling with clouds.

She hadn't brought a toothbrush, so she borrowed Susso's. She brushed with a pained look on her face and when she did the teeth on the left, she closed her eyes. Then she had a mental image of herself standing there, eyes squeezed shut, and her battered face was so detailed and clear she opened her eyes in surprise and stared at herself in the mirror. She had already seen the trickle of toothpaste running down her chin. She spat and put her mouth to the tap, rinsed her mouth out and spat again. After straightening up, she thought she saw a glimpse of something in the mirror. A shadow slinking about on the hat rack behind her. She stood stock-still with her eyes fixed on the mirror. Slowly reached out and turned off the tap.

She waited for a few seconds before putting her toothbrush down on the edge of the sink. Then she wiped her mouth and left the bathroom. She didn't turn around until she reached the stairs, but then she turned quickly. The hat rack. The clothes hanging underneath it. The shoes.

She pulled the chequered cotton curtains closed and crawled into the bed. The room was very bright; how Susso could stand it was beyond her. But maybe she tolerated the light for the same reason she didn't care what her bedroom looked like. She contemplated draping the bedspread over the window, but was too tired to get up.

She pushed her phone in under the mattress, plumped the pillow up under her cheek and felt the tranquil ticking of her pulse from inside the stuffing as she studied the texture of the wallpaper. What did Susso think about, lying here at night? Either a lot or very little. Probably very little. The idea of her lying there staring at the wall with an empty mind was so scary Diana immediately tried to turn her thoughts to something else.

She rolled over on her back and closed her eyes. Put an arm over her eyes to block out the light. What had really happened while she was brushing her teeth? She didn't want to think about that either, but was unable to escape the memory of it.

She stuck her hand in under the mattress to get her phone out. To distract herself for a while. Her fingers touched something cold. That wasn't her phone. She shifted to the side and folded the mattress up.

A gun. There was a gun under the mattress.

It was small and looked like an antique.

She stared at it but was afraid to touch it.

Then she flew into action, gathered up her clothes and grabbed them, along with the duvet and pillow, and stole down the stairs. She sprinted across the lawn, opened the door to her car and jumped in, pushed the back seat down, spread out the duvet and after lying down, folded it back over her.

Even on the diagonal, she wasn't able to stretch out fully, but she was still convinced she'd sleep better in the car. At a less than reassuring distance that was nevertheless a distance from the room Susso had filled with a dark, ominous energy Diana hadn't been fully aware of until she was removed from it.

When she woke up, it was four in the morning. Two minutes past four. The windows were fogged up; the car was filled with a grey light. She lay still, listening. Had a scratching against the metal woken her, or had that been a dream? Just then, she remembered something. A shrunken, wizened face cautiously approaching a condensation-covered windscreen, watching her with black, despondent eyes. The wrinkled face had been an unsettling shade of white. Like a foetus in a jar of formaldehyde. She figured it was something her overworked brain had dreamed up in the strange atmosphere inside the car, but she wasn't sure. She wasn't sure.

She got the car door open and stepped out with the duvet around her shoulders. There were no tracks in the film of dew beading the bonnet and the only thing moving in the pine trees were branches rocked by the wind. She snatched up her clothes, kicked the door closed, went into the house, lay down on the sofa and, against all odds, went back to sleep.

*

The percolator filled the kitchen with its bubbling; she was sitting at the table, staring at nothing. She was chilly and felt like she hadn't slept a wink. Her phone dinged. A message from her mum. K has had nightmares all night long. She's crying and asking for you. Can't reach H.

There was suddenly a knot in her stomach. She poured the coffee and sat with the mug in front of her for a while before making the call.

'How is she?'

'Hold on, I'll put her on.'

'Hi, Mummy.'

'Grandma says you had a bad dream?'

'Yes.'

'What was it, do you want to tell me?'

'No.'

'A lot of the time, you feel better if you tell someone. Because then you realise it wasn't so scary.'

'I don't want to.'

'Okay.'

'But I can tell you about another dream I had.'

'I'd like that.'

'It was like a nightmare too, but only a bit.'

'Okay.'

'It was about a turtle.'

'A turtle?'

'Mm. I found a turtle. But it was just the shell, it was empty, just like a little bowl. And when I showed it to Daddy, he said there was a turtle in it, but that it was hiding, really far in, because it was dying. And then he pulled it out and you could tell it was dying because its face was all mouldy.'

'Yuck.'

'And it smelled awful.'

'I hope Daddy threw it out.'

'I don't know. I woke up.'

'I had a bad dream too.'

'Mummy. Where are you?'

'At my friend Susso's. The one who's missing. Remember how I told you she's missing. And that I have to find her.'

'But when are you coming back?'

'Soon.'

'I want you to come back now.'

'Can I talk to Nana.'

The other end went quiet but before her mum could say anything, Diana had ended the call. She looked at the phone and noticed her thumb was trembling. Her heart rate was up because she knew she wasn't alone in the kitchen.

He was sitting on the threshold. Upright with his front paws pressed against his chest. His ears were pricked up like two long horns leaning against one another.

She waited and it seemed like the squirrel was doing the same. She put the phone down on the table.

'If you're wondering where Susso is, I can tell you,' she said.

The squirrel raised its nose as though it could divine the meaning of her words by sniffing them.

'She's in a village called Rumajärvi.'

The animal got down on all fours and stood that way for a bit before doing a one-eighty.

'I'm going up there to get her back.'

Now it was looking at her.

'And there's room in the car, if you want to come.'

She poured out her coffee and put the mug in the sink. She could feel the squirrel studying her the whole time. When she headed toward it on her way out of the kitchen, it slunk aside and quickly leapt up the stairs.

She put her shoes on and went outside, leaving the door open a crack behind her. She walked over to her car and waited; after a while, the squirrel came bounding toward her through the grass. She smiled at it then, but she didn't realise until she felt the pain in her cheek.

I had a message and when I picked up my phone from the kitchen table and saw it was from Diana, I became shamefully aware of how murky my wishes were. I was hoping it would say she hadn't found the squirrel but that she was going to stay a while and look for it.

When instead I read 'WE'RE OUTSIDE', my whole body went cold. I stared at the letters and desperately tried to interpret them to mean anything other than that she was outside my building and that the squirrel was with her. The radio was on; it was playing music that had suddenly become unbearable; after turning it off, I sat down to have a think.

We're outside. If she had had a cat, for instance, in the car with her, would she have referred to herself and the cat as a *we*? Hardly. The squirrel was already sinking its claws into her. But that was probably to be expected.

All the awful memories and corrosive guilt I had been sweeping under the rug for the past ten years washed over me; it was a while before I could muster enough strength to stand up and go outside.

One and only one car was parked outside the building, a grey Audi; when I looked at it, the door opened and Diana climbed out. She was wearing the baseball cap but no sunglasses. After watching her for a while, I crossed the street. I didn't say anything and eventually she smiled, as much as her cut lip allowed.

'Are you afraid of me?' she said.

I glanced at the car. My hand was clutching the shoulder strap of my handbag.

It came as a complete surprise to me when I walked away; it was as though my feet took charge of my body. When she called out after me, I started jogging back toward the front door, and I didn't dare to check if she was following until I had pulled it closed behind me. She wasn't; she was standing where I'd left her on the pavement, and she looked so much like Susso I froze in confusion for a few moments.

When I got back inside my flat, I locked the door. Then I sat down in the kitchen with my shoes and jacket still on. My heart was racing in my chest and I stared at my phone. I thought she would text me and nag, but she didn't and when I looked out through the balcony door, I realised the car was gone. I hadn't expected that and the relief I felt was difficult to disentangle. I hadn't managed to remove my outerwear; my heels clattered against the parquet floor as I paced around the living room, wondering what I should do. For a while, I stood on the balcony, looking out at the street. But she didn't come back.

In the end, I called Roland. I had told him what had happened to the police officers who had been dispatched to Rumajärvi, but I hadn't let him in on my and Diana's plan to go up there and now I needed to be told I'd been right not to go.

He did think I'd made the right decision.

'So you don't think I should go after her?'

'What can you possibly do, Gudrun?'

'I suppose I could talk to them.'

'All right, look, I'm going to say something to you, and it's just a hunch. Something I've been thinking. And you have to promise not to be cross with me.'

'Okay.'

'Have you considered that Susso may not be alive?'

'It's all I think about!'

'You have to ask yourself why they kidnapped her at all. If what they were after was, in fact, revenge. Either way, I don't think there's any point talking to these people.'

'So I'm just supposed to sit here?'

'If what you're saying, and what Harr and Nänne are affirming as well, is true, that this squirrel has special powers or whatever you want to call it, then maybe Diana can do what the police couldn't. So we'll have to see how she does. Or they do, rather.'

Diana sat with her hand around a can of fizzy drink in the shade under a parasol, watching the cars in the car park. One of them had Norwegian plates, so she disliked it. Like she had disliked the Norwegian girl at the till who had asked if she wanted the receipt when she paid for her petrol. She was aware it was a symptom of some kind of paranoia, but that changed nothing. She couldn't fully escape the feeling everyone up here knew who she was and where she was going.

She hadn't touched her burger and couldn't understand why she'd bought it. Her stomach seemed to have shrivelled into a pointless appendix. She gave the meat patty's rough surface an indifferent look. The napkin stuck under the plate, moving limply in the breeze. There was a couple speaking Dutch behind her. A cryptic conversation. The soft voices, the familiar but impenetrable words, the harsh *ch* sounds. She was pretty sure they were talking about the squirrel.

It had dashed about the outdoor seating area for a while, but now it was perched, motionless, on the backrest of the bench across from her. The greyish-red tufts of hair on its tail were so sparse the skin they grew from was clearly visible. The claws on its bony feet were long and curved like suture needles and just as sharp; she had felt them.

She picked up a portion of snus and pushed it in under her

lip and just as she did, she was ambushed from the flank. It was the woman from the till. She tried to shoo the squirrel away with a towel, all the while yelling at it in a chattering language that might have been Filipino. The squirrel didn't so much as flinch. It just sat there with its back arched, watching the woman. Who abruptly changed tack. She stopped waving her towel about and then backed up a few paces. She looked worn-out and depressed. Her brown cheeks pocked with acne scars. When Diana looked at her, she gestured toward the squirrel and said something. Then she retreated back inside. Since it seemed likely she would return with backup, Diana grabbed her tin of snus and can of fizzy drink and got to her feet. The Dutch couple were poring over a map and didn't look up when she passed.

The road down to Rumajärvi consisted mostly of straights that were so long they disappeared like needles in the distance. There were no houses. No signs, no poles. Just the cracked and scarred strip of pitch and gravel, running mile after mile through the monotonous spruce forest.

She drove through Paittasjärvi and soon thereafter saw the sign for Rumajärvi. Someone had vandalised the sign, written something on it in Finnish. She rolled down a small gravel road. The squirrel must have realised they were close, because it was suddenly on the dashboard. Its tail was twitching.

She reached a boom barrier and sat staring at it for a while before climbing out of the car. A padlock lay discarded in the gravel, a shiny, silver code lock. The shackle had been cut. After establishing that there was a new lock on the barrier, she picked up the old one. She absent-mindedly rotated the numbered discs while she mulled things over. Then she got back in the car and reversed up to the main road. The squirrel immediately jumped down and sat staring out the rear window; it always wanted to see where they were going. She parked next to the road and let the squirrel out; it disappeared in an instant; it was like releasing a bird. She walked back and when she reached the boom barrier, she turned off into the woods.

It was hot. She grabbed the vizor of her baseball cap and rubbed the cap against her forehead. The forest was dead silent in the heat as she crept along between the motionless spruce branches.

Before long, the dark mirror of a lake appeared among the trees, the *järvi* in Rumajärvi, and after walking a bit further, she could make out houses too. A shed down by the shore and further up, the tin roof of a house. She sank into a squat and scanned the area for people. She buried her face in her hands and the air rushing out of her nostrils with each breath felt hot against her skin. She stayed in that position until the squirrel started making a racket above her head. When she looked up, it had jumped down into the underbrush, where it rolled about, emitting squeaking sounds. On closer inspection, however, it turned out it wasn't the squirrel squeaking, but rather a swollen little lemming with dappled yellow-and-brown fur. The two animals circled each other in some kind of hostile dance that ended with the lemming disappearing like a ball among the ferns.

Diana picked the squirrel up, placed it in her kangaroo pocket and walked down toward the village. A rusty old banger was parked on the grass in front of an older house, a white Nissan Sunny, and she could see someone hiding behind it. Diana said hello, but the girl neither replied nor came out, so she walked around the car. She had seen that little face before. The mongoloid slits of her eyes, her flat nose, her thin upper lip. A textbook example of foetal alcohol syndrome. The girl had a grimy, hot-pink winter coat on over a floral-print dress and was holding the handlebar of an old-fashioned doll's pram with its canopy up.

'What's your name then?'

'Sästin.'

Diana was about to ask her the name of her doll but changed her mind after peeking in under the canopy. A squirrel was tucked in under the blanket. Both its eyes had popped out and were dangling on threads, one was a lingonberry, the other a wrinkled blueberry, and an ugly tooth glinted inside the contorted mouth.

The door to the house opened to reveal an elderly woman watching her with a severe expression.

Diana had forgotten why she was there and had to think about it for a second.

'I'm looking for a person who's supposed to be here.'

The woman waved over the child, who immediately ran in under her arm. Then she came outside. Diana followed her and was shown to a house surrounded by tarpaulins.

'She's my age,' she said, but the woman just stared at her and then left.

Sitting outside the house were two men. One was an old man with a hat and a long grey beard; she knew that was Erasmus. The man sitting next to him looked like a criminal. He was topless and had gold chains around his neck. He was holding a knife, some kind of samurai knife, which he was testing with his ring-bedecked fingers.

They watched her in silence.

'I'm looking for someone.'

'Are you from the police?'

'Is she here?'

'Who?'

'Susso.'

The old man was sitting with one leg folded over the other, bobbing his shoe up and down.

'Who's that in your pocket?' he said.

When she didn't reply, he grinned at her and then started singing: 'I have seen you, little mouse, running all about the house.'

'I'm taking her with me.'

The man with all the bling grinned languidly.

'What has done?' he said. 'Has been naughty?'

Erasmus muttered something to the man in Finnish that made him get up and shuffle into the house. Not long after, a young woman came out. She wore a cloth Alice band in her blonde hair and looked completely normal, as far as Diana could make out.

'Where is she?'

The old man watched her in silence. Then he stood up and walked toward her. He had a limp. She took a step back and when he came closer still, she took another.

While he studied her face, his tongue popped out to moisten his lips, which were unnaturally hard and dark. Suddenly, his hand shot out. Diana turned aside, shielding her pocket, because she thought he was after the squirrel. But he wasn't. He pinched her breast through her sweater and he pinched hard. She leapt back. Stared at him and then at the young woman.

'Has anyone suckled these?' he asked.

She was dumbfounded.

'Do you have children?' the woman said.

Diana barely heard the question. She was looking at the window. The man with the gold chains was moving around behind the glass and in front of him on the windowsill was a row of dolls of various heights. Some had hats on, some didn't. They looked like something that might have crawled out of a box of Christmas decorations cursed by an evil sorcerer. Because they were not still like dolls. One of them had even placed its claw-fingered little rat hands against the glass; its cheerful face was twisted by a horrifying craniofacial deformity.

'Yes,' she said quietly, 'I have children.'

'A girl,' the woman said. 'It's a girl, isn't it?'

She nodded against her will.

'How old,' the man whispered, but not to Diana.

'How old is she?'

'Four.'

'And what's her name,' the old man said.

'Kiruna,' she heard herself say.

'Kiruna,' he said, nodding slowly. 'And you live in the town of that same name then, I imagine.'

She nodded.

'At what address?'

'What?'

'What's your address?' the woman said.

'It's Duvvägen. Number fourteen.'

'If you ever come here again, we will come find you at Duvvägen fourteen and take your little girl.'

'Maybe I'll make her my maid,' the old man said, 'maybe I'll let other people use her and then maybe we'll drown her in the lake over there when we're tired of her. Who knows? No one knows.'

'But you can be sure you'll never see her again,' added the woman, who had taken a step closer. Birthmarks freckled her face and she had a sharply defined Cupid's bow. 'And if you do see her again, it will be on a stainless steel table after her body's found in a public bathroom someplace, made up like a junkie whore and with her adorable little panties stuffed so far down her throat they have to pull them out with forceps.'

Diana put a hand on her stomach. The squirrel was nothing but a hard, lifeless lump in her pocket. The old man brought his hands together in front of his chest and lowered his lips to his slender fingertips in a thoughtful gesture.

'Forget your friend,' he said.

He stroked her breasts.

'She's fine here. In fact, I'd go so far as to say she's happy.' He turned to the woman for agreement and she nodded.

'In all events, she certainly will be,' she said. 'In time. She fits in here. But you don't.'

The old man shook his head.

'Leave now, and never come back.'

Diana nodded and then she walked out unsteadily through the opening between the tarpaulins. She was breathing through her mouth, looking down at the grass and her shoes.

*

She walked and ran by turns until she reached the boom barrier, where she fell to the ground, panting heavily. Then she jumped back up. The squirrel had rolled into a ball in her pocket and when she slapped it, it curled up tighter. She put her hand in to try to grab it, but it squirmed and clawed at her. That made her rip off her sweater and hurl it away. It lay by the side of the road, like any old discarded sweater. Until it came alive. The animal moved weirdly slowly. Its nose poked out, then its head. The tufted ears. It stayed like that for a while, scanning the surroundings. Then it took two long leaps and ran up a pine tree and out onto a branch, setting it swaying.

Diana dug out her phone. It suddenly occurred to her she should warn her parents. Ask them to hide Kiruna somewhere. Her fingers were shaking. Kiruna's face behind the large digits of the clock. A row of pearl sugar for teeth. Her funny protruding ears.

At that point, she heard footsteps behind her. She turned around and peered into the forest. Was she imagining it? Moments later, she saw someone approaching through the trees. A strange woman with black hair down to her waist. She wore nothing but a knit jumper and knickers and was very thin, her legs skinny and muscular like an African long-distance runner.

'I'm leaving. I just needed a minute.'

'It's your sister, isn't it?'

Diana said nothing.

'You've come for your sister.'

'No,' she said and shook her head.

For a while, neither of them spoke.

'She's not my sister.'

'No?'

She shook her head.

'You look very alike. At first, I thought you were her.'

'She's not my sister.'

'I'm going to help you.'

Diana looked away.

'You're afraid.'

'Yes, I am. They said they were going to take my daughter if I don't get out of here. Murder her, actually.'

'They wanted to scare you.'

'And they succeeded.'

'I'm going to help you.'

'I don't want any help. I'm going home.'

'Do you know what they do to your friend? At night?'

Diana stared at her. The eyes in the emaciated face were placed unnaturally far apart and were curiously dark.

'How did you even get here?'

'Car. It's parked up there.'

'Go wait in your car.'

Diana continued up the gravel road and got into her car. Why aren't you getting out of here? she thought to herself. She tapped the key against her thigh. Do you know what they do to your friend at night? That could only mean one thing and when she imagined it, it was as though something fell apart inside her chest. Everything in there just collapsed.

She thought about Kiruna and she thought about Susso and during this struggle a memory surfaced from out of nowhere. They're at Pizzeria Laguna. Cold and pleasantly hungover, they sit down at a table. A man strides over to them, offering cutlery, rolled up in napkins. That are more yellow than white. Then he brings them plates, big, poop-brown plates, laden with pineapple and sweetcorn. There is something touching about the expectant look on the man's face and his impeccable manners and she has to fight to suppress a smile. When she realises Susso's struggling too, she starts giggling and within moments they both burst out laughing, while the poor waiter withdraws like a sad clown. They had laughed hysterically, like when they destroyed the school yearbook. It had been insuppressible and in the end, they had picked up their jackets and fled the restaurant.

A scratching on the roof brought her back. The squirrel appeared, sliding down the windscreen on all fours. When it reached the wipers, it whipped around and looked at her.

She opened the door. The squirrel slunk into the car and raced up on her backrest. She reached for the snus tin and after putting a portion under her lip, she held the tin out to the squirrel, who shied away, whether because of the gesture or the sharp, unfamiliar smell.

Just over an hour later, the woman came walking down the road. Not one car had driven by in that time. Diana opened the door and climbed out.

'I wasn't able to. I told her you were here and that I would help her leave, but she didn't want to come.'

'What do you mean she didn't want to?'

'She's awake yet not awake.'

'Then I suppose I'll have to carry her,' she heard herself say.

The woman bent down and scratched her lower calf hard. The brown, deformed nails sticking out of her toes were curved like claws.

'My God,' Diana exclaimed, 'your feet.'

'Could you do that? Could you carry her?'

'I guess we'll find out.'

'I can fire a gun. I can fire a gun from the other side of the lake. Everyone's going to wonder who's shooting. Then you can go into the house and get her.'

She followed the woman, who ran ahead of her between the spruce trees with her black hair billowing across her back like a hunted hulder. She was bafflingly fast; Diana wanted to call out to her to slow down, but was afraid to raise her voice.

Suddenly, the woman was squatting on top of a big, moss-covered boulder; there was no way of telling how she had got up there. She was pointing to a house that could be glimpsed through the trees.

'She's in there, in that house there, and she's alone. She's in the bedroom, upstairs. I'll open a window and you'll climb in through that window and then you'll go out the same way and hurry out of here.'

After she disappeared around a tarred log storage shed, Diana ran to the edge of the wood at a crouch and settled down behind a fallen tree, peeking out at the house like a child playing hide-and-seek. The squirrel darted up and down the fallen trunk. Diana kept her eyes on the house while swatting at the mosquitoes that swooped at her face in silent attack waves.

A bang and then another bang. The sound seemed to be coming from the top of a tree-covered hillock rising beyond the eastern shore of the lake; it had to be the better part of a mile away as the crow flies and at least three times that on foot. Could she really have run that far, or had the sound ricocheted? After the echo faded, a mighty silence enveloped the landscape.

Then there were voices. Someone was calling and someone else responding. Rough voices blended with shrill ones. An engine sputtered to life and moments later, a quad bike roared by between the houses, soon followed by a fiery dirt bike. A pack of wolves, three, four, five of them. A man running on stiff legs.

She watched this odd hunt pass and then stood up and raced toward the house. She ran so fast she had to catch herself with both hands when she reached the wall. She was standing in a flowerbed full of stinging nettles, pushing her fingers into the crack between the sash and the frame of a casement window; after prying the window open, she heaved herself up and crawled in over the sill, under a bobbin-lace café curtain. A parlour with wainscoting and painted wooden floor. A sofa and a removals box. A tall cabinet with open doors and emptied shelves. She leaned out through the window. The squirrel was sitting underneath it, looking up at her. She backed up two steps and it came flying in through the window.

She ran up the stairs, two steps at a time, opened a door that was standing ajar and then a closed door. A dark room. She sank to her knees by the bed.

'Susso,' she hissed. 'Wake up!'

Susso turned her head. A white patch covered one of her eyes and the other stared at her in terror.

'It's me. It's Dana.'

She peeked in under the duvet to see if she was dressed, and she was. But she showed no sign of recognising her. Diana stroked her hair, which smelled of shampoo. Her touch made Susso pull her head in under the covers. Diana dug around for her hands, but they proved impossible to catch.

At the sound of an engine outside, she walked over to the window and peered out through a gap between the blankets hung up as makeshift blackout curtains. A man in a pile jacket lumbered by with a rifle in his hand.

She waved the squirrel over, picked it up off the floor and brought it to the bed as though she were a healer and the animal a miracle crystal. She had no idea what it might do; she had probably figured it would jump down and connect with Susso somehow, but it didn't. Judging from the way it was digging its razor-sharp claws into Diana's skin, it wanted to stay with her. When she tried to shake it off, it dashed up to sit on her shoulder.

'You know what. I'm going to leave you here unless you help her.'

Its tail brushed against her cheek when the animal turned around.

'Dana,' Susso whispered.

'Yes. I'm here. Here I am, sweetie.'

'I can't see.'

'You have a patch over your eye.'

'I'm pathetically blind.'

Susso shuffled out of her dark chamber like a ghost out of a crypt; she even waved a hand about in a vain attempt to shield herself from the sunlight. Baggy sweatpants and a T-shirt in an enormous men's size. A bruise like half a moustache on her top lip. Diana took her by the hand and led her downstairs.

'We have to climb out this window. Here. We're going this way.'

She ripped down the curtain and helped Susso climb up. She was straddling the windowsill, looking down at the ground.

'There's stinging nettles.'

'Jump!'

'I'm barefoot.'

'You have to jump.'

Diana more or less shoved her out the window and then stepped both feet up on the sill and jumped after her.

They ran up toward the trees, with the squirrel bounding ahead. Susso was struggling. She staggered and fell; several times, Diana had to pull on her to make her get back up.

They had passed the boom barrier when they heard the motorcycle behind them like an ominous cornet. Diana turned around and jogged backward a few steps; after establishing that the sound of the engine was unambiguously coming their way, she shouted at Susso to go faster.

They made it out onto the main road, but not all the way back to the car.

It was him, the man with the gold chains. He overtook them, slammed on the brakes, turned in behind the car and stopped. His dirt-stained bike growled, its mudguard trembling.

Diana had stopped. Her eyes searched for the squirrel. She had glimpsed it moments before, but it was nowhere to be seen now. Susso limped up behind her.

The man's sweaty face had twisted into a grin. It was as though he was already enjoying the sadistic violence he was going to inflict on them. He tilted the motorcycle to lay it down on its side. But he never got off it.

He was looking at them, his gilded fists still around the handlebars, but there was no longer a grin on his face. After a while, he looked down at the ground. Then he suddenly turned his bike around and drove off. But not back toward the village; he went north. He leaned forward and went full throttle and his jacket inflated in the wind.

Susso was standing by the side of the road, rubbing her forehead; when Diana walked up to her, she waved her arms about angrily as if to ward off an attack by something she couldn't see.

'We're going home.'

'No! No!'

She stroked her back.

'Come on.'

After getting her into the seat, she slammed the door shut, ran around the car, jumped in and seized Susso, who was on her way out. She put her hand flat against her cheek and turned her head to face her.

'What's with you? We're going home now.'

'I don't want to.'

'What don't you want?'

She couldn't answer that question. She looked around in confusion and her fingers strayed to the patch covering her eye.

'Don't touch that,' Diana said and started the engine.

The route home via Karesuando was shorter, but following the motorcycle didn't sit right with her, so she made a U-turn and drove south, toward Pajala.

'Where is he?'

'Who?'

The squirrel who had been hiding in some unknown nook bounced up on the dashboard in response to the question. When Susso tried to pick it up, it moved out of reach and settled down to gaze out at the landscape rushing past. Then she cupped her hand under her chin and spat into it. She spat several times and then held her hand out and waited. Eventually, the squirrel went over to it. It placed its odd little fingers on her thumb and sniffed the white foam. When it was all gone, she topped it up with new saliva.

'He likes spit,' she said quietly.

Diana stared at the road and heard Susso whispering.

'Yes, it's tasty. Yes, so tasty.'

I was watching TV when Diana called, something political. I took my time picking the phone up off the coffee table and then even longer to answer it and when I did, I knew I sounded anxious. My ear filled with the sound of fast driving.

'We're on our way home,' she said.

'You are?' I said. What I actually wanted to know was who she meant by *we* and in the next moment, I found out: she was going to drive Susso to the hospital. That made me both relieved and concerned.

'What happened to her?'

'I don't think it's too bad, but I want her admitted. She's running a temperature and is dehydrated and I think she's been beaten up pretty badly. So I'm taking her over there, better safe than sorry.'

Roland had been sitting in the kitchen with a beer in his hand, reading about everything that had happened and was going to happen in the World Cup on his laptop; now he was standing in the doorway, holding his glasses, looking at me.

'They're on their way home,' I said and put the phone down on the table. 'They're going to the hospital but it's nothing serious.'

'So it's good news.'

'But it never ends. This is never going to end. Until it really ends. For real. Like this.' I picked up the remote and turned the TV off, cutting someone off mid-sentence.

'One thing at a time,' Roland said. He had walked over to the window and was peering out at the street. 'She's home now and that's cause for cheer.'

'Cheer?'

'Maybe things will get better now.'

'Or they could get worse.'

He stood with his hands in his shorts pockets. His skinny little legs were deathly white and only marginally hairier than mine.

'We have to hope for the best.'

'Sure, great idea.'

'Gudrun.'

'I'm so sick of it all,' I sobbed. 'Please understand that. I can't take much more. I can't take it.'

'But she's bringing Susso back. That means they let her go.'

'It means nothing. They always claim back what they give, and change their minds whenever they please, without warning, just like that. And even if it's true, if they leave her alone from now on, and that's the end of it. Who is it I'm getting back? It's certainly not Susso.'

'Don't say that.'

'A child that disappears never comes back.'

'Was he there?'

'Who?!'

'There's no need to snap at me.'

'Who do you mean?'

'The cult leader.'

'I don't know, she didn't say.'

He came over and sat next to me on the sofa.

'When are they getting back?'

'I don't know.'

'Then we'll have to head over to the hospital and wait. They do have a café.'

'I don't want to.'

'Sure you do.'

When we left for the hospital, I was so nervous I forgot both my handbag and my phone in the flat and after going back up, I had trouble remembering what it was I was supposed to fetch; I drew a complete blank and I stood there in the hallway, head empty, for several long seconds before I managed to corral my thoughts.

We parked outside the main entrance and I called Diana because I wasn't clear on whether they were going to the A&E entrance or somewhere else. It turned out they were already there. Diana met us in the lobby. Her shirt was dirty and her face shiny with perspiration.

'They're examining her,' she said. 'One of her eyes is damaged. Beyond repair.'

'Beyond repair?'

She nodded.

'I have to go get Kiruna,' she said and left at such a high pace she had to pull up short at the sliding doors.

The cafeteria was deserted apart from an old man sitting on a chair in the middle of the room, talking loudly and unabashedly into his mobile phone. Roland and I sat next to each other on a bench in silence.

Half an hour later, I was allowed to go in and see her. She

was asleep. At first, I thought they had shown me into the wrong room because I found it hard to believe it was her in the bed. A quarter of her face was hidden under a compress and she had a big bruise on her lip.

I quietly sat down on a chair in a corner of the room and it was a long time before I dared to look at her again. When I did, she was staring at me with her one eye. It made me flinch.

She didn't say anything, just lay there, studying me, her eye filled with a cryptic darkness, exactly the way she had done lying on my chest thirty-five years ago. In the same hospital.

Then it struck me she was practically blind without her contacts and that she might not be able to make out who I was. So I stood up and went over to her.

Her head shifted slightly on the pillow, but she didn't look away. Not wanting to spook her, I reached out very slowly before I started stroking her hair.

'It's Mum,' I said.

'You haven't changed.'

'I haven't?'

She nodded solemnly.

'I wish I could say the same.'

'You can.'

'You haven't changed,' I said and received a wan smile in return.

Every once in a while, Anders was somewhere else. He slipped inside himself and was enveloped by memories in constant flux. The cast of the life he had left behind swirled around him and the feelings they evoked obscured everything else. Words reached him as though from a different room and what he saw with his eyes was blurred and irrelevant. This lasted no more than a few moments at a time; sometimes it was just a flash, but each recurrence was horrifying.

Outside the window was the drawn-out, paralysing light and the massive silence that exerted a constant pressure on his ears. She alone could grant him relief, such as it was. With her fingertips, she could caress away the remorse twisting his features and for that reason, he stayed close to her at all times. It made him ridiculous to the others and that was likely why they were now standing outside the door, giggling.

They had been out there for a long time. It might be five in the morning, it might be four, maybe it wasn't even three; it was impossible to tell.

If they had come to fetch something from the house, whatever it may be, they should have left long ago. He didn't know who they were, but he thought he'd heard Näcken's voice.

He had pushed at Stava, but she didn't wake up and he didn't dare speak, not even softly, because then they would know they were awake, which might be interpreted as an invitation.

It was Näcken and two young men whose names he didn't know; one of them couldn't be much older than William. They forced them out of bed and ogled them while they got dressed.

They walked toward the tarpaulins, to a garage with wide-open doors. Erasmus was standing inside and the man standing next to him was Christer, the little girl's father. He was barrel-shaped and the nipples on the fleshy folds of his chest protruded through his vest top. His beard was plaited into a long finger like the beard of some Ancient Egyptian king.

Anders didn't want to enter the garage, so he was pushed inside and then he stood there next to Stava, looking at the wolf lying on the filthy concrete floor.

They had wrapped a blue nylon rope around its long muzzle and tied its paws together, the front and back separately. The animal sluggishly raised its head and looked at him, the same way it had looked at him when it had been under a spruce tree in a different time.

Erasmus spoke quietly in Finnish to a young man, who nodded and nodded and then strode off, leapt onto a quad bike and roared away.

'If you want to,' Erasmus said, 'you can remove the rope.'

Stava fell to her knees and stroked Ransu's chest, which was moving slowly up and down. She untied the knot and pulled the rope off. His maw instantly opened in what looked like a yawn.

It was not until Christer raised his arm that Anders realised he was holding a hammer, a claw hammer with a polymer grip.

The blow landed awkwardly because Stava was in the way. The avenging father shoved her aside and bent down and struck the animal's temple and then struck it again. When Stava tried to stop him, Näcken took a step forward, grabbed hold of her hair and pulled her backward.

The hammer was raised again; Anders turned away. Näcken was watching open-mouthed; sitting in his cupped hand was a bizarre, hairless creature about the size of a rat, hideously pale and with sensitive bat ears that seemed to be opening toward the unpleasant noises caused by the hammer hitting the skull, which disintegrated a little more with each blow.

When Christer was done, he put the hammer down on the workbench. His breaths were sharp and short, his hand red like a barn painter's and his vest top speckled. The pale creature sitting in Näcken's hand stared at the growing pool of blood slowly winding its way toward the drain with eyes as black as screw holes.

'Anders,' Erasmus said. 'You need to prove that I can still trust you.'

'What do you want me to do?'

The old man made an inviting gesture toward the workbench and the hammer on it.

'Please, Daddy,' Stava said.

Erasmus put a finger to his lips, hushing her.

Anders went up behind Stava and weighed the hammer in his hand. He aimed like he would with a nail; a strand of her long black hair stuck to the gory head of the hammer when he pulled his arm back to strike.

Her dad was fiddling with something in the back seat of the car; when Diana pulled into the driveway, he quickly looked up. Seeing it was her, he leaned back in and finished unbuckling the little girl from the car seat.

Kiruna ran up to her and threw herself in her arms. Diana recognised her immaculate plaits from old pictures of herself and without checking, she knew her little nails were both clean and meticulously cut.

'We were going to head out to the cabin,' he said and just then, her mother came through the front door with a cooler in one hand and the house keys in the other.

'You're back?' she said.

Diana stroked the little girl's hair and out of the corner of her eye caught her mother shooting her father an anxiously confused look, as though seeking verification that this was in fact their daughter standing in front of them and not some imposter. Then she walked over for a closer look. She put a cold hand on her unbruised cheek.

'What are you doing?'

'What do you mean?'

'You and Susso.'

She put Kiruna down on the ground.

'Susso's back. I got her back.'

'You weren't supposed to. Dad told you to leave it to the police.'

'But the police didn't do anything. Go play with Grandpa. They didn't do anything. Because they couldn't.'

'But you could?'

'Yes, evidently, since Susso's back now.'

'You can't be doing things like this, Diana, you have to think about Kiruna. What if something had happened to you? I can't understand how you can put yourself at that kind of risk, especially after what you've just been through.'

'No, I know you can't understand it.'

'Then why do you?'

'Because she's my friend.'

Her mum snorted derisively.

'That's why you don't understand. Because you don't have any friends.'

'I don't?'

'Anna-Lena and Dad. And they don't count. You've never had any real friends.'

'How would you know?'

'If you had, I would have known.'

'So that's what this is about? Friendship? You and Susso haven't been close in twenty years. Or at least fifteen.'

'You've always been really awful to Susso.'

'No, we haven't.'

'Yes, you have.'

'Either way, I don't think this is about her.'

'Oh really, what is it about then?'

'I don't know. That's what I don't understand. That side of you.'

'What side?'

'This side,' she said, tapping her cheek with her fingertips. 'It's like you want to hurt yourself. It was the same back then. When you cut class and messed around.'

'I was thrown in the boot of my own car and beaten up, I can assure you I didn't go looking for any of that.'

'But the situation, Diana, why would you end up in that situation? You have a good life, you are good together, you and Håkan, really good, and then one day you drive out to see Susso, who you haven't talked to in years, and all of a sudden, this happens.'

'It's not her fault.'

'Why is there a squirrel in your car?'

Diana turned around. The animal was scampering back and forth on the dashboard, tail bobbing.

'It's Susso's squirrel. She keeps it as a pet.'

'That girl's not well!'

She strode off toward the back of the house and her mother followed.

'I don't know what she's involved in, what kind of people she's entangled with, that cult and the website and all of that, but you have to be careful. You have to stay away from her. Can't you see that?'

Kent Sillfors was rocking his grandchild in a hammock tied between two birch trees; when Diana walked over and picked her up, he withdrew, looking dejected.

It didn't occur to her that letting the girl near the squirrel might be problematic until she was already unlocking the car door. She saw the reflection of the little girl in her arms in the window, the way she pressed herself to a person who had a distinct hint of desperation in her eyes. Glistening with sweat and exhausted, with her battered face shaded by a baseball cap like a woman in the witness protection programme on the run from some monstrous man. She could hear her parents arguing behind the house. Her mother's shrill voice, her father's rumbling one. That made her open the door. She buckled the little girl into the car seat.

'Don't worry,' she said, 'it's just a squirrel.'

She explained to the little girl that it was Susso's squirrel and that it was going to be staying in their garage while she was in the hospital and she had to promise not to tell Daddy, and the little girl nodded, electrified by the idea of keeping a secret. They crept through the laundry room whispering to each other and then carried on whispering in the kitchen.

'Wait here while I check on Daddy.'

She went upstairs. The door to their bedroom was ajar. The blinds were down and he was in bed with his work computer on his stomach. When he spotted her, he closed it and sat up. His smoothed-out face shone palely and little blemishes had broken out around the follicles on his Adam's apple. A naked hip bone was peeking out from under the covers.

'How are you feeling?'

'Where have you been?'

'Kiruna's been with Mum and Dad. And me, I went to get Susso. As I wrote on the note in the kitchen.'

'Get her from where?'

'I'll tell you about it later.'

She sat down on the edge of the bed.

'But either way, she's back now.'

'In Vittangi?'

'No, she's in the hospital. Have you had anything to eat?'

He stared at her uncomprehendingly.

'Nutrition. Have you had any nutrition lately? Because you look like it's been a while. Clinically, I would guess about three months.'

She reached over to the nightstand and picked up the jars sitting on it. After reading their labels, she held one up to him with her eyebrows raised.

'Are you out of your mind?'

'I've just had a hard time falling asleep.'

She shook the jar like a rattle.

He gritted his teeth in silence.

'I don't understand what's with you.'

'Just leave me alone.'

'Look at me. I'm home. Everything went well.'

'Yes.'

'It went well, Håkan.'

He nodded and she found his hand and squeezed it. It was warm and damp and she held it until he slowly pulled it away. He crossed his arms and stared at the wall, so she got up. She studied him for a minute. Then she gathered up the jars and left the room.

She poured yoghurt into a bowl she had placed on the table in front of the little girl.

'And we have to leave it alone. So you can't go in there. You can't go in and look at it.'

'Should we give it pine cones?'

'You think so?'

'Pine cones and squash.'

'Eat your food.'

'But I'm not hungry.'

'Did you already eat? What time is it anyway? All right. So what would you like to do, would you like to watch TV?'

The little girl said nothing; she was staring at the stairs. Diana turned around and saw him coming down the steps with one hand on the banister. His penis, dangling between his legs, was brown, as though it had been transplanted from a person with different pigmentation.

He shuffled across the kitchen floor like a somnambulist. When Diana realised he was heading for her, she straightened up and took a step back and several seconds ticked by before she raised her arms and hugged him back.

Lennart drove across the long bridge on a morning when the clouds were so low the top of the mountain looming up on the other side of the sound looked completely flat. The road stretched into a blurred haze and the silhouettes of rocky skerries out at sea glided in and out of view like dark trawlers.

Grete's house slowly appeared in solitary magnificence far out on a plain. It was an old house with pointy gables. The octagonal addition on one side of it looked like a small chapel. At the top of the tar-papered roof lantern was a spire of at least three feet. Stands of hogweed grew in the garden and if you focused on them, the house seemed to shrink to fairy-tale size.

He parked behind the motorhome, opened the door and dragged himself out. Swaths of raw moisture in the air. A tractor with a front bucket. An old Mercedes hidden under a tarpaulin partly blown off by the wind.

Frode was standing on the porch. Jaundiced and unshaven, with his hands deep in the pockets of his raincoat. His hair had retreated into a funny little tuft of wool on his forehead. The old hare was crouching by his feet, staring at the invisible world with the frozen whites of its eyes.

When Lennart approached, Frode stepped off the porch and strode off toward the garage without a word.

She was waiting in the hallway. Her withered little-girl's

hands rested on the armrests of her wheelchair; the one concealed inside a glove was distractedly fiddling with something that didn't exist.

'Did you bring her?'

'Who?'

'Uksakka.'

He shook his head.

'Did you see her?'

'I don't know. They all look the same to me.'

She wheeled herself into the dining room and he followed; the hare brought up the rear. There was a damask sofa with curved legs by the wall; he sat down on it. The old lady held her sunglasses in her hand and looked at him.

'Where is everybody?' he said and pushed the hare, who was huddling against his leg as if for warmth, away.

'Ingvill's gone. One morning, she was just gone. And I've waited for Abraham for a week now. I don't think he's coming. But I didn't think you were either. To be honest.'

'What about Fanny, and the little boy? Weren't they going to come live here with you? Wasn't that the deal?'

'It didn't turn out that way.'

'So where are they?'

'I don't know. When I found out Erasmus had taken the thurse, I gave up. I just wanted to go home. So I left them.'

Lennart looked around the room. A long dining table of oiled oak. An enormous crystal chandelier. Oil paintings of animals and people in old-timey clothing. A mountain ridge could be seen through the window.

'Skabram's dead.'

'Of course.'

'They'd left him to rot in the woods. Like a piece of fucking offal.'

'What did you expect?'

'I actually thought he'd be alive. Since he wanted me to go there. But it must have just been to torture me. To humiliate me. I heard them talking about that Myrén woman like some kind of hero. Bear killer, they called her. *Karhuntappaja*.'

'How did they find out he was in the bunker, do you know?'

'I would have thought it was her? Ingvill. Since she's disappeared.'

'I can't deny the thought has crossed my mind.' She smiled. 'All these years, I was sure she thought she was mine.'

'You see what you want to see.'

She beckoned the hare over and whispered something to it and it hopped away. After a while, Frode entered with it in his arms.

'Lennart's hungry,' she said. 'You can bring the fish Bigga brought. The cod.'

She watched him while he ate, hunched over the table.

'What did you think about when you were at the facility?'

He shrugged.

'What did you get up to then? All day.'

'Watched TV,' he said with his mouth full. 'Drank instant hot chocolate and ate Risperidone. Played Othello with a pyromaniac called Jens. It's like fucking nursery school in there, just so you know. They've painted Goofy on a column in the common room, and some other cartoon characters, I don't know their names, and underneath someone had written 'Welcome to Basket Case Nursery'. And that's what it was like. A nursery school for insane people.'

'And you put up with it for ten years.'

'Well, I was in prison in Haparanda first. Then, when I cut my arm with the bandsaw in the workshop, the second time, they transferred me. And started giving me drugs.'

'When I visited you, and told you we'd found him, that we'd found Skabram, you didn't believe me. Remember?'

He shook his head.

'You said you knew they were all dead. That you could feel it. I can feel they're gone the same way I can feel my hand's gone. That's how you put it.'

'I still feel that way.'

She grabbed hold of her wheels and drew closer.

'But you were wrong.'

'Yes.'

She watched him.

'Eventually, we'll find the others.'

'They're dead.'

'We don't know that.'

'Well, then how are you going to find them? More Goldilocks stories in the paper?'

'Exactly!'

He looked at the hare, which hopped across the floor and settled down under the table. From where it stared at him, its nose twitching violently.

'If Luttak were dead, we'd know.'

'What makes you say that?'

'Because her fur's so grey. If anyone came across such an unusual bear, dead or alive, it would be in the paper. Don't you think?'

'I don't know.'

'Trust me.'

'I think you should try to get hold of that girl Fanny instead.'

'I don't know if I dare to. There's a considerable danger that the next time you come to visit, it won't be me sitting in this chair, but rather someone who just calls themselves Grete, if you know what I mean.'

'Have you heard anything from Stava?'

Grete shook her head. She shifted in her wheelchair and straightened the blanket wrapped around her legs.

'You know who her mother is, don't you?'

'I guess I've had my suspicions,' he mumbled into his plate. Grete looked down at her hands.

'But you never said anything.'

'Does she know?'

'I think I assumed she had pieced it together. Or that some-one had told her. Maybe not in so many words, but that she'd figured it out. We had no contact at all for at least fifty years; I figured that was why. That she knew. But then she came here last spring. Lennart. Look at me.'

'I am.'

'Take off your glasses. Who am I supposed to talk to about all this, if I can't talk to you?'

'I don't know.'

'Me neither.'

He walked up the stairs and into the room she had assigned him. In it was a desk and a chair and a bed. He sat down on the bed and after gazing out the window for a while, he lay down. There was a lamp with a pressed glass base on the desk.

It was on; he looked at the matte light inside the shade.

Minutes later, he heard the patter of soft little feet outside his door. He lay stock-still, listening. Then he stood up and opened the door. The hare was sitting outside, pointed back the way it had come. Its nose was working frantically. Lennart stood with his hand on the handle, watching it.

'There's no getting rid of you, is there?'

Diana tapped her nails against the doorpost before stepping into the room.

'Hello?'

Susso had looked asleep, but now she opened her eye.

'I see you brought the whole town.'

The little girl hung back at first, but then marched over to a chair and took a seat. She kicked her legs and studied the walls, a framed painting of mountains in pastel colours, the ceiling-mounted TV, the intricate system of steel pipes and springs under the bed, the trapeze on its chain. She studiously, however, avoided looking at the patient.

'How are you feeling?'

Susso reached for the handle and pulled herself upright.

'I feel like there's something in my eye.'

'You're going to need surgery to get it out. But not here. They'll send you to Sunderbyn. Then they'll fit you with a prosthetic.'

'Really? That's great.'

'But not for another few weeks.'

'I'll have to be patient.'

'Indeed.'

'Did you know that when you have only one eye, you can see your own nose all the time? It's super annoying.'

'Are you wearing contacts now? I mean a contact. No.'

Susso shook her head.

'I haven't worn contacts in a hundred years.'

'Then we'll have to get you some. Do you know what strength you need?'

'It was my good eye they gouged out. Bastards. This one's minus three.'

'I'll sort you out. We can't have you lying around here blind as a bat.'

'I can in fact see well enough to know you don't exactly look radiant yourself.'

'My nose is broken. They're fixing it tomorrow. What?'

Kiruna was pointing to the plastic cup with the bent straw sitting on the bedside table.

'It's squash. I'm sure Susso doesn't mind sharing.'

'Go ahead,' Susso said.

The little girl went over to the bed, picked up the cup with both hands and put the straw in her mouth.

'You do seem better, though.'

'People generally do when you give them morphine. It's kind of inevitable.'

Diana reached out and gave the plastic strip around Susso's wrist a tug.

'Your voice is different. You sound like yourself now. You didn't when I came to your house.'

'I didn't?'

Diana shook her head.

'You were someone else. At least that's how it seemed to me. And your mum. And we're the people who know you best.'

Susso pulled her hand away, slowly.

'Where is he?'

'Let's talk about that later. You need to rest.'

'Why can't you just tell me where he is?'

'It.' She had lowered her voice so Kiruna wouldn't hear. 'I can tell you where *it* is.'

Susso watched her.

'It bit me. Here. Look. I've had a tetanus shot. No, I haven't. But I should.'

'Where is he?'

'At our house.'

Susso's thin fingers nervously slid up and down the side rail.

'I need him with me.'

'No, you don't. Kirri. Go out in the hallway and ask someone if you can have some more squash.'

'I don't want any more.'

'No, but Susso does. You drank all of hers.'

After the little girl left with the cup in her hands, they sat in silence for a minute. Susso turned away.

'They're going to take me again.'

'You don't know that.'

'Yes, I do.'

'I don't understand what they want with you. If they were looking for revenge for you shooting that bear, wouldn't they have taken care of that already? But you were just lying there and you can't have done much else because you have bedsores like an old peach. Maybe the eye was enough.'

'They were going to give me to someone. Because I know they took me to a cave somewhere. But I never went inside.'

'A cave?'

She nodded.

'Where, in Rumajärvi?'

'No, it was further north. In Norway.'

'By the sea? On a mountain with a bunch of bunkers and whatnot?'

Susso nodded.

'I was there too. They were going to throw me off a cliff. But then that old man who appeared in your garden came and rescued me. Don't ask me why.'

'What old man?'

'You don't remember?'

Susso shook her head.

'This little old man appeared when we were sitting on the jetty. This tall. And he was wearing a mask made of a man's face.'

Susso's mouth was thin and pressed shut and from her wide-open eye it was clear she was desperately searching her memory. Diana quickly glanced over her shoulder before leaning in and whispering.

'And he had a tail.'

Susso turned her face away. Then she heaved a deep sigh and after exhaling fully, she coughed.

'How did you get hold of him?'

'The squirrel? I drove out to your house and fetched it.'

'You went to my house?'

'Gudrun told me to.'

At that point, Kiruna returned, accompanied by a nurse who knew Diana. She was carrying a pitcher of red squash that she put down on the table.

'You can just push the button,' she said. 'If there's anything you need.'

'And here I thought you usually worked with pot-lids,' Diana said.

'They're discharging me tomorrow. I need him when I leave.'

'I don't think your mum's going to appreciate it.'

'No?'

Diana shook her head.

'Or is it that you don't want to give him up?'

'What do you mean?'

'It was a question.'

'That I'm not going to dignify with an answer.'

Susso snorted derisively and turned her eye to the ceiling.

To keep the little girl from overhearing, Diana leaned in over the bed.

'They threatened me. They said they were going to take Kiruna if I didn't get out of there and leave you with them.'

Susso said nothing.

'What if they come for her?'

'It's me they're after. You have nothing to worry about.'

Stava stepped through the door, did a quick scan of the living room and continued into the kitchen. She threw her keys down on the counter and looked out the window. Anders lingered in the hallway. There was a mirror there and a small chest of drawers and on the chest of drawers a grey corded phone. No shoes and no clothes. He carried the cardboard box by the bottom because he didn't like sticking his fingers through the handles. Not because he thought they would bite him, he just didn't want them to see his fingers and get ideas.

'You can bring them in here.'

He went into the kitchen and after putting the box down on the floor, he sat down on a chair, the only one in the room.

Stava sank into a squat. She drummed her fingers against the box. The blinds were closed, with sharp triangles where the slats had ended up askew. There was a pair of binoculars on the table. Black field binoculars with rubber eyecups.

'Who lives here?'

'Here? No one.'

'It said Flatmo on the door.'

She shot him a crooked smile.

'There's no Flatmo here.'

She was on all fours, whispering at the box.

'Should we let you out? Hm? Should we let you out?'

When she opened the lid, he turned away. He peered out through the blinds at the street below. The cars parked there. Puddles wreathed with blackened asphalt.

Out of the corner of his eye, he could see the little ones fan out across the floor. Some darted away and disappeared, others strolled around, sniffing the air with their trembling snouts. One stood dead still; Anders sensed it was looking at him, but he didn't dare check.

Stava was digging around for one that preferred to stay in the darkness of the box.

'I don't understand why we have to do this,' he said.

'You were pretty close to killing me, or did you forget?'

He sat in silence, staring at the binoculars.

'He needs to know he can trust us,' she continued. 'This is our chance to prove ourselves.'

Stava opened the refrigerator. It was empty apart from four cans of beer at the very back.

'What I did to that child,' he said, 'it wasn't me doing it. I wasn't myself. And now that Ransu doesn't exist any more, I don't think I'm capable of kidnapping someone.'

'We're not kidnapping her. We're just fetching her.'

'Fetching?'

'We're fetching her. It's our child now.'

'Do you realise how many police officers are going to be looking for her? And her mum, she's been to the village. It's the first place they're going to look, can't you see that?'

'No one's going to look for her.'

'Children going missing, that's a big deal.'

Stava closed the box and pushed it against the wall with her foot.

'We're going to make sure she knows how it's going to be. If she lets the girl go, she will have a long and not too miserable life. If she doesn't let her go, it won't be very long at all. It's that simple. A no-brainer.'

Anders said nothing. Then he got up and left the kitchen. There was a sofa in the living room; he sat down on it.

The sun was on the TV, reflecting a cold, dark version of the sparsely furnished room where he was sitting like the morose subject of an achromatic painting.

After a while, the front door slammed again.

Näcken stepped into the hallway. He shot Anders a disapproving look before walking out into the kitchen with heavy steps.

He had brought food. Tin-foil containers with greasy paper lids that he took out of a paper bag and lined up on the kitchen counter. Anders stood watching him like a hungry dog.

Näcken sat down at the table and dug in. The new smells piqued the interest of the little ones, who slunk into the kitchen, one after the other. One of the smallest ones was completely hairless and one of the shrews had ugly bald patches on its back. By kicking his boot gently and stamping his feet on the floor, Näcken kept the mice gathering around the table legs at bay.

'Be careful,' said Stava, who was standing with her back against the fridge.

Näcken glanced in under the table and when he spotted the deathly pale munchkin moving with a peculiarly hobbled gait, he stopped chewing instantly and just sat there with his mouth open. Then he bent down and offered the palm of his hand as a lift.

He let the little one down on the table top. Its face was wrinkled like a mummified mouse foetus.

'Have any more . . .' he said, making a circling motion with his index finger.

'Not that I know.'

'We'll give it a few more hours.'

'Are they home?'

'There's a car outside,' he said, chewing. 'With a car seat.'

Anders went back to the living room. Sat on the sofa staring at nothing. The only thing he could think about was the food in those tin-foil containers. After a while, Stava joined him. It was as though she'd read his mind. She handed him a container of rice and he enjoyed it so much he grunted. Which is why he barely noticed when a mouse started crawling up his leg. When he finally did notice, he froze.

'He wants to be your friend,' Stava whispered. 'Don't reject him. You'll feel better if you don't reject him.'

Diana had planned to tell Håkan what she'd been through but when she saw him sitting on the sofa with eyes that didn't seem to see as far as the floor, she realised it wouldn't just be pointless, it would be inappropriate. Like pouring petrol on a fire. He seemed stuck in the helpless state of anxiety her kidnapping had plunged him into. Sometimes, he didn't even seem fully aware she was back.

'Would you please call Irene.'

She was waiting for him to answer or at least acknowledge that he'd heard her when there was a knock on the door. He didn't like that. He flinched. Diana went into the hallway and looked out through the kitchen window. Then she opened the door.

Susso didn't say anything, just stood there. She was wearing the clothes Diana had left in a bag in her room that morning: a thin purple cotton shirt with a row of tiny buttons at the neck and a pair of dark jeans she could no longer button but that fitted Susso perfectly. Her hair was slicked back and so wet it looked black.

'I thought you were being discharged tomorrow?'

'I can't bear that place.'

'Were the contacts the right strength?'

They went into the garage. After a few moments, they

heard a noise from the car roof box suspended from the ceiling like a cocoon. Little claws pattering back and forth on the hard plastic. Diana didn't see how it got there, but suddenly the squirrel was on the workbench, with its tail like an inverse sketch of its body. Susso whispered something inaudible as she approached the animal.

'Do you have to take him?'

She went over to the workbench and fiddled with a screwdriver. She tried to catch Susso's eye, but Susso was standing with her blind side toward her.

'I'm not entirely sure what I've got myself into,' she continued. 'What I got myself into when I went to your house. And even less so when I went to get you back. So it would make me feel better if he could stay here. Just for a few days.'

'Just for a few days. You think that'll make a difference?'

'I don't know, but it would make me feel better.'

Susso had put the squirrel on her shoulder.

'They're not going to come here,' she said and then she left.

She drove to the hospital and walked through the hallways with her sunglasses on. The doctor inspecting her nose had a Polish accent and she had never seen him before, and that was a blessing. He didn't ask what had happened to her, so he had probably drawn his own conclusions. Like everyone who saw her sitting outside the treatment room with tampons shoved up her nose did. She rested the back of her head against the wall and closed her eyes. Her top lip went numb, then her bottom lip, and it felt good.

The doctor rolled across the floor on his chair and worked quickly with an air of unconcern. When he rammed his freezing instrument into her nose and set the bone, it crunched as though she'd taken a big bite of crispbread.

He inserted a temporary splint, to be removed after five days, and told her that if she was unhappy with the appearance of her nose, she would have to come back.

The first thing she did when she came home was to show Kiruna her taped nose. The little girl was sitting on the floor in her room, drawing with crayons. She gave her an indifferent look before resuming her drawing.

She heated up leftovers in the microwave and sat across from the little girl while she ate, cutting up an apple. Kiruna reached for a piece. She chewed, her little lips wet with fruit juice, and studied her mother's face.

'Does it hurt?'

'Only if I touch it.'

'Can I?'

'Yes. Ow.'

'Can we go look at the squirrel later?'

She shook her head.

'Susso picked it up.'

'I want a squirrel too.'

'They're not pets.'

'Then why does she have a pet squirrel?'

Diana picked up a piece of apple and bit it in half.

'That's a good question.'

It frightened me half to death when someone yanked the front door handle. Soon after, the doorbell started ringing and I had no trouble guessing who it was.

'I didn't expect you so soon.'

'What's the point of lying about in the hospital,' she said, 'when I can just as well lie about here.'

She leaned against the wardrobe and stepped out of one shoe and then the other by using her toes as a boot jack. I recognised the right angle her shoes formed on the hallway floor. She had always taken her shoes off that way and now it seemed like a sign she was back. Though of course I didn't have time to think about that at the time. At that moment, I was focusing all my attention on the grey figure hunkered down on her shoulder.

'Have you walked through town with him like that?'

She walked straight to the guest room without responding. It wasn't ready yet. The ironing board was out and sitting on it were piles of laundry I hadn't had time to sort out. She sat down on the chair by the desk and put her foot on my exercise ball, rolling it back and forth while glaring at me all the while; the animal on her shoulder glared too.

'Would you like me to get out the air mattress? If you want a rest.'

'Yes, that would be great.'

Roland appeared in the doorway. Susso and he nodded to each other and I noticed that her treating him so coldly upset me. But I quickly tidied that anger away for fear the squirrel would sniff it out and scratch out God knows what kind of aggressions.

'Would you mind fetching the air mattress?'

After he had shuffled off, I went into the kitchen and made coffee. Not because I wanted any but because I had a strong need to put my fingers to work and distract my mind.

Susso followed, of course. She sat down at the kitchen table and flipped through the paper. Where the squirrel was I had no idea, but it wasn't important. I sensed she had already caught hold of the thread that would eventually lead all the way to the empty grave in her garden. I had been here before. Minor invasions of my privacy and major ones. The worst one was when she interrogated me about my divorce and all the misery that followed in its wake. That was down in her flat, and it was probably the last time I set foot in there. With the squirrel as an undisclosed participant, she pumped me for one grim detail after the other. She pecked at me like a woodpecker, and the thoughts I least wanted to put into words, the insects that had crawled furthest into the wood, those were the ones she licked up first. It was bewildering and horrifying, though the horrifying part didn't hit home until afterwards. She found out things I believe no daughter should know about her mother, or her father for that matter. That being said, I think it affected me more than it did her and since that day, I find talking to her unpleasant.

'So you're living together now,' she said without looking up from the paper.

'Yes. It seemed easiest.'

I took cups out of the cupboard and put them on the counter.

'What's Minerva?' she said.

'Minerva? Isn't that a goddess?'

Susso said nothing and kept her eyes fixed on the paper.

'Is it maybe Diana,' I continued, 'but in Greek?'

Just then, Roland stepped through the door. He went into the guest room and then joined us in the kitchen. He was holding a plastic camping pump. He blew air on me until I pushed him away.

'Do you know who Minerva is?' I said.

'It's a kind of potato,' he said. 'Extremely hardy.'

Diana was out of bed before she even understood what had woken her up. She ran out of the bedroom so quickly she clipped the doorpost and staggered out into the light of the hallway.

Then he shouted again.

'Disgusting fucking bastard, I'm going to end you!'

Håkan was crouched as if about to hurl himself at the little girl, who had crawled up into a corner of her bed, where a mountain of stuffed animals surrounded her like a bizarre praetorian guard. Diana let out a roar as she lunged at him and pushed him away. She unleashed a flurry of hard punches that drove him backward. He tottered sideways but other than that, barely noticed her. His eyes shone with a searing insanity. She stepped onto the bed, pulled the little girl close and stroked her hair.

'Daddy's dreaming, he's sleepwalking and having a nightmare.'

She had expected the little body to be stiff with fear, but it wasn't. The girl didn't even look scared.

Håkan had got down on all fours; he was looking for something under the bed.

'What are you doing?'

'Just come out already!'

'Håkan!'

'It's a mouse. There's a mouse in here.'

Diana sat with her arms around the girl. The blind was up and the sun flooded the room with light.

'I'm not sure you're completely awake.'

'I saw it!'

She climbed out of the bed, sank into a squat next to him and put a hand on his back. He jolted up into sitting. He stared at her and for a few fractions of a second, she glimpsed a desperate insecurity in his eyes. Then he turned back to the little girl.

'You tell her!'

The girl's lips were tightly pressed together.

'You're scaring her.'

'Tell her!'

She shook her head defiantly.

Diana pulled on Håkan until he got to his feet.

'Come with me,' she said.

But he broke free.

'She was playing with it,' he said. 'That's why she won't say anything. I know it's in here!'

Diana stood motionless. Something about the look on his face made her hesitate. There was no trace of that pathological inertia that had held him in its grasp lately. Simply put, she recognised him, standing there in his underwear, with his hair in a tangle, staring at her. At the same time, she recalled what she'd seen through that window. A creepy ensemble of dressed-up Lilliputians, all with murine characteristics. She swallowed hard without taking her eyes off Håkan. Then she turned to the little girl.

She had lain down and her eyes were closed.

'Kirri.'

She sat down on the edge of the bed.

The little girl's eyelids fluttered and her hair was a black, tangled weave across her round cheek.

'I know you're not asleep.'

She put a hand on the little girl's arm and shook it gently.

'Hey.'

That made her bury her face into the pillow. Diana looked at Håkan. He had closed the door and shoved a blanket into the gap along the threshold; now he was scouring the floor.

'So, was it a mouse?'

'What?'

'Was it a mouse?'

'Yes, it was a mouse.'

'A regular mouse?'

He shot her a quick glance. Then he resumed his search.

'I don't want any fucking mice in here.'

'So what are you going to do?'

'What do you mean?'

'Were you planning on catching it with your bare hands?'

He paced around the room, kicking the things scattered on the floor. Teddy bears. Clothes. Books. Jigsaw puzzles. A pink princess laptop. A spherical horse that let out a crazy neigh.

'You won't find it.'

'It's in here somewhere.'

'Come with me now.'

'You don't understand.'

'What don't I understand?'

'It has to go. Okay? It can't be in here.'

'Can't it wait till morning?'

'No, it can't wait till morning.'

She dug her hands in under Kiruna to lift her up, but the little girl wanted none of it. She rolled up and whimpered into the wall. There was no question she was simulating sleep. Diana made a new attempt, this time picking up both the child and the duvet she was clinging to. She carried the little girl into the bedroom and sat her down on the bed. Kiruna was hopping mad; she almost expected her head to start spinning around.

'I want to sleep in my room, I want to sleep in my room!'

Diana closed the door and lay down next to her. She pulled her close and rocked her like she'd done when she was little. After a while, the girl relaxed and then it wasn't long before her deep, regular breath warmed Diana's neck.

The little girl was still asleep when Diana woke up. Her lips puffy like a rosy-cheeked cherub. It was past eight. Håkan's side of the bed was empty. She pulled a jumper over her head, padded out into the hallway and opened the door to Kiruna's room. He wasn't there. She popped her head into the bathroom and continued down the stairs and had soon established that he was not in the house. Nor was he in the garage nor out back. Could he have gone to work? His holiday didn't actually start until next week, or did she have that wrong? She went over to the busy wall planner and saw the line he had drawn in blue pen through his column, starting next week. But shouldn't he have said something if he'd gone to work?

She went back up to their bedroom and picked up her phone from the window sill. No messages. She stood there for a while with the phone in her hand. Then she went downstairs and into the bathroom and whipped the shower curtain aside; thankfully, he wasn't in there.

Now she could hear the sound of tiny feet from upstairs. Diana hurried up the stairs and intercepted the little girl on her way back to the bedroom with her nightgown fluttering behind her. She grabbed her arm hard.

'What's that in your hand?!'

She pried the little girl's fingers open. A ring lay in the palm of her hand. Håkan's wedding ring.

'Where did you find this?'

The girl tried to wriggle free, refusing to speak.

'Where did you get this?!' she yelled and she yelled in a way she had promised herself never to yell at her child, a real social group 3 roar it was.

Kiruna backed up until her heels hit the wall. When she saw the look on the little girl's face, she pulled herself together. She stared at the ring, as though she expected it to tell her where Håkan was, and why he had taken his wedding ring off.

'Where was it?'

The little girl raised her arm and pointed.

'Where?'

She followed the girl, who strolled into her room and pointed to one of the bedposts.

'It was on top of that?'

She nodded.

Diana looked around the room. Then she snatched up the clothes strewn about the floor and dressed the little girl without a word; when the little girl resisted, she forced her arms and legs with relentlessly hard fingers.

Gudrun's partner opened the door and he did it in nothing but a pair of shorts. A gold-mounted shark's tooth dangled on his chest. He kept his hand on the handle and watched them with raised eyebrows. Then he stepped aside and invited them in. Gudrun was sitting at the kitchen table with her hands on a newspaper. She looked pale, unbecomingly so, and was draped in a hideous tie-dye blouse that should have been left to rest in peace long ago. No one said anything and after a while, Susso appeared in the doorway.

When Roland had turned the TV on for Kiruna and closed the door, Diana sat down at the table and told them about last night's events. They listened without interrupting. Finally, she placed the ring in the middle of the table as proof.

'It's like they're priming her or something.'

'But did you see it?' Gudrun said.

She shook her head.

'I didn't have to. I saw what it did to her. She was out of control when I carried her to my bed. It was really creepy to see. It was like when she had night terrors when she was younger; I couldn't get through to her.'

'And are you sure that wasn't it?'

'What?'

'Night terrors?'

'It wasn't night terrors.'

'What do you think, Susso?'

'About what?'

'About this.'

She said nothing for a while.

'If they want her, they're going to take her. Sooner or later. There's nothing you can do.'

'But you told me they wouldn't come here,' Diana said in a voice that was on the verge of breaking. Susso looked at her with one expressionless eye, tapping the napkin holder against the table top.

'I was wrong.'

'There must be something we can do,' Gudrun said.

'The only thing you can do,' Susso said, 'is hide. But that's not such a great long-term solution.'

'I'm just trying to get through one day at a time,' Diana said.

'So where are you going to go?' Gudrun said.

'We're not telling you,' Susso replied.

Lennart was sitting in the hallway, holding Grete's aluminium crutch. They had arrived. The engine had gone silent out there. Car doors were being gently shut. The old woman was asking quiet questions and getting quiet answers and the rain was coming down hard.

Now he could hear running footsteps on the gravel. Fanny stepped in through the front door with the little boy in her arms. Her eyes took in the antiques in the room; when she spotted Lennart, she stiffened. He tapped the crutch lightly against the floor and when the boy didn't react, he tapped harder. Eventually, his big brown eyes turned to him. His hair had curled into wet knots and his tongue looked like it was on its way out of his lips like some kind of mollusc.

The old woman hobbled in through the door and continued into the dining room, with Fanny hard on her heels. After a while, Frode entered the hallway with a suitcase in his hand and a yellow IKEA bag slung over his shoulder. He put the bags down on the floor and went back outside.

The IKEA bag was full of clothes and other sundries; Lennart looked at it for a while before going over to study the contents. He poked at it with the crutch. Moved a flannel shirt that was not unfamiliar to him. A nappy decorated with colourful little animals. Another nappy and under that, the mask. Rune's mouth gaping like the mouth of a spirit about to be sucked into the netherworld.

Lennart stood stock-still, staring at the small, silvery swirls in its hair. The unevenly cut eye holes that showed the inside of the skin, stinking because of the organisms thriving in the remnants of flesh. He stuck the crutch into the bag and stirred around until Rune was no longer visible.

The rain rattled against the roof of the porch. He flared his nostrils and sniffed the air. The van was parked diagonally behind the motorhome and the car he'd stolen in Karesuando.

Stiff-backed, he trudged across the rocky yard. After a moment's hesitation, he grabbed the handle and opened the door to the back. The vicious reek of wolf's urine hurled itself at him, followed by a posse of more or less revolting smells. The armchair was in there, but there was no one sitting in it.

He closed the door and looked around. The deserted road. The tundra fading into the rain. He walked around the motorhome and past the garage and down a slope.

The kennel consisted of a log cabin, ringed by a tall, welded chain-link fence. A small lamp was burning invitingly in the window and there was even a valance curtain. There were cut-out hearts in the shutters.

There was no gate in the fence, so he walked around it.

The wolf was standing right in front of the door, watching him with eyes that were clear and calm. The same yellow eyes that had peered out from behind the mask.

'There's no one home.'

When he drew closer, the wolf pranced aside.

He tried the door. Then he opened it and bowed into the cabin. Even though the smell of smoke permeated every part of the room, he could also smell the dog-eyed old woman who had dwelt in there for an eternity, filling her days with God knows what activities.

There was a cast-iron stove and a small trestle table but no chairs. A curtain of see-through plastic strips hung in the doorway leading out to the fenced-in area. The strips were grimy and swayed languidly when the wind pulled on them.

The old-fashioned sleigh bed was full of dolls, huddling close together. They were all girls and all wore dresses and all had coiffed, shiny hair and a few of them looked very old and sensible.

The old lady's paltry clothes were hung on a hook, a tattered gingham dress and a pile jacket. Her wig had fallen down and lay on the floor like an abandoned bird's nest. Lennart picked it up and hung it back on the hook. Then he stomped his foot hard on the floor and tramped about until the tiny creatures who had been spying on him had darted out of the cabin. The last one to slink over the threshold was a field vole with a fat tail.

'You can come in if you want.'

The wolf stood outside with its long nose pointed at the wet ground, glowering at him. Then it turned its head. It had heard something; Lennart stepped out to see what it might be.

They were on their way down to the kennel. Frode was carrying the old woman on his back and Fanny was stumbling after with the little boy in her arms.

'There he is!'

When Frode had put Grete down and handed her her crutch, she waved the wolf over and eventually it padded up to her.

'This, you see, Rune, this was the home of an adorable little old lady called Uksakka. But she's gone now. And she's probably never coming back.'

Grete disappeared into the cabin.

'Come, let's go inside so you can have a look. It's very cosy! Very cosy.'

Fanny had set the boy down on the ground. He was sitting on his bottom, scratching at his bandaged cheek with his sock-wrapped hand. Lennart looked at the child and then looked away.

Kiruna had got it in her head that walking was difficult for Susso and took her task of leading her down to the cabin very seriously.

Diana hadn't been out in ages, but it was mostly the same. The diminutive red houses, scattered among the pines. The monumental brick firepit, the wagon wheel patio railing. On top of a cable reel her mother had painted lilac was a tin tub crammed full of petunias that trembled feebly in the wind and far below in the valley, the lake could be seen as a bare, grey clearing in the dense forest.

Susso had suggested they go to her dad in Riksgränsen, but Diana had been set on coming here, where she felt at least a little bit at home. She also entertained a flicker of hope that Håkan might be here. That the key was hanging on its secret nail and that the door was locked were, of course, signs to the contrary. She had a look at the neatly made beds in the bedroom and went out to the sauna, but he wasn't there either. Of course he wasn't. Even though she knew she was naïve to expect anything else, the sight of the empty guest room, which, like the sauna, was pine from floor to ceiling, filled her with cold unease. The bed where Kiruna had been conceived.

She moved on to the storage shed that housed the generator. She grabbed the recoil cord and pulled. Once the engine was running, she straightened up and contemplated the little machine. Then she went back up to the cabin. Susso was standing by the window, gazing out, her head ducked in under the valance. The squirrel had jumped up on an ancient cooking stove with a curved chimney that was sitting in the middle of the lawn. It looked funny. As though the animal felt it had come across a strange relative made of iron.

'That generator is bloody loud. It's all you hear.'

Susso didn't react.

'What do you think?'

'About what?'

'The generator. Should I turn it off?'

'I suppose that depends on the food. What did you buy?'

Diana picked up the bag of groceries and looked in it.

'Let's see. Ice cream and prawns.'

She didn't think the joke would get through, but apparently it did, because a small but unmistakeable puff of air escaped Susso's nostrils.

The little girl came inside and wanted to go on the swing and pulled Susso outside with her. Diana packed the food into the refrigerator with the squeaking of the tyre swing's chains in her ears, struggling all the while to keep the horrifying thoughts circling her like vultures at bay. There weren't too many places he could be. If only he'd taken the car. Or packed a bag. She had inventoried his clothes and shoes in the hallway and concluded that he was wearing a blazer and his new suede shoes. His wallet was gone too. But he had left his phone.

When she walked up to the car, she saw Susso standing in front of the little girl, pushing her with both hands. She opened the boot and took out the rifle and ran back to the cabin so the little girl wouldn't see it.

They sat on the patio, eating grilled hotdogs and potato salad, and then Kiruna was given permission to go to bed and watch a film. Shout if you need us, she said, and the little girl nodded without looking up.

Diana opened the door to the pantry and took out the gun and carried it outside along with a stack of blankets. Susso had pulled her feet up on the chair cushion and wrapped her arms around her knees. Diana handed her a blanket and leaned the rifle against the firepit.

'Your coffee's getting cold.'

Susso looked at her cup.

'Sterilised half cream,' Diana said and pointed with raised eyebrows to the carton on the table.

'I'm fine, thanks.'

'I bought it just for you.'

Susso didn't seem to hear.

'Remember,' Diana said, 'when we came out here with Tobe and whatshisname, Henka Rönnebro's cousin that Nuddi fooled around with, the ice hockey player.'

'Fooled around. Haven't heard that expression in a hundred years.'

'We watched horror films, *Friday the 13th*, and we got each other so worked up Nuddi was too afraid to go outside to pee, so she peed in a saucepan, and we hadn't brought any mixer, so we used instant fruit soup. The day after, there were puddles of, like, blood vomit in the snow. Remember?'

'Now you're in a horror film.'

Diana put in a snus, pressed the lid back on and tossed the tin on the table.

'True, but luckily this is as dark as it gets.'

'It's my fault.'

'What do you mean?'

'That we're here. In this horror film.'

'You didn't come looking for me.'

'No, but I could have warned you.'

'You mean you could have kept me out of it?'

'It would have been for the best.'

'Then who would have come for you?'

Susso made no reply, she just gingerly rubbed her face underneath her eye.

'How is Tobe, how much does he know?'

'How much does he know?'

Diana pointed to the pine tree where the squirrel was dashing about. Where the sun hit his fur, it shone like copper, but in the shade he was grey and the contrast between the two colours was so marked you might have thought there were two squirrels in the tree.

'Enough never to set foot in Kiruna again.'

'Is he in Luleå?'

Susso coughed and then cleared her throat and placed her fingertips on her forehead above her eye.

'Are you okay?'

'I have the world's worst fucking headache. And there's some transparent crap oozing out of my eye.'

'That's called tears. Probably because you miss Tobe.'

Susso giggled.

'Can I get you anything?'

'No, I'm good.'

'Are you sure?'

She nodded with that white square over her eye.

'Did you really think they were real? I mean, really real. When you were doing your website and all that.'

'I don't know. I wanted to. I think.'

'We were pretty hard on you.'

'You were?'

'You don't think?'

She shrugged.

Diana wrapped the blanket tighter around her and swatted at a mosquito.

'I always assumed anyone who discovered something like this would want the whole world to know about it. But that's not what it's like. It's the complete fucking opposite.'

Susso was studying her hands.

'It's so unfathomable and astonishingly horrible it utterly grinds you down. I just want to lie down and cry.'

'It's a defence mechanism.'

'Not talking about it?'

Susso pondered that for a moment.

'They hide inside animals. It's a disguise. And if you're unlucky enough to see them naked, so to speak, it'll cost you. It's as if they surround themselves with something. And you can't be involved with them without being affected by it. Whatever it is. You say you don't want to talk about it, and that's exactly it. If you get too close, they burn you up. Mentally. There's no way of telling how that ends. Just look at my sister. She's like a broken bulb.'

Diana spat her bag of snus into her hand and threw it away.

'But not you.'

'Well. He's special.'

'When I was at your house, when you were gone, I saw him. Naked, so to speak. At least I think I did. I was asleep in my car and when I woke up, I had a memory of him looking in at me. It was not a pretty sight. He's certainly cuter with fur than without, put it that way.'

'Yes, maybe he is.'

'By the way, I found a gun under your mattress. A revolver.'

There was a thud on the parasol above their heads and before Diana had any time to think about what it might have been, the squirrel had landed in the gravel next to the patio. Its tail twitched and twitched and she was suddenly fearful he might have heard what she had said and taken offence and now she was going to pay for saying he wasn't a pretty sight.

Susso studied him.

'Someone's coming,' she said.

Diana rose halfway out of her chair and craned her neck to peek out above the firepit. Then she picked up the rifle and stepped off the patio. She stood there, surveying the yard. After a while, she moved up toward the car. She stood dead still, listening and scanning the pines for movements, but could see nothing.

Susso had backed out onto the lawn so she could see the squirrel, who was now sitting on the sauna roof, at the very end of the ridge.

'What's up?'

'I don't know.'

'But something is, you're sure of that?'

While she was waiting for Susso to reply, an enigmatic logogram of sharp light glided across the red façade.

She never had time to feel scared that someone might have got inside the cabin. Because the moment she turned around and noticed the window opening, she saw the little girl. A tiny person in green pyjamas, padding away barefoot through the grass.

Diana called out and then she ran, and that made the child break into a run too, and she was fast. Diana crouched down as she ran to drop the rifle on the ground and raced after the little girl, who was on her way up the slope. Just as she caught her, the girl hurled something away, but Diana didn't see what it was. She picked her up and turned her to face her. Kiruna resisted, twisting her body and kicking and emitting a growling noise, with the teeth of her lower jaw jutting out like a riled beast. Diana knelt down in the grass and brusquely rocked her in her arms.

Susso was standing next to her with the rifle in her hands. She sank into a squat. They exchanged a look but said nothing.

Diana pushed the tangled hair out of the little girl's face, took her head in both hands and turned it so she could look into her eyes. She hadn't expected someone to be in there. But someone was. The little girl stared at her with wide-open pupils.

That made Diana smile, which caused the little girl to snort with mirth. Then she started giggling. It was so unexpected, Diana almost dropped her on the ground. The little girl lay in her lap, giggling, and it was an affected, shrill giggle she had never heard before.

'Cover her ears!'

Susso had stood up and was resting the butt of the rifle against her shoulder; Diana looked at her uncomprehendingly. Until she heard the click of the safety. Then she cupped her hands over the girl's ears.

The bang made Diana flinch. Susso reloaded, took a few steps forward and fired again. Diana didn't know what she was firing at and didn't want to.

'We have to go.'

Diana got to her feet, picked up the little girl and ran with her toward the car. The squirrel was already on the car roof. The girl wasn't giggling any more, but there was a creepy smile on her lips, which she hid behind clenched fists.

'The key.'

'Where is it?'

'In the window. Just inside the door. Get my wallet as well.'

Susso jogged toward the cabin and Diana paced around in a circle, rocking the little girl. Her eyes roved back and forth across the yard and she thought Susso was taking an awfully long time.

Eventually, she came running back with the rifle.

'I can't find it. The wallet was there, but not the key.'

'Did you check the floor?'

'It's not there.'

Diana strode off toward the cabin. Then she stopped.

'Fuck,' she said and turned around.

'What?'

'It's somewhere behind the cabin.'

Susso frowned.

'She threw it away. I saw her do it, but I didn't understand what it was.'

'Where?'

'Over there. She threw it that way.'

Diana carried the girl into the cabin, put her down on the sofa and locked the door. Then she walked over to the window and shut it. How had she managed to get it open? There was no furniture she could have climbed. She must have stepped up onto the frame to reach the top latch. She wondered who had given her that idea. And to take the key too. She shuddered. The little girl had curled up and was lying motionless with her eyes closed, but it was obvious she wasn't asleep.

She could follow Susso's movements as she wandered up and down the sloping yard with the rifle in her hands, scanning the grass.

Diana did a lap around the cabin, gathering up their things and throwing them in the suitcase. She patted her stomach and felt the phone through her fleece jacket and was just about to pull it out when a shot rang out outside. Diana ran over to the window but Susso wasn't there. Moments later, someone yanked the door handle. A hard pounding. Through the window, she could see it was Susso.

Diana let her in and locked the door.

'It's impossible,' Susso said.

'Did you find it?'

'There's too many of them.'

'Of whom?'

Susso put the rifle down on the table and rubbed her eye.

'You didn't see them?'

Diana shook her head.

'They're all over the garden. Nasty little brutes. About this size.'

'Mice?'

'Something along those lines, yeah.'

Diana walked over to the window to look out but changed her mind and pulled the curtain shut instead.

'I think I hit one before. But it's bloody hard. If only we had a shotgun.'

'Where's the squirrel?'

'Up there, I think,' she said, pointing to the roof. 'He can take care of himself.'

'But he can't help us?'

'I'm sure he's doing his best. But we have to get out of here.'

'We can run next door. There was a car there.'

'How far is it?'

'I'm not sure. Maybe five hundred yards.'

'Five hundred yards is a long way on a night like this.'

'I'm calling Dad.'

Susso picked up the rifle and took up post by the window, inching the curtain aside.

'Tell him to hurry.'

Diana was holding her phone. She had punched in her PIN and her thumbs moved confusedly over the icons before she could locate the square with the phone receiver.

'There's people out there too,' Susso said.

'If it's that blonde fucking bitch, feel free to shoot her in the face.'

'Mummy.'

The little girl was watching her and she could tell instantly from her eyes that she was herself. Diana sank into a squat next to the sofa and stroked her little head.

'I had an accident.'

The call connected. Diana quickly stood up and walked off, toward the kitchen.

'It's okay,' Susso said. 'It's happened to me too.'

'Hello? This is Eva.'

'Mum. You have to come get us.'

Silence.

'Who am I speaking to?'

'It's me!'

More silence.

'And who is that?'

'It's Diana. Can't you see it's me calling?'

'Diana . . .'

'What's wrong with you?'

'What's wrong with me? What's wrong with you?'

'Mum, listen to me.'

'What time is it anyway? Oh my goodness.'

'Can I speak to Dad?'

A long silence.

'He's not here.'

'What do you mean, not there? What are you doing?!'

'Shouldn't I be asking you that?'

'Mum. This is serious. You have to come get us.'

Now there was a deep sigh.

'Where are you?'

'We're in the cabin, you know that. We went out to the cabin!'

'And what's happened?'

'Just come get us!'

'Don't raise your voice at me.'

'But you're not getting it. You have to come get us!'

'I hope you haven't broken anything? Diana. Because I remember that time when you went out there and then a lamp was broken. And several wine glasses, the fancy wine glasses I got for my fortieth birthday, and someone had vomited in the sauna and who had to clean that up, that's right, me.'

Diana ended the call.

Susso was rummaging through the suitcase and the little girl was standing up, naked from the waist down. Her pyjama bottoms lay in a pile on the floor.

'They must have got to them. I talked to Mum and she was super weird. It was like she was drunk or fucking demented or something.'

Susso helped the girl step into a fresh pair of knickers.

'Makes sense, I was wondering how they found us here.'

'You're going to have to call Gudrun.'

I picked up my phone from the nightstand with trepidation. This is it, I thought to myself, it's happened. Hearing Susso's voice in my ear was a surprise, since it was Diana's number. She didn't sound afraid. Serious, rather. She said they were in Diana's parents' cabin in Kurravaara and that I had to come pick them up immediately.

'But what happened?'

'You have to hurry.'

'But where is it?! I don't know where their cabin is!'

'Tell them to send a pin,' said Roland, who had already got up and pulled on his trousers and was now fiddling with his watch clasp.

I was getting dressed when the message arrived.

Roland took my phone and looked at it.

'Are you ready?' he said.

We drove close enough to see Diana's car and the black tin roofs of the cabins. The sun was at world's end and the night sky was adorned with a soaring wing of gossamer streaks of ruddy clouds. Everything was so tranquil and normal it was hard to imagine there could be anything threatening in this place. But it had been clear from Susso's voice that they were in trouble and so I was on high alert. I called and said we were here and Susso said they were coming out.

Roland had killed the engine and taken off his seatbelt.

'Do you reckon it's safe to get out?' he said.

'No,' I replied, 'I wouldn't think so.'

'Then what do we do now?'

'We wait.'

'Call again.'

'They're coming.'

'Yes,' he said, craning his neck, 'someone's coming this way.'

It was the squirrel, of course. It came bounding up the slope; we watched it dash up a set of swings. Then the little beast sat up there for a second or two before darting over to the other end and scampering down the log. Now it was hopping our way.

It jumped up on the bonnet and studied us intimately through the windscreen with eyes like liquorice. It was like being in a safari vehicle, being gawked at by a cheeky monkey.

'Is he coming?' Roland said.

I pretended to be looking at my phone.

'If you don't want him in your car, you're going to have to tell him.'

'Can he hear us?'

'He can hear your thoughts.'

Now Susso and Diana were walking up from the cabin. Diana was carrying the little girl wrapped in a blanket and Susso was carrying a rifle.

Roland stepped out of the car and opened the back door on his side; when Diana put the child in the back seat, he hovered around them, wanting to help. I turned around and looked at the little girl. Her hair was so soaked with sweat, it looked black. Susso was standing with the rifle half raised as though she was about to take aim. Or threatening to. She glanced over at the trees and then I did too. I thought a bear was going to come bursting out, because I always do; sometimes they actually attack me in town and on occasion even inside my own flat. But there was no bear and nothing else either and in the end, she finally got in the car.

Roland rolled forward a few yards and then reversed to turn around. No one said anything. There was complete silence until we reached the Kurravaara road. Then Susso said:

'Where is he?'

Even though I hadn't seen the squirrel slink into the car, I had assumed it was with us. But it wasn't.

'He's not here? Diana? We have to go back!'

Roland took his time answering.

'Let's go home.'

'We have to go back!'

'I'm not going back.'

I braced for an outburst, but it didn't occur to me she might threaten him. I heard her fiddling with the rifle, then I saw the black barrel out of the corner of my eye, gliding into my field of vision.

'Turn the car around.'

Roland slowed down and pulled over. He said nothing, just sat here. After a while, he turned off the engine.

'You can't stop here,' Diana said. 'There were people at the cabin. If you stop here, they'll find us.'

'Can't you see,' I said, 'that he's a monster?'

'Turn around.'

'No, Susso. We won't. We're not going back.'

'I'll shoot you. I swear. I'll shoot you.'

Now the little girl burst out crying.

'That you would go so far as to shoot Roland only proves I'm right. He's a monster. And I don't want monsters in my car. Nor in my flat.'

Susso opened the door. But she couldn't climb out. Because Diana had grabbed the rifle.

'No, Susso. Stay here. Stay here with us.'

'Do you know what would've happened if he hadn't been there when they came? You don't want to know. We wouldn't be here if not for him.'

'No, we wouldn't,' Diana said. 'Because we would have been home. And you would have still lived in Kiruna and none of this would've happened. It's his fault we're here.'

'You don't get it.'

'That Kiruna is terrified and crying. I get that.'

'You don't get anything.'

'Can you see that she's crying?'

'He,' I said and turned around, 'is the root of all evil.'

'You know what? I feel sorry for you.'

'You shouldn't feel sorry for us. We feel sorry for you. And I know it was my fault. I haven't been strong enough. But I'm trying to be now. So I'm not giving in.'

'He saved my life. And your life too.'

'I know he saved your life. He saved your life only to destroy it. He's destroying you, Susso. You're not yourself. We don't recognise you. None of us recognises you.'

'You think it's going to stop?' She turned to Diana. 'You think it will? If you do, you're sorely mistaken. They will never stop. Not until they get what they want. And I'm not

[405]

who they're after. It's someone else in this car. Why don't you tell them what they said they were going to do to her? Or should I?'

We said nothing because she clearly had a point.

'The only one who can protect her is him. Don't you see that? Diana, don't you see that?'

'Yes,' Diana said.

'The police are powerless. And the only thing we can do is hide.'

'There are other methods,' Roland said.

'There are? Like what?'

He glanced at the side mirror.

'I'm just saying.'

'Where are we going to go? They've been to Diana's house and they've been to her parents'. So what now, are we going to yours?'

'They've been to Eva and Kent's?'

'Yes, and when they come for you, Mother, do you want the squirrel to be there or not? I'm just asking.'

I looked at Roland.

'We can stay at a hotel,' he said.

'A hotel?'

'At Ferrum.'

'Are you serious?'

He nodded.

'And then deal with this tomorrow.'

'And how are you going to deal with it?'

He started the engine.

'If you can't see a way out, you have to make one.'

*

Susso was quiet all the way home. We all were, for that matter. Both Diana and I kept an eye on the road behind us, but there was no pursuit so far as we could tell. The little girl fell asleep, of course, but when we parked behind the hotel, she woke up and was anxious and wouldn't get out of the car, and I wondered what they were going to think of us when we stepped into the lobby at half four in the morning with a crying child.

Roland and I took one room and Susso, Diana and the little girl another. They weren't next to each other but on the same floor at least.

Roland rolled himself up in a sheet and was out like a light, but I ended up sitting on the edge of the bed, still fully dressed. After just a few minutes, there was a knock on the door. She stood there watching me and I obviously knew what she wanted. I fished the key out of Roland's jacket pocket and held it out to her and she took it and left without a word.

Diana looked in through the kitchen window for a while before going up to the front door and unlocking it. The smells that greeted her cut her open; she had a sudden fit of vertigo and had to lean against the doorpost. A conglomerate of shoes on the hallway floor. His shoes weren't there, nor had she thought they would be. Cold dejection had spread through her, leaving its mark on every thought, every feeling, every second. Anything that didn't seem ominous seemed utterly meaningless.

She went upstairs and into the bedroom and looked at the unmade bed and Håkan's dead mobile phone on the bedside table. Then she went back down. The kitchen counter was piled high with dirty dishes. It smelled like something had died there, under the plates. And something sort of had. Two weeks ago, two weeks ago exactly, they had sat here eating tacos, having a lovely time. A lovely time. That life was gone forever now. After returning from Norway, she had thought she might be able to have it again at some point in the future, but not any more.

She hadn't slept many hours and her dreams had all been horrible. She had had a matter-of-fact conversation with her mother about how the most humane thing would be to put Kiruna down, as she put it, and even though she hadn't wanted to, she had acquiesced and brought the little girl to the hospital, where they had walked down a long corridor to a special room for children who were being euthanised. It had all been very pragmatic; they had been received as though they were in for a tonsillectomy. But when she was about to say goodbye to Kiruna and squeeze her hand one last time, she had, thankfully, woken up and more or less thrown herself at the little girl, holding her tight and crying quietly. Then she'd heard a tiny sound and glimpsed a shadow moving along the curtain rod and after that she hadn't been able to go back to sleep. She just dozed off from time to time. She remembered clearly how he had peered into her dream with his hideous old gnome face when she slept in her car outside Susso's house and felt almost certain he had breathed that nightmare into her, because how would her own brain be capable of producing something so awful, something that went against her most deeply rooted instincts?

And yet, she had left the little girl in the hotel room with Susso without hesitation. Because she was right. If anyone could protect her, it was him and when she left, she had been grateful he was sitting there on the desk with those watchful eyes of his.

It was only just nine, but already so warm she was sweating. She had tied her fleece jacket around her waist and rolled up the sleeves of her shirt. Their car was not in the driveway; she stepped over the hedge and walked around to the back. The patio door was open and there she was in the window.

When she stepped into the kitchen, her mum put her phone down. Diana studied her carefully.

'Where's Dad?'

'At Lakkapää,' she said and put her hand to her mouth and squeezed her lips as though they were numb.

Diana went to sit down on a chair without taking her eyes off her.

'Did anyone come by here?'

She shook her head.

'Strange thing to ask, don't you think?'

'Yes,' she said and coughed as he moved toward the kitchen counter.

'And yet you immediately shook your head.'

'Well, yes, because no one came by.'

'Ever?'

'What's the matter with you?'

'Mum.'

She came over and sat down at the table.

'What did they say?'

'Who?'

'The people who came by.'

'No one came by.'

'Then why were you so weird when I called you last night?'

'I don't know what you're talking about.'

'You don't remember me calling you?'

She shook her head.

'Fine,' Diana said and pulled out her phone. She opened the call list. 'Look. Thirty-five minutes past midnight. Kent Sillfors. Outgoing call. One minute. See?'

'Yes, but that's for your dad.'

'You picked up.'

'You know what, I don't think so. I'm usually pretty on the ball. You know I'm a light sleeper.'

Diana took hold of her hands. They were cold as wood.

'Mum. It's okay. You can tell me. I know exactly what happened to you.'

'Please don't touch me.'

The words caught her off guard. She let go and pulled her hands away. Then she sat looking at her mum, who was smiling sheepishly, with her eyes on the table top like a carefree dementia patient. Diana picked up her phone, got to her feet and left; her mum stayed seated, silent and with a disengaged look on her face.

She inserted the card into the lock and hacked at it until it clicked. The room was empty; when she realised this, she dashed out into the hallway and over to Gudrun and Roland's room. She banged the door. Susso opened and when she stepped aside, she could see Kiruna on the bed with a pillow in her arms, watching TV.

'What did they say?' Susso said.

Diana shook her head.

'Mum's completely away with the fairies. I don't know about Dad. But he's probably just as bad. We have to leave.'

'You didn't tell them we're here, did you? At the hotel?'

'Of course not. But I want to take Kiruna and go somewhere.'

'Come here,' Roland said, pushing past her into the hallway. 'I want to have a word with you.'

'No, we're leaving. We can't stay here.'

'And where are you going?'

'I don't know. We just have to get out of here.'

'I think there's another way to go about this.'

'How?!'

'Come on.'

They took the lift down to the lobby. Roland sat down on a sofa and she took a seat across from him, bewildered by his inscrutable expression. He looked severe but also amused. He got up and went to the bar and when he came back, he was carrying a sheet of A4 paper and a pen.

'I'd like to know more about that village.'

'You mean Rumajärvi?'

He leaned forward across the table and let her know with a look that she was talking unnecessarily loudly.

'I mean Rumajärvi.'

'Why?'

'Well. Even though living in this hotel is very pleasant, I don't think we can stay here for the rest of our lives. It's much too expensive. And Gudrun, she's tired. She can't take much more. It's wearing us all down. So we have to find another solution. A final solution.'

'Final?'

He glanced to the side and adjusted his watch strap by turning it around his wrist. Then he met her eyes and nodded.

'And how is that supposed to work?'

'You don't have to worry about that.'

'It's mice we're talking about. You can't even see them. You don't get it.'

'I think we should focus on this village. On Lennart Brösth and this Erasmus fellow. I find it hard to believe that these mice would have an axe to grind with you, personally, so to speak.'

'You don't understand how twisted that place is.'

'How many people live in the village?'

'I don't know.'

'Then we'll have to ask for a best guess.'

'My best guess. Maybe ten.'

'Men? Women? Children?'

'I saw one child.'

'How many are fit to fight? So to speak.'

'They're all equally twisted. The worst one, the one I was most afraid of, was a woman. Young, blonde. She was the one who told me what was going to happen to Kiruna.'

'This not knowing who they are, or even how many they are, complicates things. You want to cut the whole tumour out in one go, you know?'

'My husband,' she said. 'He's gone.'

'Yes, I heard.'

'They may have taken him. He might be there.'

'In the village?'

She nodded.

'Do you really think he is?'

'If not, where is he? Can you tell me that?'

Roland sat in silence for a moment before pressing on.

'Did you see any of those wolves when you were there? Susso reckons there might be five of them, does that sound right to you?'

'Mm.'

'What?' he said and angled his ear to her.

'Yes, that sounds about right.'

'And this Erasmus? What does he look like?'

'In his seventies. Long beard, long hair. Grey. He's pretty

short. Shorter than me. Like maybe five foot three. And he's got a limp.'

'Could you draw him for me?'

'I can't draw.'

'You could try.'

Diana took the pen and started drawing.

When she was done, he studied the picture and nodded.

'Now I want to know what it is you want us to do.'

He folded the paper and held it in his hand.

'You won't have to do anything.'

'But I don't understand. What's your plan?'

She looked at him but soon realised no answer was forthcoming on that subject. The strange thing was that he was kind of grinning at her, with his glasses perched on the tip of his nose.

'It's going to be big news, this,' he said. 'When it's discovered. And they're going to investigate it, from every angle. And do you know where that will lead them? It will lead them to Susso Myrén and it will lead them to Diana Sillfors.'

'Why?'

'Because the police were there last week. And why were they there? Who tipped them off? Your dad. What did he tell them exactly, do you know?'

She shook her head.

'He talked to Denny. He's an inspector, I think. Denny Långström. They know each other. And I think he told him Lennart Brösth might be there. And Susso, likely as not. But I don't actually know.'

'Rumajärvi's not exactly a metropolis, so they can easily check which mobile phones have connected to the masts out there recently. I assume you brought your phone when you went up there. They're going to want to know what you were doing in Rumajärvi. You have to be prepared for that. And by prepared, I mean you have to know what to say. Rambling won't do, and I don't think you'd better get trolls involved in your story.'

'Then what do you want me to say?'

'What did you tell them at the hospital when you brought Susso in?'

'I can't remember.'

'Maybe she had a boyfriend in Rumajärvi? A really scary junkie type. That you wanted to get her away from.'

'Yes, now that you mention it, that's how it was.'

'And for the rest, you keep your mouth shut.'

She nodded.

'Do you know what I mean by the three-S treatment?'

'Colloquially?'

'Colloquially.'

'Yes, I do.'

'All right then.'

Näcken slowed down and stopped by the boom barrier. Stava climbed out and opened it. Anders was in the back seat like a kid, staring out the window, and he didn't like her leaving the car. He couldn't remember where they'd been, but the lake he glimpsed between the trees awoke a memory in him and that made him afraid, so he placed a hand on his shirt and the little ones hiding underneath it.

'What are we doing here?' he said.

Näcken grinned at him.

'We're going to the circus,' he said.

'Cut it out,' Stava said.

'What circus?'

'We're not going to the circus.'

Erasmus was standing down by the lake, gazing out across the water, or maybe at the forest climbing the mountain on the other side. His feet were placed close together, his hands were folded behind his back, he wore no hat and from afar he looked like an old juniper bush.

When they approached him, a lone wolf rose from the ground. Anders stopped instantly, but Stava continued. She sank into a squat in front of the animal, who looked at her and then withdrew.

Stava spoke to her father, but it was in Sami, so he didn't understand a word. Eventually, she reached for the old man. That made the wolf lunge at her and push her to the ground. Then Erasmus left and the wolf followed.

Anders rubbed his cheek. There was something weird about his cheek. It was like touching someone else's cheek. He went closer to the small, rolled-up body and standing there looking at her, he felt like an animal coming across roadkill by the side of a highway. A certain level of wonder and a dash of worry. Other than that, nothing. Her black hair wound through the grass like some kind of strange and suffocating plant. He sat down and looked at it; then he touched it gingerly.

Lennart stood there with the boy on his arm, turning the sunglasses display rack.

'What about these, how do you like these?' He turned his face to the boy, whose hand instinctively shot out, but he was prepared and pulled his head away. He leaned forward and studied himself in the small mirror.

'Not these? All right. Aren't you the picky one?'

He pushed the temples back into the holes in the rack and pulled out another pair.

'What do you say to these then? Like a rock star, eh? Like Elvis Presley!'

He went over to the till, pulled out his wallet and threw it down on the counter. It was made of leather with a gold clasp. The man picked it up and looked inside.

'This is Norwegian money, I can't take that.'

'Sure you can.'

'No, I can't.'

'You can take as much as you like.'

'I'm sorry.'

Without taking his eyes off the man, he put the sunglasses and the yoghurt pots and the bananas in his pocket. Then he picked up his wallet and walked toward the exit.

The man had caught up by the time the doors slid open to

let him out. Another man was approaching at a run between the shelves. They started circling him.

Lennart could hear himself breathing heavily through his nose.

He reached out for the young man who had refused his money and after he had backed himself into the evening papers with a terrified look on his face, he caught hold of him with his massive hand. He squeezed his childishly weak throat. At first, the man tried to wrest free, but then his face turned red and he helplessly started scratching and touching anything he could reach: the sleeve of Lennart's jacket, his zipper, his buttons, the boy. In the end, he was simply wiggling his fingers in the air as if performing a hexing so petrifying it was only ever used as a last resort. Lennart let go and tossed him aside. The man crashed into a shelf and lay there, sucking air into his lungs with long, hissing breaths.

He went out to the van and buckled the child in and started the engine and turned out onto the road. After driving for a while, he glanced at the child. His plaster had come off. It was dangling like an open hatch door. The wound was a nasty-looking hole through his cheek, about half an inch across. It looked more like an acid injury than something he'd scratched open.

Lennart put his stump on the wheel and stuck the plaster back on. Then he fished a banana out of his jacket pocket.

'Here you go. And if you're going to be peeling bananas one-handed, there's one thing you have to get straight: they're easier to open from this end. See? People open them from this end, but that's wrong. Or maybe not wrong, but it's harder. Dig in.'

The car was parked behind the petrol station, seemingly deliberately tucked away. It was a Chevy, a very long and pompous hatchback with light wood panelling on the sides. There was a doll's head with sooty angel's hair on the tow ball; I thought it looked creepy.

Roland climbed out and went over to talk to someone sitting in it. I couldn't see who it was; all I could see was a leg sticking out the door. Camouflage trousers, white with a grey and black woodland pattern.

I'd felt sick all morning and now it washed over me again, like a cold undertow. Roland had told me not to come, but I had been too restless to stay at the hotel. A hundred yards from my own flat, which felt odd in an incredibly enervating way. Besides, being around Diana and her little girl made me feel awful. Not to mention Susso, and even more so her flame-coloured rat, which was never where you thought it would be.

Parked under the sign displaying the fuel prices was a lorry with the text 'Rönnberg's Fish' on it and next to that a cart that was a kiosk and from which Harr was now walking toward us. Tall and lanky and comically bow-legged. He had traded his hat in for a baseball cap.

He stopped briefly and bent down to me like a traffic

officer and I had no choice but to roll down my window. He was holding a paper plate and had food both in his mouth and his beard. Little clumps of mashed potato that moved when he chewed. He grinned and pointed to the Chevy with his plastic fork.

'I've bought CDs for you.'

'CDs?'

'My album.'

'Yes, the one with the bus.'

'Exactly, the one with the bus. Twenty copies. I reckon that'll do you.'

I nodded, which made him doff his cap and walk on.

I was surprised it wasn't that guy Ensimmäinen who climbed out of the car, but a young man in his twenties. I had no idea who he was and was angry with Roland for not telling me he had involved yet another person, and a young one at that, with everything that entailed.

They stood there, talking. It didn't seem to be a discussion. They laughed fairly often and hard and I thought that was inappropriate given what they were about to do. Though I suppose it was a way of releasing some tension. It struck me I had never seen Roland with friends before, or other men of any description, but I wasn't sure if that was because of him or me.

After a few minutes, he returned. He climbed into his seat and rummaged around the centre console, eventually pulling out a phone charger. The string of a reflector was entangled in the spiral cord; he sighed through his nose and started untangling it.

'Who's that guy?'

'Pontus. It's Harr's lad.'

'So he's going too?'

'He's going too.'

'Why didn't you tell me that?'

'Because I didn't know he was coming.'

I stayed in the car, mulling things over. Then I opened the door and went over to join them. That was, obviously, an incredible intrusion. Pontus smiled at me, but in an awkward way. His strawberry-blonde hair was shaped into a scraggly mohawk. I grabbed his shirtsleeve and pulled him aside.

'I don't know what your dad's told you about this undertaking or whatever we should call it, but I want you to be aware that it's going to be dangerous in ways you can't imagine.'

'Don't scare the boy,' Harr said.

Pontus looked at me with one eye, squeezing the other shut against the sun.

'I know it's dangerous all right.'

'It's not just that. There's other aspects. If you get blood on your hands, you'll never be able to get it off.' I showed him my open hands and he looked at them.

'I just want to help.'

'And that's very sweet of you, of course. But you have to think about yourself too. And you don't know what you're getting yourself into. This is going to make you miserable, I promise you.'

A van with Lithuanian plates came driving toward us. The door opened and Ensimmäinen jumped out. His hair was braided and hung down his back like a rope. He opened the Chevy's boot, which was like a door, and pulled out a shotgun and a rifle with a scope the size of a wine bottle. That was too much for me. A wave of nausea washed over me and I got back in the car.

After the van left, Roland came back to our car.

'All right then,' he said. 'You hungry?'

'Please don't talk about food. I want to throw up.'

I could feel him watching me.

'What's in the bag?' I said.

He looked at the carrier bag he had placed in the back seat and then he looked back at me.

'CDs.'

I nodded.

'Want to have a listen?'

'No, Roland, I don't want to have a listen.'

'Then what do you want to do?'

'Just let me sit here for a while.'

He went over to the petrol station and when he came back, I was feeling a bit better; I could even give him a small smile. He held out a paper cup of coffee and I accepted it. Then, surprisingly, he handed me a chocolate bar as well. And a cold bottle of mineral water that he put between my thighs.

He took the cup out of my hand and slurped down some of the coffee. Then he gave me the cup back; it was like my hand was a cupholder.

'We can't just sit around here,' he said and started the car.

We drove into Vittangi and ambled around without really knowing where to go. Several of the pavements had been demolished and there were a lot of sand heaps and traffic cones. It was warm; I could feel sweat breaking out underneath my bosom. A pitch-black child with an oversized helmet pedalled by on a bicycle; I believe that was the only person we saw.

The pizzeria was housed on the ground floor of a yellow wooden house. The awnings above the windows were so old their stripes were all but indistinguishable. The front steps had been removed to accommodate the roadworks, leaving the front door a foot and a half above ground level. To make this unmistakeably obvious, the entrance had been cordoned off with a piece of string with red and yellow plastic flags on.

The outdoor serving area was a fenced-in wooden deck with picnic tables and parasols; we sat down. We were the only guests. My feet were killing me; taking my shoes off made me moan with pleasure. Thankfully, a breeze was blowing from the river, which was, to my delight, actually visible between the houses. Roland went inside to buy a beer and I moved the ashtray, an upside-down terracotta pot on a saucer, to another table. A tower of beer crates loomed next to the door. A watering can with a rose hung on the wall and there was a number of planters, but they had nothing but dirt in them. Dry old dirt. And cigarette butts.

Roland nursed his bottle of beer, reading the paper with his hand spread over the pages the wind was trying to fold every which way.

'When Jerker Persson went out to weed his garden early one morning, he made what can only be called an unusual discovery. A few feet away, Herman the camel was munching on his lawn.'

It was as though my ears were blocked.

'A camel?' I heard myself say.

He nodded.

'In Boden.'

He read on and took a sip from his bottle.

'Western Farm. Bloody stupid nonsense.'

Anders was kneeling on a cardboard box with galvanised staples in his hands. They were attaching chicken wire to a frame of pressure-treated wood held together with nail plates. It was going to be a kennel, Stava had told him. She was doing the carpentry. Every hammer blow made him blink.

Now she was sitting with her palm extended toward him. Instead of putting a staple in it, he grabbed it. She looked at him. Then she put the hammer down and wiped her forehead with her arm.

'Anders,' she said quietly.

In a fit of profound confusion, he pulled her strong, coarse little hand closer, clutching and bending over it as though he were praying; he stayed in that position until she pulled her hand away.

Then he straightened and began gathering up the staples that had scattered across the grass. Näcken, who was working on the other side of the frame, was watching him with a look of revulsion on his face.

He knew he looked horrible these days and from time to time, he would touch his own face. Feel his cheek, which was taut and weird.

The dog house was a red box with a tar-paper roof. The girl called Kerstin was rooting around in there and just then, she stuck her head out the little door and waved. The wave was for Ipa, who was approaching on a quad bike with sheets of rusty steel mesh trembling on its trailer.

She turned in the front yard and got off. Erasmus helped her unload. He had his hat on but was otherwise naked to the waist. His arms were boyishly sinewy and there was a butterfly of greyish-white hair on his chest.

'Is it nice in there?' Ipa said.

'Oooh yes,' came the reply from inside the doghouse.

'Do you think she'll like it?'

'I want to live here too.'

'It's the new girl's house. But if you're nice to her, she might let you into her house sometimes.'

'Anders,' Erasmus called.

Anders stayed seated for a while, anxious, before crawling across the grass toward the old man, who was sitting on a plastic chair in the shade of the house.

'You know what I think, I think you should bite Stava.'

'You want me to bite her,' he slurred.

'Yes, give her a proper bite.'

Anders crawled back. He knew he was supposed to do something, but not what it was. Then he spotted Erasmus, who was watching him, and remembered. He bit her arm. Stava cursed and shoved him back. Erasmus and Näcken laughed.

'You broke the skin,' she said, examining the mark on her arm.

Anders wanted to know what Erasmus thought of that, that he'd bitten her hard enough to break the skin. He turned expectantly to the old man. Then he noticed Erasmus had lost his hat and that his head with its long grey hair was drooping to one side as though he'd suddenly fallen into a deep sleep. One eye stared at nothing and where the other one had been, there was nothing but a dark hole.

Näcken had sprung to his feet. He stared at the lifeless body. His hammer hit the ground and he clapped both hands to his throat. He coughed up bloody froth and staggered aside. Then he took a few steps in the opposite direction. His legs buckled and he collapsed, right on top of the bed of clattering steel mesh.

Ipa had dashed toward the quad bike and leapt onto it, but that was as far as she got. She lay slumped over the handlebar.

Anders had heard the bangs, but it took him a while to realise someone was shooting at them. When he did, he dropped to his stomach in the grass.

'It's the police,' he said. 'The police are shooting at us!'

'No,' Stava said, 'it's not the police.'

'It wasn't me, it wasn't me.'

Stava tugged at him, trying to get him to stand up, but he refused. Several rifles were firing from up in the woods; it sounded like a firing range.

'If you don't come right now, you're on your own.'

'Tell them it wasn't me!'

He hid his head under his arms and shut his eyes tight and lay that way until everything had gone so quiet around him all he could hear was his own laboured breathing. He had no idea how much time had elapsed. He raised his head and looked around. The heavy tread of Näcken's boots. The glop spattered across the board-and-batten wall behind the elder's lifeless body dripping slowly onto the ground like some kind of sap. Of Ipa's head, resting on the quad bike's handlebar, only the lower half remained. Everything below her nose was intact; her soft, delicate lips expressed an indifference that seemed unsettling in the context. The silence rumbled inside him. The little ones who so loved to comfort him were nowhere to be seen. Stava was gone too.

The pale oval of a face was visible through the doghouse door. Anders stared at the little girl. Then he got up and dashed over at a crouch. He crawled in and made a space for himself next to the child, who shifted further in and sat with her knees pulled into her chest, watching him guardedly.

'Let's just sit here for a bit,' he whispered. 'Until it stops.'

After a while, his eyes were drawn to a shadow stretched out in the grass. At first, he thought someone was standing outside, studying the devastation, but after a long time passed without the shadow moving, he figured it must belong to a tree or some such that he hadn't noticed earlier.

Just then, it slid sideways.

He turned to the girl, holding his index finger to his lips.

A grey-bearded man whose face was shaded by a camou-flage baseball cap peered in through the opening.

'Well now,' he said. 'There you are.'

He didn't look hostile at all. Friendly, if anything.

'I'm not really supposed to be here,' Anders said.

The man mumbled something inaudible and straightened up. He was holding a rifle by his hip, a shotgun, a gas-operated, semi-automatic shotgun with a chequered forend. The barrel had a ventilated rib and red front sight and Anders saw the red dot being aimed at him and then he saw nothing else.

It was incomprehensible to me that Roland could eat, and a pizza at that. Or a Bedouin pancake, as he called it with a veiled smile. I had pushed my chair back and was glancing at him askance as though it were cheese-crusted roadkill he was cutting up with his knife and fork. It turned my stomach. And he could tell. Because he pushed his plate over with a grin behind his moustache.

'Care for a bite?'

'I'm good, thanks.'

He looked out at the street, chewing.

'Pretty dead around here.'

'They may never come back.'

'Whatever happened to that graphite mine?'

'Don't you get that, Roland?'

'What?'

'They may never come back.'

He put his cutlery down on his plate. He picked up a napkin he had trapped under his beer bottle and wiped his lips. Then he crossed his arms and studied me. A string of gold glinted inside the collar of his polo shirt.

'I hardly think us worrying about it will help.'

'It bothers me that you're not worried at all.'

'It's going to be fine.'

'Stop saying that; you have no way of knowing that.'

He crumpled up his napkin and leaned forward and pushed it down the neck of his bottle.

'I have such a strong feeling it's going to work out, you might as well call it knowing.'

'And I have a strong feeling it's not going to work out and that it's going to make everything worse. I'm the only one who knows exactly what kind of forces they are dealing with. I heard you laughing and talking about silver bullets and whatever else. Like it was a joke! Like you don't think this is real.'

'They've crossed paths with the squirrel, and I've told them about the wolves the girls saw in the village. So I'd say they have a pretty good idea of what they're dealing with.'

'And you're just sitting there, gorging yourself on that disgusting pizza.'

'It wasn't even a little bit disgusting.'

'And how long can it take! How long have we been sitting here!'

'Gudrun. These lads, they've never let me down and they never will. There's something almost religious about it. About our relationship. It's not properly of this world.'

'Religious?'

'My eyes bloody well tear up when I talk about it.'

At that moment, his phone, which was sitting on the table, emitted a signal, the heroically tooting blast of a horn from Sherwood Forest. He held the phone up to me to inform me he had received a text.

'Is it them?'

He pushed his glasses up to his forehead.

'Yep.'

We drove back to the petrol station. Roland climbed into the Chevy and I drove behind him and that hideous doll's head. He set out toward Pajala, which I thought was odd, and I found passing the turnoff to Susso's house even odder.

After a few miles, we turned down a forest road that we followed to a clearcut. There was nothing there, and I suppose that was the idea.

Unable as I was to stay in the car, I got out and walked up and down the road in the stagnant heat. Roland stood gazing out across the devastated landscape and I could tell he was in no mood to talk.

After more than thirty minutes, I thought it was odd they hadn't come and was just about to ask him to check his phone for more texts when I remembered we had both turned our phones off at the pizzeria.

Then the van came creeping toward us. All three of them were in the front seat, like a gang of slit-eyed copper thieves; the impression seemed deliberately evoked. Harr was in the middle; as they drew near, he held something up for us to see.

It was a shaggy grey wolf's head, pulled halfway out of a supermarket carrier bag. Its tongue lolled out of its gaping maw and Harr stuck his tongue out and grimaced in an attempt to mimic the animal's simultaneously aggressive and helpless attitude.

That didn't sit well with me. I don't know why. I instinctively felt it was wrong to make fun of the wolf and that Harr would pay for it, sooner or later.

After getting out of the car, he held the bag out to me and I was so caught off guard I took it. The head was unexpectedly heavy; it was like he'd handed me a bowling ball in a bag.

'That one, let me tell you, that one you should stuff and mount and put up in your shop. As a warning to others.'

'I think I'd rather not.'

'But if that makes them leave you alone?'

'I don't think that would be the reaction.'

'No?'

'No. And it's also incredibly illegal.'

'You're right, of course. How can I not have thought of that?'

I only then realised he was mocking me. His crooked front teeth glinted under the overhang of his moustache when he smiled. Roland opened the bag and looked in it.

'What do you reckon, Rolle, shouldn't she put it up in her shop?'

'What a bloody brute.'

'Yep. Less cocky now, though.'

Ensimmäinen took the rifles out of the van and put them in the hatchback's boot and Pontus had squatted down to unscrew the licence plate.

'Take a gander at this,' Harr said.

The rest of the wolf was lying on the metal floor in the back of the van.

He grabbed its hind legs and pulled the body closer. Then he held up one of its front paws and stepped aside so we could see it. There was an oblong patch of skin on it with no fur. The skin was reddish and marbled and there seemed to be something repulsively spongy about it.

'This,' he said, scraping it with his thumb, 'is probably the only sign of something being amiss.'

'Was it like this?'

'Nah, his head was still attached when we ran into each other.'

'But weren't there more of them?' Roland said.

Harr shook his head.

'But Susso said there were more,' I said.

'This was the only one we saw. And I actually killed it in self-defence. He came at us like a rabid dog.'

'And Lennart Brösth, was he there?'

He shook his head.

'What about the woman in the wheelchair?'

'No wheelchairs,' he said and closed the doors.

The reply left me lost for words. I must have looked unsteady, because Roland suddenly grabbed hold of my arm.

'But you don't understand . . .'

Harr was leaning against the van. He'd taken off his baseball cap and was looking into it, rubbing his thumb against the sweatband. His scalp shone underneath the strands of hair pulled tight over his head. Ensimmäinen unscrewed the cap of a plastic petrol canister and poured the contents into the cab of the van with a completely neutral look on his face; it looked like he was watering plants.

'This doesn't solve anything!'

'At least this Erasmus bloke,' Harr said, 'definitely won't bother you any more. And no one else in that village either. I swear it, on all that is sacred.'

Ensimmäinen pushed the door shut.

'*Mun aika mennä on,*' he said.

Harr put his cap back on. He touched the vizor and winked at me and then he grabbed the carrier bag with the wolf's head and walked off toward his car.

*

It was unclear to me why they had to torch the van; wasn't that just going to attract unwanted attention? And what if the flames spread and started a forest fire? It had been very dry lately. These and many other questions I put to Roland as we drove back home, but he made no answer, just sat with his hands on the wheel, staring straight ahead.

'Why do you think he took that head?'

I noticed him grinning, almost imperceptibly.

'He wouldn't be dumb enough to stuff it, would he?'

'Stuff what?'

'The head!'

Now he frowned.

'What head?'

Susso was sitting in the armchair with her legs on the bed, watching her. She never looked away and Diana was filled with a strong urge to hurt her. Physically. Grab the nearest object and hurl it at her. Wrestle her to the ground and push her thumb into her eye. Into her healthy eye. And she could obviously tell. Because now she smiled.

'I'm just telling you what Mum told me.'

'You're bloody smiling.'

'Only because you're so worked up. You should see your-self, it's like there's one of those thunder clouds above your head. Like in a comic book.'

'I'm worked up because you're smiling. So your smile started it!'

'I'm sorry. I didn't realise I was smiling.'

'Okay, great, that's all fine then.'

'I understand that you're feeling bad about it. On several levels.'

'No, you don't. You don't have a family. You have no fuck-ing idea. And the worst part is that you're enjoying this.'

Susso looked down.

'We said we weren't ever going to get married,' she said. 'Traitor. The only reason you're using your name is that he didn't want to be called Hellström.'

'Well, you got it your way. I have no husband and soon I won't have a child either.'

'I promise you I'll never let them take her.'

'Now we're both at rock bottom. Just like the old days. You've dragged me down into your crap.'

'I didn't come looking for you.'

'Goddamn it, Susso. Go fuck yourself.'

Susso put her feet down so Diana could pass. She pushed the curtain aside and looked out the window. The shadows from the cumulus clouds above Kiirunavaara had absorbed the mountain's compact darkness and smeared it out in long tentacles, reaching in across the Bolagsområdet neighbourhood toward the town centre. Just below the hotel was a small park. In it rose the sculpture called *Talande Tecken*. A mining pick casting an ominously long and thin shadow across the stones. The fountain was a circle with a pipe in the middle from which water spurted out in iridescent sectors that evoked the streaks of an iris. She hadn't known the fountain resembled an eye. Because she had never seen it from above before.

'I've never been here before,' she said.

'Where?'

'At Ferrum.'

'It's called memory lapses,' Susso said. 'I assure you we've been here several times.'

'I mean at the hotel. In a room.'

Susso peered at her, waiting for her to go on.

'Isn't that weird?'

'Not really.'

'All right, but it feels weird.'

She lay down on the bed, with her back against the headboard.

'Remember that time we went to Laguna and started laughing at the man who worked there. Or maybe not at him, maybe more at the entire situation. Remember that?'

'That we went to Laguna?'

'You have to. We laughed so hard we almost died. You even wet yourself.'

'I did?'

Diana nodded.

Susso shook her head.

'I don't remember as much as you do, Diana.'

'Of course you do. You just remember different things. I've noticed the same thing with Håkan. I remember things from when Kiruna was little that he has no recollection of. And vice versa. And by the way, there's a hole in your sock.'

Susso wiggled her toes.

'They're your socks.'

Diana was quiet for a while, studying Susso's foot.

'Is it going to pass?'

'Not unless you darn it.'

'I mean with Håkan.'

'He's probably permanently changed. If you ask me.'

'Maybe it would be better, in the long run, if he owned up to what he did. If he faced the consequences.'

'I don't think so.'

'It would be easier to live with, I reckon. Afterwards.'

Susso shook her head.

'That's no way to think. When they're involved,' she said, pointing to the top of the wardrobe, 'different rules apply. You just have to accept it.'

'He said he was over it.'

'What?'

'That I cheated on him.'

A brief knock on the door. Susso shot Diana a quick glance before getting up. She opened the door and Gudrun entered. Her hair tangled and her cheeks pale. She looked around.

'Where's the girl?'

'She's watching TV. In your room.'

At that, she sighed and sat down at the foot of the bed. She removed her handbag and put it next to her. Diana and Susso waited in silence for her to say something.

'Well,' she said, 'it's over now.'

Then it was as if she couldn't get anything else out.

'Are you sure?' Diana said.

She cleared her throat.

'We're not going to talk about this. At all. Do you understand me, Susso? Not another word about this.' She wagged her pudgy little finger. 'The police are going to want to talk to both of you, sooner or later, and it would be better for everyone involved if you knew nothing. We've talked about this. You had a junkie boyfriend in Rumajärvi whose name you can barely remember, and you went up there and fetched her. That's all. Any other information you may want, you'll have to get from the papers when they start writing about what happened. Which may not be for a while.'

Diana held the little girl's hand in hers and neither of them spoke. They walked through the church grounds.

'Do you think there are any more birds?' she said. 'Baby birds.'

When she received no response, she stopped.

'Do you?'

Diana sank into a squat and looked the little girl in the eyes.

'Should we have a look?'

She pushed part of a shrubbery aside.

'Baby birds, where are you? Hello?'

The little girl stayed on the footpath, watching her with unexpectedly grown-up eyes, full of contempt. As though she were looking at an old alcoholic answering the call of nature in the middle of the park.

Diana climbed back out of the greenery, full of despair that she immediately pushed back down. She grabbed the little girl's hand and walked on as though nothing had happened. They followed Lasarettsgatan past the hospital and strolled down Kyrkogatan. The little girl turned a few times to look at the building where she knew both her parents worked, but she didn't say anything and neither did Diana.

Håkan had been missing for four days now and Kiruna hadn't asked about him once. She didn't know what to think of that. It could be she was angry with him for being ill and then disappearing and had rejected him. That was going to leave a big mark. And those mice that had lured her into the night. What kind of nebulous harm they may have done to her was more than she could bear to think about.

As soon as they stepped through the door, she did a lap of the house in search of Håkan, but he wasn't there. She held his phone in her hand and had a confused thought about needing to charge it so he could call. The little girl lingered in the hallway. She hadn't taken her shoes off.

[440]

'I don't want to be here,' she said.

'Why do you say that?'

'Because I don't.'

Diana felt anger growing inside her.

'We live here. Take your shoes off.'

That made the child plunk herself down on the floor. She put her arms on her knees and pushed her head out like a sulky little monkey.

'Where do you think we should go then? I'm sure Daddy will be home any minute. And we have to be here when he comes.'

'No, we don't.'

'Yes, we do.'

'I want to go to the cabin.'

'What did you say?'

'I want to go to Nana's cabin.'

'Why would we go there?'

'It's fun there.'

Diana squatted down in front of the girl. Her little shoes had elastic no-tie laces; she dug her fingers in under the ties to loosen them.

'But we're not going. We're staying here. Until Daddy comes home.'

'I want to go to Nana's cabin.'

'So you said. But we're not going to.'

'I want to go to Nana's cabin.'

'That's enough.'

'I want to go to Nana's cabin.'

'I don't want to hear any more out of you.'

'I want to go to Nana's cabin.'

'Kiruna. Stop it!'

'I want to go to Nana's cabin. I want to go to Nana's cabin. I want to go to Nana's cabin.'

Her hand shot out and covered the little girl's mouth. When she tried to free her lips by yanking her head back, Diana held her head in place with one hand and pressed the other hard against her mouth.

'Stop it,' she said and felt her eyes welling up with tears.

As soon as she removed her hand, it started again. 'I want to go to Nana's cabin. I want to go to Nana's cabin. I want to go to Nana's cabin.'

Diana stood up and locked the front door. Then she picked up the incessantly rambling girl, carried her upstairs and put her down on the floor in her room.

'Now stop it! Do you hear me? Stop it!'

The little girl didn't stop and eventually Diana left the room and closed the door. There was no key in the lock, so she fetched the key from the door to her and Håkan's bedroom. Kiruna was on her way out into the hallway with her monotonous message, so she shoved her back inside and closed and locked the door. Then she picked up the phone and called Gudrun.

'Can I talk to Susso.'

'She's still at the hotel.'

'Okay, I'll call her there.'

'What's wrong?'

'It's nothing. I just wanted a word.'

She dialled the number of the hotel and was put through. The receiver was picked up but no one spoke, there was just a rushing sound.

'Hello? Susso?'

'Yes.'

'Why didn't you say anything?'

'I didn't know who it was.'

'What are you doing?'

'Nothing. Watching TV.'

'Kiruna's acting really weird. She's going on and on about going to the cabin. I can't get through to her, it's really scary and I don't know what to do.'

'I'm on my way.'

After she hung up, she walked over to the door. Nothing but silence on the other side. Not a peep, and that made her anxious. She unlocked the door and opened it. For one brief, horrifying moment, she thought the little girl was gone. Then she realised she had crawled in behind the easel and box of play clothes, from which the sparkling wings of her elf costume were jutting out.

'Mummy,' she said. 'What's wrong with me?'

She wanted to tell her there was nothing wrong with her, but couldn't get so much as a word out; instead she closed the door and went down to the kitchen.

She cleared the table, loaded the dishwasher and started it. Then she filled the sink with hot water and washing-up liquid. After doing all the dishes and building a mountain of mugs and saucepans and plates on the drying rack, she poured herself a glass of red wine and chugged it and then she had another.

'You bastards,' she said. 'You bastards.'

Lennart lay in bed with both shoes and clothes on, staring up at the hotel room ceiling. The curtains, which ran all the way from the ceiling to the floor, were closed. There was a clock on the TV, but he couldn't see what the red digits said. He could hear where the little boy was at all times because he breathed loudly through his mouth as he crawled across the carpet like a snuffling little pig. From time to time, he stood up, but never for long. It might have been a game Lennart didn't understand.

He heaved himself off the bed, stepped over the bananas he'd placed on the floor and went into the bathroom. The ceiling light turned on automatically. It was a big, fully tiled bathroom with underfloor heating. The counter with the sink in it was so long a grown man could stretch out on it. There were individually wrapped soaps and tiny bottles of shampoo and other muck. Even toothbrushes. But no razors.

He plugged the bathtub drain and turned the tap on and then sat down on the toilet seat, contemplating the water as it rose. The little boy probably wondered what the rushing sound was, because he appeared outside the door and stood there on all fours, staring. Lennart signalled with a nod that he was welcome to come in, but he didn't seem to understand. He just stared at the tap and the water rushing out of it.

When the water was four inches from the edge, Lennart turned it off. For a long while he sat motionless, looking at the tub.

The little boy stood up, leaning on the bed with his chubby arms. His knees buckled. He opened his mouth wide and the unhealed wound on his cheek gaped like an extra mouth, deformed and ugly. Lennart picked him up and carried him into the harsh light of the bathroom. The sight of the bath seemed to make the little boy happy, because he gurgled out sounds that were probably meant to approximate words.

He lowered the boy into the water and watched his eyes grow wide under the surface. His arms and legs flailed. Lennart's big, aged hand spread out across the child's ribcage like a murderous starfish.

'It's better this way,' he mumbled, 'drowning's not so bad.'

A stream of pearls rushed out of his open mouth. The little boy's scrotum was big and blueish and his penis, which was waggling up and down, looked like some kind of caterpillar with an exotic way of moving.

'Soon you'll sleep. It's almost over.'

At that point, he realised the sock with its duct-tape cuff had come off. It bobbed around the choppy water like a little boat. Lennart stared at the hand the sock had concealed. One second passed. Two seconds. Then he grabbed hold of the boy's arm and pulled him up.

The child lay on the tiles, coughing and gagging with his eyes squeezed shut. His face was darker than the rest of his plump body, which glistened with water. Lennart backed up against the door without taking his eyes off the hand that had been hidden.

It looked like the other hand. Pink and soft and perfectly formed like a doll's. The nails were longer, but there was nothing wrong with them, they just hadn't been trimmed.

Here it came. The little boy had rolled over on his side and he was crying. Not with terrible force like a baby, but quietly and inwardly.

Lennart had continued to move backward out of the room. He held his soaked arm helplessly pressed against his stomach as though it had been maimed. He looked around. His glasses were on the table. He put them on, grabbed the carrier bag with his wallet and car keys and strode toward the door. Then he turned around and switched the TV on. He turned the sound up as far as it would go; it was a newscast. He lumbered out into the hallway and left the door wide open behind him; when he reached the lift, he could still hear the sound of the TV. A young man and a young woman were found dead in a hotel room in Luleå on Thursday. The police suspect they had been using one or several new internet drugs, often a lethal combination.

He stepped into the lift and rode it down to the lobby. Passed the reception desk with his eyes rigidly fixed on the glass doors of the exit. He climbed into the sauna-like heat of the car and looked through the windscreen, which was stippled with crushed insects. Then he looked at the empty car seat. There were French fries on it, dried-up yellow sticks on the greasy cover. He picked one of the sticks up, put it in his mouth and chewed. Then he picked up another. Then he started the car and drove away.

Diana saw her through the window. She came striding up the street at a brisk pace. The neighbour's golden retriever, which lay slumped on their lawn, raised its head. Then it got up. But it didn't bark. Instead it bolted, around the corner. In that moment, when she saw Susso approaching their house with the squirrel like some kind of Japanese pocket monster on her shoulder, she was overcome with conflicting emotions. No one else in the entire world could help and that made her want to hug Susso, hard, as though she'd been lost in the wilderness and against all odds had run into her best friend in a four-by-four with GPS. But she also wanted to yell at her. Hit her, actually. Not least for what she had told her about Håkan. The way she had told her. Like she was talking about some randomer. Like she didn't get or care that it was Diana's husband. And she was afraid in a way she hadn't been before. Not of Susso, exactly, but of the warped reality and the dark context she was a part of. When she hurried to the door, she didn't know if it was to open it or lock it.

She opened it, of course.

Susso stood there looking at her with her one dark eye, and the animal on her shoulder looked at her too. Its long, needle-like whiskers were pointing every which way like beams from a light source.

'I don't know what's wrong with her.'

Susso stepped into the hallway. With a supporting hand on the trellis, she took off her shoes.

'I can tell you there's no one here, at least,' she said.

She went upstairs and Diana followed.

The door was open. After Diana established that Kiruna was not in her room, she yanked open the bathroom door. She wasn't in there either. Nor in the bedroom, nor in the study.

'Dana.'

Susso was squatting on the floor in the little girl's room. Diana got down on all fours and looked under the bed. And there she was, on her back. Diana buried her face in her hands. The relief at the little girl not being missing lasted for no more than a second.

'Why are you under your bed?' Susso asked.

'Because I want to,' the little girl replied.

'And why do you want to?'

'Because Mummy's mean.'

'In what way is she mean?'

'I don't want to be here.'

'Then come out.'

'I mean at home.'

'Then where do you want to be?'

'In the cabin. Where we were.'

'How come?'

'Because it's fun there.'

'What's so fun there?'

The girl said nothing.

'What's so fun there?'

'We were going to play.'

'You were going to play?'

'Yes.'

'Who were you going to play with?'

Instead of replying, she started fiddling with the underside of the bed. Ran her fingers along the slats and pressed her hand in between them, pushing the mattress up.

'Who were you going to play with?'

'I don't know their names.'

'But they're little, aren't they?'

Susso leaned closer and looked at the little girl, who had turned her face to her and nodded.

'Then I know exactly who you mean. And I can tell you right now that they're not good friends to have.'

'Yes, they are. They're fun.'

'Do you want to know what they did to another girl who thought they were fun? They ate her.'

'I don't believe you.'

'No?'

'They're too small to do that.'

'Well, they ate part of her. They started with the eyes, because they're the tastiest. Then the lips, because they're soft and very delicious too. Then they munched through her cheeks, but from the inside out, and then it looked like the little girl had three mouths that were always screaming.'

'Is that true?'

'It's true.'

'Mummy?'

'Yes.'

'Is that true?'

'It's true.'

I counted the days, every single one, and when I had reached a number I felt was improbably high, I started hoping that what had happened in Rumajärvi would never be discovered. I prayed to the ravens and the carrion beetle. The devouring bacteria of decay and the white shroud of winter. They were, in fact, not hopes, but fantasies, which I allowed myself to be seduced by, and on occasion I took them so far I briefly doubted there even was a village by the name of Rumajärvi. The path to that kind of doubt was well trodden, of course. Having spent countless sleepless nights pondering the line between reality and what lay beyond it and how reliable my senses and the memories built on what they perceived could possibly be, I had dismantled the partitions in my brain to the point where doubt had free rein. When this happens, madness is not far behind, and there's only one thing to do: you have to put yourself in a state of denial.

During the day, I manned the shop, as ever, serving customers, as ever, and at night I watched TV, as ever.

Is it called the calm before the storm or the calm after the storm? I always forget. Maybe it's calm both before and after. It has to be, really, relatively speaking. Either way, it was calm. Roland and I talked exclusively about practical matters and barely about that either, and I felt like someone else.

The days were hot. Unnecessarily, miserably hot. The sun beat down on the town square like on a Mediterranean piazza and people came into the shop to cool down. Stood there half naked, reviving. A lot of tourists were surprised at the heat that refused to subside. How did the sun do it? Both day and night. Not just tourists, for that matter. Sixten Kalla was sitting on the bench out in the foyer, saying they were having record lows in Abisko.

'Record lows?' I said.

'No, I meant the opposite, obviously.'

'Yes, I figured.'

'It's hot like a desert up there.'

'Have you been up?'

'No, but I've been to the Kalahari,' he said and grinned at me from under his baseball cap, and I didn't get the joke until afterwards, I was so dazed and confused.

'Just look at what happened up in Karesuando,' he continued. 'There was one of those bloodbaths up there, you must've heard?'

The news hit me like a cudgel and I was completely stunned and could only manage to shake my head.

'They slaughtered a whole village. It was on the news this morning.'

I closed the shop, even though it was just two. Then I sat behind the counter, reading on my phone, which was shaking in my hand. Seven dead. Shot. A mass murderer matching Mattias Flink's record from 1994. It said nothing about Lennart Brösth. Granted, Harr had told me he hadn't been there, but I'd had hopes.

It was for the little girl, I told myself. Sooner or later, they would have taken the little girl. And they would never have left Susso alone. This was the only way.

I went home and called Roland but then I changed my mind and texted him instead. Have you seen the news? I wrote. The reply was instantaneous. An angry smiley. Not the yellow little man with the sullen mouth, the red, angry one, like a furious tomato. What was I supposed to make of that? I wanted to talk about what had happened, but he went out to his cabin in Holmajärvi to make himself unreachable. It made me red and angry.

I sat there alone in the kitchen, utterly convinced the police had already figured out that the person behind the Rumajärvi bloodbath was a sixty-nine-year-old woman in Kiruna. When the doorbell rang, I jumped, because I was so certain it was the police that when I opened the door, I was already holding my handbag ready to go with them.

But it wasn't the police, it was Susso.

She was wearing shorts and a tank top so it was obvious the squirrel wasn't with her. That was actually even more surprising than her visit.

'Come in,' I said and we went into the kitchen.

She sat down at the table.

'You've caught the sun,' I said.

She gave her upper arm an uninterested look and put her fingertips against her skin to see if they left marks. Then she looked at me.

'Håkan's back,' she said.

'Would you like coffee?' I said.

I had already got the tin out.

'Where has he been?'

'He doesn't know.'

I filled the pot with water and poured it into the tank. Then I put the pot on the warming plate and pushed the button.

'He doesn't know?'

She shook her head.

'And you're sure of that?'

'We're sure of that.'

'How does he seem, does he seem stable?'

'What's the opposite of stable? Labile? He's crying and so on. And he doesn't understand jokes. He doesn't understand much of anything, it seems. It's like he's not there.'

'So a bit like Cecilia?'

'Yes.'

'Has he said anything? About what happened?'

'What do you mean?'

'You know what I mean. About what happened at your house. When you and Diana were missing.'

She shook her head.

'And the little girl?' I said and set cups out on the table.

'She seems better. But I have a hunch she's play-acting.'

'That's nice to hear,' I said and poured coffee into the cups. 'I'm afraid I don't have any cream. And no milk either.'

'So I figured I might stay here for a while.'

'Here?'

She nodded.

'Where, in the small room?'

'Yes.'

'All right. Well, I guess I'll have to run it by Roland.'

'Where is he anyway?'

'He's in his cabin. He took my car and went to his cabin and he's out there navel-gazing. Eh? What a gem I found.'

'Seems to me he has his qualities.'

'It's so typically male to just take off.'

'Well, then you'll be happy to have me moving in instead.'

'Of course, but don't you think it's going to be a bit cramped?'

'Mum. I'm kidding.'

'You are?'

She nodded and I put a hand on my chest and laughed, and then she smiled.

We sat there chatting and it was more or less like it used to be, back when Susso lived in the flat below mine. I asked her how her eye felt and she said it felt like nothing.

Eventually, I asked her if she'd seen the news, and she had but it was clear she didn't want to talk about it, which we weren't supposed to, according to our agreement. But I couldn't help myself.

'Have the police been in touch with you?'

'With me? How would they get in touch with me? I haven't been home.'

'Diana then. Sooner or later, you will be brought in for questioning. You have to be prepared.'

'No one's going to bring me in,' she said and lifted her eyebrow up with the tip of her middle finger to adjust her prosthesis. Then she looked out the window and smiled like she was planning a crime.

'Where is he?' I said.

'Who?'

'Him,' I said and showed how tall he was with my hand.

'You can't talk about him either?'

'I don't know about can. There's resistance. Did you have a name for him?'

She shook her head.

'Sure you did. You told me his name was Skrotta.'

'Come on. That's a lie.'

I studied her and suddenly slipped into a memory.

'I remember when you were little,' I said. 'You might have been eight, nine years old, and you told me you skipped the word beer when you sang Christmas songs in school, do you remember? There's a line in "Here We Come A-wassailing" or whatever. But when it was time for that word, you were silent. Because you hated alcohol and drinking so much you couldn't let the word pass your little lips. That's kind of how it feels, I reckon. It's like your mouth is blocked.'

'How do you remember something like that?' she said softly.

'How do I remember? How could I forget? It's just so you.'

She was holding her cup but hadn't so much as sipped her coffee yet; it was probably ice cold by now.

'He's with Diana's parents.'

'Is he going to stay there?'

'No. I think we'll be heading home in a few days.'

We sat in silence for a while. Then I said:

'How are Kent and Eva anyway?'

'I don't know.'

'You don't know?'

She shook her head.

'But surely Diana's been over?'

'She's been busy with her own things. So I don't think so.'

'Maybe I should talk to them.'

Susso got to her feet and stood there looking at me with her living eye and her dead eye and I didn't know which one to focus on. It looked like she was about to say something mean but chose to bite her tongue.

Then she left. The front door slammed shut and I sat at the table with my hands on the table top, gazing out the window. As usual, my eyes were drawn to the mine. Sometimes I think it looks like one of those Mesopotamian ziggurats and sometimes the kind of flat-topped mountains you see in westerns. Now I fancied I could see the mountain itself, with its levelled summit. Like some kind of melancholy mirage from days long gone. I could glimpse the city hall steeple with its blue bandage between the downy birch trees in Ferrum Park. They were finally renovating the clock, which had stood still for an eternity. The wind turbines on Viscaria were standing still too. A sparse sprinkling of small, deathly pale flowers that no one wanted to pick. In the distant wilderness. Outside my window.